First published in the United Kingdom in 2006 by Manuscript & Publishing Agency Ltd.
The Forge, Hewish, Weston super Mare, Somerset, BS24 6RS.
This edition published 2006

ISBN 1-905412-13-4

Papers used by Manuscript & Publishing Agency Ltd are natural, recyclable products made from wood
grown in sustainable forests. The manufacturing processes conform to the environmental regulations of
the country of origin.

The Uncertanties of Morning

of

Morning

Recollections of a Wartime Boyhood

Keith Taylor

Manuscript Publishing Agency

For my daughter Lynne and sons Stuart and Scott.

I like pigs. Dogs look up on us. Cats look down on us. Pigs treat us as equal.

Sir Winston Churchill (1874-1965)

Sheltered Child

Star spun sky with siren howling,
Stray dogs hurrying out of sight.
Cosy close to neighbours sheltering
In a fist of candlelight.

We did not see the high street burning,
Or the smoke that screened the night.
Did not see the black walls falling
Debris in the morning light.

We did not hear the injured screaming,
Did not have to count the dead.
Only heard the 'all clear' sounding,
Urging shocked survivors back to bed.

Ken Swallow

PREFACE

The downstairs rooms are ablaze with yellow light. The curtains drawn across the french windows to keep out the black, vertical frames of night.

Mum and Aunty are in the kitchen. One is washing the tea pots, the other drying. I now know the sounds of the cupboard doors opening and closing as they put the usual plates and dishes away but are arranging others alongside the draining board for when my sister Betty and Dad come home.

My fascinating friend the dining room fire, with its myriad coloured flames emanating from the gradually dwindling black base of coal or coke invites me again to the hearth. Here I kneel for seconds only, until I'm nudged by the need to check the pig I drew earlier on the wallpaper at the foot of the stairs. What I have to do is to decide whether or not the pig has a squiggly enough tail and this need lures me, pencil in hand, out of the open door and into the hall.

I have never seen a pig but I have seen pictures of them in books, and Aunty has recently read me the story of *The Three Little Pigs* so that is how I know they have curly tails.

I know, too, that I have the snout right and I've given mine pointed ears. It has short, thick legs and a fat body. But the tail.......?

Two or three steps out of the dining room door and I see something nasty. Something so threatening that I can no longer put one foot in front of the other. Something that conceives a knot of fear that lingers cold within the well of my tummy. It has straight sides and is hiding unsuccessfully behind the thick fawn curtain It is the same colour as the night! So what is it doing inside the house?

In a quavering voice I call out, 'Mum! Aunty! What's that thing there?'

Aunty, slim, white haired and always smiling, comes to my side. 'Where?' she asks softly.

'*There*!' I emphasise, while pointing to my leering enemy. *'There,'* I say again.

'Oh, that! That's a blackout curtain. I put it up this afternoon.'

'Oh, but I don't like it, Aunty. It frightens me.'

'Well, we all have to have blackout curtains now, I'm afraid.'

'But why do we *have* to?'

'Because there's a war on.'

'What's a war on?' I ask.

CHAPTER 1

To trace the location associated with this wartime memoir, one needs to be looking at a map of Great Britain, particularly the eastern side of England and the wide indentation called The Wash.

About ninety or so miles inland from there stands Nottingham, a city associated with the legend of Robin Hood and the lace trade.

Two or three miles north-west of the city centre, Wollaton Hall, an Elizabethan country seat built between 1580-1588, presides over acres of now diminished park land due to the estate being sold to the City of Nottingham Corporation in May 1925, following the deaths of Lord and Lady Middleton who had owned in total some 4,164 mixed acres of land.

Tenant farms, dairies and timber yards were sold by auction alongside colliers' cottages, allotment gardens and plots suitable for building. Sections of a long planned wide road, known as The Boulevard System, were also cut and extended north-west from the flood plain of the River Trent at Lenton and Dunkirk to the relatively steep foothills of Bestwood and Mapperley.

The Boulevard system today is described as a dual carriageway divided by a grassy central reservation. However, for the first fifty or so years the pavements and central reservation were shaded by quick growing lime trees and regimentally fenced allotment gardens.

The section passing through Wollaton was called Middleton Boulevard, whereas the long section from a colliery community lane called Radford Bridge Road to the Boulevard's termination point at Arnold and Daybrook was named Western Boulevard.

It was along this route, but connected to the mining community by a series of footpaths, or 'pads' as they were known locally, that a tract of land was purchased by several building firms from the Middleton Estate catalogue during the estate's auction.

The land tract was described as allotment gardens which, according to my mother, were interlaced with clear water streams. Nearby and also sold by auction was Black Covert Plantation, where pheasants had been reared for the autumn and winter shoots popular with shooting parties. The Estate's sales catalogue described these combined plots of land as 'Fields No. 1068 - 1070 - 1098 - 1095, and the overall area was listed as LOT 373. Once purchased and the building firms moved in, four roads were cut directly off from that section of Western Boulevard.

Beechdale Road progressed west for several miles to meet the ridges of Nottingham's highest points at Bilborough and Strelley, whereas two short cul-de-sacs, each comprising of perhaps twenty-five detached houses, were named Franklyn Gardens and Westholme Gardens and contrasted with the fourth cutting Chalfont Drive, which is where this memoir begins....

Chalfont Drive to my eyes headed directly into the westering sun. After two rows of detached houses were built, for several hundred yards or so along its grey pavements the road petered out and a pleasantly green wilderness of disused allotments, cattle grazed fields and three horizon blocking woods took over. Where the last of the detached houses finished, a dirt track known as Colliers Pad on one side and Cherry Orchard the other connected Chalfont to the mining community at Radford Woodhouse.

The house in which I was born in April 1938 was not owned by my parents but my father's sister, Amy. She had married Charles Shaw, a professional photographer and lace maker, who in 1913-14 was invited to visit the Middleton's nearby country seat at Wollaton to photograph the 'state occasion and festivities surrounding the visit of King George 'V'.

However, as to how and when Amy met Charles Shaw has become lost within the corridors of time. Nevertheless, by asking my family, over the years the picture of a devoted but childless couple gradually emerged.

I inherited my father's passion for exploring and wandering the countryside, which may have something to do with the Taylors' ancestors having a hundred or so years before given up their village or hamlet livelihoods and made fresh lives for themselves in the then relative security of the city, and the lace and hosiery trades in particular.

Grandad Taylor, was employed as a foreman twist hand in the lace industry. Gaps already begin to appear here in the family tapestry because the truth is I never knew him, or *of* him. A rift, never healed, had occurred between my paternal grandparents and my mother and father before I was born.

Amy I do know had been a 'flapper-girl', or 'Charleston waller' as she once put it, and all three children were brought up on classical music and taught to play the piano. They were, as one might term them today, 'into opera'. It would not be unreasonable to suggest that Amy met her husband-to-be, Charles Shaw, at a dance or concert.

Charles Shaw was, I understand, a tall, dark haired man who wore glasses. He had inherited from his parents several terraced houses and two shops situated in the Heanor-Marlpool districts of Derbyshire. The rents accumulated from this, and perhaps other sources of invested income, allowed him the freedom to study and become a professional photographer.

Before they moved to the first of the detached houses to be built on Chalfont Drive, Amy and Charles Shaw bought and lived above a sweet and confectionery shop on Lincoln Street in the parish of Basford. My late sister Betty, ten years my senior, remembered the sweet shop days well.

Lincoln Street and all the surrounding streets were linked to poverty. Few children going into 'Shaw's Sweets and Confectioners' could afford bags of dolly mixtures or sherbet dips but Amy, who served every day except Sunday, saw to it that the 'street urchins' (as these children were often unreasonably called) had more than their weighed out share of sweets in their bags.

'Aunt Amy, bless her. She gave more sweets and ice-creams away than she actually sold,' smiled Betty, recalling Aunt Amy in later years.

My mother, father and sister Betty lived about a hundred yards from Lincoln Street, in a back-to-back terraced house with a communal yard and tap. Long demolished, that tight little community was known as Alice Square. There Betty had the friendships of our cousins, Sylvia, Peggy, Alice, Rene and Jack, who with their mother lived nearby.

The three families were close and how my mother, father and sister became residents of Alice Square may have had something to do with my father's itinerant attitude towards employment. He was never without a job. However, once he had learned that job and knew the ins and outs of it he then began looking for something else - a new challenge, another of his traits that I have inherited.

In her formative years, Betty spent some time with Aunt Amy and Uncle Charlie at the shop on Lincoln Street. On the hot, long summer evenings, Aunt Amy frequently took her and my girl cousins to the nearby Vernon Park where they fed the ducks and ornamental waterfowl. Here paddled a Muscovy, a black and white type duck with a red bill wattle and eye-patch. Because it could be told apart from the others, the Muscovy was called 'Joey' by Betty, her cousins and the park-keeper. In the depths of winter they went next door to the Vernon Cinema to watch a silent film but returned to feed an often ice-bound 'Joey'.

Tiring perhaps of Alice Square and wanting something better for their daughter, my parents moved about half a mile along the road and into a semi-detached rented house on Roderick Street. My cousins-to-be also moved, to a house with a front and rear garden at Stockhill Circus.

Amy and Charles Shaw in the meantime, and with the proximity of Wollaton Park in mind, set their sights upon the first house to be built on Chalfont Drive. They had with them as pets two sulphur crested cockatoos and a black Newfoundland dog, called Jerry. When they finally moved into the house, the cockatoos were allowed to fly freely in the sitting room and Jerry was given a wall corner in which to sleep. This corner backed onto the big red and black tiled kitchen baking ovens.

Working together throughout the weekends and evenings, my father and Uncle Charlie laid out the gardens. The rear garden boundary was defined, by hedgerows, whereas the front had a wire fence along one side and privet the other. The front was enhanced by a wall of locally quarried stone. The house comprised of a front porch, wide hall and stairway, a front lounge, sitting room and kitchen with fitted cupboards and cold slab scullery. At the foot of the stairs beside the front door was a cloakroom, where the electricity meter was also stored. Upstairs was a small bedroom situated above the front porch, two double bedrooms, bathroom, separate toilet, wide landing, blanket chest and storeroom.

Betty remembered early visits there and in particular Aunt Amy and Uncle Charlie dressing Jerry in children's clothes, which included a cap and placing a pipe between his huge silken jowls, then photographing him. By contrast, Betty disliked intensely having to eat at the table with two sulphur crested cockatoos flying about the room whenever she was taken to Chalfont Drive by my mother.

Tragedy intervened. Uncle Charlie died. He was still relatively young but I know nothing more than that. The year would have been around 1936-37 and I was conceived in the summer of that year, my parents third attempt to bring a boy into the world, although I was not to learn that I would have had two brothers, Louis and Gordon, until I was eight or nine. Ironically, it was not a member of my family who gently conveyed this startling fact to me but a boyhood friend. Thus further gaps began to appear in the family tapestry and for a considerable time.

I was due to be born at Roderick Street, but Amy dreaded living alone and paid my parents a visit. Out there along the Boulevards she knew no one. In view of these circumstances, she asked if they would care to move again and share the Chalfont Drive house with her. Amy was willing to sleep in the little bedroom above the front door, therefore my sister could have the big bay-fronted bedroom and my parents the equally spacious bedroom at the back.

After the move, Betty, still a schoolgirl, attended the Player School situated some two or three miles on the edge of the Aspley and Bilborough estates. However, when the Bilborough girls learned that she lived 'in a posh house off Western Boulevard' Betty was dragged repeatedly into the girls' toilets during playtimes and going home times, and had needles and knitting needles stuck into her arms, legs and beneath her fingernails. Although she was carrying me, my mother in one of her infrequent but raging tempers confronted the school's headmistress and wrote to the school governors. She heard nothing. So taking the matter into her own hands, she arranged for Betty to be transferred to what is now The Middleton School which was closer to home and adjacent to the 'posh Boulevards'.

Meantime Jerry, the black Newfoundland, had aged and had to be put down. Newfoundlands are relatively short lived dogs. Lord Byron, the much fêted poet and bygone owner of the not too distant Newstead Abbey, erected an unbelievably large monument to 'Boatswain', his dog of the same breed.

Because Betty and I were due to be living at the house, Aunt Amy also parted with her free-flying cockatoos. Whether she placed an advertisement in the cage bird enthusiasts' column of the local evening newspaper, or negotiated for them to be installed in the Nottingham Arboretum aviaries, I have never known for certain.

The Arboretum aviaries had certainly influenced Amy when she was a girl, particularly since she once lived less than a mile away and birds and animals, as I intend to enlarge upon later, became very much a part of all of our lives. Therefore I cannot imagine Amy having the cockatoos put down if they were healthy and free of disease. In any case, there was a caged African Green parrot installed at the house when I was born. This leaves me with the impression that Amy was not willing to give up her pets entirely, despite her brother and his family being as keen to move into Chalfont Drive as she was to have them live with her.

CHAPTER 2

By 1935-36 most of Britain's adult population regarded continuing war with Germany as a foregone conclusion. Gas masks were being mass-produced and plans were underway for installing communal and neighbourhood garden air raid shelters throughout the British cities, towns and suburbs.

In Nottingham the Chief Constable, Athelston Popkess, in his dual role as War Department Co-ordinator, accepted the delivery of 500,000 gas masks. Householders by 1939 learnt, through press releases and radio news bulletins, that 65,000 to 75,000 people were eligible under the National Insurance Act for updated air raid shelters, this eligibility depending on earnings less than £250 per annum but with a further allowance of £50 for each child.

On 14th July 1939 various counties throughout Great Britain suffered the first wave of air raids. From that date protective measures escalated. In suburbs pavement side streets were painted with white rings, should people find or feel themselves stranded during the envisaged 'black-outs'; workmen dug trenches and erected air raid shelters; and both men and women, employees and volunteers, spent days and sometimes weeks loading, unloading and stacking sandbags, as did the nurses and staff of all the British hospitals. Most civic buildings had sandbags stacked around the main and back entrances, including the splendid and centralised administrative centre of Nottingham known as The Council House.

On the morning of September 1939, German troops entered Poland, ransacked and occupied certain territories. Great Britain, with Prime Minister Neville Chamberlain at the helm, issued Germany with an ultimatum to withdraw. But the ultimatum was ignored. Germany was holding fast.

At 11.15 a.m. on 3rd September, Neville Chamberlain made his long remembered and historic broadcast to the nation, 'this country is at war with Germany'. A week or so later the troops of the British Expeditionary Force were sent across the Channel where in France they joined with the French Militia and were marched to defensive positions along the Belgian border.

War historians have since emphasised that while this company of regular soldiers with its re-trained reservists were trained well for the battlefield, they were inadequately equipped.

Evacuations followed next, with pregnant women, young mothers and children being seconded from the major cities to what were considered to be safer zones so far as the threat of intensive bombings was concerned.

Nottingham's Goose Fair held on the first weekend in October was cancelled for the first time since the First World War but, surprisingly, only for the sixth time since the horrors of the plague in and around the seventeenth century.

On 28th November, it was announced that due to petrol rationing the horse-drawn cart, van and lorry would be put back on the road. Horse sales were held and firms' representatives sought the horse handler's advice and bought horses. Considerably more horses were used for freighting by various railway companies than by other concerns, with the London, Midland and Scottish Railway Company claiming a seven thousand horse and van fleet throughout the British Isles.

Road signs bearing the illuminated words 'CROSS HERE' were in force although fewer people than can be imagined were aware that the signs also illuminated the lower part of a pedestrian's body when she or she was crossing the road in relative darkness.

Christmas 1939 saw people giving as presents manufactured wallets for holding ration books and identity cards, while walking sticks and illuminated brooches were popular. Word was broadcast and published nationally informing all householders that regarding the family Christmas dinner, 'large bird poultry' such as geese and turkeys would be in short supply, whereas chickens, ducks and game birds were readily available and pheasants the cheapest ever to have crossed each butcher's and poulterer's counter. By January 8th 1940, food rationing was officially enforced. On producing the relevant ration book, everyone was entitled to 4 ounces of bacon or ham and 12 ounces of sugar. Butter, margarine, cooking fats and cheese were also rationed.

CHAPTER 3

My earliest recollection is that of being in a pram which had been wheeled into the sunlight shining through the glass panels of the front door. Ahead of me down the cream wallpapered hall the kitchen door was propped open, thus revealing two women wearing pale blue smocks and white aprons. Both worked side by side at the sink and wooden draining board.

The one who lifted and carried me the most was singing about someone called 'My Little Angeline'. She had dark brown hair which she wore in a net, was solidly built and round faced. Her eyes were wide and blue. Periodically she conversed with her companion who turned immediately and smiled whenever I made a sound. This lady was slim, had white hair and greyish blue eyes.

A sense of well-being prevailed as I struggled within my harness and attempted to prop myself up against the smooth white pillows, the *soft white* pillows. Yet I enjoyed the hemmed-in feeling made by blankets keeping me safe and apart from the adult world beyond.

I was by then aware of the bond I maintained with the blue-eyed woman who taught me to make a grunting sound when I needed to use my potty and until I could say the word kept pointing to herself and saying, 'Mum'. She then pointed to me and repeatedly said, 'Keith, Keith,' until to her satisfaction I was trying out both words and succeeding.

Eventually I learned that the white haired woman's name was 'Aunty' or 'Aunt Amy' and the smiling small featured girl whose neat face was framed by masses of brown hair was similarly bonded to Mum. Her name was Betty, my sister.

Much less frequently, came Dad. Like Betty, he was small featured, blue-eyed, lean and whippy with white hair, sparse at the crown. I became gradually aware that he, Mum, Betty and I were an immediate family, whereas kind, gentle and ever patient Aunt Amy was someone who remained slightly apart.

Whenever Dad lifted me into his arms or up to his shoulder I examined his cufflinks, tie, collar studs and the shiny grey waistcoat that matched his perfectly creased trousers. His black shoes always shone immaculately. His gold pocket watch I loved and was frequently asking to see it. With his one free hand, Dad would flick open the watch and show me the hands and figures while speaking in terms of time. 'One o'clock, see Little Man? Now that's two o'clock.'

Dad seldom referred to me as Keith but preferred instead to address me as Little Man. When I was at his shoulder, I sometimes caught a glimpse of myself in the ornately framed mirror placed above the tortoiseshell tiled hearth and fireplace. I was blond haired, round faced, blue-eyed and wore short trousers and long sleeved pullovers or jumpers that in the evenings Mum, Aunty or Betty knitted. On the mantlepiece stood two beautiful candlesticks made of walnut but with silver plinths and holders. Years later I was told they had been given as wedding presents to Mum and Dad by his twin brother Albert and wife Alice.

The other occupant of the house was Polly, the African green parrot. Her cage stood on Aunty's sewing machine next to which was positioned an armchair, part of the three-piece suite.

Whenever I jumped onto the armchair or climbed onto Aunty's lap in readiness for a story or nursery rhyme, Polly would spring to life and shuffle along to my end of her perch screeching defensively at the top of her voice.

Polly frightened rather than fascinated me. I didn't like the look of her sharply hooked grey bill, especially since I knew she had nipped Aunty's fingers and wrists on several occasions. Moreover, Polly had drawn blood. Her hazel eye seemed to blaze with a hidden fury.

Why then, if the parrot was aggressive, did we have to keep it? Why couldn't we take it outside, open the cage door and let it fly away? Aunty shook her head while explaining that Polly might not survive. Might not know how to find the nuts and fruits she needed and which Aunty bought bagged from a shop.

Then I was asking how Polly came to be sitting on a perch in a cage. Using one of the several books she bought for me each month, Aunty showed me pictures of jungles; palm trees above which the sun blazed. She explained that sometimes jungles steamed like our kitchen on Monday washday mornings.

In these jungles nuts and fruit grew and the monkeys and parrots that lived in the trees fed on them. Jungles, however, were far away from where we lived, in the hot countries across the sea. With one slender manicured finger, Aunty pointed out the sea. Sometimes people like ourselves - white people - met the black people who lived in these jungles and exchanged or traded goods as another picture indicated. Sometimes these goods consisted of monkeys and parrots the black men caught singly and in traps.

When the white men had collected enough of whatever they had gone to the jungles to trade, they came back across the sea to this country. If the monkeys and parrots hadn't died on the way, they were then sold on to pet or animal dealers who shipped them by rail yet again to the pet shops in the towns and cities where they were wanted. That, apparently, was how Aunty came by Polly.

By then I was plaguing her with another question. What had she meant when she said, 'hadn't died on the way?'

Aunty, I noticed, smiled quickly at Mum. 'That's when your life comes to an end,' she said.

'What? Everybody's?'

'Yes, I'm afraid so.'

'What? Even my life?'

'Yes, everybody's one day.'

'But to die — ?'

'Means you go to sleep and don't wake up again.'

B-but, I like it here, Aunty. *I* don't want to die.'

'Oh, you aren't going to die yet. You die when you're very old, not when you're very young.'

Aunty then miraculously produced a picture from my book called 'Rip Van Winkle'. The picture depicted a man in a woolly hat with a pom-pom at the end, laying on his back, clothed but with his bare feet sticking out of the blankets at the end of the bed. He had a long, white beard tapering almost to his waist and a self-satisfied expression on his slumbering face.

'When you're an old man you look like that when you die,' said Aunty.

I nodded while thinking, well at least you are smiling as Rip Van Winkle was smiling. So dying couldn't be *too* bad, could it?

When some afternoons Aunty needed to use the sewing machine, she would carefully lift Polly's cage and put it on the floor. Polly shrieked repeatedly and I found the sounds offensive to the ear. Sometimes she struck out and nipped Aunty's fingers. Fascinated, I used to watch Aunty mending a tear in Betty's school blouse or Mum's smock as she worked the treadle wheel with one foot.

Beneath the sewing machine Aunty also kept her most treasured possession, a wind-up gramophone. Usually she played her records in the evening just before I was taken to bed, or less frequently on an overcast week-day morning when she had cleared her sewing backlog and helped Mum prepare the midday meal.

Taking the records from the varnished cabinet, Aunty dusted the play deck before carefully placing three or four records onto the table alongside it. The record sleeves were dull brown but the name of the company and label was encircled either in blue or dark red, each with a small gold lettering which seemed to tell Aunty a great deal.

I was particularly fascinated by the HMV record label which featured a dog, a white terrier with black ears, sitting beside and listening into a speaker. Aunty explained that HMV stood for His Master's Voice to which the terrier was apparently listening. I had not by then seen a dog. However, that record label alone illustrated the fact that it was an animal associated with people in the same way that Polly was associated with our family. Moreover, a dog's human benefactor was known as its master.

Each record was so fragile Aunty explained that you had to withdraw them from the sleeve very, very carefully. I smelled the celluloid and liked it. Tilting one record gingerly, Aunty showed me the narrow circular grooves and told me that was where the voices came from. They were in there, safe and clean, although it was imperative that the record didn't get scratched. When the record was on the turntable, Aunty had then to check or insert the needle and carefully put the arm down to the desk.

Her favourite records were basically arias from the opera 'Madam Butterfly'. She had seen the opera performed, several times, with Uncle Charlie. Uncle Charlie who to my mind, grey bearded and sleeping with his hands clasped over his tummy and wearing that self-satisfied smile on his face, was like Rip Van Winkle. Yet who, sadly, I would never see because he was not going to waken ever again.

Of course, I knew nothing about 'Madam Butterfly' but I did like music; the arias. Polly was, incidentally, always on her best behaviour when Aunty had the gramophone playing, whereas Betty I recall used to sneak quietly up to her bedroom to do some tidying as she would quietly explain to Aunty.

There were times, however, when Aunty forgot to wind up the gramophone and it was then that the voices became slurred and distorted, until she grasped the handle and wound it for half a minute or so as the turntable revs again co-ordinated.

Another of Aunty's favourite records was of Jeanette MacDonald and Nelson Eddie singing 'The Indian Love Call'. She had every one of their recordings and played them all.

There was another lovely tune that when he was in the bathroom Dad used to whistle called 'Vilja, an aria from Franz Lehar's operetta 'The Merry Widow', to which Aunty stood listening transfixed. And Dad, to my amazement, had only to round his lips to have the same sound, *the same tune* come from between them.

Sometimes Dad would whistle 'Vilja' when in the dining room he had me balanced on his shoulder and, if he lowered me, still whistling, I would see the quiet laughter filtering pleasantly through his warm blue eyes and make up my mind that when I was a grown man like him I would whistle that same tune.

A piece of music lodged itself into my mind in the same way that 'Vilja' was lodged into Dad's and 'Indian Love Call' into Aunty's. Despite the sunlight and the heat that Saturday, we had been indoors again and listening to *different records*. 'The Blue Danube' by Johann Strauss was playing and I became instantly obsessed by the piece, particularly since both Dad and Aunty took it in turns to waltz around the room holding me in their arms. When each revolution finished, I pleaded 'Gain, Aunty. 'Gain.'

Never one to refuse, Aunty repeatedly played that record time after time. I couldn't whistle, whereas I had learnt to sing 'da de da' fashion and was singing, or *imagining* I was singing.

There was a side porch attached to the kitchen which led out into the yard. To the left of the porch was the coal house. Just to the right, placed in a recess below the gauze covered pantry window, stood the dustbin; unseen until it was wanted. A turn left by Dad's woodshed took you into the rear garden, a turn right into the front. The yard was always cool in the summer and below freezing on most days in the winter due to it being shut out from the sun.

Opposite the side or 'back' porch was the windowless side of the house lived in by our neighbours, Herbert and Marjorie Teather. The thick front privet hedge bordering their house Mr. Teather agreed to cut back and front because he liked the hedge high, as most people thereabouts liked privacy. A high hedge was an indication of their *wanting* privacy. Consequently, Mr. Teather was cutting the front hedge with a pair of shears when I repeatedly performed my renderings of 'The Blue Danube Waltz'. Craning over Dad's shoulder I saw Mr. Teather, darkly suited and with the shears drooping beside his trouser legs as he strode smiling widely towards me.

'My word! You're beginning your choral lessons early, young fellow. Why, we'll have you in the church choir before long,' he grinned, tickling my chin.

When Mr. Teather returned to his cutting and Dad carried me into the house, Mum at the baking ovens told me as if I had suddenly become an adult that Mr. Teather was the lay preacher at St. Margaret's Church situated about three-quarters of a mile away. He was also a deputy school headmaster. 'You will be going to Mr. Teather's school one day,' said Mum.

I looked at her while thinking how she knew that. How did Mum know where I was going? Because as far as I was concerned, I wasn't going anywhere. Home with her, Dad, Betty and Aunty; that was surely the only place to which I would be going; and staying.

CHAPTER 4

Realising the intensity of German aggression in January 1940, the British First Lord of the Admiralty, Winston Churchill, sought the opinions of Europe's neutral state leaders and stressed his hopes that they would fight alongside the British.

By early April, Winston Churchill, by then the new Prime Minister, established a war cabinet and appointed Lord Beaverbrook as the Aircraft Production Minister. The position of Minister of Food was filled by Lord Woolton.

Norway and Denmark were invaded by German troops who stormed and seized the leading ports. In northern Norway the British Navy met the Germans near Narvik, a long established port. Naval battles took place over a three-day period during which the Germans lost ten of their twenty destroyer fleet. The British Navy also sank three German cruisers. The British Forces then landed in Norway and fought alongside the Norwegians. The German Forces withdrew.

In May 1940, the British and French were holding defensive positions in northern France. Winston Churchill formed a coalition government.Albert Alexander, became First Lord of the Admiralty; Clement Atlee, who was awarded the office of Lord Privy Seal; Lord Halifax accepted the appointment of Foreign Secretary and Ernest Bevan that of Minister of Labour.

When the Germans were invading Luxembourg, the Netherlands and Belgium, Winston Churchill in the House of Commons made his 'blood, toil, tears and sweat' speech, as it became known and the future for Great Britain looked bleak.

By the middle of May 1940, recruitment began for those many elderly men and women who had already seen action in the First World War but were active enough to form individual or home defensives. They were signed up under the Local Defence Volunteers banner but were later called The Home Guard.

Meanwhile, the Germans had bombed the port of Rotterdam, thus causing the Dutch Army to surrender. From late May until early June, some 338,000 troops of the British, Belgian and French regiments were evacuated from Dunkirk, France in a memorable but fearful armada of boats which, although small, proved seaworthy and were supplied by the British.

The Germans were advancing and had all but encircled the Allied Forces occupying north-eastern France. During this evacuation, the Belgian Army surrendered to the Germans and King Leopold III was arrested.

***

'Joey Duck has died,' Aunty announced as she read the newspaper one evening. That was another one gone to sleep forever! She then showed me a newspaper photograph of a mound of earth positioned in a pond side shrubbery. 'That's Joey Duck's grave,' she chimed.

So Joey was buried in the soil near some bushes and people were taking flowers. Did I want to go? Early the following evening I was taken along the Boulevards in a pushchair. My first outing and only to Joey Duck's grave in Vernon Park.

Mum wore a grey gabardine, belted raincoat and Aunty a long russet overcoat with a high collar, but a weather coat in the sense that it came almost down to her ankles.

I knew about Joey Duck but didn't know what a car was, although I sensed somehow that it wasn't a flesh and blood being. It was not until I saw a car door open and the driver step out, however, that I realised a car was a form of transport like a pram or pushchair.

Joey Duck's grave looked exactly as it had appeared in the newspaper photograph.

We stared at it for seconds only but looked longer at the foliage reflected pond, railed with a long island.

On the walk home I was aware of the sky darkening and when we arrived balked inwardly when I realised that Betty and Dad were there and switching on the lights before drawing curtains.

'We've been to Joey Duck's grave,' I announced importantly.

Laughing from his fireside chair, Dad reached out and hauled me onto his knee. Betty by comparison just said, 'Oh yes,' and again escaped quietly upstairs.

Betty, however, was at the helm of my pushchair on the Saturday afternoon that she and her friends decided to meet and walk Colliers Pad and for a short distance along Beechdale Road to a block of shops, the rooftops of which could just be seen from Mum and Dad's rear bedroom window.

We were going to Starbucks to buy sweets, Betty told me. She and her friends, Barbara, Kathleen and Jean, were so busy talking and laughing as they pushed me in the pushchair that they failed to point out the exceptionally high elm just to the right of the Colliers Pad ditch which years before was known as 'The Tallest Tree in Nottinghamshire'. Families had walked from the city to picnic on the field beside it. Youthful Radford Woodhouse colliers had staged illegal whippet races or 'flappin' gaffs' here and gambled at cards in the humps and hollows of the field that was so named. In retrospect, my sister and her friends probably knew nothing of those days. Hadn't been told, or forgotten if they had. I was to learn about the elm in the months ahead.

When we reached Starbucks, one or two of the girls stayed beside the pushchair then took it in turns to go in and buy sweets. Barbara and Kathleen were neighbours and lived closer to the fields and disused allotments than Betty and I, who were once described as living 'in the middle house' although it had been the first of the houses to be built. Around the same height, all four girls wore neat jackets and pleated skirts, shared their sweets around while laughing and giggling. But Jean, who lived on Westholme Gardens, the next road, was the one who spoke longest to me while I was fastened in the pushchair. Jean's hair was luxurious brown, thick and crimped beautifully down to her shoulders. Her face was oval, her complexion pink, eyes blue, lips wide; sensuous. She was, I sensed, the adventurous member of the quartet. The daring leader.

I think all four girls were well into their school senior years and talking of leaving and taking up night school classes to each gain a secretarial position. They wanted to become secretaries. Attend business colleges. With hindsight, I would say that Jean was the type who would have married the boss or his son. Pushchair bound though I was, I liked Jean immediately. I became aware of her holding the pushchair handles and talking to me.

Kathleen and Barbara's fathers worked in the offices of John Player and Sons Imperial Tobacco Company, situated to the east and about a mile beyond the far side of Western Boulevard. Each morning and afternoon they walked to work together, dressed in suits, wearing trilbies and each carrying a raincoat folded over the left arm.

Kathleen's complexion was very like her father's, whereas Barbara resembled her father facially. Barbara's father addressed those he met on the pavement by name, whereas Kathleen's father smiled and ventured brightly but singularly, 'Hello-o.'

Mum several times told me that when Kathleen's family had not long moved into the house, a tawny owl flew from the thicketed hedgerows of Cherry Orchard Lane that could be seen from Kathleen's bedroom window, settled on the window ledge and
attempted to attack its reflection which it mistook for that of a rival.

On hearing the rapping of glass and the caterwauling, her parents had gone up the stairs to investigate, switched on the bedroom light and glimpsed the owl before it flew back to the thickets.

Behind the houses opposite stretched the tight but extensive maze of allotments called the New Aspley Gardens. Those behind the houses across from the one in which we Taylors lived were laid out orchard fashion and although I was not to know it then because I slept with Mum and Dad in the back bedroom, the apple and pear blossoms enhanced the outlook considerably during the months of spring.

That Saturday trip to Starbucks the girls had undertaken without a warning from their respective parents because it was considered relatively safe to be walking along Colliers Pad, due to the area being flat and houses flanked the Beechdale Road pavements. Cherry Orchard Lane was a different matter. High rambling hedgerows either side of the winding dirt track. Disused allotments one side. The fields of Aspley Hall Farm the other. Reason enough for Mum one day to warn Betty that there was a man on the prowl along Cherry Orchard Lane.

On overhearing this warning, I didn't ask what 'on the prowl' meant. Somehow I seemed to know. Lingering. Exploring the thickets and field side ditch. Looking at people, although I had no idea why. Being generally and alarmingly up to no good. So Cherry Orchard was deemed forbidden territory. Yet in my case, only for a relatively short time.

CHAPTER 5

Being born and brought up in one of the poorest quarters of Nottingham had furnished Mum with a penchant for several colloquial terms that had probably been used among the people of the communal yard fraternities for generations. For instance, if Dad or I wanted help or needed to arrange something we were working on and asked Mum if she could spare a minute, she would assist willingly enough but mutter as she came into the room, 'Oh, you are a Mickey drippin'!'

If it was Aunty or Betty seeking help or advice, Mum similarly muttered, 'Oh, you are a Wet Emma!'

One morning when she was dusting early in the front room, Mum glimpsed from behind the net curtains two of John Player's office staff striding by in their suits and trilbies and called out to Aunty preparing my breakfast in the kitchen. 'Hey, Amy! Come and look at Mr. Ellis! He's wearing a new suit! He's "Cock 'o the North" this morning!'

If matters were going well about the house, Mum would never refer to the situation as such but answer Aunty's question. 'No I don't need any help Amy, thanks. Everything's going absolutely "Hey Johnny Robin" today.'

When I asked Mum if she knew the title of the signature tune to the weekday noon radio show called Workers' Playtime, which was always blaring in the background, she put her head to one side, thought for a second, then told me the tune was called "Climbing Up The Wall to See a Cock Spider", which I didn't believe then any more than I do today. Yet Mum sang out that line along with the music and surprisingly it fitted.

Spending much time looking at books on the settee or scrambling about in Aunty's armchair when Polly's fiendish voice permitted, I became attracted to the green leafy world beyond the french windows and noticed at intervals two or three small brown birds flying between the garden rockery and the roof. Betty told me they were house sparrows. One hot Saturday afternoon, she took me by the hand and helped me wobble unsteadily out of the house into the yard and along to the cement block seat in front of the windows. She walked carefully and held my hand firmly. Her voice was assuring, maternal. When we were on the window seat, Betty then pointed up to the drainpipe and there in its crook beneath the guttering I saw the sparrow's nest, a round ball with streamers of hay and dried grass trailing out into the breeze.

Our neighbours, the Bennets, had built a sizeable shed up to the edge of our lawn. Where the shed ended the usual low privet hedge continued to the end of their garden and ours. Mum and Aunty called this rear corner of the house "Bennets Corner". The house sparrow pairs nesting in the crook of our drainpipe and that of our neighbour's had acres of garden space in which to search for their food. There were also the gardens on the other side of the road and the allotments beyond through which to forage.

Time and time again, Betty and I watched the brown birds flying steeply up to their nests in which, Betty told me, a brood of young sparrows waited for their parents to go in with food.

'Where do the young sparrows come from?' I asked.

Betty lost no time in explaining that each young bird, whatever its eventual size and shape, came from an egg. In my mind I immediately saw the hen's egg I sometimes had boiled for breakfast. Eggs, so far as I knew then, came from the kitchen but were laid by a bird called a hen.

'So when we eat an egg, are we eating a baby bird?' I asked.

'Well, not exactly,' Betty replied, while emphasising that the yolk we eat is also eaten by the baby bird during its time of development in the egg.

'How does it get out of the egg?' was my next question and after Betty explained that it breaks through with its beak, she went to the mossy bricked drain, fumbled about and returned with several fragments of shell cradled in the palm of one hand. The fragments were dull, white streaked or flecked with brownish grey. Betty said that we would keep the fragments and put them in an empty matchbox.

The hen sparrows chirped, while the black throated cock birds, Betty pointed out, paraded along the guttering and roof tiles, fluffing themselves into sizeable balls and jerking their upright tails. 'Showing off,' smiled Betty.

A week or so later on another hot Saturday afternoon, we went again to the window seat Betty and I, because the previous day I had watched, by peeping over the back of the settee, several young sparrows hopping about the rockery. There were three or four fledgling sparrows exploring the area in front of the french windows. Downy grey fronted baubles with brown flickering wings. Their calls, with which I soon familiarised myself indoors and out, varied from a single high pitched "chip" to a long drawn out "cheep" delivered about three octaves lower.

Leaving me on the seat, Betty went into Dad's woodshed and returned with three or four wicker baskets pebble-dashed with the stains of strawberries or raspberries. She informed me in her gentle maternal way that she was just going into the house for a minute. So I sat watching the sparrows, noticing how when an adult sparrow flew down with food each youngster quivered its wings and hopped forward calling, intent on attracting the food bearer's attention.

Smiling, Betty returned. In the base of each basket she had spread a layer of cotton wool. Placing the baskets on the edge of the rockery, she then knelt and gently picked up a baby sparrow. They were all lost she said. All needing a home. Those baskets lined with cotton wool? They were going to be new homes for each of the fledgling sparrows.

Intrigued, I stared at the neat bundle of grey down and brown feathers resting in the palm of Betty's hand, turning its head in one direction and then the other while still calling "chip, chip" but never once attempting to struggle free. The delicacy of its yellow sashed bill, the rounded head, and expression of sheer innocence centralised within its dark oval eye were reasons enough for an unfamiliar warmth to stir within the pit of my stomach. With an extended little finger, I gently caressed the back of the sparrow's head. Then Betty suggested I held the sparrow in the palm of my hand. The sparrow seemed weightless as the tiny feet and claws sought purchase against the contours of my skin.

In the meantime, Betty lifted another sparrow fledgling from the rockery and placed it into a strawberry basket.

Suddenly, I detected a rhythm pulsating effortlessly from my fledgling and told Betty that it was bouncing inside. As I spoke I saw my sister as I had seen her several times bouncing a ball against the yard wall.

'That's the heartbeat you can feel. You mustn't touch it beyond that which you're doing now. But that's its heartbeat. That's what's keeping it alive. You've got a heart like these baby sparrows and so have I,' Betty explained.

When she took the fledgling carefully from my hand and eased it into a basket, Betty put her hand to my chest, felt about and said, 'There it is! Feel that? That's where your heart is.' Lifting one of my hands, she showed me the underside of my wrist and had me feel the pulse beat. 'All this. It tells us we're alive,' smiled Betty.

When each of the four or five fledgling sparrows were sitting in a strawberry basket placed on the window seat, we stole away and back to the dining room. Wecould look at them over the back of the settee, said Betty.

Mum and Aunty were as usual in the kitchen washing and drying the pots, while the saliva forming scents of newly baked bread flooded through the kitchen making me want to stay.

When I told Mum the fledgling sparrows were lost, she retaliated, 'Lost! They're not lost! You shouldn't be touching them. Shouldn't be interfering. Their mother might not keep coming back with food if you do. You might frighten her away.'

'But *Betty* says they're lost,' I insisted.

Mum's blue eyes momentarily criticised Betty as she continued, 'Oh, I know. Everything's lost according to your sister. She's brought more dogs here on her way home from school than I've ever known in my life.'

'But where are the dogs?'

'They're gone. Like I've always told Betty they would go. She used to bring a dog home, we'd give it a meal on a plate and then off it would go, back home.'

'Back home?'

'Yes, back home. Because it wasn't lost any more than those baby sparrows are lost.'

That having been said, Betty ushered me into the dining room where we watched the parent sparrows feeding their brood even though each was snuggled in its Betty-selected strawberry basket.

Regarding the dogs my sister brought home, in the times which I am attempting to describe it was not uncommon to see dogs singly roaming the streets and crescents. People let their dogs out first thing in a morning and the dogs returned, no doubt when they were hungry or had patrolled their self-elected territories. There was also much less traffic on the roads and therefore little danger of the dog getting run over or causing an accident.

Before breakfast the next day, Betty and I looked over the back of the settee and saw five empty baskets on the window seat. In each was an indentation, a hollow made by the fledgling sparrows' bodies when they nestled into the relative comfort of the cotton wool base.

Out across the lawn and perched among the apple and plum tree branches were sparrow families, one of which we hoped was "ours"; the one into whose lives we had interfered the previous day.

Despite our compatibility in the garden and elsewhere, Betty and I occasionally quarrelled in the early morning.

Mum always awoke and carried me downstairs, where she would dress me while Aunty put out the breakfast. Because both Betty and Dad had left for school and work, respectively, I usually ate breakfast alone. On Saturday and Sunday mornings, however, I was joined by Betty. On being awakened by Mum, she would don a navy blue housecoat and slippers, go into the bathroom, splash cold water onto her face, then come down.

Quite often she looked pale, piqued and proved unwilling to make conversation. Occasionally, she would answer my question with a glib or cynical remark which puzzled me, for the sister whom I was to know later in the day was not at all like that. Just the opposite, in fact.

One Saturday morning, immediately after breakfast, I reached for a book which Betty slid immediately from my gaze while uttering, 'That's mine.'

'I only wanted to look at it.'

'You can't. I said it's mine,' admonished Betty, snatching up the book and sinking onto the settee.

Burning with a sudden and inwardly frightening anger, I lunged forward and began flaying Betty with my fists aiming for her face which she protected with the book while yelling, 'Mum! Mum!' Her yells, however, only incited me further. I regarded her face, shoulders and body as targets but when Mum came into the room, Betty grabbed my shoulders, flung me aside and stood book in hand before marching out of the room.

On another occasion when Betty told me to "go and eat coke", I bombarded her with settee cushions, my cheeks again on fire as I piled and stuffed the recurring round of cushions into her face with such force that Mum had to pull me off.

There dawned one of Betty's school going mornings when Mum was dressing me as usual. Turning from combing her hair in the mirror, Betty yelled, 'Mum! Stop treating my little brother like a doll! Teach him how to dress himself, for goodness sake! He's not a doll! Do you hear?'

In all the fifty odd future years that I was to know her, I never saw Mum look so guilty or have known her back down from an argument or altercation. She stubbornly never once regarded herself as having been rebuked. That morning proved the exception.

Mum was stunned. Her eyes lowered, face flushed. Guilt flared through my inner being for allowing Mum to dress me and not voluntary to dress myself.

The next morning Mum was by my side and instructing me on which buttons to fasten and zips to pull, while Betty watched us from the breakfast table. When I told Betty that I could dress myself, she grinned that warm maternal, yet slightly mischievous grin that I had come to love and said, 'Of course you can do it. *Of course you can,* You're a big boy now, not a baby. Not Mum's little doll.'

Once she had left the breakfast table, gone upstairs, washed, cleaned her teeth, dressed and brushed her hair, Betty returned to the room obviously feeling much better.

Once those early morning storm sessions were over, Betty shared everything with me. I recall kneeling on the carpet beside the hearth and watching her playing snobs, catching the dull red, green and blue squares on the back of her hand. We also attempted a children's magazine crossword or two. But the mainstay of our afternoons in together for both Betty and I was books. We loved them. And after and between reading sessions, we kept our books beneath the settee and armchair cushions because there wasn't a bookcase in the house.

The first book I perused for any length of time was *The Children of the New Forest* by Captain Marryat. Betty's copy had a thick red cover and she pointed out the page numbers and showed me both the book's binding and the spine. She further explained that books were put together at a printers and by a machine. That was why we, the readers, needed to be careful when we were handling them, because if roughly handled a book could come apart.

Pointing in turn to each of the relatively few illustrations, Betty told me about the English Civil War. The Roundheads and Cavaliers. She showed me a picture of the King, Charles I, and Prince Rupert. Moreover, she told me that the Civil War had actually taken place many years before in the countryside not far from our home. The book's only coloured page carried an illustration of two long haired men riding side by side. When Betty told me that one of the men was Prince Rupert, I imagined him riding with his colleague along Colliers Pad and Cherry Orchard at the top of the road.

Betty obviously discussed books with her friends, Kathleen and Barbara, and also the "Kittoes" - as Mum used to call them - and the Pearce sisters. Perhaps occasionally she loaned them out because she used to write in her small, neat hand on the inside cover of each volume —

> *"If this book should dare to roam,*
> *Just box its ears and send it home."*

In the bottom right-hand corner of the page Betty wrote her name and address. It was important that everyone knew their name and address she said, to which remark Aunty added that it would be very useful in the future, especially if the Germans invaded Great Britain.

So far as I was concerned, this last remark was falling on deaf ears. That was grown up talk. I didn't know, or *want* to know, about the Germans invading Great Britain. My address, however, was a different matter. On alternative days I sat on either Aunty's or Betty's lap and had them point out to me —

(Number)   CHALFONT DRIVE,
                       WESTERN BOULEVARD,
                       NOTTINGHAM.

Each time that we picked up the book that is what we studied. Our address.

'So if someone in the future asks who you are, then you say, ' "I'm Keith Taylor" and give them your address,' Aunty explained, as indeed did Betty.

But who was going to ask? I would be with Mum, or Dad, or Betty, or Aunty. I would *always* be with one or other of these members of my family. So why was it so important that I tell someone else?

'Well, you never know,' said Aunty in answer to this question when she was working on her sewing machine, 'You just never know.'

I knew my name and address all right, but I was going to live with my family until I was an old man like Rip Van Winkle and my heart stopped beating. Like the fledgling sparrow would die when its heart stopped beating. We would be smiling and in my case I would be sporting a long white beard. So who would be wanting to know my name and address in the meantime?

***

In June 1940, Italy declared war on Britain and France. On the fourteenth of that month the Germans swarmed into Paris and days later France signed a double zoned armistice with Germany.

Incidents, withdrawals and invasions not directly threatening to the British people occurred for a further year.

By 13th August the German Air Force (Luftwaffe) had made nearly 1800 sorties against the Royal Air Force in what was shortly to become known as the Battle of

Britain. By comparison, the Royal Air Force made 975 sorties after which the Luftwaffe, for two weeks, bombed all the airfields, the associated aircraft and installations manned by the Royal Air Force.

On 23rd August the Luftwaffe bombed London throughout the night and again on the 25th the Royal Air Force retaliated by bombing Berlin.

Two nights later, the Luftwaffe bombed *twenty-one* British cities and towns. London was again targeted on 7th September, the forerunner of a long-term and terrifying campaign that became nationally known as The Blitz.

By November, the Luftwaffe were bombing Southampton, Bristol, Birmingham, Coventry, Liverpool and Glasgow.

Demonstrations occurred in many city streets, particularly London, due to Italy's proclamation of war, and stones were hurled and the windows smashed of Italian cafés and gents barbers. Some Italian shopkeepers removed their shop signs, but those who were known were shunned and in some instances discriminated against. Occasionally, the neighbour of an Italian shopkeeper erected a sign indicating that "THIS SHOP IS BRITISH".

CHAPTER 6

The Children of the New Forest had me wishing that we too had a cottage in the woods. We had to make do with Colliers Pad, the stones, ruts and surrounding vegetation that I studied when tightly grasping Aunty's hand I walked with her to the off-licence situated on a street corner of the coal mining community at nearly Radford Woodhouse.

The streets of this community nestled into a curve of railway embankment, comprised of ninety-eight terraced houses, a chapel and the off-licence.

My mind, after Saturday and Sunday when I saw more of Dad and Betty, was gradually settling into a routine and I began associating mine and Aunty's yeast buying visits to the off-licence with first thing after tea on a Monday.

I loved the little shop. Its chiming doorbell and brass handle which I couldn't reach. Its windows cluttered with wash powders, soap, sweeping brushes and mops. Then once inside, the low beamed snugness. The gleam of the bacon machine, the smells of smoked bacon, yeast and something indescribable but to which my nostrils were instantly receptive.

'Ale! That's what you can smell, young fella. Good, wholesome, hearty English brewed ale,' laughed white haired Mrs. Kirk, the shopkeeper, when she heard me telling Aunty how much I liked the smell.

The moment I left the breakfast table each morning, I went to Aunty's armchair or the settee, lifted the cushion and took from beneath it a book. Or if I saw *The Daily Sketch* newspaper on the settee or a corner of the table, I would kneel in my chair if Mum or Aunty had removed the table cloth and not only scan the pages, but attempt to pick out certain words like London and read them out aloud.

Some of the words I did not understand but if they were nouns or names and a photograph appeared alongside, then I would associate the name as a word with the image or newspaper photograph. King is probably the first name that I learnt to associate in this way, as with Mum and sometimes Aunty or Betty, I invented my own quiz game called "Who's That?".

Seeing a photograph in the newspaper, I would stab it with a forefinger and ask, 'Who's that?' and when one or other of the women answered 'The King', they would then point out the name in the accompanying caption. Thus over the days I became aware that the King was called "George the Sixth" and his wife "Queen Elizabeth". The taller very distinguished looking lady who was sometimes photographed with them was the King's mother, Queen Mary.

Quite often the Royal Family were photographed on a balcony, which I learned from Betty fronted their London home known as Buckingham Palace. Betty chose, however, not to tell me that this Royal residence was bombed on 10th September 1940, or perhaps at the time I was looking at the photographs the bombing had still to occur.

The Queen was then prompted into publicly saying, 'I'm glad we've been bombed. It makes me feel I can look the East End in the face.'

The two little girls accompanying the King and Queen were, Betty explained, their children, the Princesses Elizabeth and Margaret.

Intrigued by the Royal couple's robes of office, I then asked Betty what the funny

28

things on their heads were called. When Betty explained that these were crowns, I told her in all honesty that I wouldn't like to wear one because they looked too heavy, whereupon Betty confided that she wouldn't like to be a Queen either and have to sit on a throne all day and wait for someone to come with a question or message.

The Daily Sketch also featured a cartoon character called Dagwood, he of the lank frame and morose expression who always had three sprigs of hair springing out from the crown of his head. Dagwood I also read out aloud but the name of his wife Daisy was a little more difficult. However, Mum came and stood over me, tea towel in hand and items of cutlery gleaming between the folds, and helped me pronounce and read the name.

Later that day, I surprised myself and Aunty upon whose lap I was sitting by reading out the title of the book we happened to be looking at. 'Marco Polo,' I murmured uncertainly, while a delighted Aunty enthused —

'Good boy! Good boy!'

The rest of the book I left to her because I wanted to listen to the story, *have it read to me* rather than struggle with the words myself.

After *Marco Polo*, Aunty then produced *My Alphabet* and together, seemingly for hours, she pointed out the letters and we read them together before she persuaded me to read them out to her and eventually a beaming Mum who forever seemed to be going to and from the kitchen.

One morning when I read from the *Daily Sketch* the word Nazi out aloud, Mum came up behind me, pretended to scan the war connected article, and squinting discreetly removed the entire newspaper from my gaze.

Her concern was repeated when I gazed at the monochrome print of a slender nosed man with a black moustache. Beneath the print were two words which I struggled to decipher, ADOLF HITLER. On this occasion, Mum was less discreet as she removed the newspaper.

'Does that say "Adolf Hitler"?' I asked.

'Yes, but you don't want to be reading about and looking at pictures of *him*,' she replied curtly.

'Why not?'

'Because he's the man who's started the war.'

'*Why* has he started the war?'

'Because he wants our country and other countries besides his own.'

'Why does he?'

'He's greedy, that's why?'

'He wants to own the world,' Aunty cut in.

'And we're not going to let him. Is that right?'

'That's right. This is our country, our island. Hitler comes from Germany, not far I shouldn't think from where Strauss wrote your beloved *Blue Danube Waltz*. He's nothing to do with us though, Hitler. We don't want him here and we're not having him,' Aunty continued.

'But if Hitler's a German - a Gerry, what are we?'

'British. We are British people living in Great Britain. Hitler is a Gerry, a Nazi, who comes from Germany,' Aunty explained as she handed me the recent book on Magellan's voyage to replace the newspaper Mum had edged from my gaze.

Then I heard Mum saying, 'That's enough for now, Amy. Don't tell him anything more about the war please.'

'But he has to know. He has a *right* to know.'

'Not at his tender age, I don't think he has. No just leave it at that please, Amy.'

Some things were happening beyond my home about which I wasn't supposed to know. Nasty things by the sounds of it! Well, *The Daily Sketch* would tell me what *they* were. If I couldn't read the words, I could at least look at the pictures before Mum whisked the newspaper from my gaze. And when it was whisked from my gaze, where did Mum put *The Daily Sketch*? If she didn't place it high, I'd probably find it in the tall gas meter cupboard, or the shoe cleaning cupboard beside the ringer and Monday morning's washtub. One day when there was no one in the kitchen, I would go and look. But was there a time of day when either Aunty or Mum weren't in the kitchen?

If my perusals of Adolf Hitler roused Mum from her repetitive chores in the kitchen, so did the voice of the world-renowned tenor, Richard Tauber, whom she recognised the instant she heard him projecting his every smooth rendering of *My Heart and I* from the wireless. Cutlery, plates or tea towel in hand, Mum would rush girlishly into the dining room and stand beside the wireless, head turned slightly to one side or blue eyes seemingly concentrating on the garden beyond the french windows. Other tenors, other singers failed to move Mum in the same way and I fell to considering why. What was special about Richard Tauber? Come to think of it, why did Aunty make so much of her Nelson Eddy and Jeanette MacDonald *Indian Love Call* recording? And again, Dad when he was shaving in the bathroom or digging or planting fruit trees in the garden for something he called "The War Effort", why did he always whistle *Vilja*? But then what about me? I still loved listening to Johann Strauss' *The Blue Danube Waltz*. So was everyone in the world affected by voices and orchestrations in the same way?

In later life Mum mentioned a relative who at the age of eighty-three collapsed and died on the stage of a Nottingham music hall while singing and entertaining an audience. From which side of the family he originated she failed to mention, if indeed she intended to tell me because not only did Mum choose to keep news of the war from me but matters relating to death, dying and family arguments, the prospects of visiting the dentist or one day becoming a soldier myself.

By contrast, she was keen for me to see the world beyond the windows: the foliaged trees, shape of clouds, a blue tit or great tit perched and feeding from a knob of lard or suet suspended by a string from the lower branches of a garden pear tree.

One Monday after tea, Aunty donned her long russet overcoat despite the continuing sunlight and told me that I could go with her to Cunnah's, the newsagent's and post office situated in the block of shops on Middleton Boulevard. There were some items of stationery she wanted to buy and maybe for me a pop-up book with characters that sprang upright when you turned the pages but to which there was very little by way of a story attached.

The possible lack of a story or rhyme secretly disappointed me but the thought of going for a walk with Aunty, who could resist it!

We walked 'over the top,' as Aunty frequently referred to Colliers Pad, then to Mr. Kirk's to buy yeast for the Tuesday afternoon baking session. Men in caps, white shirts and with their trousers supported by braces sat outside the street doorways or in twos and threes along the kerbside. Here and there we glimpsed one riding a bicycle. They nodded. Put up a hand. Smiled or called out.

'Do you know them, Aunty?' I queried.

'No, it's just the way some people are. Besides which, I once heard it said that war brings people closer together and I can well believe it now,' Aunty replied.

Halfway along Radford Bridge Road, built in amongst the houses to the right was a newsagent's and a fish and chip shop. To the left, where the streets finished, allotments spanned the width of land between Radford Bridge Road and the council houses of Southwold Drive, which like the road on which we lived opened out onto sylvan Western Boulevard.

Presently we came to houses like our own, detached and with walls built from local stone. Intriguing to me was a rambling white farmhouse which had once belonged to the Middleton Estates, its last tenant being Mr. Jack Matthews who had also maintained the lime kiln site on which the allotments had since been built.

'But if it's a farmhouse, where are the cows and the pigs and the sheep and the chickens, Aunty?'

'Oh, they all went when the estate was sold. And the fields were here where the houses and gardens and road is. We're walking on them now.'

Later in life, when I was researching for a local history publication on the area, I learned that the dairy herd used to be driven twice daily along this road at the top of which a five barred gate marked the boundary of an agricultural, boat building and mining community combined. With Aunty that evening I drew in my breath for perhaps the second or third time when I saw the long, reedy backwater of the Nottingham canal edging towards the post and rail fence where the last of the houses terminated on the right.

Between the backwater's end and the last house wall a narrow path curved up an exceptionally steep bank to the lock gates and towpath beyond. I gazed enraptured at the mirrored water. The masses of reed stems quivering slightly in the breeze. The long grasses and wild flowers of the nearside bank. Then to my disappointment, the canal became screened by a solid fence made from railway sleepers placed upright. There was a gate in the fence and several outbuildings, for this was the British Waterways' boat building and repair yard. Opposite stood Pear Tree Cottage, a red roofed house with its main doorway facing east and imposing because it was also twice the size of the house in which I lived with my family and Aunty. It had always been - and perhaps still was - the home of the boat repair and canal maintenance foreman and his family.

The road then brought Aunty and I to the canal bridge and the point at which Radford Bridge Road joined the Western and Middleton Boulevards.

Certainly there were rows of lime trees here and grass inlaid central reservations. But between the Middleton Boulevard shops and the trolley bus parked in front and at the thirty-nine bus terminus stood a cement ramp or wall. Before yet another question sprang from my lips, Aunty explained that the barricade was one of several erected along those green foliaged miles of the Nottingham ring road. There was a gap just wide enough for the thirty-nine bus to pass through. Should a convoy of German tanks, or the Wehrmacht, attempt the same manoeuvre because of the width and bulk of each machine they would find themselves thwarted and possibly surrendering into British hands.

'Are the Germans here already then, Aunty?' I chirped.

'No, not yet. They haven't set foot on British soil as far as we know. But barricades like this are known as a precaution. Just in case they do.'

Aunty then pointed to the John Player's bonded warehouse situated in the Nottingham direction and about a quarter of a mile away. 'They've painted that black, look, so that the Luftwaffe pilots can't pick it out so easily when they're coming over on a bombing raid.'

'A bombing raid! What's... ?'

'Oh, never mind about that for now, Keith. Let's go across to Cunnah's and buy my writing pad and envelopes and your pop-up book.'

A novelty though it soon proved, the pop-up book came second to the blue exercise book Aunty also bought for me. A lined book in which I could write and that had a series of involved looking times tables printed on its inside covers. The back outer cover was like none I have seen since, for imprinted within the cover's overall blue background was the sharp black outlined illustration of a red deer stag.

Back at home with Aunty and in the armchair beside bad tempered Polly's case, I studied the illustration.

The stag was depicted sideways on, its head swung around and uplifted as it gazed nervously in my direction. The eyes held the expression of fear; uncertainty. The ears were pointed. The curved neck carried a full mane. The shoulders positioned muscularly and just above the dorsal line of its back. The stag's rear quarters were rounded. Its tail short, prominent. Legs long and slender. Antlers upsweeping, symmetrical in shape. The points or tines twelve in all, equally matched either side.

Aunty told me that a stag bearing twelve equally matching tines was called a Royal. In the background was a stretch of water - a loch as Aunty explained, and a range of mountains.

'That's Scotland. The Highlands where the red deer live. But there are red deer in the park here, just beyond Radford Woodhouse and the Middleton Boulevard shops,' Aunty concluded while drawing me snugly into the side of her hip.

'Are there? When can we — ?'

'Well, perhaps tomorrow evening, straight after tea if the weather stays fine,' smiled Aunty.

Aunty was, as always, as good as her word. The following evening we ventured beyond Cunnah's and the Harrow Road School where Betty was by then a pupil, to a green railed high fence and gateway positioned between a row of houses. This, explained Aunty, was Wollaton Park where Lord and Lady Middleton had once lived in the Elizabethan mansion screened by late summer foliage.

The trees were basically oaks and we were walking a track known as Digby Avenue. There was a wood to our right and in the long grasses of a spinney a hundred or so yards away a herd of red deer hinds couched and cudded, while others stood nibbling the low hanging tree foliage.

I studied the shapes of their jaw lines and muzzles. The pointed ears flickering because, Aunty said, the flies and midges were bothering them.

The coats of the deer were smooth and red which is how they became so named. In autumn and winter their coats thickened so that they could withstand the cold and driving rain especially in Scotland, Aunty explained.

Glancing at the brooding clouds, Aunty continued. 'Actually, it's coming on to rain now. So I think we should be turning for home, even though I have my umbrella.'

We arrived home just as the rain began slanting silver across the many squared panes of the french windows.

Dad and Betty were home from work and late school activities, respectively, and at the table eating together. Eagerly, I relayed mine and Aunty's latest adventure. Noticing before hearing the rain coming down heavier, Mum said as she came into the room, 'There'll probably be less chance of a bombing raid if it rains all night,' to which Betty glumly answered —

'But there's always tomorrow night.'

Collectively then, the family realised that I was with them and fell silent, at least until I asked, 'What do the deer do when its raining, Aunty?'

'Stand under the trees until it stops,' she answered.

Mum then addressing me said, 'Well I'll get your hot milk and tot of whisky ready for your night-time drink,' and went into the kitchen.

After Aunty had played her latest recording, she produced another and watched my face as I listened to the soothing orchestration of *In a Monastery Garden*, because every now and again the bird impersonator and world-famous whistler, Ronnie Ronalde, gave his rendering of a blackbird's song. The notes were rambling, repetitive, yet sublime in their deliverance. Aunty told me to imagine a summer's evening and the monastery walls overhung with greenery, the garden borders bedecked in summer flowers. 'If you close your eyes you can see the bees hovering over the flower heads, all in your mind,' whispered Aunty.

But as soon as I closed my eyes, Mum nudged my finger tips and proffered my mug of hot milk laced with whisky. 'Sip that while you're imagining,' Mum cajoled.

The whisky? There was enough in that mug of milk to ensure that I wouldn't open my eyes again until Mum announced that breakfast was ready the following morning. And that had been, and continued to be, the pattern for many weeks and months apparently.

Tears, however, moistened my eyes due not to the whisky fumes, but on that particular occasion the blackbird's song. It was the equivalent of Strauss, Richard Tauber, or any human form of music.

Where could I hear a blackbird singing like that? I asked.

Dad told me that he heard them earlier in the year at first light (which because of my whisky-drugged state I never experienced) and again when he was walking home along Western Boulevard in the evening. He heard blackbird after blackbird after blackbird. Yes, they came into our garden, onto our lawns and perched in the branches of our fruit trees. They sang from the Boulevard limes and the housing estate rooftops. They also hunted for food and reared their young in the nests hidden in the hedgerows of the New Aspley Gardens, positioned behind the houses on the opposite side of the road and which Betty and Aunty could see from their bedroom windows.

Aunty then pointed out as tears continued to moisten my eyelids that Ronnie Ronalde was indeed a clever man because he could imitate a blackbird. So he must have studied blackbirds. Thought blackbirds. Particularly the blackbird's larynx.

Before succumbing to the whisky drug completely, I had two more questions to ask, 'What is a monastery?'

'It's a place where monks live.'

'What is a monk?'

'Oh *Keith*, surely it's time Mum took you up to bed now,' shrilled Betty defensively.

Bedtime it may well have been, but I wasn't going to be carried up the stairs until the blackbird had ceased whistling!

Eventually, the combined effects of whisky and daily exhaustion took their toll and like every night I slept, although *too* soundly some may think. In the meantime, the family and families throughout Great Britain, France, Germany and Poland no doubt settled in to face the darkness, the possible horrors and devastation of those many nights that preceded the uncertainties of morning.

When I saw photographs of a hairless man smoking a cigar, I stabbed it with a forefinger and asked, 'Who's that?'

Mum, squinting slightly, answered 'Winston Churchill.'

She or Aunty then pointed to his name and together and slowly we read it out.

There were many photographs of the Dunkirk evacuation and I asked Mum who had taken them.

'Photo journalists, I should think,' she answered, and I immediately realised or *knew* that they were not in uniform and to some degree this realisation intrigued me. I liked the idea of taking photographs for newspapers and still made much of *The Daily Sketch* pages while eating my porridge breakfast. But I also regarded breakfast as an unnecessary chore, although I enjoyed eating at the table with the entire family around midday each Sunday. That was unless I was rebuked by Betty who would suddenly hiss, 'Sit up straight. Come *on*! Straighten your back. You don't sit slouched over your plate like that.'

Startled, I would wriggle on my chair while exclaiming, 'Well *I* do, so shut up you! *Shut up*!

On another occasion I felt belittled because Betty pointed out that I wasn't holding my knife and fork properly.

'You hold them like *this*. Not like that! Where do you think you are? *I'll* tell you off if no one else here will?'

With my ears and cheeks burning, I assessed the proximity of my weapons - the settee cushions, while answering Betty with, 'Shan't!' Yet I attempted to hold my knife and fork as she demanded and once she saw this, my sister calmed. I could have eaten slices of beef or lamb swathed with deep brown home-made gravy and vegetables for the rest of my life and was still chewing when the family were gathering up the pots and clearing the table.

Apart from Betty's occasional rebuke, I regarded the dinner table as a very comfortable place to be. But one Sunday lunchtime I lifted from the side of my plate and swallowed a lump of mustard. God! Within seconds I lost control of my knife and fork, posture and almost my entire being. My throat was on fire! My eyes were running. And I couldn't stop coughing.

Betty remained at the table but Mum or Aunty hurried to the kitchen as I yelped and yelled until a glass of water was placed before me.

'Sip it slowly,' someone advised.

Slowly! I seemed to have drained it in five seconds. Nor did I touch mustard again for some years.

Was being in the war out there worse than swallowing a lump of mustard? I later wondered.

For a birthday, Mum or Aunty knitted me a green, long sleeved jumper with two stags emblazoned on the chest motif fashion. They were so pleased with it that the next thing I heard related again to photography. Betty and I were going to be photographed at Freckletons Studios in the centre of Nottingham.

The resulting photograph was going to be framed and hung on the dining room wall. Moreover, I could take, if I carried it under my arm, a cuddly toy spaniel which was also another present.

Mum and Aunty accompanied Betty and I to Freckletons. It was my first experience of a room in a city, although not a comfortable room because a man in a dark suit and carrying a tripod kept telling us in which direction to look. Eventually he pointed to a toy bird in a cage. 'Look up at that bird, Keith and Betty.'

As we did I thought of Polly.

The bus journeys to and from the city were also the first I can recall. For me they held no interest for I wanted to get home to my books.

On alighting at the Middleton Boulevard terminus we had then a mile or so to walk. But not through Radford Woodhouse. Betty didn't particularly like going that way, and so we walked the Boulevards.

Someone said, 'I hope there won't be a daylight air raid.'

To me, however, this meant little for I was still anxious to get back to my nursery rhymes and the story of Dick Whittington.

Halfway through each week, Mum or Aunty made a rabbit pie and served it with hot gravy and three or four portions of vegetables, one of which was always potatoes. The rabbit, usually one but sometimes two, was delivered to the front door by a lean man who wore a cloth cap, glasses and had silvery white hair. He had at one time lived in a communal yard like Mum and Dad, except that the yard of his childhood was attached to Lord and Lady Middleton's estate at nearby Wollaton.

'It was a hovel existence, more or less,' was how the man described his early days to Mum as rabbit dangling from his fingers he stood talking to her at the front door, while fascinated I stood beside her and noticed that the eyes of the dead rabbit were wide open. Mum, and indeed everyone in the house, used to refer to everyone by name but the names of this man and his sidekick we never learned. Consequently, we referred to them as The Rabbit Men.

They were, in retrospect, the first true countrymen I had seen. Sometimes alternating between brown or black overcoats, grey trousers and black shoes, and always hunched as they trundled between them a two-wheeled cart piled with snared rabbits up the middle of the road.

'They don't look very smart,' said Aunty pushing her fingers through her hair as she stood one lunchtime behind the front room net curtains watching them.

'Well, poor lads, I don't suppose they can afford to go around each wearing top hats and swallow tailed coats if they're only selling rabbits,' chuckled Mum.

Besides the rabbits dangling from his fingers, the Rabbit Man carried a knife the handle of which protruded from his overcoat pocket

'One rabbit or two today, madam?' the Rabbit Man usually asked.

When Mum had made her choice, he would then grasp the handle of his knife while asking, 'Do you want me to cut its feet off? Or shall I leave them on so it can run you out of debt?' When after seconds the man produced the knife, he added, 'I'll cut the eyes out for yer if yer want, missus. Or do yer want me to leave em in? See yer through to next Saturday?'

'Oh, I can handle a rabbit, skin it, do the lot,' Mum smiled as the man handed her the one or two rabbits for which she paid him one shilling and sixpence each.

There dawned a day when Polly attacked Aunty and badly lacerated her hand for the last time. Throughout the morning while Mum was at the shops, Aunty's hand smelled of Dettol or iodine and Mum had bandaged it.

Polly, the parrot, had in the last weeks shrieked unbearably whenever anyone went near her cage. And the shrieks became louder with each passing day.

'It's wrong for people to keep birds in cages,' Aunty murmured sadly, although she did agree that Polly was a fiend who when at first she was allowed to fly freely around the room, clawed at the family's faces and once Betty was so shocked she went up to her bedroom and refused to come down. Aunty in the more recent times began to tire of having her hands bandaged. She therefore made the decision that on this particular weekday with the dinner pots and dishes washed, stacked and glistening on the draining board, we were taking Polly in a bag to somewhere called the PDSA and have someone deftly stick a needle into her body so that she would sleep forever. Moreover, we were not bringing her back home.

This was explained as Mum helped me on with my jacket and coat, then took my little navy cap from the peg and placed it onto my head.

'Do you want to see Polly for one last time?' asked Mum.

Polly was, as usual, on her perch but rocking backwards and forward in a strange and menacing rhythm. On seeing me, she swore in an avian fashion and sidled to my side of the cage. I was aware of her clawed feet and hooked bill. Then she shrieked......shrieked......shrieked.

Wearing her long russet overcoat and carrying a leather bag with a silver zip across the top, Aunty entered the room and made straight for Polly's cage. Aunty, I noticed, was not wearing gloves.

'Keith, come into the hall out of the way,' Mum urged from her position beside the dining room door. I was surprised at the tremor in Mum's voice. Once I was in the hall, Mum closed the door. We heard the clank of cage bars. Then Polly began shrieking and again in my mind I saw her hooked beak, agape and revealing her pinkish-blue tongue.

In an effort to erase this image from my mind, I studied the door panels, all beautifully sheened with mottled woodwork so that you were almost afraid to touch and leave your fingerprints on them.

'It's walnut,' said Mum in answer to my question.

When, with Polly shrieking in the background, I asked Mum who had varnished all the doors, picture rails, stair banisters and skirting boards in the house, she told me it was Dad. The toilet and bathroom doors to the right at the top of the landing, however, he had painted cream.

When the door of Polly's cage clanked shut for the last time, I knew that there would be sunflower seeds and husks from Polly's feeding trough scattered all over Aunty's sewing machine.

Polly had fallen silent. It was a marvellous silence. Well deserved. Then the dining room door opened and Aunty came out brandishing the zipped bag. She smiled but looked white and shaken. 'I think Polly and me are *both* suffering from shock,' she said.

The sight of blood streaming down the back of Aunty's pale, blue veined hand startled me.

Mum went upstairs and returned with the iodine bottle and a white tin containing plasters and bandages. Mum's eyes were very wide, very blue. Her cheeks red. Her expression registering concern. She told me to stand beside the bag while she bandaged Aunty's hand in the kitchen.

Stand near the bag! Could Polly - would Polly - fly out? She had always been a prisoner, in a succession of crates and cages and now a zipped up bag.

Wearing hats and coats and with Mum carrying an umbrella, Mum and Aunty came from the kitchen. Aunty picked up the bag and as we turned the key in the door lock, I noticed how red and highly polished were the tiles in the front porch. There were no buses and so we had to walk those two or so miles to the PDSA and back, which entailed an overall journey of around five miles. This was the longest walk I had undertaken to date.

We walked to Colliers Pad and along by The Tallest Tree and the Humps and Hollows field. At the far end a lane or track led across the fields to the woods at the back of Cunnah's shop on Beechdale Road. The track was greyish blue, the colour, Aunty explained, of coal dust. On the track, with their backs to us, two people rode horses as in Captain Marryat's novel *The Children of the New Forest* the overdressed Prince Rupert had been portrayed.

Once across Beechdale Road and down the slope by the houses and beneath the railway bridge we arrived at the mining community. As we walked the flagstone pavement alongside Jackie Matthews spacious white farmhouse, Aunty pointed to a group of heavy birds, 'Geese, Keith. Look. I bet they paddle on the canal at the back. Remember the nursery rhyme? How does it go?

"Goosey Goosey Gander
Where do you wander?......'   enthused Aunty.

'Why is the canal at the back, though?' I asked.

'Oh, but it isn't, not all the way. Look here,' said Aunty.

We walked the flagstone pavement for another five or six houses to where a narrow path left the roadside and progressed up the steep grassy bank to the flight of lock gates.

Next to the path the long backwater flowed widely from the widely mirrored canal pound and fringed the bank of reeds and meadow grass that was separated from the road by a post and rail fence.

Suddenly I wanted to stay; there beside the reeds, the lock gates and the water. Felt somehow *compelled* to stay. While peering at the water between the supports of the post and rail fence, I little realised that I would be spending many hours exploring this fourteen mile long waterway in the years to come.

But it was ancestral memory speaking on that first and all future visits to the canal, although some fifty odd years were to pass before I learned that some of the Bonsers, on my mother's side of the family, had been narrowboat people who journeyed weekly along the Cromford Canal in Derbyshire and lived in a Derbyshire canal side community known as Pinxton Wharf.

My great grandparents may have been narrowboat people, although if Mum was ever aware of this she never related the possibility perhaps because, like many working-class people at the bottom of the wage scale in those days, she was ashamed of the poverty associated with her family background.

When while carrying Polly we passed the backwater arm, the canal became closed from view by the fence made from railway sleepers, placed close together and dug deeply into the ground. When I peered through the occasional and narrow cracks in the railway sleeper fence, I saw the outbuildings of the barge and narrowboat repair yard and my first vessel, a grey barge, moored close to the bank. Aunty and Mum explained to me what they were, while adding that the last narrowboat had journeyed down the canal to its termination point on the River Trent some five or six years previously.

'The canal is now what they call derelict but you can still walk alongside it,' Mum confirmed.

By the Crown Hotel we crossed the canal bridge and I was aware of the Middleton Boulevard shops and particularly Cunnah's, on that occasion screened by trees.

We had then to walk the long bend known as Middleton Boulevard which like the more familiar and adjoining Western Boulevard had a wide grassed central reservation and four lines of matured lime trees continuing along its length.

Most of the properties fronting the Boulevard were bungalows, council owned at the time and individual in style. Each stood in a separate garden bordered by privet hedges.

Occasionally we passed a spinney of tall pine or oak trees and Aunty explained that these had once stood in the enclosed confines of the by then much reduced Wollaton Park.

A steep hill then took us to a small traffic island at the junction of Derby Road. How much further, I wondered? Again I glimpsed the barricades placed almost across the width of the sixteen mile road connecting Nottingham to Derby.

The cars and flat backed lorries travelling the roads in those days, I should add, were infrequent to the point of hearing them long before they came into view. 'Car coming!' we would exclaim.

The pace of both Mum and Aunty was of course hindered by me who had said farewell to the pram and pushchair. Yet never had I walked so far.

Clifton Boulevard plunged steeply downhill. Over to the right, across the Boulevard which had been planted with fewer trees, stretched acres of high rolling fields inset with a sandstone bluff. This tract of land was known, nor surprisingly, as Highfields.

Several sleek black horses grazed here but different horses in appearance to the ones I had seen earlier. They had, Mum explained, docked tails and were used in funeral corteges, something which I suddenly wanted to know nothing about. Before the funeral firm had rented the fields for grazing their horses, however, I learned in later years that the family who owned the land and lived in a secluded mansion nearby used to graze and breed a herd of black Highland cattle on these fields. They had fresh bloodstock brought in from the Scottish breeders to the nearby station by rail.

James Shipstone, the local brewer, lived beyond the secluded mansion but in a similarly ornate house surrounded by lawns and beech trees.

The first people to move into the bungalows on Middleton Boulevard remembered James Shipstone, by then an elderly man, walking briskly along the pavement swinging his black, silver tipped walking stick and raising his trilby to everyone he passed, while his chauffeur drove one of the brewer's Rolls Royces slowly alongside so that when it rained or he became tired, James Shipstone halted the Rolls and travelled the three or four miles along the Boulevard in style. James Shipstone's brewery, incidentally, was situated about two miles north-east of our home.

With Mum and Aunty that afternoon I became fascinated by the contours of the quarry. The geological layers. Roots of oak and beech trees exposed, yet embedded into the earth.

Eventually, we came to a T junction, houses and buildings connected to the community districts of Lenton and Dunkirk. We turned left. I enthused at the steep hump of Abbey Bridge which took the road over the hidden canal. Then we were at the farmhouse.

It was a fascinating old building with a tiled roof, green window shutters and pear trees extending along its outer walls, as Mum pointed out. The outbuildings had been bulldozed aside and several benches were arranged along the low walls of the yard. A sign outside informed us that we had arrived at The People's Dispensary For Sick Animals. Mum decided that she and I should sit outside. Aunty agreed and took the bag containing Polly into the farmhouse surgery.

Mum was staring ahead. In retrospect, I realise she was looking at the roofs of Cloister Square, the communal yard beside the canal and in which, as a girl, she used to play. Here she and her sisters ventured along the canal towpath and around lock gates and when the girls saw a narrowboat and its fore-tethered horse approaching, they ran home and begged sugar lumps from their mother. These they fed to the horse.

In her ninetieth year, Mum, still with wide blue eyes and a retentive memory, told me that the canal horses were beaten and general treated badly. 'Poor things. Animal cruelty just didn't come in to it,' she sighed.

Presently the farmhouse door opened and Aunty came out carrying the bag. She walked with a white smocked man beside her. Aunty always appeared tall to me, but as she stood talking to this man - the vet as Mum explained - she seemed to be addressing his chin. The vet was like most men of the times, white haired. He also wore darkly rimmed glasses and was stooped.

Between them they had decided to open Polly's bag outside rather than risk the parrot attacking people in the surgery. Tentatively, the vet took the bag from Aunty's grasp. Aunty's expression registered concern. The vet carefully unzipped the bag. I sat, as I think Aunty stood, with bated breath. Pausing, the vet placed his hand gingerly inside the bag. Aunty stepped back. The vet withdrew his hand from the bag. He then lifted Polly; inert. A bundle of dark green feathers. He and Aunty exchanged a few words, then Aunty smiled, nodded and taking the empty bag walked towards us.

'Was Polly — ?' Mum began.

'Suffocated. On the way down here. There was no air in the bag so the poor bird suffocated,' Aunty explained as Mum and I walked beside her. Suffocated? I had to ask. Polly, due to the lack of air in the bag, had gone to sleep of her own accord. The vet had said, 'Well this parrot isn't going to hurt anyone again,' when he withdrew Polly's body. So suffocation, I surmised, had to do with not getting air! I inhaled deeply. And again!

'Are you all right, Keith?' queried Mum as we turned for home. I answered in the affirmative because I could feel the air around me entering my nostrils. Was aware of what I now knew to be my chest and lungs.

CHAPTER 7

Dinnertime for a working-class family like ourselves was not in the evening but between twelve thirty to one in the early afternoon.

On quite a number of Sundays, soon after Mum and Aunty had cleared away the dishes and Dad returned to the garden, mine and Betty's cousins arrived having walked the three or so miles from their home at Stockhill.

The family bond was strong and remained that way until each of the girls married and moved away to raise families of their own.

The instant Mum heard the front door open and knuckles gently wrapping the glass, she almost ran from the kitchen to greet her nieces and open the door of the small lobby situated beside the front door so that they could hang up their coats. There were no formalities; it was a family welcome. Much laughter, talk and general warmth exuding in a way that I have seldom known since.

None of the downstairs rooms were closed to my cousins, although the front room or lounge as I was to discover in later years was usually reserved for party occasions and formal discussions.

Sylvia frequently led the way from the lobby to the kitchen or dining room, always laughing and referring to Mum as Aunty. Sylvia, tall, slim, with laughing blue eyes and a mass of tight blonde curls crowning her head. Like her mother, whom I was not to meet for some years, she was fair skinned, freckled and often dressed in a blue two or three-piece skirted outfit or a splendid sky blue dress spotted with white which also boasted white cuffs and collar.

Sylvia was narrow waisted, supple, athletic and surprisingly strong, as on most of her visits I discovered to my cost because, much though I disliked it, she could barely resist tickling me.

She was, like my sister Betty, around the school leaving age and her methods of trapping me into confinement varied, even though I several times crept and hid beneath the dining room table. Sometimes she would sit beside me on the settee, look at the books and discuss the stories and nursery rhymes, then suddenly clamp me into her hip with surprising speed and force before the tickling sessions began. Or she occasionally stood over me, reaching down to carefully thumb through a book. Then her long, steel hard hands suddenly clamped against my shoulders and she would sit whilst again keeping me restrained.

I laughed, I wriggled. Pleaded for her to stop. But her tormenting fingertips plunged repeatedly backwards and forwards as she tickled me around the waist and hips. Sometimes I feared she would never stop, kick out and wriggle in retaliation though I did. Betty and my other cousins usually stood giggling in the background. No one, except Mum, made a move to help.

'He's ticklish, ticklish, ticklish, ticklish,' Sylvia would chant while I would yell and scream — 'Stop it! Oh, stop it! Sylvia, stop it!'

On one or two occasions, Mum came to my aid. Sometimes she had been laughing with the girls in the kitchen and around the big red and black ovens, for Sunday afternoon was cake, tart and pastry making afternoon.

I could hear Mum's deep belly laugh, then mercifully she would appear in the doorway, fingers stained with dough or white with flour, as she pleaded,

'Oh Sylvia! Don't tickle our Keith for too long, he's only just finished his dinner.'

For the first few minutes of my cousins' visits it became a battle of wits between Sylvia and I. But once the tickling session was over, then Sylvia treated me as an equal as she did everyone else.

Rene was the quieter of the four sisters. Oval faced, blue eyed, blonde hair to the neck of her blouse. She wore two pieces to her blouse and spoke softly with emphasis and was often serious in expression.

With Mum she discussed kitchen chores, recipes, baking sessions and the sewing and embroidery techniques she had been taught at school. When Rene joined me on the settee and flicked through one of my books, she would ask me what the story or rhyme was about in the manner of a gently coaxing schoolteacher. She would quite often ask if I was comfortable, wanted more milk or sugar in my tea, and where I would be going with Mum and Aunty the following day.

Peggy was a dark blond, perhaps closer to light brown. I recall her wearing her hair often down to her shoulders. Her face was full cheeked like her sister Rene's. Her greyish blue eyes warm, expressive. Her nose neat and her mouth and lips well-shaped. Quite often, with her sisters, myself and Betty, Peggy would sit staring into the fire and begin softly singing the songs she had heard on the Sunday lunchtime wireless programme.

In those days a group of Western cowboys and cowgirls sang around a microphone and Peggy, like myself in the years to come, quickly latched onto song words.

Around the fireside then the girls sang such songs as "Candy Kisses" or "Cowboy Down In Calico", and a great favourite of mine and Sylvia's, "I've Got Spurs That Jingle, Jangle Jingle".

On hot summer days, Mum and Aunty handed out deck-chairs so that we could sit in the garden, and whether summer or autumn I would hear such terms as 'when we lived in Alice Square' frequently used. But the war? Never once do I recall them mentioning it.

Alice was the vivacious sister. Tall, slim, hair sleek midnight black like her father Tom's, a hard working, hard drinking Cinderhill collier. Summer or winter alike, Alice's skin was lightly tanned. Her features were small, eyes blue; flashing. Mouth generous. Teeth even and exceedingly white. When Alice laughed, she threw back her head thus exposing her slender, tawny throat and her laughter was deep, sensual, as her voice was naturally and attractively husky.

Like all young girls of around that time, they wore long skirted two-pieces in the spring, autumn and winter but in the summer, Alice and Peggy in particular, sported short sleeved blouses, often pink or pale blue.

Mum was always careful to check that they hadn't come through Cherry Orchard because 'the man' was still on the prowl. Nor did she want them to go home that way.

'You'll be safer walking along the Boulevards to Nuthall Road, especially if there's an air raid,' Mum often advised them, at which the girls would insist, 'We will, Aunty. We will, honest.'

But Mum never wanted the girls to leave and they stayed for Sunday tea. If the afternoon was sunny or mild, despite their long walk from Stockhill to Chalfont Drive and the equally long walk back, they would take me to Wollaton Park.

By the time that I could walk any worthwhile distance, the autumn was in. When the girls took me to Wollaton Park, Aunty stayed home to help Mum with the cake baking and jelly making sessions. Dad, while always acknowledging the girls' arrival, was often digging in the garden, brown jacket open and wearing grey flannel trousers the bottoms of which were tucked into his wellingtons.

He put up a tool shed. He planted apple, pear and plum trees. He hauled bags of lime and compost down the garden on a wheelbarrow. Yet he always appeared immaculate in creased trousers, clean white shirt and charcoal grey waistcoat by the time we returned for tea.

Despite the war, each season continued unhindered. With Betty and my cousins talking and towering above me, I smelt the season before I saw it. Inhaled the aromatic tangs of leaf decay and wizened autumnal fruits before I walked the oak ride known as Digby Avenue.

We were all by this time wearing heavier coats and perhaps one or two of us gloves. I had a cap that seemed too big. Consequently, I was aware of its peak. Grinning, Sylvia told me that I might become cross-eyed.

The low temperatures failed in persuading us to hurry. In Wollaton Park there was too much to see. Too much to do. And, in the case of the girls, still much to say. We searched through the leaf litter for walnuts and picked up acorns, some of which bore the minute teeth marks of a red squirrel or the single slit made by a pheasant's bill as the long tailed game birds, which I hadn't by then seen, scratched over the ground for edible morsels including the addictive layers of beech mast.

Over to the right loomed an open wood, clear of ground layer, that was fenced by chestnut palings wired together and at intervals held in check by strong upright posts. On each side a gap had been cut into the fencing, as cousin Rene explained, to allow the deer to go into the wood to search like the pheasants for acorns and beech mast.

There was a group of hinds and calves nuzzling through the dead leaves, their coats buffish-grey but with the conspicuous pale fawn patches flaring on their rear quarters.

Sylvia indicated that we should cross to the deer gap and here we found several tufts of deer fur which had been brushed from the animals' coats as they passed beneath the lower rung of the fence. The tufts of deer fur were long and greyish-brown at first glance, but bearing traces of auburn, black and silver when held up to the light.

On Wollaton Park I was aware of height, the outspreading tree branches, the differing textures of tree bark and trunks. The occasional, but not unpleasant, whiffs of rotting timber.

When Digby Avenue ended, a steep grassy hill interspersed with oak, lime and an occasional prunus or ornamental cherry tree swept up to the solid and ornate entrance of Wollaton Hall. Built for Francis Willoughby (1546-1596) who was descended from a wealthy trader in wool and woad, the formal wide stepped entrance of the Hall faced north.

Other than the name Middleton Boulevard, I had not heard of the Willoughby descendants who had resided at Wollaton and, not surprisingly, throughout my formative years I associated the building only with the natural history museum's collection of mammals, birds, fish and fossils that were housed there.

On Sundays the Museum was open from two in the afternoon until four-thirty. But each day regardless, all children were required to be accompanied by an adult. The fact that Betty and my girl cousins were under-age seemed to go unnoticed by the attendants, but had they been boys the only way for them to have gained admittance would have entailed a long wait outside the Hall until a kindly couple or family accepted their request to take them in.

Two canons were mounted at the top of the first flight of steps, muzzles tilted slightly as if challenging the north wind. As Betty or one of the girls gently ushered me by I touched the spokes and wheel rims without realising that canons had once been used as weapons of war.

The steps ceased at a narrow entrance blocked when the museum was locked and closed by a stud bordered door, made from oak perhaps. Three or four steps then took one to this entrance and into the double-tiered gallery, which was cold, stone grey and the highest room I had entered or dreamt existed.

When I heard Betty and the girls exchanging comments about the families who had lived there, I thought of me, Betty, Dad, Mum and Aunty. Why would we *want* to live in so big a house as this? Could you really call it home?

Then all such thoughts were forgotten when on the wall either side the main arch leading into the Great Hall I saw the row of big game hunting trophies. Thompson's gazelles, beisa oryx, eland, water buffalo and the huge and awesome head of an American buffalo or bison, each centralised on a beautifully mounted shield and solidly presented with plaques beneath giving a date and location for when and where the unfortunate animals were shot.

The serrated horns of the antelopes gleamed black and appeared artificial, except that they were not. The bison's domed head and curly mass of forelock I badly wanted to stroke.

Stepping beneath the arch into the Great Hall which had served as the Middleton's formal dining room, the era of Victorian-Edwardian taxidermy appeared before us as we stood before dioramas containing wart hogs and sloth bears, a pair of kangaroos and koala bears, a magnificent leopard and a zebra mare modelled braced as she stood suckling a foal.

In hushed notes, yet from which far-carrying echoes seemed mysteriously to emanate, Sylvia explained that all mother animals fed their young on milk, even the human female like our mothers. Then Peggy, I think it was, pointed to the pouch gaping like a darkly furred purse in the female kangaroo's belly and told me, or perhaps us all, that the female kangaroo carried and nursed her baby in there. Moreover, a baby kangaroo was known as a 'Joey'. *That*, I decided, was something I was going to tell Mum and Dad when we were all home at tea-time.

Along one wall, and backed by magnificent paintings depicting the natural habitat of each species, was the collection of British Mammals.

Here I learned what bats looked like and that otters were aquatic mammals, belonging to the stoat, badger and weasel family. Each animal group was displayed in the context of a family: male, female and young.

Except for the glass front of each case intervening, the fox clubs were able to be stroked, the dog fox and vixen sleek, graceful, especially about the head and ears. Then I learned from one of the girls that a fox's tail was called 'a brush'.

Sylvia read most of the informative notices, sometimes out loud —

"Red squirrels are denizens of Wollaton Park." One line informed us. As we carried acorns and husks of beech mast engraved with squirrel teeth marks in our overcoat pockets, I surmised that the word denizen meant lived and Sylvia beaming while ruffling my hair enthused, 'Good boy! Good boy! Yes, you're right! Did you hear that Betty! Keith asked ....'

In the seconds that followed, however, I was attempting to read some of the labels for myself.

The pairs of eyes assigned to each animal came from a special firm (Watkins and Doncaster), Rene had once read, and the tongues of the animals, where shown, were modelled on the original tongues some samples of which were periodically kept in ice, she added. The skins and teeth were real enough, though, and each animal was measured from nose tip to tail tip in order to gain a true likeness.

The man who modelled the animals and painted the backgrounds, while also including tree branches, masses of jungle grass or stands of gorse and bracken, was called a taxidermist.

'Where does he work?'

'Through one of those big doors, I should think.'

The doors were closed in such a way that the word PRIVATE mounted upon a plaque was not needed, for in the times which I am attempting to describe an open door carried an invitation whereas a closed one bore the opposite effect and was treated accordingly.

In a hidden gallery, well-lit once we had stepped around the colonnades, we found ourselves staring up at the snarling countenance of an orang-utang. Then two chimpanzees. And in the third case, triumphant, tall and flaring viciously in a corner, the considered "star" of the museum's entire collection, a male gorilla. (This in recent years has been considered by anthropologists to be a relatively poor likeness).

The girls pushed one another in front of it, while giggling and exclaiming in shivering voices, 'King Kong! He's not getting me! Or, 'Where's Tarzan? Perhaps he'll come to rescue us, swinging through the trees!'

Obviously, I had heard of neither but during such incidents as those, chose uncharacteristically to ask nothing.

The bird gallery was as equally intriguing: a pair of dunnocks feeding a three-quarter grown baby cuckoo; the skylarks with their exquisite nest and tiny eggs; a magpie stealing an egg from a pheasant's nest; gannets, guillemots, a golden eagle, pheasants ptarmigan in both summer and winter plumage, pink footed geese.

The two species of pied woodpecker, tree-creeper and nuthatch, along with a pair of woodcock, Britain's largest inland wader, all carried the line - "denizen of Wollaton Park" within the mounted description. And again I savoured the word "denizen".

On the homeward walk, sometimes beneath the mist-swathed oaks I recaptured the way in which the oak leaves, stands of holly, flowering gorse and even berries had been beautifully preserved in each of the habitat cases.

Throughout the war, Dad was employed as an airframe fitter by the firm AUR-OF based at the expansive Langar Aerodrome situated in the Vale of Belvoir (pronounced *Beaver*) in Leicestershire. This was one of the leading aircraft repair depots in the British Isles.

To get there he had to walk about three-quarters of a mile to the Middleton Boulevard shops, catch a thirty-nine bus and travel to Huntingdon Street near the centre of Nottingham. Here he would board one of the several buses provided for the many employees of AUR-OF and return by the same modes of transport each morning, and sometimes on Saturday morning. Consequently, I saw little of him during the week but made up for this occupational hazard each weekend.

Most Sunday mornings Dad took me on countryside walks but when I was still small he left this to Betty and our girl cousins while continuing to lay out the garden.

One Sunday afternoon, for some unexplained reason, Dad chose to settle into his fireside chair while I thumbed through my books on the settee.

I had not seen Dad sleeping before, his head turned slightly away from both me and the french windows. An expression of contentment was on his face as he relaxed in his immaculate attire and black shoes, arms folded across his chest.

Had I been an artist, I would have outlined his face; the play of light across hi scheekbones.

In the kitchen where Mum was rolling out pastry and making jam tarts for tea, I heard the girls, Sylvia, Rene, Alice and Betty talking and laughing. I wondered then if Mum was doing to them what she sometimes did to me: putting the clean rolling pin across the top of my head when I gazed up from her hips, or waving her flour swathed fingers in my direction thus forcing me to seek cover around her long skirted waistline.

Suddenly, the women lowered their voices. They went into the hall. Then the dining room door silently opened and the girls stood with rapt expressions on their faces, softly mouthing a single utterance, 'Ah.' They were looking at Dad. Looking *lovingly* at Dad. A wave of pleasure flared through me then because I could see that they loved him.

Mum's eyes, however, were dancing with mischief. Quietly she eased around the front of Dad, still sleeping prone, fingers interlocked across his tummy, legs stretched out with one ankle crossed over the other, close to the hearth and fender.

Amazed, I watched Mum step into the hearth and with one hand resting on the chimney breast, put her hand over the flames then jam a forefinger quickly up the chimney. She withdrew her finger just as quickly having collected a conspicuous swab of soot.

With unaccustomed grace, Mum then swung sideways and deftly placed the soot swab onto Dad's small but muscular nose.

Suddenly I was burning with anger. Not with my equally surprised cousins, but with Mum because, I suppose, her action had challenged Dad's dignity.

Unable to contain myself, I shrilled, 'Dad! Wake up! Look what Mum's put on your nose!'

His blue eyes flashed in the light. He could not help but see the swab of soot. But other than slide one hand down to his trouser pocket, Dad remained immobile. From his pocket he tugged a clean white handkerchief, removed the soot from his nose, and said quietly, 'There you are. You can put that in with tomorrow's washing.'

On accepting the handkerchief, Mum was quiet; resigned. Her mood of mischief lived and died within minutes.

Turning she and the girls trooped back into the kitchen. Dad, in the meantime, looked across at me, winked, then closed his eyes...... .

CHAPTER 8

In return for a non-monetary lease of bases in the Caribbean and Newfoundland, the United States sold fifty destroyer ships to the British Royal Navy. The ships were then used in the war.

By September 1940, a branch of the German artillery was based in France and shelling the towns and depots situated along the shorelines of south-east England, and Dover in particular.

The name Adolf Hitler was seldom out of the national and regional newspapers. On October 4th Hitler met, for consultation, the Italian Prime Minister, Benito Mussolini, in the Alps and learned three days later that his troops had control over the Romanian oil fields due to prior negotiations.

By October 12th, Hitler changed tactics and ordered the Luftwaffe to bomb London and other English cities. On November 14th and 15th Coventry was bombed. Twelve armament factories, the famed cathedral and sections of the city centre were reduced to debris. The dead totalled 380, the injured 865.

On the 16th the British Royal Air Force made a retaliatory move and bombed the German city of Hamburg. Meanwhile, in the Atlantic airborne radar monitored by the Royal Air Force located the first German U boat and on 20th November Britain signed an agreement with the United States of America citing that whatever technical knowledge was gained between the two countries, it would be shared and used according to its immediate or future values.

* * *

One of those Sunday afternoon walks to Wollaton Park with Betty and our girl cousins influenced my life for at least the next twenty-four years.

We were as usual collecting acorns and beechmast when a sandy first cross terrier with a curly tail loped ungainly through the tussocks from the direction of the rabbit warren situated in a half circle fronting Gorsebed Wood, over to our right. The half circle of broken low hilly ground, along which lines of lime and oak had been planted some three or four hundred years ago, was known to the estate workers as The Recess.

The terrier, although overweight, had followed its natural instincts and been burrowing for rabbits there.

Without hesitation, the terrier came over to us as Betty and Sylvia stooped over it murmuring endearments, patting and stroking. Then to my surprise, the terrier sought me out. Snuffling and panting, its jaws agape revealing tongue and teeth the dog leapt up at my face and began licking. Protesting and intolerant of its hot tongue coming into contact with my skin, I grabbed Rene and Sylvia's overcoats and tried to squeeze between their hips.

The terrier, at least half my height, came on wanting a fuss. In the confusion, I seized Rene's overcoat belt, forced her to turn and slipped through the gap made by two parting bodies. Taking one or other of the girls' hands while still yelling in protest, I literally put the terrier behind me and a matter of paces later the incident was forgotten. Or so I thought.

Back at the house two or so hours later, however, Mum while ladling green salad onto our tea-time plates, asked if I had behaved myself.

'Oh yes. He always does. But he's frightened of dogs,' said one of the girls.

I had that afternoon probably regarded the dog's open mouth and gleaming teeth as a threat, in the same way that I had regarded Polly's hooked bill as a threat. Like most people, boys and men especially, I disliked surprise then as I do today. I also dislike having things, no matter what, thrust upon me. That dog, I instantly decided, had indeed thrust *itself* upon me. Consequently, I protested. But how could I explain this to my parents and Aunty? Moreover, why did I have to explain it to them, or anyone? Nevertheless, words were said and fortunately for me, although I was too young to realise it at the time, there were repercussions.

The midweek afternoon was overcast to the point of describing it as black. Just off to our right the coal or coke stacked dining room fire seethed with red light and life.

It felt good being home. Sitting again on Aunty's lap as between us we read and discussed the story of Dick Whittington.

I very much liked the idea of walking along fenceless roads and by the milestones to London, knapsack on my back, black cat at my heel, as the illustrations depicted.

'And what did the bells say? Asked Aunty.

' "Turn again Whittington. Turn again",' we chanted together.

The darkness made me think of the night. Black night. The Germans. Yet there was no one in the house except Aunty and myself. I knew that Betty was attending school and Dad was out working at Langar Aerodrome. But Mum? Where was Mum?

'Aunty, where's Mum? I asked.

'Oh, she'll be back soon. She's gone a long way out on a double-decker bus to a farm at a place called Underwood.'

'What's she gone there for?'

'She's gone to buy a puppy.'

'A puppy?'

'A baby dog.'

What! screamed my mind. *A dog!* Why buy me a dog when they knew I didn't *want* a dog? Didn't *like* dogs? Didn't like things forcing themselves upon me?

'It's not coming here, is it?' I queried.

'Oh, yes. It will only be a baby. A little tiny thing. There was a litter of puppies advertised for sale in last evening's newspaper and so we thought it a good idea to have one. It will help cure your fear anyway.'

Cure my fear! I didn't *want* my fear cured, because I didn't *want* a dog around me. Snuffling. Licking. Its tongue hot and wet. Its paws padding my chest and nearly knocking me over. I didn't want one!

'But I don't *want* one. Don't *want* one, Aunty,' I protested.

Aunty shrugged, smiled, her hair very white against the failing light, and said, 'Oh well, we'll just have to see.'

Temper then surged through me. Yes we *would* have to see. When it comes, *if* it comes, Mum can just take the puppy back where it came *from*.

We continued with the story for a sentence or two before Aunty observed, 'I'll have to draw the curtains and put on the light in a minute. I can hardly see to read.'

Then we heard the swing and thrust of the front door opening.

'Here's your Mum,' smiled Aunty.

I waited, ready to jump onto a chair and sit in protest on the dining room table if the dog came plunging in and licking me.

Smiling and still wearing her grey gabardine raincoat, Mum came into the room. She was carrying the brown zip-up bag in which Polly had suffocated, except on this occasion the zip was undone.

Tensed, I waited for the dog's assault. It never occurred. Looking at Mum I asked, thinking she had changed her mind, 'Where's the dog, Mum?'

'He's here. Look!'

She held up the bag and a furry dome shaped head peeped above the zip. 'He's been on a double-decker bus with me this afternoon,' cooed Mum.

He was a six-week old puppy, a black and tan. His eyes friendly, dark. His muzzle snub. A tan line ventured between his eyes then cascaded either side of his muzzle to his throat and jaw-line. His stubby legs were tan. His coat black. In due time I learned that he was a mongrel. A first cross; Airedale crossed with Welsh terrier.

'Do you want to stroke him?' asked Mum.

'I don't. And I don't want to see him again,' I admonished.

Mum looked nonplussed. Shrugging, she took the bag and the puppy into the kitchen.

Easing me gently from her lap, Aunty said, 'Right, we'll draw the curtains then see about getting some tea ready.'

'Don't let the puppy come near me,' I warned. I was aware then of my feet, my shoes. The unpleasant threat of having to kick out.

In the kitchen the puppy, whining and more frightened than I was frustrated and angry, was gently placed into a round wicker dog basket positioned beneath the washday mangle.

In the evening Betty looked at me, grinned and said, 'We've decided to name our puppy Scamp.'

'I don't care! I'm not calling it anything. I don't want it near me, ever!'

The next morning I was standing near the breakfast table. Aunty had still to rise. Dad and Betty had gone to work. It was dark outside. The curtains were drawn across the french windows and the room lights were on.

'I'll let Scamp come to the fire while you're having your breakfast,' Mum announced.

'No! I'm not having him in here!' I stormed and forced Mum to take me up into her arms as Scamp trundled curiously from the kitchen and stood in the open doorway of the dining room.

A black and tan furry bundle, rotund and short legged, he recognised Mum who coaxed him with, 'Come on Scamp.' The puppy stood whining before wagging his miniature walking stick of a tail.

I asked why he was making those sounds, to which Mum explained that he was frightened, feeling lost, having spent the first night of his young life alone.

In retrospect, Scamp would have been fussed and fondled by each member of the family after I had been taken to bed and before I awoke. But I lacked both foresight and hindsight and so was not aware that he may already have settled beside the hearth.

Mum explained that Scamp had only known his mother and her milk, the shuffling and pushing and perhaps nipping of his litter companions, and the warm scents of the hay and straw layered stable in which he was born. But now he was experiencing fear and uncertainty. He was missing his mother, much like I would miss my family if suddenly I was taken away.

I listened. I sympathised. Yet I still rejected the possibility of Scamp coming near me. He had teeth, Mum explained. Of course he had teeth, which was why she and Aunty would bring home bones from the butcher's for him to chew on. Scamp wouldn't bite us though. He was one of the family now. Betty had sat nursing him in her lap beside the fire last night.

I was unrepentant. If Mum wanted me to eat my breakfast, Scamp must go back into the kitchen I told her. I did not want to see him again.

During the six weeks that I banished Scamp from my life, I was made fully aware of the cinema. If I wasn't taken twice a week, I was at least taken once. We were all cinema-conscious but never actually went as a family. That is to say that Betty occasionally took me accompanied often by Sylvia and Rene or she went with her friends, Kathleen and Barbara. At around the age of thirteen or fourteen, Betty may well have felt that she had outgrown being accompanied by her elders.

There were six cinemas situated within walking distance of the house, four of which were plush and two considered secondary or "flea-pits". These two we avoided unless Aunty shrugged and insisted that we went, which we did at least twice.

The Forum, situated about a mile away along Aspley Lane, was one of Dad's favourites. Some starlit Saturday nights I think he enjoyed the walk with Mum and I as much as he enjoyed the film. Rather than walk the unlit and closely thicketed Cherry Orchard in the darkness, my parents with me in the middle and holding a hand between them chose the relatively wide route along the Boulevards to the Aspley Lane traffic island.

There were allotment gardens on either side. Closed up for the night. Silent but sometimes with smells of newly dug over soil pleasantly teasing the nostrils. Everything was uniform. The line of unbroken high fences made from wooden palings. The privet and hawthorn hedges, all summer trimmed to around the same height. The lime trees planted along the Boulevard's grass verge and central reservation. All in a line the length and width of the entire Boulevard, as I was to discover in the years ahead. Cars and lorries were so few you could hear them approaching half a mile away.

At the traffic island we turned left by more allotments, the end of Cherry Orchard and the night blackened fields of Aspley Hall Farm.

The vicarage stood in tightly fenced grounds to the fore, a relatively new building erected like the red stoned yet quite splendid St. Margaret's Church opposite, some thirteen years before I was born. As we passed the church and vicarage, Mum always explained that our neighbour Mr. Teather held services there each Sunday. Yet, as if she thought I was already aware of the Christian faith or any form of religion, she never indicated how or why.

The farm outbuildings and inner courtyard cottages also came to the pavement's edge but were hidden by a wall. One only saw the blue tiled roofs and a layer or two of red brick underneath. Now that I know more about such fascinating places, I expect that besides the stables, grooms quarters, coach sheds
and granary, several workers' cottages, the dairy, brewery, game room and perhaps

even a bakery were clustered beyond the walls. In all probability there was a propagation yard and outbuildings because, being a country gentleman's residence, Aspley Hall was surrounded by ornamental gardens.

The formal entrance to Aspley Hall was tree-lined. The Hall farmhouse, stockyards and splendid Dutch barn were situated about five hundred yards from the road. A field grazed by a herd of Dairy Shorthorn cattle and bordered by a hedgerow the length of the drive, but with a post and rail fence along Aspley Lane, stretched away to the right. To look into the field, Dad and I used to scramble up the steep bank and peer between the rails while negotiating the trunks and roots of seven once magnificent elm trees which, Mum explained, were locally known as The Seven Sisters.

A family fruit and vegetable propagation business called Lamberts filled several dozen acres on the opposite side of Aspley Lane.

Disappointment then accompanied me along most of the direct route to The Forum because on the left side of Aspley Lane the widened pavement bordered row after row of shops, while on the right a vast but neat and orderly estate of council houses added a touch of homeliness to the night. About three-quarters of the way along the row of shops stood a confectioner's and newsagent's. Here Dad would buy chocolate for Mum and himself and dolly mixtures for me.

There was always a twinkle in his eyes when Dad handed me the sweet bag, screw wrapped tightly at the neck. Moreover, in recent years meeting my cousin Rene in the centre of Nottingham, she recalled —

'You know, Keith, right from the time we ever knew your Dad, he never once called at the house without bringing each one of us a bag of dolly mixtures. He was the most thoughtful, kindest man I have ever known.'

The dolly mixtures that Dad took to the house of my cousin's he may have purchased at his sister Amy's shop. As for his generosity, I became one of the several people on Dad's receiving end in the years ahead and can therefore vouch for the fact that he was indeed very much a giver rather than a taker.

It was at The Forum Cinema that I became embroiled with a mass of monochrome images. *The Pathe News* with its narrator's swift and informative voice, just a shade too loud for my liking, informing us of the atrocities taking place both abroad and closer to home. Then the main film, sometimes cherub faced cowboy Gene Autrey riding Champion, a magnificent black horse with a white blaze. A singing cowboy whose sidekick Smiley Burnett rode a white mare with a single black eye patch which earned her the name "Black-eyed Nell". Dad rocked backwards and forwards in his seat with laughter at the slapstick antics of Laurel and Hardy. Mum, by comparison, sat back in her seat controlled, while quietly submitting to her low but unmistakable belly laugh.

Mum's favourite child actor was Shirley Temple. Her most memorable film to that date was the screen adaptation of Margaret Mitchell's *Gone With The Wind*. She, Dad and Aunty had, as youngsters grown up with the cinema. On those walks home they told me about the silent films, which I could never imagine, and in particular Charlie Chaplin and Gene Autrey's predecessor, Tom Mix.

Mum also listed the wireless and sometime screen star Jessie Matthews amongst her and Aunty's favourites, while insisting that when I was learning to talk I called this lady Jessie Matches.

It was atThe Forum that the three of us viewed with all seriousness the classic John Ford Western *Stagecoach*, which on the starlit walk home Mum said she thought was almost equal to *Gone With The Wind* in riveting one to the seat. This again was the American West in monochrome. A dramatic travelogue featuring arid landscapes, dust, galloping horses, warring Apaches. John Wayne starring as the Ringo Kid was, to my young eyes, so intense an actor that I thought for minutes I was looking in on a world squeezed in between the life that was being put before me and the war, sequences of which I had seen on the cinema newsreels and attempted to read about in *The Daily Sketch.*

Mum was taken with the acting of Claire Trevor who played Dallas and for the first time I heard mentioned an American town in existence throughout the era in which the film was set, Lordsburg.

When on that particular homeward walk Dad explained that the American West as we had seen it portrayed on the screen that evening had actually existed, my imagination ran riot. One second I was Curly, the stagecoach driver. The next the tall, long striding Ringo Kid bringing down an Apache with every rifle shot. And thirdly, I was an Apache with paint pony beneath me; cumbersome, dust shrouded stagecoach and its passengers ahead.

Piecing together place names that I struggled to read in the newspapers or heard mentioned on the cinema screen, I concluded that south of Nottingham my natal city were miles of farmland then a city called Coventry. Beyond Coventry was spread Hitler's main target: London. Around the edge of the British isles were The White Cliffs of Dover about which a film of the same name had been released and a strong voiced woman, so unlike Shirley Temple, had recorded the title song. The woman's name, I learned eventually, was Vera Lynne.

Across the sea, almost directly opposite Dover, was France and then Germany. The French, I understood, had given in to the Germans. But the war apart, somewhere out towards the sun where it was forever hot lived colonies of black people some of whom trapped and sold parrots and monkeys to white people who kept the birds and animals in cages.

Then somewhere else, perhaps across another sea, stretched a vast country called America where the Ringo Kid and hordes of Apache warriors had once roamed. That is how the world atlas began forming within my mind.

As the days darkened, I was told that a newcomer was due to visit the house. Like Rip Van Winkle he sported a white beard, but wore a red gown and hood trimmed around the sides with white. A kindly, red faced man, he came across the starlit sky in a sleigh pulled by four reindeer, the sleigh packed to the hilt with presents for children all over the world.

'All over the world? Does Santa Clause give presents to the children in Germany as well?' I piped.

'Yes, but over there I think he's known as St. Nicholas. And *we* have another name for him, too. Sometimes he's known as Father Christmas,' smiled Aunty.

It seemed incredible that a nice old man would want to visit all the world's children, although he obviously enjoyed the sleigh ride across the sky.

'But how does Santa Clause know what each boy or girl wants for Christmas?' I queried.

'Oh, he knows somehow. I don't exactly know how, but he knows all right . You and the children throughout the world won't be disappointed,' Aunty assured.

I told her then that nice man though Santa was, I didn't want to see him because I wouldn't know what to say other than thank him for the presents. Then I learned that he came when everyone was asleep. Moreover, *he came down the chimney* when everyone was asleep. Had been doing for years, according to Betty!

News of Santa's visit on Christmas Eve coincided with another snippet of information that set Aunty bustling with excitement. The Boulevard at the end of Chalfont Drive was to be connected to the City of Nottingham, via a bus service. A double-decker bus. The number thirteen. The terminus was to be alongside the block of shops on Beechdale Road.

'Near Starbuck's,' I overheard Aunty telling Mum and Betty. We were to catch it between two lime trees, outside of a detached house with a half-timbered upper structure and lived in by the Howard family.

How Mum and Aunty knew the names of some people living thereabouts and not others, I could never ascertain.

The bus company's inaugural trip was scheduled for a Monday but it was on the Tuesday or Wednesday afternoon of that week that Aunty took me to Nottingham on the thirteen and whilst shopping pointed out Santa Claus. He was appearing in a Nottingham departmental store for a few days before going back to wherever he came in readiness to return with all the presents. But again I made it clear to Aunty that I had no wish to meet him. Just the presents would do, I decided, especially if mine were books.

The city streets were filled with hurrying, overcoated people, none of whom spoke, acknowledged or gave the slightest indication that they had seen Aunty and I walking amongst them.

Holding Aunty's hand, I enthused at the Christmas displays in the shop windows but calmed when on Clumber Street Aunty pointed to Beecroft's Store and said, 'There's Santa again! Look! See him?'

I couldn't see him but answered in the affirmative. A similar incident occurred on a gale-seething Monday about a week later.

In the early afternoon, Mum or Aunty saw beyond the front room net curtains a white dove perched across the road and on the roof of a house belonging to the Jebbuts. Mum picked me up while Aunty pointed to the dove. I saw wet roofs gleaming against a background of black scudding clouds and the branches of five young rowan trees on the Cameron's garden opposite, swishing and twirling in the throes of the gale. But of the white dove I saw nothing yet told Aunty that I could see it because, I suppose, I wanted to get on with other things.

'It's the "Dove of Peace",' said Aunty, as Mum lowered me to the carpet.

'Then let's hope it's doing some good out there,' murmured Mum reflectively.

Early on Christmas Eve I sat sipping whisky and milk in an armchair facing the fire, while studying my new red bootee slippers and reflecting on how much darker they were than the child's pink dressing gown I was wearing over my pyjamas.

There was surely an extra voice mingling with those of Mum and Aunty in the kitchen? I knew it wasn't Betty's, so who...... ? Surely it wasn't Santa arriving ahead of his time? What was I going to say to him? Where could I run and hide? As the dining room door opened, I sipped my warm drink and stared at the flames leaping high and golden yellow into the chimney breast.

'Keith, this is Mrs. Teather come to bring you a Christmas present,' Mum announced.

I turned as Mrs. Teather pulled out one of the two visitors' chairs positioned backs to the wall to the fireside on my left. She was, of course, our neighbour. Younger than Mum and Aunty, her mass of black wavy hair cascading to her shoulders, becoming here and there finely touched with grey. Her complexion was pink, Eyes small, blue, forever echoing with a warm and pleasant laughter. Her nose was aquiline. Lips well-shaped, mouth wide, teeth even and startlingly white.

The Teathers were a childless couple. But I was in little doubt that, like Santa Clause, Mrs. Teather - or Marjorie as she was known to Mum - loved children.

Her voice was soft; gentle. I knew even then that if a woman existed who other than Mum wanted to lift and hold me close to her green overcoated body, I would have no objection providing it was Mrs. Teather.

'What's that you're drinking with your milk, Keith?' Mrs. Teather asked.

'It's whikky,' I replied.

It was then I noticed and momentarily studied her fine cheekbones, curling eyelashes and hair tumbling over the back of her collar.

'Actually, I've come ahead of Santa Claus. I'm here with presents for Betty and yourself,' Mrs. Teather beamed while putting two wrapped and colour tied parcels onto my lap.

After taking another sip of milk and whisky, I placed the mug on the stool beside my chair, thanked Mrs. Teather and began to undo the parcels.

In each was a book. The title, author and subject of the first escapes me completely. I recall the tangible smell of print, then the pleasure of seeing the cover which depicted an elf, a mouse and, I think, a hedgehog in the colours of black, white and red.

The elf's name was Rodney Bennett. He lived in a wood among the tree roots, grass blades, dead leaves and beneath the parasols of fly algaeic fungi. The mouse and the hedgehog were his friends.

As mum conversed with Mrs. Teather, she looked first at Mum and then at me, and then *longer* at me and then at Mum.

'Could you read a few words out to me, Keith?' asked Mrs. Teather.

I read out the elf's name, Rodney Bennett, and others that I could decipher. I even attempted a sentence or two. Eventually, I arrived at five words that whether I read them to myself or out to Mrs. Teather caused the hairs to arise, strangely cold, on the back of my neck. The words were "in the dead of night".

Whether the author's creative ability or my subconscious awareness of the war prompted this reaction, to this day I cannot explain.

The words were aloof - secretive, yet described the blackness, cold and unfriendly, beyond the curtained french windows. "In the dead of night". These words had such an effect that I began secretly wishing I had written them myself. *Someone* had written them. But who? And why, *how,* had this man or woman through putting these five words onto paper acquired the ability to arrest me and perhaps his or other her child readers? How had they so ably projected darkness, secrecy, the midnight chill that I was yet to know?

I wanted to ask Mrs. Teather or Mum this question but knew somehow that neither would be able to answer it. I therefore kept the words to myself, locked within the box of my mind.

Yet after breakfast with the family on Christmas Day morning I found myself reaching for the sentence again. Santa Claus had not only called but had left and assembled for me a model Hornby electric train. Mum had stood a glass of port beside the hearth for Santa and the glass was now empty. So I was *certain* he had been.

The Hornby train kept me occupied for some of that festive day and our girl cousins coming for tea throughout the evening. Yet still those words kept drifting back in my mind — "In the dead of night. In the......".

CHAPTER 9

JANUARY 1941. Franklin D. Roosevelt, President of the United States, placed an embargo of gasoline and iron on Japan. He also inaugurated the Office of Production Management aligned to the Second World War and responsible for contracting all matters relating to defence and conducive to the United States and Great Britain.

On the 22nd Tobruk, a Libyan port previously held by the Italians, was commandeered by the British Western Desert Force led by Lieutenant General Richard O'Connor. On 7th March this same force laid siege across Italian controlled Ethiopia and had the Italians literally running before them.

Meanwhile, the Luftwaffe ceased bombing Royal Air Force stations and turned their attentions again on London.

In Libya the British 8th Army lost El Algheila, an important staging post to the Italian and German forces commanded by General Erwin Rommel.

By mid-April, the British forces had seized the Ethiopian capital Addis Ababa from the Italians after a lengthy battle in which many casualties were lost on both sides.

At night the aircraft factories situated near Coventry were targeted by German bombers.

***

One Tuesday morning, Aunty and I walked to Kirk's off-licence to buy the yeast needed for the afternoon's bread-making session. When we returned along Colliers Pad and stepped onto the pavement at its junction with Three Nail Tree I saw with some trepidation that Chalfont Drive, the road on which we lived, was not entirely deserted. Sitting at the gates of their owner's houses and each about a hundred yards apart were three dogs. Different in size and colour but positioned like pavement statues.

Fortunately, they were on the opposite pavement to that which Aunty and I had to walk. The nearest was also the biggest. A red setter, explained Aunty. His name was Paddy Williamson.

When we were opposite him, Aunty stopped and as if Paddy was a human being, she called out, 'Good morning Paddy Williamson.'

Paddy stood, wagging his great tail.

'Come here then. Let's have a look at you,' coaxed Aunty.

The big leggy setter needed no second bidding.

'He's pleased to see us, look,' said Aunty.

'How do you know that?' I piped while tightening my hold on her hand.

'He's wagging his tail. Come here then boy.'

Transfixed, I stood as Paddy's opened jaws displaying the rows of white teeth and sideways lolling tongue came closer. Were closing in on me. Then Paddy's moist nose probed my hands and fingers and I found myself fondling his silken jaw-line in a way that to a stranger might have suggested that, except for my size, I had been handling dogs for years.

The setter's legs were long and trimmed with fur, his shoulders high; powerful. His back half silken, half shaggy.

Paddy Williamson. He just wanted us to make a fuss of him. I delighted in his probing muzzle. Tongue smooth against the back of my hand. The long yet barely discernible whiskers.

Aunty gently took Paddy's jaw between her hands and opened the setter's mouth. His teeth were strong, white and varied in size and shape.

'You're in splendid condition,' she murmured, while patting Paddy reassuringly.

When she next lifted the shopping bag, Paddy, his tail still wagging, turned his back on us and loped across to his front gate.

Next we came to Rover Jebbutt, smaller than Paddy but a lithe, strong dog for all that. A springer spaniel well past his prime.

At Aunty's call he came over. Chocolate and brown with long down turned ears. Aunty called Rover's shortened tail a rudder. His eyes were slightly bloodshot.

'It's because he's an old dog,' Aunty explained.

'What? Older than me, Aunty?'

'Oh yes, and so is Paddy Williamson.'

Incredible! Everything and everyone was older than me!

When we arrived at our front gate, Aunty called our third dog, Bruno Cameron.

A black mongrel with upright pointed ears, Bruno's coat was sleek, smooth and his stubby wagging tail shorter than that of Rover Jebbutt. And although he was about the size of the dog that unnerved me in Wollaton Park, Bruno did not jump at me.

'I can do anything with dogs. I might not be so good with Polly parrots but I can do anything with dogs,' smiled Aunty as she unlatched our front gate.

'Your Dad's the same with horses, you know. He wanted to be a jockey when he was a youngster. Can't walk by a field if there are horses in it. He has to call them over. He doesn't feed them because they don't belong to him, but he can't resist patting and stroking them.'

I was surprised because no one had told me that before, not even Dad.

That evening I was playing on the hearth rug in front of the fire with some plastic or metal miniature animals Aunty had bought from Cunnah's. Betty and Aunty were tidying up the sewing machine which they had used together, and Dad was in his armchair reading the local evening newspapers. Mum was, I think, in the kitchen preparing my mug of hot milk laced with whisky.

Minutes later Aunty and Betty, who was arranging a dress or school gym slip on a coat hanger, looked across at me then took the hanger and its garment up to her room.

In the short time it took her to return, Aunty showed me the "secret" drawer fitted into the side of the sewing machine where she kept her needles and bobbins of cotton and I was reminded of the minute cupboard fitted into the underside of her gramophone where she kept her record needles.

When Betty returned, she said, 'Keith, how would you like to come and see Scamp?' and I was immediately on my feet and following her outstretched hand as she walked through to the kitchen.

Scamp was curled in a blanket placed like a nest within a circular wicker basket. He had, Betty explained, been out with Dad for a long walk and was by then tired. So used to people entering and leaving the kitchen had Scamp become that he remained with his muzzle tucked into his flank, a much bigger, longer bodied dog than when Mum brought him to the house.

Together Betty and I knelt beside Scamp's basket.

'Hello, Scamp. I've brought someone to see you,' Betty half whispered in her soft caressing voice.

Scamp's black dorsal fur was coarse; his jaws, throat, and under parts and legs pale tan, which also fringed his ears and eyebrows and the underside of his long curly tail. On the top of his head, just offset from his ears, two patches of russet resembled couplet islands surrounded by a coal black sea.

Scamp licked Betty's outstretched fingers and then mine as Dad, Aunty and Mum stood behind us peering around the door.

I reached out for Scamp's fur, rich, deep in texture yet at the same time glossy and warm, and began stroking him. As I stroked him and he laid his broad muzzle into the palm of my free hand, I spoke his name over and over again.

The next morning's awakening image was Scamp and, surprisingly, I awoke before Mum came into the room to tell me as usual it was morning.

The sight of a porridge breakfast on the table and a highly banked fire roaring up the chimney was a foregone conclusion. While pulling the green stag motif sweater over my head, I felt an unfamiliar nudge at my elbow. Scamp! He was standing alongside me, eager to thrust his heavy muzzle into my hands as Paddy Williamson had done with Aunty.

As I embraced Scamp around the neck he sank to his haunches, then surprised me by rolling onto his back, fawn tummy to the ceiling. Kneeling on the red carpet, I tickled Scamp's tummy as he remained prone, his jaw-line partially hidden by fawn whiskers, mouth shaped like a pleasurable grimace, fawn forelegs bent at the knee or knuckle joints.

As I leaned far enough forward, I inhaled a body warm smell. But coming from where? From Scamp's paws? Taking one paw gently in my hand and kneeling, I bent closer and sniffed it. The paw smelt warm, his pads warmer. I counted Scamp's toes, studied his claws. Asked Mum what the claw was called set up the leg joint and away from the others. Mum told me it was a "dew" claw.

When I tickled Scamp's tummy a second time, his wagging tail thumped rhythmically against the carpet. A minute or so later, Mum came to the dining room door and said, 'Eat your breakfast Keith and oh, by the way, we thought you weren't going to take to dogs.'

On the mornings when I had a fried breakfast, Scamp sat head height to my knees and each time Mum returned to the kitchen I slid a bacon rind down to his jaws or a crust of fried bread. I loved to feel his warm breath, hot tongue and hear the saliva smacking rhythm of his jaws followed by the occasional and single gulp sound Scamp made when he swallowed.

There dawned a Sunday morning in which the pale sky appeared swarthy against the first snowfall of my life. Close to the french window step, tiny patterns of sparrow prints trailed around the rockery stones as the birds picked up the bread crumbs scattered by Mum or Aunty.

When Betty and I finished breakfast, Dad suggested he and I took Scamp on his lead for a walk along Collier's Pad. Each morning before he went to work Dad did this but I was unaware of it and thought this Sunday morning's walk was one of Scamp's first. It was the first experience of snow for us both.

Mum insisted that besides an overcoat and cap I wore a scarf. Dad, however, told her gently to "stop whittling", we were not going to be out for long.

The three of us stepped into the unfamiliar grey, black and white world. That is except for Teather's two high and wide laurel bushes, one of which blazed green, to the left of our front garden gate.

As we walked over the unblemished and glaring white layer, I sensed the solitude. The ominous silence. Skeletal ranks of briar thickets filled the land tracts between the houses and fields. The Humps and Hollows Field was transformed into a tract of freezing ice-withholding tundra. The elm, the tallest tree in the county, was black on one side of the trunk and white the other.

Dad let Scamp off the lead and the dog pivoted away. Sniffing here. Sneezing there. Lifting a hind leg. Then moving on. The brown underside of his long curling tail serving as a beacon guiding us across this frozen yet strangely exciting place.

Suddenly, the picture of the storybook elf Rodney Bennett came to mind and prompted me to exclaim, 'I expect the little field-mice will be surprised when they come out of their little holes tonight, Dad!'

'Yes, I expect they will,' smiled Dad.

Scamp eventually came towards us, pausing beside a twig or solidified grass clump to lift a leg and transform the snow to yellow.

By then it was snowing, and fast. Suddenly, Scamp approached the edge of a ditch side bramble break and a dozen or so darkly plumaged birds flew up and swung towards the colourless mass of sky.

'Starlings,' Dad confirmed.

We found the spot where they had been huddled. The grass was biscuit coloured and green here, which meant the starlings had pitched down just ahead of the last snowfall.

Dad nodded in agreement, then put up his coat collar and reached down to mine, while explaining, 'Blizzard coming on, let's get back to the fire.'

As we crunched towards the house, the sense of remoteness prevailed. Yet everywhere there was movement created by this eyelash dampening screen of snow.

At Three Nail Tree we stood while Dad called Scamp over and put him on his lead. Snowflakes collected swiftly along the dorsal ridge of Scamp's back and settled in the furry tufts above his half closed eyes and whiskers. Once clear of the fields, Scamp decided he was in a hurry to get home.

At the gatepost of the first house, Keetley's, he stopped. Dad turned, shook the lead and coaxed gently, 'Come on, Scamp.'

At the second set of gates Scamp stopped as if saying, 'This will do fine.'

Dad coaxed him on. Gatepost and gatepost. Obviously Scamp didn't care for snow any more than he failed to associate houses, other than our own, with people. Dad had such patience. Scamp stopped with his legs braced at every gatepost, his head down as if determined to thwart the oncoming snow. Dad never once raised his voice.

I quietly enthused at the way snow almost hid my shoes.

Scamp halted at Teather's gate. When Dad unclasped the gate latch, he also let Scamp off the lead and my new black and tan friend made fresh tracks as he bounded to the back porch and shook the snow from his coat.

The comforts of awakening on those mornings after each snowfall and during the eventual thaw were occasionally punctuated by moments of horror and sadness when over breakfast, and with Scamp ever beside me, I looked at the photographs in *The Daily Sketch.*

There were photographs of aircraft, ships, ack ack guns, bombing carnage, fire, ambulance and first-aid crews at work, as well as those depicting hundreds of children queuing up at street-based soup kitchens.

I read out the words Red Cross and Salvation Army. Like most of my generation, I was unaware that we had already survived two or three bombing raids.

The first local air raid took place on August 30th 1940. Nottingham's fourth air raid occurred on 19th January 1941. Two bombs were dropped on the far side of the city at Colwick, a village and suburban area close to the River Trent.

We, as children, had no conception of the risks, fears and sorrows the clear night skies could bring. To us war was being played out in newspaper photographs and on the *Pathe News* cinema newsreels. It was, like the austere winter days, a grey, black and dull white war.

People were dying and bombs were being dropped, but at places labelled within our minds as a "somewhere else".

Further visits to The Forum cinema with Mum and Dad furnished me with the words of two songs to add to my relatively scant repertoire. The first was Smiley Burnett's rendering of *I'm A Cowboy* and the second breezily sung and catchy *Woodpecker Song*, sung by Gene Autrey as he rode his horse directly into the screen.

The voice of the *Pathe News* narrator was loud as the deliverance was urgent, as again I viewed carnage, bombings and squadrons of aircraft, none of which I could positively identify.

For some unfathomed reason, I became particularly interested in aircraft carriers and marvelled at the take-off procedures made by aircraft with intriguing yet, to me, barely memorable names. Like many, I was always glad when the *Pathe News* came to an end because the voice of truth also ceased and I was able to revert again to the worlds of fantasy and animation.

One Saturday afternoon, which was particularly overcast but with the glow from the dining room fire inviting Scamp and I to block off the heat so that no one else could gain pleasure from it, according to Mum, the time four p.m. and the radio lured Betty down from the bedroom.

Dressed in a grey sweater and green pleated skirt, Betty pulled a chair from the table and sat one knee over the other gazing at the flames, as I often did myself, in readiness for a special wireless programme. And another voice.

'It's called *Bing Sings*,' Betty murmured in answer to my question. While talking with her I noticed the play of firelight upon her soft cuppable cheeks; her blue eyes so bright and expressive against the firelight's glow; brown hair trimmed boyish fashion but thick, wavy with feather soft curls brushing her sweater collar.

Betty was ready to worship this man with the strange name of Bing, in the same way Mum worshipped the tenor, Richard Tauber and the screen actors, Frederick March and Clark Gable, and with the same exuberance Aunty reserved for Nelson Eddy and Ivor Novello. Compared with these two last mentioned singers, Bing had a different voice and sang different types of songs. About Ireland mostly..... another "somewhere", sounding green and homely and another pointer on the map of the world continuing to form within my mind.

Bing Crosby? An American, explained Betty. Had made some films with a comedian, Bob Hope, and these she would be taking me to see with cousin Sylvia perhaps, or Rene.

On further Saturdays as we settled with Scamp in readiness for *Bing Sings*, Betty showed me a photograph of the singer. It was in a monthly magazine she ordered from Briddocks, a newsagent's situated near the city centre. The magazine was called *Silver Screen* and vied for attention on the newsagent's shelves with its rival *Filmgoer*.

Bing on the photograph looked as I had imagined him. He was also the first man I had seen smoking a pipe.

Bob Hope, whose photograph appeared in *Filmgoer*, looked nothing like I imagined him. But Betty apparently loved his wisecracks and deadpan humour, describing him as being 'very funny'.

I found it difficult to put down either one of Betty's monthly film magazines and when no one was in the room I turned to the full page portraits of such film stars as Alice Faye, Veronica Lake and Rita Hayworth.

Besides their facial structures and hairstyles, I memorised their gowns and necklaces while wondering how much these items cost, who had bought them for the stars and why I never saw Mum, Aunty or Betty dressed in such a manner.

In retrospect, I wasn't ready for Bob Hope. Yet it seems I had always been ready for Bing Crosby, because less than twenty years later I was imitating him, along with Frank Sinatra, Dean Martin, Matt Munro and Tony Bennet, at nightclubs in Nottingham, Leicester and London.

New and different voices continued to come into my life, not the least of which were the Walt Disney animation of Mickey Mouse, Donald Duck and a maverick, slow-thinking hound dog called Goofy, who also appeared in a weekly comic called *Film Fun*.

Aunty then introduced me to another Walt Disney character when with Mum she took me to *The Lenos* cinema to see the film *Bambi*.

The *Lenos* was situated near Aunty and Dad's former home on the edge of Bobbersmill, and so overcoated and again muffled in scarves we walked beneath the streetlights to the busy thoroughfare of Radford Boulevard and the welcoming foyer standing out among the lit and busy shops.

There were signs, established by the roadside, bearing the words CROSS HERE. These were designed to help pedestrians in the event of a black-out preceding air raid. I thought the signs friendly but failed to discover until the war was over that they also illuminated the lower part of a pedestrian's body, thus informing the driver of a vehicle that someone was about to cross, if not already crossing

Beyond the rush and purr of trolley buses, the cinema foyer continued to beckon. I read the sign *BAMBI* then as Aunty collected our tickets at the foyer, noticed Mum intently reading the chalked sentences on a blackboard.

'What's all that say?' I piped.

'It's........it's........just a list telling us what to do if the air raid siren goes and where the nearest shelters are situated.'

'Is there going to be an air raid then?'

'Not tonight,' smiled Aunty as she joined us, brandishing the tickets and indicating that we should follow the usherette waiting with her torch at the ready.

Until the main film started, however, I was aware that the cinema had a ceiling beyond which was the roof. Immediately above the roof was the sky. I then thought of the aircraft squadrons we saw in monochrome on the *Pathe News*.

Not infrequently, a newsreel showed bombs being released or parachutists and although I was born in wartime, I knew instinctively that under normal conditions such reckless procedures did not, *would not* take place.

The famed Disney film was an animated adventure story centred around the life of a deer fawn. It was also educational in the documentary sense because it depicted the wildlife of a North American forest.

The scenes of Bambi, aided by Thumper the rabbit, attempting to walk on the surface of a frozen pond; his awe at meeting the great stag known as The King of The Forest; and the animals fleeing from the forest fire, I vividly remember to this day. The animated voices, and huge, long lashed eyes of Disney's main characters, be they stag, skunk or wide old owl, fascinated me in the same way.

On that particular evening, however, my own eyes pricked with warm tears when Bambi's mother Feline was shot by a hunter and I could sense a thread of excitement pulsating through Mum when the stags paraded, bounding fashion through the forest glades.

Yet something bothered me about *Bambi* that I could not have explained at the time, but which I now realise had to do with the original story. Written by German born Felix Salten, the novel *Bambi* was published by Jonathan Cape in 1928. It was considered "an animal story of insight". Salten wrote several more books embracing natural themes and each was illustrated by an artist with an awareness of animal structure and instinct.

At the time the Walt Disney adaptation of *Bambi* was touring British cinemas, Salten was probably penning *A Forest World* which to my mind was the finest of his works. And the illustrator, whose name as a boy I failed to learn, was equally outstanding. Salten wrote basically about the wildlife of the German forests where, as in Britain, the red deer and roe deer roam at will. The illustrator or illustrators of his books had drawn both these deer species for *A Forest World* illustrations equalling the superlative work of sporting artist, Raoul Millias, and the detailed correctness of Victorian artist, Edwin Landseer.

With the American cinema-going public in mind, the Walt Disney adaptation featured the native white tailed deer, the buck's antlers of which are thrust forward rather than upwards like the red deer, but I had not by then seen an illustration of a white tailed deer. Consequently, and as a realist in his formative years, I was under the impression that the Disney animators had deviated from the natural form and wondered why.

As we walked home that winter evening the images created by a German author, but about whom we knew nothing, played across my mind while Mum and Aunty seemed to be taking it in turns to scan the skies because they too had German originated images in mind, but of a different form.

One Saturday evening as the days became noticeably longer and brighter, the entire family decided to embark on a cross-country walk to the wool dynasty village of Wollaton.

For the grown-ups no doubt it was looked upon as a steady stroll, but for me it was a walk because I had to take two or three strides compared to their one. Consequently, one or other of the group stood sideways at intervals waiting for me to catch up.

Bypassing the familiar block of shops in which Starbuck's was centralised, we continued up Beechdale Road which at the beginning of the twentieth century was "a strikingly beautiful tract of countryside" according to one local resident, who described the beech spinneys enhancing the cattle grazed dale and blazing russet against those bygone autumn skies.

Beechdale Road terminated at a traffic island but our unmarked route to Wollaton was by way of a stony lane, uphill to the railway bridge over on our left.

The lane was steep banked on either wide. We were therefore aware of tree roots, green moss on tree trunks, ground ivy, small birds like dunnocks and robins, and myriad budding tree branches forming an elongated arch overhead.

Between the railway and the bridge over the canal stood houses, soon to be semi-targeted by Luftwaffe pilots because of their proximity to the railway, while green fields stretched away to the right.

Eventually the hedgerows ceased and a smallholding dominated by a farmhouse of red brick and lived in, I think, by the Heap's family overlooked the lock gates and pounds of the canal stretch extending a mile or so north of Radford Woodhouse.

Throughout the walk we were looking at history, although I was only aware that buildings had been erected at a "sometime in the past", likewise the canal. Nor did I realise, of course, that most of the woods and spinneys had been planted with game preservation in mind.

Turning to face Nottingham's erratic skyline we looked at the canal, its circular pounds at different levels divided by lock gates. The towpath silent, deserted in the low evening sunlight but grass bordered, hedged and secretively inviting.

I learned that the lock gated staircase, once known to the narrowboat people as The Wollaton Flight, was masterminded by canal engineer, William Jessop. The original plan had been to take the canal through the flat country of Beeston and Lenton Abbey. Lord Middleton, being one of the company's chief shareholders, insisted that the waterway arm swung directly south-east of his walled estate and progressed for a further two or so miles to his colliery. This objective resulted in the staircase of fourteen lock gates being installed at a cost of thirty thousand pounds beyond the previously agreed financial limit. The canal was then used as a coal transportation route for the next hundred and forty two years.

Historical facts such as these, however, were not to hand that evening. What we remarked upon were the beds of aquatic weed; the play of sunlight on the ripples; the fluting of blackbirds and song thrushes from the marshy but compact covert which had been planted alongside, perhaps to screen the sawmills operated by the company of R.F. Rand and W. Brown which is how the lane came to be called Brown's Woodyard and after the war, Woodyard Lane.

At the time of which I am writing fourteen men were employed at the woodyard, including two Polish refugees.

The Brown's were contracted to fell timber on most of the large country estates throughout the English Midlands and the Welsh borders. Once trimmed, the tree trunks were sold to the colliery companies and used for pit props.

Standing at the gate, Dad pointed to the stacks of timber while I inhaled the heady scents of resin and sawdust mixed with those of freshly oiled machinery.

I wondered why Dad had preferred going out every day on two buses to Langar Aerodrome when a twenty minute walk would take him to Brown's and home again in the evening. He needn't have worried about getting home before an air raid if he worked at Brown's Woodyard, besides which we could all see more of him in the evenings and at the weekends.

Suddenly, Aunty exclaimed, 'Hey look at the ground, it's moving?'

Beyond the sawmills and woodyard the stony lane curved between the outbuildings and the foreman's cottage on the left and the tightly fenced wood on the right. Here the ground surface was black and shiny and - yes - Aunty was right; moving!

Betty began striding carefully along the fenced woodside, while saying, 'Careful. Careful. Try not to tread on any of these.'

Any of what?

'What are they?' I yelled.

'Frogs! Baby frogs! Hundreds and thousands of them!' yelled Betty as we tried to walk through the vast concourse of tiny amphibians.

The previous summer they had been tadpoles and throughout the winter had hibernated in the mud at the bottom of the lake hidden deep within the wood. That evening they were journeying overland, making their way to all the nooks, niches and crannies throughout the woodyard outbuildings and stables. Once clear of the frog army I smelt something, pungent and not at all unpleasant.

'Pigs,' said Dad swinging me onto his shoulder and crossing to the half opened door of one of the laneside stables.

They were nestled in bales of straw. Four pinkish-white pigs. Pink snouted, pointed eared, poker eyed.

Betty chose to stroll on while saying that she didn't like the smell, but I couldn't think why. And I was able to compare them with my drawing at the foot of the stairs. I decided then that - yes - I had it about right.

Paddocks interspersed with cart sheds and a white mansion, as Mum described it, called The Lawns continued by the laneside until its terminate point with Wollaton Road at which we turned right. Three hundred yards on the road forked.

This was, I think, new country to Aunty and my parents.

We took the right-hand fork called Russell Drive, bordered either side by fine detached houses and built at around the same time as the one in which we lived. Russell Drive was lined each side with beech trees. After a time, I became bored by its sameness and in my mind returned to the canal bridge at Brown's Woodyard and wondered what it was like being a pig.

We trailed on until the road forks met and couplets of cottages rose buttress like within the thickly hedged fields on our right. Around the bend, out of sight, was the main road canal bridge to which Dad and I were to walk and return home by way of the towpath on future Sunday mornings. That evening no mention was made of its proximity, thus in retrospect I have gained the impression that if the three women were aware of the canal they chose not to take that route home perhaps due to inappropriate footwear.

Dad saw them first, then Mum. Smiling, they swung sideways and directed me to a five barred gate.

'Horses! Horses! Here they come,' grinned Dad.

He whistled. He clicked his tongue. But such persuasions were not needed for the horses, a motley of magnificent bays and chestnuts, some with white blazes, came up to the gate. When I assessed the size scale of each horse as Dad swung me up to pat and stroke their probing muzzles, I experienced a sense of relief in that there *was* a gate between us.

The necks of well-groomed horses were, I discovered, sleek as cushion covers as I stroked them while Dad pointed out the whereabouts of the hock and fetlock on the horse standing nearest to us. He told Betty and I that whereas we humans are measured according to feet and inches, horses in terms of height were measured in hands.

'These are about fourteen and a half hands high,' he explained quietly yet excitedly.

When eventually I glimpsed the size of the horse's teeth, I withdrew my hands from the top bars of the gate and clambered down. They weren't quite as proportionally big as the dragon's teeth I had seen in picture books, but surely they were the next thing to it! And when the horses snorted and blew through their nostrils as if seeking attention, I half expected them to breath fire into our faces.

Dad explained the difference between a bay and a chestnut then as we moved away told Betty and I that he had always wanted to be a jockey but he was just a little too heavy.

'So instead he became a footballer and cricketer,' Mum told us.

'Yes, but being a jockey was my foremost ambition,' Dad admitted.

As we took the right-hand fork through Wollaton village it occurred to me, as it had possibly occurred to Betty, that in front of that five barred farm gate we had learned more about Dad than on any other previous occasion, obviously because he had been so moved by the presence of the horses.

When he recognised the village cricket ground beyond the hedge to our right, Dad again became quietly excited and also probably nostalgic for the days of his wiry framed and athletic youth.

It was when we reached the magnificent chestnut tree by the sports ground entrance, standing to this day, that Aunty broke into her rendition of *Under the Spreading Chestnut Tree* and danced a little as she sang the song that I had first heard Jessie Matthews singing on a *Workers' Playtime* wireless programme. In those days, I should add, the radio was called the wireless by most listeners and announcers.

Dusk was coming in, darkening the stonework of the village cottages yet highlighting the whitewashed exterior of *The Admiral Rodney* public house in the village square.

There was not a soul to be seen. Nor on the future Sunday mornings when I was walked that way by Betty or Dad. Every door was firmly closed. There was not a discernible crack in any set of curtains or the tinkle of a piano resounding from a parlour and out onto the pavement. The entire village it seemed had closed, locked and bolted their doors against the war. Or perhaps the world. All that mattered was the hearth surrounding snugness which the majority of the villagers were probably celebrating.

History was again on either side of us, although I was still unaware of it. Cottages were lived in by people. Had been built long before my time. That was all that I knew and was *content* to know.

The chantry house we therefore passed without realising that it probably dated from 1470, and the house next door and directly opposite the church had been the residence for the church caretakers and in later years The Reverend Russell's groom and coachman. St. Leonard's Church with its interior arches dating from the Middle Ages and Norman style doorway was the second place of worship I had seen, but even then its purpose was not explained to me. Into this same category could be placed *The Admiral Rodney* public house, the centralised village pump which historians insist has never provided water, the yew trees screening the silent rectory, the walls and buildings erected from stonework that could again date back to the Middle Ages.

As we progressed down the wall-sided and tree-lined Church Hill, a new and pleasantly repetitive sound held my attention. When we were then level with the boundary wall of Wollaton Park, I became aware of a lodge house situated behind locked green gates. Above and around the lodge house twenty splendid oaks opened their branches to the ever-changing formations of cloud. In these and three great ash trees positioned outside the park wall and immediately above us much activity was taking place.

Some forty or fifty pairs of rooks had nests positioned like brown twiggy islands set within a sea of tree branches and sky high above the lodge house and the detached houses, facing the park and on the opposite side of the road.

Among the green budding foliage rook pairs gathered at their respective nests to feed the young, left to find more food or flew in with an unidentifiable morsel clasped in their bills. Some pairs were hopping through the twigs and branches, or head nodding in partnership on elongated boughs.

For minutes I walked transfixed, my eyes to the treetops. The rook conversations carried past the second set of lodge gates. Easy if slightly raucous avian talk. Community geared conversation that I could have listened to all night but which, unbeknown to me, the people living opposite and around the park complained bitterly to the point of even suggesting the trees be felled so that the rooks nested somewhere else in the years ahead.My obvious lack of height, however, prevented me from seeing the prisoner-of-war camp and its overseeing army units maintained by the War Department on the other side of the park wall. The camp was not pointed out to me. Perhaps even the four adults wanted to ignore the threat of war on such a splendid evening. Instead of the war, we talked in the deepening dusk of Scamp waiting back at home. Wondering where we were, as Mum put it.

Each evening after dark, Dad put Scamp to his lead and took him along Colliers Pad a little before bed-time then again when Mum was cooking breakfast and Aunty, Betty and I were still in bed around six each morning.

As we walked I envisaged Scamp's high curling tail thumping against the door of the kitchen based gas meter cupboard where Dad hooked his lead. And I knew that the following morning Scamp would be waiting at the foot of the stairs as I tentatively, yet excitedly, made my way down to face the excited probing of his broad, bewhiskered muzzle.

CHAPTER 10

A strange jogging sensation penetrated my sleep, a sensation similar to the experience of being tossed repeatedly in a blanket.

I awoke discovering that I was indeed in a blanket. Warm, blanketed and nestled in Dad's arms.

We were outside! In the black night! On the back garden path!

People were hurrying in front of us and people filing behind, their exclamations deafened by the continual roar of engines.

'W-what's happening, Dad?' I gasped.

'We're going to the air raid shelter, Little Man. There's an air raid,' Dad murmured.

'The Germans! Have they come?'

'Yes, there look.'

Dad stood for a moment and swung me lightly and slightly towards the starlit sky. The Luftwaffe bombers, bulky, evil black and menacing all horizons droned threateningly above.

Encircling Dad's neck, while noticing he was wearing his suit and trilby, I hoisted myself to the height of his shoulder and yelled, 'Go away! Go away you naughty misters!' But to my dismay, the bombers continued to cross the tapestry of the stars.

'C'mon, Fran, for goodness sake,' urged Mum.

She and Aunty carried candles and blankets in their apron fronted pockets. Mum held Scamp, straining on his lead.

'Where's Betty? Where's Betty?' I queried.

'In the air raid shelter lighting candles for us all,' Mum hastily explained.

The air raid shelter was of the type I had not seen before or have seen since. Made from local Bulwell stone, its entrance resembled a cave. The roof was concealed, it's ceiling supported by galvanised iron. Someone, perhaps Dad, Uncle Charlie or a workman, had thoughtfully cemented a washing-line post above the entrance; it was a secure base. A personalised shelter of the Anderson type, I think.

Then lowering his head, Dad carried me down the three steps. I smelt galvanised iron, dampness and acrid tangs of the sandbags stowed beneath the wooden benches either side.

Betty was speaking softly to everyone as she lit the candles and handed them around. Scamp barked. Mum shortened his lead with one hand while distributing blankets as best she could with the other.

His back to the house, garden and slowly departing Luftwaffe, Dad sat me on his knee and wrapped the blanket around my body, legs and slipper-clad feet.

There were people squeezed into the air raid shelter whom I didn't know. In retrospect, one family may have been Mr. and Mrs. Fisher and their daughter, Dorianne. Their garden backed onto our own and Teather's and a gap had been made in the high thick privet hedge in order for them to get through.

Once the candles were lit, I recognised Mr. Teather settling in opposite Dad and I saw Mrs. Teather. She was wearing her dark green overcoat, her high cheekbones distinguishable in the candlelight, her head back, resting against the wall of galvanised iron and concrete.

Beyond the air raid shelter the droning of Luftwaffe bomber engines could be heard. Mrs. Teather closed her eyes then opened them. Even in the candlelight I could see that they were very blue. Her hands were crossed on her lap where rested the thickest book I had ever seen.

'Mrs. Teather, are those stories in that?' I asked hopefully.

'Of a kind Keith, of a kind,' she smiled.

'What is it called?' I urged.

'It's the Bible, Keith,' she softly replied.

Judging by the hush that followed, the Bible was something about which I had not heard but which was special.

Mrs. Teather smiled across at me, her teeth, white and even in the semi-darkness. But quite clearly there were not to be any stories.

Suddenly, a thunderous explosion resounded. And another. Someone sobbed or caught their breath. Scamp turned towards Mum and Dad and sitting on his haunches thrust his muzzle between their bodies.

'Scamp's hiding,' I said.

Her hands still on the Bible, Mrs. Teather continued to smile but did not answer. No one answered. Everyone was listening.

Again an explosion heightened our fears, dominated the night. Then Mr. Teather stood, as best he could, his eyes wide, face comically persuading, hands lifted as if he was about to conduct an orchestra. 'Right, let's sing *Ten Green Bottles*, shall we? Here we go. After three,' he suggested.

Without further hesitation, the air raid shelter's occupants, our neighbours burst into song. Singing. Singing. While a few miles away the Luftwaffe settled over and bombed the centre of Nottingham and also its suburbs, just as earlier that night they had bombed the City of Sheffield.

'Again!' someone demanded when, against the continual background of bombs exploding, the song came to an end. 'Only louder!'

'Blow the Gerries!' someone else yelled defiantly.

This time, because while being jogged on Dad's knee I had heard the song once, I joined in as best I could. Next the grown-ups and Betty singing *It's a Long Way to Tipperary*, after which I became sleepy, bombings or no bombings.

When I next awoke I was still in Dad's arms and being carried towards the house. The house which still stood, as all the surrounding houses were, standing.

'Have the Gerries gone, Dad?' I piped.

'Yes, we've had the "All Clear",' he confirmed, then smiled in a fond but relieved kind of way when I added —

'Well, I didn't hear it.'

The air smelt of smoke. Hot smoke. I sensed tension in the atmosphere.

Hurrying ahead of us, Mum entered the house by the kitchen first and switched on the light. As she turned to take me from Dad, I saw there were tears in her eyes. 'Oh those poor people. Those poor souls,' she murmured. I wondered who she meant.

'I hope my sister Nelly and her family are all right. One of the bombs sounded as if it was dropped right over their place,' she said.

'They'll be all right,' murmured Dad.

'Then there's my brothers, John and Fred, and their families. They all live out that way, you know.'

'I know, I know. But I think they'll be all right. We'll know better in the morning,' Dad answered softly.

Very few houses were connected by telephone in those times. People learned of disasters and such by word of mouth, or by contacting the police and the air raid wardens if someone was missing.

When I awoke in the morning, my first thought as usual was Scamp. Like most of my generation, I had still no conception of the sorrow, stress and misery hundreds of people were experiencing in two or more English cities, due to the terrifying missiles the Luftwaffe had released against a spectacular but lethal background of stars the previous night.

As a child I was not concerned with dates appertaining to the calendar year but while studying the wartime and blitz accounts in the Nottingham Local Studies Library in recent years, I have surmised that due to the large number of Luftwaffe bombers that I was shown by Dad on that first occasion, the date and time was most probably the small hours spanning 8th and 9th May 1941.

The city's population, most of whom were retiring for the night, heard the air raid sirens at around 12.30 a.m. on Friday, May 9th, and seven minutes later the "Blitz of Nottingham" began.

The city's first air raid casualty was, ironically, a newly born baby killed in the air raid of August 30th 1940 and of which I was totally unaware, the evening's mug of warmed milk liberally laced with whisky having obviously put me out.

Another air raid occurred on January 15th 1941 of which I knew nothing. The blitz on May 8th of that year, however, was staged by no fewer than 95 enemy bombers, which is why I have associated my experience with that date due to there having been so many aircraft in the sky when Dad paused on the path to show me the threat that hung literally above us.

The next morning's *Daily Sketch* featured as usual photographs of the Royal Family and Winston Churchill, and if the blitzed cities of Nottingham and Sheffield were mentioned I was not made aware of it. Even less was I made aware of the horrific blitz accounts in the following evening's two newspapers *The Nottingham Evening Post* and *Evening News* which Dad purchased at a Nottingham newsagent's on his way home each evening.

The newspapers I only saw when they were opened and seemingly spread across Dad's lap as in his fireside armchair he read or perused them after he had eaten.

By May I doubt that there would have been a fire blazing in the hearth but the armchairs were always positioned on each side of it and I was usually playing with my tiny metal farm animals or Hornby train set, with Dad's black shiny shoes positioned in the style of one foot across the other as he read the newspaper but never allowed me to see the few captions that I habitually endeavoured to read or the photographs such as I was accustomed to seeing first thing in the morning.

I realise now that Dad was reading such expressions as buildings "going down like packs of cards" printed alongside photographs of buildings with collapsed floors, wall partitions smashed together, windows blown out and roofs teetering and sagging on a few remaining brackets and support beams.

There were also photographs of workmen, soldiers and air raid wardens searching through the brick and mortar rubble, while no doubt discussing how best and when they were going to dismantle the building without causing further injury. Like the cinema's newsreels, the newspaper photographs depicted carnage in black, grey and white. Such coverage and photographs alarmed "the sheltered children" of my generation but perhaps only for seconds or a minute at the most, because we had our toys to play with, books to read and further questions to ask our long-suffering siblings. The adult fears and miseries. The anxieties that were heightened when each night crept in. The understandable hysterics of some and instinctive boldness of others were not conveyed to us by word of mouth or even fully by newspaper photographs.

As poet Ken Swallow puts it "we did not see the black walls falling", anymore than we could imagine the air raid wardens and Red Cross personnel out there in the among the scents of brick dust, singed wood and much else, searching through piles of rubble, calling out and clambering over the almost unidentifiable remains of houses, commercial and civic buildings in their attempts to retrieve the dead and injured.

We had no conception of the courage or the pain both physical and mental that was experienced at an alarming rate beyond those printed newspaper reports and photographs. A bombing raid to us was something that happened last night but might not happen tomorrow. Holding the newspaper as if it were a protective yet informative barrier, Dad read of students helping workmen and air raid wardens sift through piles of singed debris, of the untrained householders who had formed chains and continually handed buckets of water to one another in their attempts to put out the fire.

One of Nottingham's main casualties, which is mentioned to this day, was the Co-operative Bakery situated on a north bend of the Trent just downstream from the nationally famous Trent Bridge. Close to the bakery was a railway bridge, which may well have been the Luftwaffe's target. If this were the case, then not one of the several highly explosive bombs released above it hit that target. Instead the bombs all but demolished the Co-operative Bakery and killed forty-nine shift workers huddled in the firm's air raid shelter. The building was reduced to a tomb of bricks, mortar and tons of flour.

An estimated four hundred highly explosive bombs incendiaries and oil bombs, were dropped over Nottingham throughout that long remembered raid when the Meadow Lane football ground was hit and forty people killed in nearby West Bridgford. In addition, two Anglican churches, a University textile and knitting machinery college, a Masonic Hall and the magnificent Old University College on Shakespeare Street, once attended by the novelist D.H. Lawrence, were bombed along with a particularly ancient building, the Moot Hall.

Dad, in his fireside chair, had seen much as like many men and women he went through the city to catch the connecting bus to Belvoir that morning. He had heard the verbal accounts, the local wireless bulletins perhaps, but by the late evening and with the newspaper spread before him the collated evidence of the debris wandering journalists no doubt horrified him as it had everyone else.

Incendiary bombs had all but desecrated the Trent Bridge cricket ground.

Stunned wardens and reserve volunteers related to newspaper reporters how they and others had seen the stone pillar supports of buildings teeter seconds before the buildings collapsed. Of window frames blown inwards or outwards.

Of those many people injured by splinters of flying glass. Of the sudden fires and the choking veils of smoke.

Dad was, no doubt, aware that almost everyone working on rescuing souls and hosing down buildings with water used from rooftop storage tanks wore gas masks but which, ironically, I have since been told, served as something of a hindrance. Yet what was the alternative? That evening's newspaper accounts concluded with paragraphs relating to a newspaper reporter's visit to the People's Dispensary for Sick Animals. All the dogs that were taken in with injuries or suffering from shock had recovered. Only one had to be put down due to it suffering a crushed ribcage.

When Dad finally put the newspaper pages together that evening, he obviously realised that we had experienced a narrow escape. But like most of his generation and former generations, the fears of war were firmly lodged into the back of his mind. There was no escaping it. Every adult person in Europe, let alone Britain, was in some way affected by the war. Air-frame fitters like Dad were reminded of it each time the shattered body of an aircraft was towed before them on the airfield at Langar.

The meanders of the River Trent, glittering like a necklace in the moonlight, had literally served as a guiding light to those Luftwaffe pilots then as in the air raids to follow, which brought the overall total of attacks on Nottingham to eleven.

Silently, Dad continued to read the newspaper and as he turned each page I lifted my head from the toys and wondered why his brow had become so furrowed. But he was taking in more accounts of the devastation. The Cavendish Cinema bombed......a West Bridgford shopkeeper who after his shop windows were shattered and a wall had caved in, put up a notice indicating that I'M BLASTED OPEN! The Registrar's Office bombed. The warden of a boys' club leaving an air raid shelter to see a space of flattened rubble where an hour earlier his house had stood. Air raid wardens and Red Cross workers digging a woman out from a bombed shelter. Unusual sights like a wireless positioned on a low table or a then popular indoor plant called an aspidistra standing, as if resolute, within an intact vase and holding the attentions of both rescue crews and journalists.

One of the worst eye-witness accounts was given by a man who turned as a bomb hit a block of four houses. As the houses merged into a fireball of bricks, mortar and dust, the body of a pyjama-clad man and his bed were blown through the roof. The body was eventually brought down from the roof of the next house and the skeletal remains of the bed dismantled from the branches of a tree, which miraculously survived, in the neighbouring garden. The double tragedy emerged when a five-year old boy, presumably the man's son, was discovered among the rubble.

To children like myself who were toddlers at the onset of the war, the truth was still kept under verbal wraps, and understandably.

When one learned of a bombing or group of bombings, one gained the impression they had taken place some distance away. That they were isolated incidents.

The pain and suffering of the injured, both physically and mentally, was beyond our reasoning; our realms of thought. Consequently, it was the adults who suffered.....the survivors as well as the wounded, the injured and those who so gallantly had striven to help them. As sheltered children, we were not told things that would make us suffer. And each morning, as the West Bridgford shopkeeper had "blasted well" implied, life continued as usual with the books, toy animals and, in my case, daily round of stories read from books screening the threat conceived immediately our parents and their generation thought of and mentioned the word tomorrow.

CHAPTER 11

On 10ᵗʰ May 1941 the House of Commons, Westminster, was destroyed when incendiary bombs were dropped ceaselessly across London. On the same day the deputy leader of the Nazi Party, Rudolf Hess, was flown secretly to Scotland, his mission being to discuss proposals for peace. Instead he was arrested and regarded as a prisoner-of-war.

Off the coast of Greenland on 24ᵗʰ May, the British battle cruiser *HMS Hood* was sunk by the German battleship *Bismark*. Three days later out in the Atlantic various Royal Navy units located the *Bismark* and sank her.

On 1ˢᵗ June utility furniture and clothing were introduced to the British shops and markets, and clothes were rationed.

In the United States, by the 28ᵗʰ, President Franklin D. Roosevelt had established the office of Scientific Research and Development.

By July the newspapers carried reports of Soviet troops, whose units had been defeated by the Germans in the Baltic States, the USSR and Poland holding their own against more German military units on the original Polish frontier. Two days after the Germans were forced back from Leningrad, the USSR signed a mutual aid agreement with Great Britain.

In August 1941, the British Royal Air Force Chiefs displayed their consternation when after studying aerial photographs it was discovered that the bomber pilots seldom found their targets. The answer, the Royal Air Chiefs decided, was to research deeply into all systems directly involved with radar navigation.

***

My walks with Aunty to the off-licence were interrupted on the Monday evening she set off alone wearing her russet overcoat and carrying a zipped up leather bag with the promise that she would wave to me from Colliers Pad if I looked out of the back bedroom window, which indeed I did. The heat was pleasant and everywhere, except the rows of houses on Westholme Gardens and backing onto our own, was green foliated or in the case of the lawns, newly mown.

I noticed as I leaned out of the open window that sections of brown paintwork was peeling on the window ledges and Mum, who joined me, explained that this was largely due to the heat. The sparrow's nest was still trailing its lengths of interwoven grass and string. The "chip-chip" calls of sparrows continually carried from the guttering to the rockery.

We looked into the light, the low golden evening light, and presently saw her; Aunty. Still russet coated, slim and slightly stooped, walking against the green blazing background of the Humps and Hollows field.

'She's not taken her coat off, bless her,' said Mum.

Then Aunty was looking in our direction and waving a startlingly white cloth, an ornamental cloth with which she used to cover the top deck of the tea trolley, which was never used but stood in the hall where my pram used to stand. At times she brandished the cloth rather than waved it and I imagined her laughing and smiling.

The very next Monday tea-time I was not leaning out of the window but walking at Aunty's side. Going to buy yeast for the Tuesday afternoon bread-making session.

On one of those stifling but sunlit Monday evenings, Aunty shed her russet overcoat and after depositing the yeast in the kitchen walked back with me along Colliers Pad to the Humps and Hollows Field.

At the corner of Colliers Pad where the dirt path began, four detached houses backed onto the field. Beyond them were fields and woods for as far as the eye would allow. An elm stood on the corner near the first of these relatively isolated houses and I was fascinated by the three long rusted nails some bygone Radford Woodhouse youth perhaps had positioned there in order to climb into the crack of the elm's widespread boughs. In later life I learned that this elm had been appropriately called Three Nail Tree by the Radford Woodhouse fraternity. The hedgeless ditchside was almost hidden by ranks of dog's mercury, docks, dandelions, cow parsley and other members of the umbellifer family.

When we reached The Tallest Tree in Nottinghamshire, Aunty pointed out a narrow path connecting the ditch banks to the cowslip and clover studded carpet of The Humps and Hollows Field. Here she had picnicked in her young days, sometimes with Uncle Charlie, but when she was a girl quite often with her brothers Albert and Frances, who was of course my father.

Aunty sank down into the grasses and I alongside her. Blackbird cocks fluted from the hedgerow thickets and disused allotments at our backs. Cowslip heads trembled in the threads of a breeze while above us a bird, unseen, poured out its repetitive yet never tiresome song.

'Skylark,' said Aunty, smiling, pointing in answer to my question.

She pointed but at first I couldn't pick out the songster. The sky was vast; blue. The gatherings of cumulus cloud, white, misshapen. Was this the sky of the entire world, I wondered?

Presently I followed Aunty's pointing finger. A dark speck was hovering and holding its own in the vastness. The lark was, Aunty explained, singing because of the sun, the light. It may also have been singing to advertise its territory here on the ground, perhaps to other skylarks.

Eventually, and as Aunty prophesied, the lark came drifting gradually down, describing wide spirals whilst still singing. Then suddenly the singing ceased and the lark was dropping....dropping....to its nest in the tussocks. Except that skylarks don't land directly at the nest but settle some feet away then sprint furtively to the tussock or the imprint of a cow or horse made in the grasses and where the tiny youngsters are nestled and awaiting food.

'There could be four or five pairs nesting on this one field alone,' smiled Aunty.

Home was forgotten. I was sitting among the clovers and wildflowers listening to the skylarks with Aunty. This was all that I needed. We stayed, sitting, listening and watching the inflamed disc of sunlight sinking imperceptibly behind the woods.

Eventually, and sadly, Aunty said that it was time we ought to be going, before the dusk settled in.

When I pointed again to the sun, she said, 'Yes, this is the time we would be leaving for home after we had picnicked here. And this light is what your dad always calls "the westering light", and I think it's lovely, don't you?'

'But the skylarks, Aunty.....?'

'They'll be singing tomorrow. As soon as the sun rises and perhaps before. They'll be singing,' she assured me.

I asked Mum why Aunty and I had been alone on the Humps and Hollows Field, much as I had enjoyed it. Where were the men who had hammered three nails into the trunk of the elm?

'Probably overseas. Been called up. They could be soldiers now, a lot of them. Soldiers or sailors or airmen fighting for our country,' replied Mum sadly.

Sitting me in their laps, Betty or Aunty pointed to the words of each sentence as they read them out to me. I began to see the pattern. A line of words was called a sentence. A group of sentences helped move along a story. I wondered then what Captain Marryat looked like, where he lived. How and why he had interwoven his novels into true historical accounts.

Presently I was looking at the words and illustrations of Don Quixote and listening enthralled to the adventures of a sea captain called Magellan. I learned also that our country, Great Britain, was surrounded by water and therefore called an island, like Robinson Crusoe's island.

The sea was vast. Stretched for miles. Therefore, Aunty told Betty, if the Germans attempted to invade us they would probably be turned back by our own fleets, our own ships. Moreover, between Germany and Great Britain was not only the sea but France, a country about which Betty was learning at school. Consequently, it would take the Germans a long time to reach our shores, if indeed they ever contemplated it. Betty nodded in satisfaction as I climbed yet again onto Aunty's lap, while persuading, 'Read me this one please, Aunty.'

'Yes, well I'll read it *with* you. We'll read it together,' she answered.

Desperate to display my independence, I pleaded with Aunty and Mum to reverse roles and to let me go to buy yeast from Kirk's off-licence the following Monday. The heat wave persisted and was therefore on my side. Aunty was willing to allow me out alone for the first time but, of course, the final decision rested with Mum. Now as a parent myself, I realise that she must have been understandably apprehensive about allowing me to go. And who could have blamed her? But, surprisingly, she relented. Not, however, before Mum issued me with the instructions that I was *not* and she meant *not* to speak to anyone between the house and the Kirk's off-licence.

When I arrived, I was to ask for "three ounces of yeast, please" and give Mrs. Kirk the sixpence Mum had pressed into my hand.

'She will give you three pennies change. Or it might be a threepenny bit,' Mum added.

Reversing roles of course meant taking the white cloth and waving it. Aunty was still going to wave with another white cloth and from the back bedroom window as Mum and I had done.

And so I set off on my first journey alone.

Saying their goodbyes and calling out, 'Don't forget what we've told you,' Aunty and Mum saw me off at the front door.

Once I had latched the gate, I was aware of the space around me. Space on either side. There was no one to speak with. No hand to hold.

"Three ounces of yeast, please." Would I......*could I* remember that?

Passing the first tract of disused allotments, I turned left by Three Nail Tree. Blackbird cocks were fluting, the skylarks high and singing. The Humps and Hollows field yellow swathed with cowslips and buttercups as before. The track curved slightly after I had passed The Tallest Tree. Here I turned and saw a white cloth dangling and swinging from a rear bedroom window.

Mum and Aunty. That was our house.

Quickly I unfolded the white cloth I was carrying and the breeze came in and all but covered me with it. I fought the cloth, gathered it up where I could and moved my arms in the waving motion. For seconds I was free until the cloth again engulfed me. Mum and Aunty were signalling though, so that was a good sign.

I trekked on towards Beechdale Road with its singularly long-stemmed ragworts flowering between the cracks in its concrete block surface. Houses faced me from the opposite pavement, Colliers Pad, the trees and fields at my back.

At the kerb I stopped and exercised the road drill I had been taught — Radford Bridge Road, with detached houses on one side and newly-built pre-fabs the other, dipped between two heavily thicketed embankments to the railway bridge. This was dark, shaded and stony underfoot, but the main road of Radford Woodhouse tapered into the distance beyond. Two steps took me over the pavement on the left and beside the walled gardens and backyards of the colliery fraternity.

I glimpsed woodshed after woodshed in these rear gardens but little realised they either housed ferrets, canaries or homing pigeons. If I had realised this, I would have lingered. Knocked, no doubt, on the door of a complete stranger and asked to see their charges.

"Three ounces of yeast, please.'

I turned the corner of Vane Street and standing on tiptoe flicked the brass door latch. The bell chimed and as I opened the door those intoxicating off-licence smells infiltrated my nostrils.

'Hello, young man! Have you managed the door all right?'

The voice was a gruff one. *That wasn't Mrs. Kirk!*

'Yes, thank you.'

The man had black hair parted on one side, a wrinkled forehead and was wearing a white shirt and blue patterned tie behind his grey, long sleeved smock.

'Is...is....Mrs. Kirk in, please?' I piped.

'She's having her tea just now, little fella. I'm Mr. Kirk though, so it's all right. What can I get for yer?'

I swallowed. What was it? Oh......

'Can I have three ounces of yeast, please?'

'Three ounces of yeast? Why certainly.' Mr. Kirk smiled and ventured, 'You're not a Woodhouse lad though, are yer?'

'No, I live on Chalfont Drive.'

'Oh aye, o'er that way,' shrugged Mr. Kirk as he placed nodules of yeast into a brightly polished scale pan.

When next he met my fascinated gaze, Mr. Kirk startled me beyond words because he had only one eye. The other was lidded, but closed. Only one eye! Wait till I get home and tell Mum and Aunty that Mr. Kirk has only one eye!

Mr. Kirk's smile was warm and kindly and as he gave me the yeast in one hand and the change which I had to grasp with the same hand because I was carrying the white cloth, he said, 'I'll come round and open the door for yer son. Now don't speak to anybody between here and Chalfont Drive, will you?'

Thanking Mr. Kirk and assuring him that I wouldn't, I left the off-licence and hurried towards the railway bridge.

My goodness! Wait till I told Mum and Aunty that Mr. Kirk……..

In retrospect, I realise that Mum must have been going quietly out of her mind when she lost sight of me at the end of Colliers Pad. Those fifteen or twenty, perhaps thirty minutes must have seemed like a month…….*a year.*

Nor could I wave the engulfing cloth with the change and yeast clasped in the opposite hand.

When I reached the front door, Mum and Aunty crowded into the porch their faces alight.

'Mum! Mr. Kirk's only got one eye!' I announced, excitedly.

'Oh, I know,' said Mum taking the yeast, change and white cloth from my hands.

Disappointment plunged to the soles of my feet. How *did* she know?

'He lost it in a pit accident, a mining disaster,' smiled Mum ushering me into the dining room.'Oh it must have been years ago. '

CHAPTER 12

Besides locks on the front and back doors, a further sense of security occurred when a massive pair of black painted lattice gates were erected between our house and Teather's. They were solid and lasted throughout our stay at Chalfont Drive. Except for early Saturday mornings when the milkman and his mate called for the milk money and were each given a mug of tea by Mum, the gates were always securely bolted on the inside. In all, these gates were about twelve feet height but the narrow hinged gate which opened into the yard and rear garden was lifted about eighteen inches from the ground. Consequently, Scamp could thrust his muzzle beneath when he heard someone opening the front garden gate and usually he began barking and growling if the visitor was not a neighbour or member of the family.

Whichever one of the two rabbit men called appeared nervous of Scamp, although all they could see was his bewhiskered muzzle. The postman undoubtedly shared the same uncomfortable experience, although Scamp to my knowledge never bit anyone. But to a stranger, because he looked up at them as he was barking, he obviously appeared intimidating.

When he was let off the lead, Scamp was usually well-behaved but he developed a trait for chasing a few cyclists who came by. A fast growing dog, perhaps half the size of a German Shepherd, he would race across at a bicycle without hesitation and snap and snarl at the cyclist's feet and the pedals.

Dad thought it was the almost inaudible whirr of the bicycle tyres that set Scamp in motion and the instant Dad firmly called out, 'Scamp, come here!' Scamp swung away and approached Dad, slinking fashion and sometimes with his tail between his legs. It was then that Dad hissed, 'Dash you! Dash you! You'll get a good kick in the face one day, my lad.' And at some date in the future Scamp was to collide with a passing vehicle or receive a stunning kick which changed the shape of his face and muzzle for several weeks, so swollen did they become. But he never overcame this trait even when he was an ageing dog.

It was at around the time the gates were fixed securely to the house that Scamp's wicker basket, or the remains of it, had to be thrown into the bin due to him having chewed most of it until the basket was almost unrecognisable. Mum said it was because Scamp was teething but, in retrospect, it was because of Scamp's persistent displays of energy coupled with the need to be doing something. As I mentioned early, according to Mum he was an Airedale-Welsh Terrier first cross and the Airedale I have since learned is closely related to the otter hound.

As he matured, Scamp took on the appearance of an otter hound and when occasionally at sunset Dad took me up to the remains of the field on the corner of Cherry Orchard Lane where he released Scamp from the lead, the dog immediately broke through the slender paths dividing the nettles and thistles and made for an oak rising from the hedgerow about three hundred yards away.

Beyond the oak and the gaps either side of it, a long field ran parallel with Cherry Orchard Lane and it was in this field, brown furrowed in the winter or blazing golden with wheat or barley throughout the summer, that Scamp most evenings put up several hares. Russet coated with dark long ears, the hares were always aware of Scamp approaching and he hunted them as a hound hunts, by scent, with his muzzle to the earth.

The hares were away before Scamp eventually lifted his muzzle and saw them but he remained following their scent trails from the laneside ditch and across to the attractive spinneys of elm and beech in the adjacent fields.

Dad watched Scamp from the pavement. Sometimes he picked me up so that I could follow Scamp's scent trailing progress. Then after twenty minutes, Dad gave out a long and tuneful five syllable whistle which on hearing it turned Scamp immediately.

As we waited, I watched Dad looking at the sunset and once when I asked, 'What are you looking at Dad?' he replied —

'The sunset Little Man. There are never two the same, you know. Every one is different. And if there's a sunset tomorrow night it will be different from the one we are looking at tonight, you see. Memorise the shapes of the clouds now and look at them again tomorrow. And the sky, it could be orange or pink or red, but it won't be *exactly* the same as the sky that we're looking at now.'

Scamp's tongue lolled sideways over his jaws when he returned to Dad and I, and the expression in his eyes gave me the impression that he was laughing. Face on, however, and due to his unfaltering lion-like walk, Scamp would certainly make a man think twice about harming me if I was alone and his bark, as we discovered, literally stopped callers in their tracks.

One warm sunlit afternoon, my cousin Peggy came to see us. As a young girl she was a calm and collected person. Throughout that particular visit she appeared serious and thoughtful, or to some extent worried perhaps.

My memory fails here but she may well have volunteered to serve in Her Majesty's Forces, as did her sisters Rene and Alice.

As Peggy conversed with Mum, I studied, as an artist would study, the roundness of her face with its well-shaped nose and full lips, and her wide expressive eyes. She reminded me of Betty's friend Jean who lived on the next road, except that her words were well-measured compared to the usual exuberant outbursts I had come to expect from girls of around that age.

Peggy's hair was also similar to Jean's. A rich mass of deep brown, making me want to reach out and touch it. Eventually, Peggy suggested she and I should go for a walk to the top of the road, to look at the fields. She held my hand, walked slowly and spoke softly. Here we listened to the skylarks and watched for a time the breeze furled rhythms of the long grasses, ranks of cow parsley, thistles and poppies.

We walked towards the woods that from our front garden gate pleasantly blocked the sunset horizon, except on that particular day, and due both to the light and the season, the woods were green and the sky flawless blue. We were not going *into* the woods Peggy quietly informed me, although we might go to the barbed wire fence surrounding them and look in.

We stopped to look at the red and white liveried dairy Shorthorn cattle cropping the grass and Peggy picked cowslips and the long stemmed flowers of the camomile. As Peggy picked the flowers, so she smelt and gently caressed their petals while arranging them into bunches or "posies"; one for herself, one for Mum, one for Aunty.

Eventually, Peggy told me that she thought it was about time we made our way home and that she wanted anyway to keep the flowers looking fresh. I was quietly surprised. Disappointed perhaps. The shock occurred, however, when walking towards the house and again holding Peggy's free hand I heard a man yell sharply and a piercing crack that, despite the distant bombings, I had not before heard the like. Spinning on our heels, Peggy and I watched a great full foliaged elm tree teeter then crash sideways to the ground.

We stood mesmerised. Then when the dust cloud cleared, we saw the men, dwarfed by the elm's size, standing around it.

'Peggy, what are they *doing*?' I shrilled.

'Chopping down the trees.'

'Why, though?'

'It's all to do with the "war effort", I suppose. But trees that size Keith must be *hundreds* of years old.'

I stared across the fields at the blue sky space where minutes before a great tree had stood. Then came the questions. Poor Peggy!

What do men use to chop down trees? *Why* do they chop down trees? Did they *have* to chop down trees? For how long can trees live if they are *not* chopped down?

Dutifully and as ever gently composed, Peggy answered each of my questions as best she could so that by the time we reached the front garden gate I had become aware of the relationship between trees and the earth and woodcutters - as they were then called - and trees.

Later that afternoon Peggy prepared to leave, she swept me up into her strong young arms and when Mum and Aunty came to say their goodbyes I detected a sadness filtering through the eyes of all three women. Peggy lowered me to the ground, hugged Mum, hugged Aunty, tweaked my fingers, then in a twirl of summer dress she was hurrying down the road towards the Boulevard without once looking back.

Mum lifted a finger to her eyes as she returned to the kitchen, while I poured out the ingredients of the tree shock to Aunty.

Basically, I think was wondering why men should be so intent on felling trees on so beautiful a day. Aunty then told me that she would have a walk up that way with me the following afternoon.

Could she - *would she* - stop the woodcutters?

Aunty shook her head and told me that she didn't think she would be able to do that, at which admission I experienced both surprise and disappointment. The following afternoon, however, she would take me up to the Beechdale fields and talk with the woodcutters if only to find out what they were about.

The sky space was wider that afternoon. More trees had been felled.

'A whole spinney of elms, felled in less than a week!' Aunty exclaimed.

The breeze was again furling the grasses, the sky cloudless blue and the larks singing as if there would be no tomorrow.

'We'll speak to the man in charge. He'll be wearing either a trilby hat or a bowler.'

'Why, Aunty?'

'To set himself apart from the rest. It's always been the tradition, at least in mine and your Dad's time. The rest of the woodcutters will be wearing flat caps, you see.'

As we approached the woodcutters, I saw that one or two of the men were bearded.

'Beards? They are traditionally worn by this breed of man too. Woodcutters and gamekeepers. They wear beards,' Aunty explained.

The men with flat caps were trimming and sawing off the tree branches and piling them unceremoniously onto a flat backed lorry, which to my horror had made tracks in the field grass.

As I expected, none of the woodcutters looked alike in close up as they had at distance. Their faces, large hands and muscular arms carried the same mahogany tones as the dining room table from which we ate. Their teeth gleamed white. Their brows were half shaded by the rims or peaks of their hats. Waistcoats were draped out or hooked onto the sides of the lorry.

Aunty had not seen a lorry used for transporting timber because in her younger days timber had been stacked and bound to a long cart pulled by four horses.

Aunty greeted the men and the one who touched the rim of his bower, bowed slightly and addressed Aunty as "Missis", came forward.

Woodcutters? Yes, that used to be the old name for men like themselves all right. But now they were known as timber contractors and they had been contracted by the Government to fell all the trees in the spinneys and down to the edge of the new road which would, in effect, be a private extension of Chalfont Drive, the road on which we lived, by a certain date.

The reason was, the tree contractor explained, because the Government - the War Department, were building a complex of high security offices here. He then pointed in the direction Peggy and I had walked the previous day. Here three or four lorries were parked and alongside them, the lorries having earlier that day been unloaded, were stacked rolls of barbed wire, paving stones and fence posts. Security boxes, or *offices*, were going to be built at each side of the security gates and the people who would eventually work there would need to show passes when each morning they entered the premises.

If we wanted to go to the farm and the woods, the foreman continued, pointing north towards Aspley Hall, we would have to "go round".

The foreman then took a map from his pocket and unrolling it gave one end to Aunty. As he and she studied it, I noticed the workmen lifting their waistcoats from the lorry and dusting them down.

Turning to me, one grizzled man with a silver-white beard and kindly brown eyes, jolted me to his attention by asking, 'Do you know how old a tree is son? I bet you don't. Well come here and I'll show you its life rings, one for each year..'

Joining the man, he put a hand to my shoulder and guided me to the bole of a felled elm. Amid the pleasant yet destructive tangs of sawdust, he pointed out the life rings. Circling, saw-edged and recording in growth the storms, the winters, the summers and each seasonal cycle the tree had known.

I touched the tree bark and loved its texture; slightly rough, uneven, yet a surface attractive and teasing to my fingertips. 'Has *this* tree seen many changes then?'

'Yes, son. More than we'll ever know. He's been looking out across these fields perhaps since the day they were enclosed, has this mighty tree. If he could talk, my word he'd tell you everything about what's happened around here. Packed to the hilt with history he would be, like a book full of interesting pages.'

Before us was beauty crushed by devastation. Around me were people talking about trees, future security and, less appropriately, the horrors of war.

It was then I thought of the elm alongside Collier's Pad. The tree known locally as "The Tallest Tree in Nottinghamshire". I nudged Aunty, asked her and the man if this tree was going to be allowed to live.

'Oh, he's safe enough. Out of our area that one and he's still got a few years to go yet, like me,' smiled the silver bearded man.

Beyond the Humps and Hollows Field, however, the land had been compulsorily purchased by the War Department. We would not be allowed to wander there and this included the track on which I had seen the couple riding the horses.

'There's going to be a row of houses fronting Beechdale Road along there. It's been sold to a local builder that strip of land,' the foreman told us.

Eventually, Aunty thanked the men and took my hand. The men touched the peaks of their caps or, in the foreman's case, the front of his bowler. As we turned towards home I wondered how it must feel to be sporting a black or silver beard.

'Yes, times they are a changing all right. We've got lorries hauling the timber now.

I've got a feeling the old cart horse has had his day,' mused Aunty sadly as we crossed the field.

At last we had the answer. It all had to do with the war - and change. Even elms had to be felled in times of war. They had to die, like soldiers, airmen and women, and sailors had to die. But was war reason enough for trees and people to die? That question I did not pester Aunty with but kept to myself, hoping that one day I might parallel it with a satisfactory answer.

The smaller of the two rabbit-catchers, the one with the round ended nose and forehead lines, told Aunty as she took two dangling rabbits from him about a German, or "Gerry", aircraft that had been shot down, apparently in our natal county.

When it came plunging nose first out of the sky, the aircraft was already alight. By the time it became half buried in the meadow grass, the incendiary bombs were exploding one after the other. The entire casement became a huge bonfire.

'Did the pilot manage to bail out?' asked Aunty.

'Not according to last night's newspaper. He was probably killed by bullets when he was up in the air anyway,' the rabbit-catcher replied.

I thought then of the parachutists I saw on the *Pathe News* coming down......down..... Then the pilot rolling to one side when he reached the ground.

'Ah! It's no good for nobody is war!' the rabbit-catcher exclaimed, touching the rim of his trilby in farewell.

'Yes, you're right there. Yet knowing the world as I think I now know it, I can't help thinking that somebody's having a good time somewhere,' Aunty replied.

CHAPTER 13

In the Summer of 1941, the BBC suggested that German occupied countries use the V for Victory sign, three dots and a dash, as a symbol of Morse code. Moreover, the Corporation further suggested that when accosted by or within close proximity of the Nazis, people should hum or whistle the opening bars of Beethoven's 5th Symphony.

In September Franklin D. Roosevelt, the American President, declared "no mercy" assaults on Italian and German vessels located in United States waters. The United States then launched a "Liberty Ship", an emergency freighting vessel carrying supply cargoes requested by Britain. Several days later Franklin D. Roosevelt joined Winston Churchill at a London-based conference, where both signed The Atlantic Charter which ensured the continuation of aid and further support of both countries throughout the war.

In the shortening days of October, *Kearny,* the U.S. destroyer, was hit off the coast of Ireland when all American ships were listed as German U boat targets. Meanwhile, the cities around and within marching distance of Moscow fell to the assault of several German Army divisions.

On October 13th, Nuremberg, a prosperous German city, was bombed by the British Royal Air Force. On the 31st all 115 crewmen aboard the United States destroyer *Reuben James* perished during a German U boat assault. In the meantime, the Germany Amy divisions continued to invade parts of the USSR while gaining power in Kharkov, a city of prestige situated in the Ukraine.

***

On a mid-week afternoon of teeming rain, Aunty took me on a number 13 bus to the city. The bus stop was still partially sheltered by heavily foliaged lime trees.

Aunty walked steadily, attempting to hold the umbrella over me as well as herself, her long russet overcoat nurturing familiarity and, for myself, well-being just so long as I was beside her.

The sounds of the rain intrigued me. The puddle dimpling rhythm, coupled with the gentle yet repetitive pattering on the top of the umbrella. I also nurtured the awareness of being sheltered, of having - as usual - someone to look after me. And I hoped secretly that it would always remain that way.

There were puddles around the base of every third or fourth tree. Aunty also saw them and remarked that after such a long hot summer the trees were, at last, having 'a good long drink.'

I asked why the trees wanted to drink and then why we had rain.

Aunty explained that it was all part of nature's pattern. If there was no rain we would not have fruit and vegetables, nor milk from the cows. No wildflowers in the fields. No grass and 'no lovely green trees.'

So it *was* important, the rain. The deluge that rippled and sang parallel with the kerbstones while silvering the surface of the road.

'There will be more rain now because the autumn is almost with us. That is when the leaves all change colour before the wind comes and blows them from the trees,' Aunty continued.

In Nottingham that afternoon she bought two or three pairs of galoshes, or waterproof shoes. One pair for herself, another for Mum and a small pair for me.

'For when we have to go splashing across to the shops,' she told me.

As usual, I came home with a book and was planning to read it and look at the pictures at the table that night while at the same time attempting to erase thoughts of darkness and the Germans from my mind.

I imagined them patrolling the road beyond the front gate, Chalfont Drive, not daring to approach the house because of Scamp. They were in peak capped uniform, erect, grim in expression and ready to accost, *or kill*, anyone approaching who failed to reply to their challenge with the password "Heil Hitler!".

The black night and grey or pale blue uniformed Germans were, to my mind, synonymous. I was looking at the book but thinking, *worrying about perhaps*, the enemy Mum I knew would not submit to if the Germans foolishly disregarding Scamp broke down the front door. She would stand hurling kitchen sink missiles at them before they before they had chance to draw their guns!

Then I remembered that the front door was securely locked with the curtain and blackout curtain further ensuring our safety. Yet, I asked myself, wouldn't one be safer living in an isolated cottage in the New Forest like Captain Marryat's storybook children?

Minutes past. Then with his dorsal hairs standing on end. Scamp rose growling from beside my chair. He was staring at the dining room door.

'Scamp?' I queried.

Surely not the Germans attempting to break the front door down!? My heart quickened.

Then I heard an unfriendly sound. A key turning in the front door lock which when I realised a member of the family had arrived home reverted within my mind and became an instantly *friendly* sound. Mum and Aunty left the kitchen, opened the dining room door and stood looking down the hall. Ready to engage in an affray, Scamp, his curled banner of a tail erect, padded swiftly and stiffly out to the hall still growling.

'It's all right Scamp. It's only your Dad,' chuckled Mum.

And Dad it was, but in different attire. The front door locked behind him and coming into the room wearing khaki well-pressed trousers, which after sniffing them caused Scamp to sneeze and sneeze again, and a soldier's uniform the hat of which he whisked from his head as grinning he sat on one of the two visitor chairs facing the dining room table.

Alarmed, I shrilled, 'Dad, you're not going to fight in the war are you?'

'Not this time Little Man. I was a soldier in the First World War, but now I'm too old to serve my country and so I've joined the Home Guard,' he grinned, while pointing to his white hair.

Rising from the chair while fondling Scamp, Dad returned to the hall, bent, sighed then stood in the dining room doorway smiling and holding a pack in one hand and a rifle in the other.

I could hardly speak! *A rifle! Brought to the house!*

Dad sat again, put the pack down for Scamp to sniff and continue sneezing upon, then resting the butt to the carpet he studied the rifle.

'It's taller than me,' was my first reaction.

Saturday night visits to the cinema had given me an idea of how the rifle looked in the hands of film stars Tim Holt and Charles Starrett, but to have one positioned alongside me was quite a different matter.

A rifle was not, as the cinema screen so often interpreted, a long black manageable stick. It was besides a killing weapon, a manufactured item that was skilfully designed and ornately crafted.

Dad showed me the barrel, breech and stock. Weighed the rifle in his hands, then still holding it handed a portion of the barrel to me. It was not a lightweight rifle and certainly unmanageable as far as I was concerned.

Recent museum visits have convinced me that the rifle was probably a Lee Enfield 303 which was the standard British Army model until 1942 when the MK1 404 Lee Enfield was tested and issued with the accompanying bayonet.

If I carried the rifle on my shoulder like the snow-plodding hunter I saw in a Walt Disney cartoon, a portion of it would trail after me, have to be dragged, I mused. But then I silently consoled myself with the realisation that I was neither a hunter or a soldier and was again able to look at the rifle through the eyes of an outsider and as an object that would remain something to look at and admire but thankfully never handle.

Dad's uniform, from the black shiny boots in which I could see the pink blurred reflection of my face, to the webbing belt with its minute pockets and pouches, might well have been a banner bearing the words THE NAZIS ARE COMING, except that this quietly laughing man whose very presence coincided with an almost overwhelming need to learn more about him played down any such thoughts.

He was taking the war, as all the grown-ups seemed to be taking it, on the chin or squarely in the face and despite the occasional horrific setback, life was going on for Dad and everyone as before. "Live now and hope for better days tomorrow" seemed to serve as the national motto.

Dad's Home Guard Unit Headquarters were situated behind a splendid half-timber fronted house called "The Gables" in the single road village of Strelley, some two and a half to three miles west of our house and on the edge of the D.H. Lawrence country.

Two regular buses, a 16 and 30, caught at the first traffic island beyond the New Aspley Gardens would have taken him part way before the buses diverted through the council estates of Aspley, Bilborough and Broxtowe. But knowing Dad as I believe I knew him, I suspect he walked, rifle to his shoulder, both ways to and from the Home Guard training unit. Later between the blankets, despite the darkness and silence of the room, a feeling of utter security and well-being enveloped me.

The two lattice gates were bolted day and night to keep intruders from the yard. Scamp's bark alone stopped people in their tracks. And now a rifle with its accompanying ammunition belt had been placed in the lobby beside the locked front door and where the boxes of gas masks were stacked. What I failed to take into consideration was the ceiling beyond which was the roof and the sky, and the threat that could become a startling reality if and when the Luftwaffe were again ordered to take advantage of the stars.

Another rainy afternoon, Aunty had to go to the solicitors with regard to my late Uncle Charlie's properties situated on Burnt House Road, Heanor. During the morning nursery rhyme and story sessions she agreed that if I was a good boy and sat quietly in the waiting room while she was in Mr. Sutcliffe's office, I could go to Nottingham with her.

I had one Saturday afternoon already demonstrated that I could sit quietly in a chair when Aunty and Mum took me with them to Clay's, a dress shop situated in the busy Radford community called Denman Street.

The afternoon was overcast, like many at around that time, and to make matters worse, and I suspect using their clothing coupons, Mum and Aunty both purchased black dresses or two pieces. I think now that a funeral was imminent, but who and on which side of the family the deceased had belonged I had no idea.

Nor were the two women particularly upset because as they came and went to the changing rooms they giggled, pirouetted or wiggled their hips like the film star dancer Carmen Miranda, particularly Mum for whom I began to experience some embarrassment.

Yet quietly as I had promised, and bored in the extreme because we were on the second or third floor and I couldn't look out of the windows due to them being covered in dust or whitewashed, I can't remember which, I sat in the chair.

When after what seemed a long time, however, Mum and Aunty took their selected garments to the cash desk and the assistant produced pieces of brown paper, lengths of string and a blob or two of sealing wax, my mood lightened. But I had at least demonstrated to Aunty that I could sit quietly on a chair and, surprisingly for the whole family I would think, not ask a single question.

Waiting for the number 13 bus then on that rainy afternoon, I was aware of leaves breaking from the limes and being carried away by the wind. We were wearing our new galoshes and the rain and wind increasing in velocity made our wait for the bus all the more exciting.

Listening again to the rain pounding the umbrella, I noticed the saturated autumn tinted foliage casting a greenish shadow across Aunty's knuckles, bony and pale as she clasped the umbrella.

Several other people were waiting for the bus, but whether men or women memory fails me here. When at last with splashing tyres the 13 arrived, the other people allowed Aunty and I onto the bus first and eagerly, because I wanted to see everything from a comfortable height, I climbed the stairs.

When she saw that the seats were hard and wooden, or near to it, Aunty uttered a word that I found fascinating —

'Utility,' she murmured.

'What's that mean, Aunty?'

'Oh, it's to do with the War Effort. These are makeshift seats, inexpensive and without proper upholstery due to the war.'

'Utility,' I repeated, and again. Yes, I decided, that was definitely a word worth latching on to.

Denizen. One of the other words not associated with the war that I wanted to remember. Sylvia reminded me of it when, again in the Bird Room of the Natural History Museum at Wollaton Hall, she read the explanatory label positioned beneath a habitat case which displayed a tawny owl. The owl's plumage was rufous, the down and feathers soft looking and strokable right down to the taloned feet which, between the claws of one foot, grasped a woodmouse.

The background scene was an autumnal woodland glade. The floor of the display case was littered with dead leaves, grass tufts, fly algae and a wedge of bracket fungi adhered to the stump of a silver birch.

Woods, I thought, looked very intriguing places. But then as we eased from the tiered cases around the walls of the rooms, I heard Sylvia telling her sisters and Betty that owls can turn their heads without moving the body due to a large muscle positioned at the base of the neck.

The word denizen had again referred to the tawny owl's foothold in the woods of Wollaton Park, the woods which could be seen from the museum windows. I was, however, unaware that a pair nested most years in the hollowed trunk of a once magnificent ash tree rising from the Cherry Orchard ditch side situated six or seven hundred yards from the house in which we lived. The autumn was well advanced on that particular Saturday afternoon visit to Wollaton Hall and park. As usual, we had arrived with acorns, sweet chestnuts and fewer walnuts stuffed into our coat pockets.

After visiting the Hall we toured the paths of the formal gardens, our backs to home. The mysterious looking lake and its surrounding woods nestled undisturbed in the distant south-westerly hollow of our still unexplored parklands. The old deer park had been transformed into an eighteen hole golf course divided by Lime Avenue, the formal entrance drive.

The existing woods and coverts, however, had remained untouched and were included into the landscape with the upsweeping Arbour Hill and the skyline wood of the same name blocking the easterly horizon. The red deer remained roaming at will throughout their ancestrally favoured folds of land, spinneys and coverts, and grazed the open greens.

From the blue exercise book Aunty had given me I knew that the stags roared, lorded over the hinds and occasionally became involved in antler interlocking battles during the autumn. Nor were such battles totally confined to the book.

Crossing a wooden bridge spanning the dry moat or ha-ha, and which I found easier than climbing and descending the steps of the Hall's formal entrance and cedar lawn tract of the gardens, I heard an unfamiliar rattling as my cousins guided me onto the narrow path dividing the ha-ha from the golf course. Just off to our right a herd of hinds and followers grazed.

Then Alice gasped, 'Stags. Look! Fighting!'

On a hillock stood my "first" stag. Poised. Coat reddish-brown with upsweeping antlers symmetrically shaped. Below him in a sandy hollow a buff coated and red coated stag struggled with antlers interlocked and bodies sidling and twisting, heads and shoulders pushing and maned necks straining as each attempted to retain a hold on its opponent. I stood mesmerised.

The battling stags, some thirty to forty feet away, described a circle. Flesh, muscle, sinew and blood drove them along with testicular driven aggression, although I was of course unaware of this. I watched their slender, cloven hooves seeking purchase within the turfy, leaf-strewn grass. Divots of earth lifted into the air until their battle path was darkly patterned, scored and the top layers of turf unrecognisable. I saw that the heaving, tensed muscles of the stag's rear quarters and seasonally pronounced shoulders were their driving forces and the antlers their weapons.

Heedless of my protests, the girls hurried me along the moatside path towards a spinney positioned where Lime Avenue climbed, as the bygone coaches of the gentry would have climbed, up the hill's easterly side to the north facing lawns below the Hall's high-stepped formal entrance. Behind us we heard a far carrying roar, resonant, threatening.

'That's it! The fight's over. One of the stags will have disentangled and bounded away,' said Rene or Sylvia.

On arriving home my first words were, 'We've seen two stags fighting.'

I told everyone, Scamp included.

Later the following week when I again mentioned the incident to Aunty, she reached for the blue exercise book bearing the stag illustration and another on world facts and feats which, although intriguing, I was less familiar with. The artist who produced the stag illustration for the original blue exercise book had provided a background of rocks, heather, a loch and mountains, which I hadn't before dwelt upon. I then likened the picture to the background diorama studies in the Bird and Mammal Rooms at Wollaton Hall.

'What's that?' I asked.

'A loch,' said Aunty. 'A Scottish lake.'

And so my questions continued, as stabbing the variously illustrated natural elements with my forefinger I learned that the entire illustration carried a setting describing a moorland and mountain scene in Scotland, which according to Aunty, whose turn it was to point, was 'that way' while pointing to the front of the house which like Wollaton Hall faced the cold north.

'No, I can't take you there because it's such a long, long way. You have to go by train,' Aunty explained, while adding, 'But one day when you're a man, you may go yourself.'

'I will, Aunty. *I will*,' I assured her.

In the second book was an illustration of two stags with their antlers interlocked as I had seen the battling pair the previous weekend.

'That's how they were Aunty! *That's how we saw them!'* I enthused.

Together we read the caption explaining that not only did stags use their antlers to fight in this manner but that sometimes they became interlocked and could not withdraw. Consequently, and as in Scotland when the winter weather set it, they remained perhaps grazing due to their entrapped but lowered heads until the heavy snows came and they died of starvation, still interlocked.

When the caption mentioned the word "skeleton", Aunty gently explained that the flesh would rot away leaving only the stags' skeletons still locked together.

It was then I realised that the bones of our arms, legs, feet, hips and ribcage were somewhat like antlers. Yet I was quietly horrified at the thought of flesh decaying - dying away,

CHAPTER 14

Throughout their frequent meetings, Winston Churchill and Franklin D. Roosevelt agreed to deal with the German threat ahead of the Japanese threat, despite the latter forces having well and truly entered the war and established air and military bases in French Indo-China.

On 13ᵗʰ November 1941, the much saluted British aircraft carrier *Ark Royal* was targeted by a German U boat, a U81 submarine, and subsequently torpedoed close to Gibraltar. The aircraft carrier took a day to sink, during which crew members of the British Mediterranean Fleet fought for or considered their chances of survival. But throughout, the British Navy morale was reportedly at an all time low.

On December 7ᵗʰ, the United States Pacific Fleet succumbed to a surprise attack by the Japanese at Pearl Harbour, Hawaii. The Fleet's Commander, Admiral H.E. Kimmel, admitted to being unprepared for such an attack. Dismissed within days of this admission, he was replaced by Chester Nimitz. Meanwhile, Anthony Eden, the British Foreign Secretary, flew to Moscow where he discussed and helped reformulate the military situation with Joseph Stalin, the Soviet leader.

***

Never once did I seem to have a free moment. If Betty wasn't teaching me the time or, along with Dad, showing me how to tie my shoelaces, Aunty was reading me stories and jogging me on her knee while singing our newly founded Noah's Ark song *The Animals Went in Two-by-Two* to the tune of *When Johnny Comes Marching Home*. Moreover, when they were available, Aunty had purchased from Cunnah's two miniature hippopotamuses, two elephants, zebras and giraffes. Accordingly, and on rainy afternoons with Scamp sitting on his haunches looking on, we acted out the scenario on Aunty's sewing machine top with an impromptu Ark she had made out of cardboard.

Each morning's *Daily Sketch* provided more new names to read. Another Ark, *The Ark Royal*, being one along with the standard photograph of that once magnificent aircraft carrier.

Stalin was another name I read out loud along with Anthony Eden, the Christian names of which Aunty broke up for me along with that of Admiral Kimmel.

One evening Dad, seated in his Home Guard uniform, showed me how to count money. Just putting two halfpennies, a few penny coins and a shilling on the table, we chanted together —

'Two halfpennies make one penny.
Twelve pennies make one shilling.
Twenty shillings make one pound.'

The *Daily Sketch* photographs not directly associated with the war usually featured members of the Royal Family, particularly the two little girl Princesses. Although they were princesses, they wore overcoats like everyone else I pointed out to Betty, who agreed that it was obviously better to be a prince or princess than a king and queen and have to sit, she again assured me, on a throne wearing a crown all day while waiting for men like Winston Churchill to send messages via a lesser man about what was happening in the war.

The Princesses Elizabeth and Margaret often had walking beside them two or three small, light coated dogs with pointed muzzles and upright ears. Mum told me these were called Welsh corgis. The girls' expressions indicated that they were fond of these relatively small dogs, as I was fond of my rangy Scamp. Yet there was something unexplainable about the corgis and their way of life that had me wondering if they were dogs in the sense that Scamp was a dog.

When I attempted to explain this to Betty, she replied, 'No, they're not the same. These are *Royal* dogs. They live in the State apartments at Buckingham Palace and Sandringham and I bet when they die there will be gravestones put up for them. But *we* couldn't put a gravestone up for Scamp. Then again, I can't see him enjoying life in a State apartment anyway so he's perhaps better off living with us,' Betty assured.

Scamp's life, like my own, was gradually changing, although I was not so much aware of it as the rest of the family.

In the early morning darkness Dad used to take Scamp up to Three Nail Tree and let him off his lead. After Scamp had done what was required of him, Dad brought him home. Then as Scamp gained canine independence, Dad walked slowly behind him *carrying* the lead, returning to the front gate ahead of Scamp. Gradually, Dad just walked out to the front gate, opened it and left it open so that Scamp went up to the land tract around Three Nail Tree and returned alone. On his return he would whine at the front door and Dad and Mum, busy with breakfast and in Mum's case packing Dad's sandwiches, would let him in.

When Dad had gone to work, Mum would then prepare Betty's breakfast and when Betty was down eating or getting ready for school, Mum then woke me. So Scamp saw each of us by turn. Aunty continued to rise in her own good time, probably around eight or half past, and she and Mum had a brief breakfast together. Scamp then was gradually acquiring new ground and on the few occasions I watched him pacing lion-like in the direction of Three Nail Tree, not one of the other dogs sitting on the opposite side of the pavement and outside their respective owner's gates went out to greet or challenge him.

On passing these dogs, Scamp was ready to do battle. The fur on his shoulders and dorsal fur on his back rose and his muzzle puckered into a silent growl, while his tail was lifted high and shaped like a three-quarter handled walking stick.

To my eyes Scamp was holding his own. In reality he was taking in and acquiring territory: the left side pavement of Chalfont Drive; the disused allotments; Colliers Pad and its ditch; the Humps and Hollows field; back-tracking across Chalfont Drive to the half field and the long hare field beyond; then a four or five hundred yard stretch of Cherry Orchard, to return and leave his scent on the bramble thickets on his rival's side of the pavement before re-crossing to his natal side of Chalfont Drive. All these land tracts Scamp regarded as his canine domain. He had no challengers.

This territory he covered each morning after Dad let him out about five-thirty. Then if Mum or Aunty let him out around mid-morning - which wasn't often - he took an hour out to patrol his territory again. In the late evening after a day's work repairing aircraft bodies damaged by enemy aircraft, then perhaps a stint with the Home Guard volunteers, Dad took Scamp up to the half field and hare field before retiring with Mum for the night.

Having acquired this knowledge through observation alone, I somehow knew that the Royal corgis would not need this sense of territorial ownership and freedom in the same way as Scamp. But little did I realise that I was also comparing the needs of a dog, or dogs, with those of a dog which had been closely bred and carried both the bloodstock and instincts of a hound.

Each morning the pages of the *Daily Sketch* increased my awareness of the atrocities of war, the size of the world - particularly Europe, and the comparable land mass of Great Britain.

I had never seen, let alone perused, a map and although I had heard of maps, I thought that only army generals and Royal Air Force pilots carried them. Ordinary people like myself and the storybook character Dick Whittington were guided to the places they wanted to visit by milestones positioned along the roadsides and with arrows pointing in the direction they should be heading. At least according to the illustrations in my book.

Intrigued, I knelt on a chair at the table, the pages of the *Daily Sketch* spread before me and attempted to break down such place names as Birmingham, Coventry and Oxford. But what I examined most carefully were such photographs as the vapour trails of enemy aircraft; art gallery curators and staff loading famous paintings into removal vans for safer storage; the people of the London pavements, some exceptionally well-dressed, hurrying to an air raid shelter; the queues of children, each child looking worried - *frightened,* and with a boxed gas mask fixed around his or her shoulders being led to a place of safety, a centre for evacuees or a railway station.

There were also photographs of children and parents waving goodbye; soldiers walking, each with his wife or girlfriend, again presumably to a railway station; statues in Piccadilly Circus and Trafalgar Square being protected by timber boards. I wondered if the world was always like this.

Soon after tea on those winter nights, with the curtains carefully drawn across the french windows and my awareness of the darkness beyond, Mum switched on the wireless and while she and Aunty were washing the pots I listened to the stories told by a man called "Uncle Mac", who had a lovely deep voice and whom I liked although he and I had never met.

The programme was called *Children's Hour* and from it and the remarks made by Uncle Mac, I learned that again Christmas was on the way.

Yes, my elders and family confirmed, Santa would be coming and *soon!*

On Christmas Eve when *Children's Hour* had finished Mrs. Teather came, as she had the previous year, and presented me with two books. My cup of warmed milk and whisky had still to be put in front of me.

As in my pyjamas, dressing gown and red slippers I exchanged pleasantries with Mrs. Teather, the thought suddenly occurred that if it was a starlit night and there was a bombing raid Santa Clause might not get through! He might have to turn back due to the Luftwaffe bombers! Had that ever happened? And what if his sleigh and reindeer *collided* with a Luftwaffe bomber? How on earth could he distribute presents to children throughout the world?

When Mrs. Teather had left I sat with my warmed milk and whisky while wondering how many other children *there were* in the world. Did Santa Clause visit the Princesses Elizabeth and Margaret at Sandringham and Buckingham

Palace? How did he know at which Royal household the Princesses were staying anyway? And how many sacks of presents did he carry in his sleigh? Surely not just one! Not for all the children in the world?

I thought then of Santa's reindeer team and compared them with the stags I had watched battling the previous autumn. Those stags couldn't travel across the sky anymore than I could myself. Anymore than could Scamp. Anymore than could I if I were holding Aunty's or Betty's hand. People had to have machines like aircraft in order to cross the sky, surely?

And yet, I thought, if Mum puts the glass of port in the hearth again as she did the previous Christmas....and we rise and find the glass empty......?

Hugging my pillow slip filled with presents downstairs on Christmas morning, with Scamp poised and wagging his tail beside the bottom stair, I decided to check on the drinking glass that by my reckoning should have been standing in the hearth. *And standing in the hearth it was; empty!* I then checked the hearth for soot. There was not a sprinkling. Not a suggestion. But surely by the time Santa had climbed down all the house chimneys in the world, had a glass of port, left his presents, then climbed back up the chimneys, he would be covered with soot? This question, however, I kept to myself.

Betty had trimmed the dining room with tinsel and streamers and holly sprigs were affixed to the ornate mirror positioned over the fireplace and adhered to the candleholders. Cards adorned the mantelpiece and the top of Aunty's sewing machine. Christmas breakfast was as much a formal affair as Christmas dinner, with all the family sitting at the table and Betty failing to chastise my eating posture and manner in which I held my knife and fork. Christmas morning I spent in the dining room with Dad and Scamp, who sat beside me while I crayoned in my newly acquired crayoning books and read sentences while showing Dad the illustrations in *Gulliver's Travels* or *The Tailor and the Mouse.*

Dad, when he wasn't conversing with me, was content to sit in his armchair beside the constantly roaring fire. He dozed. He sipped whisky. Yet his smile was instant the moment I approached him with such questions as, 'Dad, have you seen this in my book?' Or, 'Dad, did you know that.......?'

His answer was as gentle as his smile, 'Oh yes, Little Man, that's good.' Or, 'No I didn't know that, Little Man. Do you know anymore about it?'

Betty spent most of Christmas morning in her bedroom and into which I was never allowed. That Christmas lunchtime the table's central occupant was a goose from one of the villages like Colston Bassett, Carr Colston or Cropwell Bishop, bought by Dad who acquired it from one of his several work colleagues who ran smallholdings out that way.

'Geese have more fat on them than chickens and turkeys,' Mum pointed out as she sliced the layer of breast and belly fat away in readiness for Dad to carve and share out the bird.

The sheer crafted beauty of the carving knife and fork fascinated me and I asked where items of cutlery were made, although my wording was something along the lines of, 'Where do they make knives and forks, then?'

Someone replied, 'Sheffield.'

It was then I remembered hearing that the City of Sheffield was blitzed on the same night as my natal Nottingham.

92

Betty told me that the tail of a table bird is called a parson's nose, then asked me to pull the wishbone with her. What I wished for, of course, escapes my mind completely because I was relatively content with everyone and everything around me. But I remember closing my eyes as I was told by Betty to do and leaning back to pull the bone perhaps further than was necessary.

In my portion of the Christmas pudding I found a coin, a threepenny bit, as did Aunty and about which we had been warned lest we swallow them. Betty was luckier and brandished a shiny sixpence.

That afternoon as expected our girl cousins arrived and because it was Christmas, I expect everyone was exercising their best behaviour as it was the only time in which cousin Sylvia refrained from catching hold of and tickling me sometimes almost to the point of exhaustion.

Both downstairs rooms, the front, as we called the north facing room, and the dining room were opened in the afternoon with fires blazing in the hearths.

Scamp, unused to the front room, travelled from one to the other but finally chose to lay down under the dining room table where he could still enjoy the heat of the fire. When he stayed beside anyone for any length of time, it was beside me or Dad.

The girls went from room to room, showing each other bracelets and necklaces that one or other of their parents had bought which again aroused my suspicions about Santa Claus.

At teatime, to my surprise, Dad and Mum pulled out the extensions to the dining room table which until that time I had been unaware of, and then everyone of us sat to tea, the curtains drawn, the hall and rooms ablaze with light, and Scamp shut away in the kitchen so that he couldn't pursue his habit of what Mum called 'begging under the table'.

After tea, despite Mum and Aunty's protests, the girls helped clear the table. Then Aunty or Dad carried the gramophone into the front room along with the bowls of nuts, fruit, plates and nutcrackers. It was into this room that we all gathered. There was a table, chairs, sideboard, three-piece suite, wall-to-wall carpeting and truly beautiful mottle tiled fireplace. Mum built up the fire in the dining room for later in the night and to provide the house with hot water, then shut the door. She also gently banished Scamp, again to the kitchen, while explaining that the music, the song scores and arrangements may prove 'too much for his ears'.

Here around the hearth Dad poured the glasses of port and sherry and sipped from a small glass of whisky. If he thought one of his nieces was not comfortably seated or likely to feel the warmth from the fire, he asked her if she would like to change places with him. Usually my cousin and his niece answered, 'No, it's all right Uncle Fran, thank you. I'm all right here, honest.'

To me it seemed strange hearing Dad being addressed as Uncle Fran.

When we were all settled, Betty would then hand around two of her presents, both film annuals: *The Silver Screen Annual* and *The Film Review Annual*, both of which fascinated me until Mum announced that, so far as I was concerned, it was bedtime.

I was fascinated first and foremost by the film titles, the majority of which meant little or nothing and had me wondering why the film had been so called. I was also intrigued by the names of some of the actors and the photographs, of course, from each of the films named as well as the portraits, the majority of which bore no resemblance to anyone I had by then seen.

Mum's favourite child actors were Shirley Temple and Mickey Rooney. Dad preferred the cowboys, the Westerners like Tim Holt, Charles Starrett and the lean, laconic and immensely popular Gary Cooper. He was also looking forward to seeing a then unreleased version of *Tarzan of the Apes*, for he had read the book by Edgar Rice Burrows just as he had read the novel *White Fang* by Jack London.

Both of Betty's film annuals, as they were called, referred to the films made over the past year and it was then I learned that Robert Donat had starred in *Goodbye Mr. Chips* and Joan Fontaine in the film based on the Daphne du Maurier novel *Rebecca*. Henry Fonda had played the lead in *The Grapes of Wrath* and Betty's favourites, Bob Hope and Bing Crosby, in *The Road to Singapore*.

Dad promised to take me to see *The Thief of Baghdad*, a film produced by Alexander Corda and starring Sabu. This film was throughout Word War I regarded as an epic. The Technicolor photography, special effects and direction also ensured that it won an Academy award.

For quite sometime I studied a photograph of Gary Cooper and Barbara Stanwyck, the stars of *Meet John Doe*, then compared the facial differences of Orson Wells and Joseph Cotton, both of whom starred in *Citizen Kane*. And the same for the still picture of Humphrey Bogart, Sydney Greenstreet and Peter Lorre, whose glassy-eyed expression conceived a chill down my spine, starring in *The Maltese Falcon*.

I especially liked the film title *How Green was my Valley* and memorised the name of one of its actors, Walter Pidgeon. But I was baffled, while admiring the profile of Ida Lupino and the creased brow expression of Humphrey Bogart, why a film should be called *High Sierra*. It sounded like a place. In America perhaps, because the background looked like those I had seen in the Gene Autrey films. But what had it to do with? What was the film *about*? Just grown-up people sitting around talking?

Then I came across a film title that really set me thinking. The film was called *Christmas in July*. I considered that a silly title. Christmas was in midwinter, here in England, America and perhaps other places from what I had heard. Christmas had to do with expecting Santa Claus. Unwrapping presents. Sitting with one's family and relatives around the fire and out of the cold.

July was surely a hot month in midsummer?

Betty confirmed this but only laughed and continued talking with our cousins when asked why a film had been called *Christmas in July.*

And so the question was left unanswered. It *remained* unanswered, much like the question to which I was slowly attempting to answer myself - was there *really* someone called Santa Clause?

When I was in bed sleeping, warmed again by blankets and whisky, the girls stayed for another hour or so because they had a long walk to their home at Stockhill. But upstairs asleep though I was, I knew they would not go home empty-handed for Mum and Aunty gave them each a slab of Christmas cake and a tin of jam and lemon curd tarts with mince pies. This was again confirmed later in life when I met my ever smiling cousin Rene in the centre of Nottingham and whose long-term memory has proven as acute as my own.

CHAPTER 15

Japanese forces captured Kuala Lumpur in Malaya, then made ready for a successful assault on Rangoon which took place in March 1942.

By February the British forces defeated along the Malayan Peninsular by the Japanese sought sanctuary at Singapore, a well-manned naval base.

On the 11th and 12th bad weather prevented the British Navy and Royal Air Force from destroying two German battle cruisers which used the English Channel as an escape route back to their base in Germany.

On the 15th the naval base of Singapore surrendered to the Japanese. An incredible seventy thousand soldiers and airmen of the Commonwealth and Great Britain were included in this surrender, which devastated the Prime Minister Winston Churchill.

On March 28th the medieval city and port of Lübeck in north Germany was bombed by the Royal Air Force, leaving only remnants of medievalism to be toured and photographed in the peacetime years of the future.

***

Gradually I realised that Christmas and weekends apart my life was gradually forming or being formed into a routine. This had, however, to fit in with the routines of the house or, to be more precise, the routines of Mum and Aunty.

The seven day week, I understood, began on Sunday, the morning of which Dad or Betty usually walked me to Strelley Village or around Wollaton while Aunty and Mum brushed the carpets and mats, dusted the furniture and fittings or, in Betty's case, straightened her bedroom. It was before Dad and I left, sometimes with Scamp, a morning of little to say and much to do. A morning for using window leathers, polish and dusters seemingly within minutes of the family breakfast pots being cleared from the table.

For my part, Sunday was countryside awareness day, although between the road on which we lived and the village of Strelley there stretched the lovely meadows, coverts and horizon blocking woods of Aspley Hall then the mile and a half of roadsides flanked by shops and houses that we passed on the way to *The Forum* Cinema.

Beyond that point was a fabrics and knitwear factory, more shops, a pub called *The Beacon*, council houses, fronting a recreation ground, then a traffic island and a direct route to the village but with roads leading off to the various housing estates once the traffic island was negotiated. It was a gentle but unmistakably uphill walk to Strelley where the meadows were broad, the hedgerows high and prolific, the estate houses and cottages appearing at intervals often with a track leading from field gate to front door.

I studied the varied shapes of the trees and peeped down the narrow track beside The Gables, at the rear of which the Home Guard Unit where Dad was assigned stood tucked back in a 'small copse' as he described the semi-circle of trees. During the winter there was little to be seen. The cattle, for instance, were in huge, straw filled barns attached to the stockyards.

I suspect that Dad was hoping to see a few horses but they too were stabled rather than grazing the fields.

When usually cold and having each worked up an appetite, Dad and I returned home to listen to Gracie Fields singing over the radio. Sometimes she would be entertaining the troops. A talented lady from Rochdale, Lancashire, she sang at different mediums such ballads as *Danny Boy*, her signature tune *Sally (Pride of Our Alley)* and comedy numbers like *The Biggest Aspidistra in the World*.

Sunday afternoon, as I have previously described, we expected our girl cousins and Mum's nieces. On Sunday nights in the winter, I poured over books or sat playing with metal farm animals and fences at the table while in the background, usually around eight and 'same spot on the dial' as the show's host put it, the *Carroll Levis and his Discoveries Show* was broadcast. This was a talent show designed to feature acts that initially were suitable for the wireless.

The voice and mode of speech metered by the show's host, Carroll Levis, fascinated me to the point of me asking Mum why Carroll Levis spoke differently to everyone else. Mum then explained that he was Canadian.

On more than one Sunday evening, without quite understanding either plot or dialogue, I listened to a play. One in particular fired my imagination due to the background sounds of the sea, the shrilling of the wind, the creaking of ship's timbers or oars positioned in the row locks.

By listening to the dialogue, I learned that smugglers signalled with lanterns along the black coastline of Cornwall. The play was an adaptation of Daphne du Maurier's *Jamaica Inn*. So vivid had the broadcast sounds and voices entered my thoughts on that occasion, that smugglers hiding from the troopers in hidden caves and the flickering of flames lighting up the cave walls were the last things I remembered before my tot of whisky and milk lulled me off to sleep that night.

For me Sunday was over, although it was not so for Dad. Tucked into a side street close to the railway and River Leen at Bobbersmill was a pub called *The Nag's Head*. As one came along Nuthall Road from the direction of Nottingham, this pub was fronted by another, *The Wheatsheaf*. Only in retrospect did I learn why Dad preferred the first pub to the second. It was because quite a number of the children he had attended school with went there, as grown-ups of course; adults with children of their own. And it was here, although I was not aware of it, that Dad came into his own because not only was he fêted for his prowess on the local football pitches of his youth but also his skills as a left-handed spin bowler and batsman on the cricket field.

Dad was, as in recent years I have come to understand, what might be termed locally famous and perhaps the more so because at *The Nag's Head* he was also the Saturday and Sunday evening pianist.

He played the Victorian-Edwardian *Home Sweet Home* and togetherness type sing-alongs, although I and, who knows, perhaps Betty were unaware of this.

The Nag's Head was no more than fifteen minutes' walk from the house and I imagine now Dad, a lone figure dressed in a good suit, gabardine raincoat and wearing his beloved trilby, walking Grassington Road, one side fringed by detached houses and the other the railed confines of the John Player Company recreation ground which since the Enclosures Act had been known as Seven Springs Field.

This had been a local beauty spot sought by summer afternoon picnickers, until the owner and founder of the nationally famous tobacco company acquired the field in 1913 and transformed it into a sizeable recreation ground with a

Tudoresque pavilion facing south two years later.

By the time Dad and Mum moved into the Chalfont Drive house with Aunty, the regimental row of Lombardy poplar trees extending along the recreation ground's fenced eastern periphery were matured and created a soothing if not mystical type of song on days and nights of high wind. This song Dad probably blended with those he had been playing on the piano at *The Nag's Head*, as perhaps slightly inebriated he walked the lonely light dimmed route along Grassington Road then up Holbeck Road to cross the wide, tree-lined Western Boulevard and then strode the Chalfont Drive pavement to home.

When on Monday morning I awoke, usually around a quarter to eight, Dad had already left for work. Betty had earlier joined Mum at the breakfast table and was by that time getting ready for school.

The downstairs rooms of the house, and particularly the hall and landing, were ablaze with light. For seconds as she lifted me from the bed, I again became Mum's flesh and blood doll. But, always at the foot of the stairs, Scamp was waiting, his tail thumping excitedly in readiness for my long and never forgotten ritual greeting. Kneeling, I hugged Scamp, pressed his head and muzzle into my chest and when I stood into the cleft of my hip, as I murmured my endearments before taking my place at the breakfast table.

If I happened to forget that it was Monday and someone chose to blindfold me, I could have told them what day it was due to the aromatic tangs of washing powder, soapsuds and, I suspect, Reckitts Dolly Blue, that emanated from the kitchen from which Scamp was temporarily banished. Not that he minded on wash day, because the soapsuds caused him to sneeze and the mangle, beneath which he slept each night on a mat, was dragged from its position beside the wall and used to squeeze the surplus water from the clothes accordingly. Consequently, the floor tiles were also damp and as Mum went back and forth with the food and drink items for my breakfast she would often chuckle, while admitting that she was 'paddling in and out.'

I can still see the washtub as I write. Higher than both Scamp and myself. Dull grey in colour. Friendless but needed, especially first thing Monday morning. The ponch which Mum used to pulverise the soaking clothes and bedding, was rusted brass in colour and fitted with rings of yellow copper. The gripping tool, the name of which I have forgotten, which Mum used to pull the clothes from the steaming hot water, was simply designed yet obviously made by a craftsman.

On Monday with the fire roaring at my back, I would breakfast without seeing much of Mum because she was so busy. This situation was by contrast beneficial to both Scamp and I for, although forbidden, I continued to feed him under the table. Here he would sit, his long pale whiskers touching my bare knees and his moist muzzle sometimes gently probing my knees, quietly begging for bits of egg white or slivers of bacon to be put in front of his muzzle and which he swiftly gulped down in the manner of all pack animals. Scamp was, of course, hidden by the large wide tablecloth. But Mum was always suspicious and I'm sure knew that I was lying when I told her that I was *not* feeding Scamp under the table.

Scamp and I would go to the hearth, Scamp to sit on his haunches, me kneeling beside him, one arm around his neck. He seemed mesmerised by the flames and literally stared at the strange play of light, colour and power flickering before his eyes as it disappeared up the chimney. On at least two mornings of each week

Mum would tell me to move Scamp from the fire because the heat and the vividness of the flames could eventually render him blind.

Gently grasping Scamp's studded collar, I did as I was asked but without protest or challenge disbelieved Mum. *My* dog wasn't going to go blind anymore than he was going to die! *My dog* was immortal!

Throughout those weekday mornings I never saw Aunty at the breakfast table. Only on Sunday did she join us. Possibly then, Mum took Aunty's breakfast up to the bedroom, or at least a cup of tea?

Aunty somehow *filtered* into the early morning scene. Smiling - *always smiling* - and sometimes turning the wringer as I stood watching the soaking garments of all shapes and sizes appear folded and flattened from between the double rollers, the silver-green water pouring back into the wash tub beneath.

It was after the clothes had been put through the mangle or wringer and piled neatly and folded into the ironing basket that the next chore of the morning was tackled.

There were no "elevenses". No breaks for coffee. The working-class wives and mothers of those wartime years just hadn't the time.

Shopping was the next chore. Always on a Monday and Wednesday and sometimes on a Friday. Primarily to Hoggs, the grocer's, a net and sheen windowed little shop situated on a street corner of the undeniably hilly Churchfield Lane, Radford This sprawling and industrial district is still referred to as "Radfud" by we Nottinghamians. Local historians have suggested that the name in Anglo-Saxon times probably indicated the red (or clay founded) crossing place (or ford) in the river, the river being the then considerably widened and marshy River Leen.

About three-quarters of a mile away the compact community of Radford Woodhouse could be similarly linked to these times, for Woodhouse denotes "a wooden house and meeting place in the forest".

The residents of West Nottingham had walked, often as young couples or with their families on picnics, this once scenic route from Hyson Green to the fields overlaid by the housing estates on which we by then lived, my parents and Aunty Amy and Uncle Charlie amongst them. Now Aunty and Mum were with shopping bags taking the same route two and sometimes three mornings a week and with the scenery much changed.

After leaving home, shopping bags in hand, we walked beneath the rows of lime trees and across Western Boulevard at a forty-five degree angle. In the winter the limes appeared regimental and in fog and rain austere.

In one of the wide fronted houses on the opposite side of the Boulevard to where we lived but to which we crossed, Nottingham's Chief Constable Athelston Popkess resided when time and national duties allowed. This fact was perhaps not made public to the people of the city and surrounding suburbs until after the war was over. I was never made aware of it and I cannot recall anyone in the house mentioning it. At least not in my presence.

Once we had crossed Western Boulevard and glimpsed once or twice a passing car, but seldom three or four, we turned the corner into Northdown Road.

There were several roads leading off Northdown, at least four of which I was to know well in the years ahead. But these apart from Northdown curved relatively narrowly and with semi-detached houses either side, while above the rooftops some half to three-quarters of a mile away rose the great square and many windowed mountain of the John Player Imperial Tobacco Company. If the wind was blowing from the east, there on Northdown Road one could smell the tobacco in perhaps both its raw and manufactured state.

My first reaction was to confront and stroke the black dog which sat, like a figurine, outside the lattice gates of its owner's home each morning. The dog I would describe as a totally black collie. Mum, however, told me that she thought it a first cross - a mongrel, like Scamp. A black Labrador and collie cross. Mum also told me that I should never touch a strange dog, a dog which I didn't know. If a dog came up to me, that was a different matter. But if I went up to a dog it might misinterpret my intentions, however well-meant, and bite me. The glossy furred figurine then remained as such, occasionally glancing in our direction but never coming towards us or wagging its tail.

Three hundred yards or so down from the black dog's pavement position, a snicket directed us left between two houses and along a field path with the Bobbersmill allotments coming in to our left and a high railway bridge, built some ten or twelve years before the war, invited us to ascend the twenty or twenty-five steep cement and side walled steps, which were cornered halfway along, to the allotment holders' unmade road above.

Mum explained that this was known locally as New Bridge by her generation. Before there were no steps. Consequently, one had to turn left and walk alongside the embankment and between the high hedged allotment gardens until the bank tapered then gave way so that the walker and very occasional cyclist could make a turn right and then walk over the railway lines via this cobblestone track. When one had climbed these steps and turned right, then again, the railway bridge had to be crossed and the track taken beside the railway on the right with the allotments screened by a fence of upright railway sleepers to the left.

It was, and remained for many years, one of the most unsightly routes or tracks imaginable. Yet like many corners of Radford, or old Radford as the district is now sometimes known, New Bridge and its unlovely approaches was in the then future to be mentioned in the novels and stories of another locally wandering boy ten years my senior. His name was Alan Sillitoe.

On this repetitive, birdless and featureless stretch of the lane, at least we heard the clatterings made by railway trucks being shunted and saw men loading or unloading the freight wagons.

Eventually the track descended to the same level as the railway, and over and between the boundary of the post and rail fence I attempted to read the place names emblazoned in white on the truck sides. Names like Burnley, Pinxton, Toton or Nottingham Victoria. Short, solid names. Yet not at all like those mentioned in the songs Bing Crosby featured in his Saturday afternoon wireless programme.

The freight-loading men on seeing Mum, Aunty and I, turned, waved and occasionally shouted 'Good Morning!' Some referred to Mum and Aunty as 'Missus' and me as 'Little Fella'. They were all so cheerful. Vulnerable, so far as a daylight bombing raid was concerned and probably in a line of fire, yet always laughing and talking.

Each man wore a cloth cap, duffle coat or grey suit. There was not a young man among them. The thickness of their waistlines and grey plumes of hair that refused to be trapped beneath their caps explained that. And as we walked, I watched the bodily co-ordination of each man. Watched them twist and bend and straighten and lift and twist and bend and straighten. Did they have to do that all day long, I wondered, and thought afterwards of Dad and his colleagues attempting to repair the war ribboned aircraft that were returned to Langar aerodrome.

Curiosity one morning prompted me to find a hole in the railway sleeper fence to the left of the track, for I *just had to know* what the fence screened.

Disappointed, I explained to Mum and Aunty that all I could see were piles of shale extracted from the nearby Bobbersmill Pit, as the colliery was known, and a line of sapling Lombardy poplar trees.

Where the cobblestones finished, the lane swept gently to the left and became a dirt road or, more precisely, a cart track. To the right the loading bays and export warehouse of the Player's Imperial Tobacco Company hid the railway. Usually in each of the six or eight loading bays stood a cart horse, facing the track because both the horse and cart had been backed into the bay, blinkered and feeding from a nosebag. Mum told me that each nosebag was half filled with the oats on which horses loved to feed.

I then asked why there were high walls and solid equally high gates fronting each bay and subsequently the entire building, and Aunty explained that the gates were locked to keep prowlers out at night.

To our left beyond a low wall stretched a green ungrazed and unmanaged field, centralised by a ruined mill perhaps sixty to eighty feet high and built of red stone, unlike the boundary wall which was hewn from locally quarried stone.

In near disbelief, on that or one of the other early occasions that I walked to the shops with Mum and Aunty, I listened as Mum explained that this had once served at the island tower for the boating lake and pleasure gardens that used to be here. *Used to be,* my mind echoed. That phrase again. *'Long before I was born',* is what she actually meant! Who and where was I when, as Mum explained, couples rowed out in boats at dusk beneath festooning strings of fairly lights before having a drink and meal at the waterside café, of which by then there was no trace?

There was not a hint of sentiment in Mum's explanation, although I think there may have been if Dad had been explaining the site to me.

The pleasure gardens had been owned by a local businessman who on realising that firms of bleachers and dyers had before his time become established along the banks of the River Leen and made use of the fast current, accordingly had the river dammed so that he too could use the water for his boating lake.

From what I have since been told, the lake and pleasure gardens were well-established and patronised throughout the First World War but by the time of this the Second World War, all had fallen derelict. There was a ditch-line of water below the wall onto which one morning I climbed to look, much to Mum's consternation, and that was it. The rest was field grass. But, I suspect, a good breeding habitat for frogs and toads.

The site became known afterwards as Radford Folly.

In the loading bays on the right and close to where the River Leen almost merged for several yards only with the red cobblestones of St. Peter's Street, dray men loaded huge flat boxes, packed tightly with cigarettes. The wood surrounds of each box or packing case looked new and the tight lengths of banding glittered occasionally in the morning light.

After several trips along this route with Mum and Aunty, and in later years with Dad, I knew instinctively that I couldn't get lost.

St. Peter's Street merged with the previously described trudge of Churchfield Lane at the end of the New Bridge track.

So far as Mum and Aunty were concerned, that section of the shopping route was over with until half an hour or so later we retraced our steps for home.

To me, however, or rather to my ears, another place beckoned because at the far end of the Radford Folly field a lane, used then by the colliers of the Bobbersmill Pit, cut off to the left and followed the River Leen upstream.

What I heard each time that I walked by the end of this lane was the thunder song of something I had still not seen. A waterfall. As if determined to shield this bygone attraction from the prying eyes of little boys, some unknown authority had decided to screen it with a high barrier of green painted corrugated iron, although, as I was to discover in later years, the waterfall could be seen if one walked for a few yards along the lane.

I loved hearing the water cascading over the sill of the weir and learned that in the summer it was quieter than in the winter or after heavy rain, when the tumult increased and to my young ears - roared fiercely like a great angry and uncontrollable monster.

Attempt though I did to persuade Mum to stop so that I could see the waterfall, my pleadings fell on deaf ears. To stop and look would take seconds, at the most a minute of our time, but Mum remained tight-lipped and walking. In retrospect, she may have been harbouring a memory to do with a pleasant afternoon picnic at the pleasure ground or, in contrast, a sad incident which she understandably chose not to dwell upon.

The alder and willow trees beside the hidden waterfall rose above the brick-built and slate roofed building in which the cigarette company's many horses were stabled.

At the end of the lane, the river was shallow off to the right and fenced by railings. Four or five square buildings had been built on a tract of barren flood bank. Air raid shelters, Mum or Aunty informed me.

Before crossing the red cobblestone road to continue up Churchfield Lane, we had to check in case flat backed lorries or trucks were being driven down.

The clip-clop of horses' hooves resounded throughout the yards and walls, when frequently a horse and dray was guided to or from the tobacco company. Each and every day piles of horse manure darkened the cobbles until someone came from one of the nearby terraced houses with a brush and dustpan, swept up the manure and spread it on the plots and borders of their small garden.

On these Mondays when Mum and Aunty had so much to do, one or the other of them habitually described the walk up Churchfield lane as 'a slog'. Contrasts occurred in buildings and habitation on both sides of the road. For instance, the rail fronted office block looked across at the old seventeenth or eighteenth century buildings of a farm and stable yard called Worthingtons.

Other than rubble and half-opened stable doors, there was nothing to be seen there except perhaps a strand of ivy or ragwort growing from an occasional crack in the brickwork. And one would have thought the offices of The Imperial Tobacco Company to have been deserted. Here, and unbeknown to me at the time, hundreds of export duty forms were filled out and stamped prior to vast quantities of cigarettes being consigned for destinations that were probably a daily or weekly conclusion to the many clerks involved, but of which I had never heard.

The wage and pensions offices were also installed in that block to which our neighbours and other employees walked and returned to Chalfont Drive twice a day, having set out at first light and probably with the latest broadcast news of the war on their minds.

Thirty yards up neat terraced houses in rows of four or six fronted the road, each with a low wall made from locally quarried stone and a single wrought iron gate separating the porched front door and front room or lounge window from the pavement.

Letterboxes gleamed in the morning light. The tiles of each porch were red, looking immaculate and scrubbed and toned with polish at least once a week, the wife or mother of the family having to kneel to do the job.

Styles of curtains differed and in about every other window a figurine had been placed, usually an Alsatian dog looking inwards at the occupants of the room or a girl, one hand to her ample hip, the other balancing the goldfish bowl positioned on the crown of her head. These were, I discovered in later years, mass-produced ornaments and the type that were given away as fairground prizes. Nevertheless, each in every home seemed to delight, or be treasured, by someone.

Opposite the houses the grey walls of the church loomed. On the higher ground above them the broad towered church with its clock of gold or imitation gold figures and numerals faced east. In days gone by, it had obviously appeared splendidly presiding over the fields. But by the time Mum and Aunty were born, the factories and yards of The Imperial Tobacco Company were blocking out the morning intended sunlight.

A scattering of lime and beech trees surrounded the church. Mystified, I asked what the gaunt grey stones were sticking out of the ground. 'Gravestones marking the spot where someone is buried,' Aunty told me. Shuddering inwardly, I asked nothing more.

CHAPTER 16

Before entering the first shop, Hoggs the Grocer's, we had on each visit to pass several horses and carts parked by the roadside and facing downhill. The time was usually around ten a.m. and both the carters and the horses were indulging in a well-earned rest because, Mum told me, their workday had begun at seven.

The carters were already in the café opposite Hoggs when we drew level with the blinkered horses, each of which had its muzzle buried firmly into a nosebag fixed to the bridle. They champed quietly on a feast of oats.

Most of the carters' horses, *the workhorses* as Mum rightly called them, were bays with black manes and forelocks. Occasionally one sported a long white blaze. They smelt of hay, harnessing leather and warm urine.

Each time that we passed I gleaned something of the workhorse and carter's world. The intricacies of the harness. The featherings on the horses' hocks. The cart shafts and the spokes of the four beautifully balanced and painted cartwheels.

The Imperial Tobacco Company's blue faced clock with golden numerals faced the carters' café as if to always remind the carters of the hour and the mission for which they were paid. Its message, in working-class terms, could be psychologically interpreted as "Don't get too carried away, lads."

Almost opposite the factory's clock, the white faced church tower clock with black numerals chimed the half hour. It was this clock, and surprisingly not the factory clock, according to Mum, that we occasionally heard tolling like a hollowed bell on certain nights when the wind was blowing in the direction of our home.

Hoggs the grocer's, with its brass handled door and more intimately resounding bell than those of the clocks I have previously described, was always immaculate. Everything gleamed and shone from the brass door handle to the regularly scrubbed counters. One could see the pinkish blaze and distorted reflection of his or her face in the scale pans and the scale weights which were neatly stacked but ready for immediate use. Not a single smear was to be seen on either of the shop windows or the bacon and ham display case situated alongside the equally immaculate bacon slicing machine.

The moment we entered I secretly inhaled, because I had still to discover an aroma so saliva creating and nostril teasing as that of smoked bacon.

Every shelf behind the counter was stocked heavily with tinned fruit, vegetables and various meats. An eye-catching pyramid display of tins filled the street corner windows. Wash powders, cleansing powders, canisters and various detergents were crated or box stacked in the corridor between the shop and the Hoggs' living quarters or home. That Mr. and Mrs. Hogg worked long and hard at their trade was glaringly obvious to every customer entering the shop.

Both husband and wife wore crisp, white smocks. Mr. Hogg was dark skinned. His dark eyes were wide and a small neat moustache complemented his black hair, which was always creamed down, cut short around the sides and parted neatly in the centre.

Mrs. Hogg was also dark haired and slightly built. She was nothing like as tall as her husband. Her skin was smooth like that of my sister Betty. Her nose slender and slightly bridged. Her eyes brown. Mouth and lips well-shaped and generous.

Husband and wife worked together. One read out the items from the customer's order, and at the same time clipped the relative coupons, of which I had little understanding, out of the ration book while the other took the item from the fixture and placed it on the counter in front of the customer.

Even the scissors used to neatly clip the coupons from the weekly allocated page of the book glittered in the small shop's faltering light. I heard such words as lard, sugar, dried peas, prunes and golden syrup being read out and memorised the words as the bag and tins were put on the counter well above my nose.

The Tate and Lyle lettering on the blue sugar bags I soon became familiar with and also the wordless oil-proof wrappings around the squares and sections of butter or cheese.

Sardines and pilchards were, I knew, shiny skinned fish packed tightly into tins. When they were placed tinned and colourful on the counter, I envisaged eating them with toast, a blazing fire in the hearth, the curtains drawn across the french windows and *Uncle Mac's* voice emanating from the front grid of the wireless, as around five in the afternoon he read out a *Children's Hour* story.

The counter section on which Hoggs reckoned up and priced the items had a varnished top. Both husband and wife reckoned up in pencil and when not using them rested their pencils behind the ear.

I especially liked hearing the scissors clipping coupons out of the ration book. Mrs. Hogg usually applied herself to this task.

One set of ration books were buff coloured, another set blue and another green. The blue, Mum pointed out, were mine and Betty's. The talk between the grocer, his wife and the customer usually referred to the latest atrocity of war. I heard Coventry, Birmingham and, of course, London mentioned, along with the names of such men as Churchill, Mussolini and Hitler.

Powerful sounding names assigned to men in powerful positions. There were no Smiths, Browns, Jones or Taylors among them, I noticed.

As I stood patiently in the shop, I additionally wondered why these men had made themselves known to the world. Why had they *needed* to make themselves known? Why weren't they content to be airframe fitters like Dad or grocers like Mr. Hogg? Why didn't they want to load drays or railway trucks? Do some gardening? Go to the cinema on Saturday night?

Did they like cowboy films? Or Laurel and Hardy? Did they as boys go to the grocer's with their respective mothers? What was it about someone that made them so special their names were on the lips of hundreds and thousands of people living in other countries?

When the groceries were on the counter before Mum, Aunty and I, Mr. and Mrs. Hogg packed them into a cardboard box or two cardboard boxes, one for Mum to carry and one for Aunty. If it was raining, they placed a sheet or two of newspaper across the top and closed the flaps to keep the items dry.

With me between them, Mum and Aunty left the shop. But Mum always called again with me on a Wednesday and sometimes, because we always walked the way, on a Friday. And in the morning, seldom the afternoon.

The carters had usually finished their snacks and mugs of tea by the time we left Hoggs. Often each carter was with his horse, removing its nosebag while calling it George or Dobbin or Kitty before swinging up onto the front of the dray, lifting the reins at which on hearing the carter's sideway click of his tongue the horse would move off.

Whether the carts had brakes or were braked while the carters went to the café, I never really knew. If, as happened on a Wednesday or Friday, the carters were in the café when Mum and I walked by to continue shopping on Hartley Road, they waved, lifted their tea mugs and called out, 'Mornin' Missus! Morning' young 'un!'

Like the railwaymen, the carters all looked alike to me. Middle-aged to elderly, many of them having survived the First World War, they wore cloth caps and dingy suits or overalls.

The café, when the door was open, remained hazed with cigarette smoke and must have stank of tobacco. Inside, at the back of the counter with its fronted glass case where cakes and pastries were displayed, was a sign stuck on the wall bearing the words:

"Tis the carter's café
Run by Jack
Whose cakes and pastries
No bad points lack."

Then the third clock of our Monday walk to the shops appeared. Positioned on the wall alongside the notice was the clock which Mum told me wasn't working and had a cracked face, further emphasised by a notice pinned beneath which indicated that there was —

"NO TIC HERE"

Tic was, of course, a term commonly used in those days for any form of credit facility.

The walk home from Hoggs was mostly downhill but I could tell that the boxes of groceries were heavy. Mum and Aunty each needed two hands for carrying a box and were not, therefore, able to shield themselves, me or the groceries while holding an umbrella. Mum, the stockier of the two, also carried a leather bag and in the evening I would hear one or other of them telling Dad or Betty that they '…came home loaded.'

The walk home was less interesting. The railwaymen having loaded or unloaded the trucks and the train, like them had moved elsewhere.

Scamp never barked when we came home because, Mum or Aunty explained, he knew us. After greeting us, Scamp would then be let into the rear garden into which Mum or Aunty would also go to test the sheets, blankets, rugs and items of clothing pegged out on the exceptionally long clothes line.

The food items they would pack into the pantry, situated under the stairs and alongside the back door and porch. Meat, cheese and milk were placed on the cold slab and occasionally lightly covered. The pantry window had a gauze grille covering which allowed in a constant, but regulated, flow of air. The cupboard where Scamp's lead was affixed to a hook was kept firmly shut. The pantry floor, like the kitchen and front porch, was red tiled.

While they were preparing dinner, Mum and Aunty switched on the radio and we listened to *Workers' Playtime*, always with both the kitchen and dining room doors open so that the songs and jokes could be hard in both rooms.

It was due to this broadcasting of this popular show that I, and others of my generation, learned the names and inadvertently studied the repartee of such comedians and comediennes as Betty Driver, Max Miller or Charlie Chester, neither of the latter I particularly liked, even less the way they delivered their respective jokes.

Bud Flanagan and Chesney Allen, however, I warmed too immediately as, seemingly, did everyone else. And again I wondered how these two characters were so called. Bud, I could just about accept. But Chesney? Surely that wasn't his real name?

Smiling, Aunty told me that she thought it was. Even though I was not present at the factory staged concert, I could sense the audience participation over the airwaves. The factory 'girls and boys', as the comedian compère called them, were always *with* Flanagan and Allen. And by *with*, I mean that they hung on to their every word.

When the simplistic yet catchy song *Run Rabbit* ended, one of the performers suggested an encore, with everyone joining in. *How* those factory workers joined in!

'You wouldn't think there was a war on, would you?' said Mum to Aunty, as she wandered into the dining room while at the same time drying a cluster of knives, forks and spoons with a tea towel. Mum's eyes, I noticed, were glistening with tears.

People, the audience, laughed loud and long throughout those *Worker's Playtime* sessions. The Germans were advancing west and at a rapid pace? *So what!?* Who was cowering? Who was *prepared* to cower? The song lines of another Flanagan and Allen song, *Who Do You Think You're Kidding, Mister Hitler?* said all.

Monday afternoon was ironing afternoon if the clothes on the garden strung line had by then dried. If not, then the chore was slotted into Tuesday, the afternoon of which the bread was always made and then baked in the big red and black bordered ovens beside the kitchen sink. That said, I was seldom if ever ignored. Mum I think it must have been, made and rolled out the dough while Aunty sat me on her knee and not only read me stories but continued teaching me to read.

Occasionally on a Monday I was told, usually by Mum, that a woman called Mrs. Doughty was coming. How Mum knew this, I could never ascertain. The thought of Mum having written to Mrs. Doughty never occurred to me. I was aware even less that people wrote and sent letters.

I knew that many leaflets to do with safeguarding a household were occasionally posted through a letterbox, but directly and usually by an Air Raid Warden or perhaps a member of the Women's Voluntary Service. I also knew that five or six mornings a week the *Daily Sketch* was delivered to the house, although the thought of someone having got soaked in order to have delivered it never once entered my head.

The *Daily Sketch* appeared, informative and dry, and that was it. But Mrs. Doughty........? How did she and Mum communicate?

A maternal woman with back-swept hair fastened at the nape, wearing glasses and always a long dark overcoat, Mrs. Doughty came, usually just after we had eaten at around twelve-thirty.

Like the rabbit sellers, she came to the front door and admitted to being afraid of Scamp's bark. Scamp, however, was always shut out in the yard.

Her eyes were quick, dark blue, and her skin a smooth yellowish-white. She greeted me warmly. Her smile was wide.

When she was shown into the dining room, Mrs. Doughty sat on one of the two visitors' chairs facing the table. Her sitting position was that of resting her hands in her lap or entwining her fingers but only once because, apart from Scamp's bark, she was not unduly nervous. Mum knew her from way back. Perhaps from their communal yard and single shared water tap days in Alice Square. But by wartime Mrs. Doughty and her large family were settled into a council house or one of the estates Dad and I skirted when we walked to Strelley.

Usually, Mum provided her friend with a cup of tea then went up the stairs. It was then that Mrs. Doughty conversed gently with Aunty or asked me if I had been to anywhere or done anything nice. By that I think Mrs. Doughty meant interesting.

When Mum returned to the room, it was always with a bundle of clothes clasped to her bosom. Sometimes she returned for a second bundle while smiling as if she was about to undue her Christmas presents, Mrs. Doughty rolled and stowed long coats, shirts, cardigans and dresses into a bag and holdall in the efficient manner of all worldly and maternal women.

When with bags packed Mrs Doughty stood, she faced Mum and while emphatically thanking her lifted her purse from her pocket.

'Oh, no, no. I don't want paying for them. It's a pleasure seeing them go to somebody who really needs them,' Mum would say.

'Well, I'm ever so grateful. *Ever so grateful,*' Mrs. Doughty would say, after which Mum advised her to go along the Boulevard when she walked to catch a 16 or 30 bus at Aspley Lane, because *"The Man"* was still prowling the ditchside thickets of Cherry Orchard Lane.

Calling out her goodbyes, Mrs. Doughty then walked to the front door with Mum. Here they engaged in a private and low voiced conversation, perhaps for one or two minutes, before Mum opened the door.

On one occasion when Mum returned to the room after Mrs. Doughty had called, I asked her why she gave mine and Betty's cast-off clothes to Mrs. Doughty.

'Because she's got a big family and is very poor. You must always do your best in this life to help people who are less better off then yourself,' Mum replied.

Monday afternoon then continued with story and reading sessions for Aunty and I, with Scamp beside us, while Mum ironed in the kitchen perhaps for the next two hours.

The reading and storytelling sessions continued often throughout Tuesday morning. With Aunty I continued repeating my name and address, putting coins together in what Aunty called 'our shillings and pence' sessions, and attempting to read sentences from *Dick Whittington* or *The Story of Hansel and Gretel* with its splendid accompanying illustrations.

Later, perhaps sometime in the afternoon when the kitchen held tightly to its mouth-watering aromas of newly baked bread, Aunty walked me in the direction of Wollaton Park and to Cunnah's.

Here she may have had some business to attend to, perhaps to do with National Savings Stamps or War Bonds. One afternoon as we drew level with the canal's reedy backwater, a youth appeared carrying a home-made harpoon in one hand. On the end of harpoon wriggled a glistening, weed scented eel. Eels tasted good, the youth triumphed. He lived in the Radford Woodhouse community and both he and his father had harpooned eels in this backwater on previous occasions. In the spring they also searched the reed fringes and took eggs from the moorhens in bids to supplement the wartime breakfast and dinner tables.

As I studied the snakelike fish with the golden, black pupil eyes, I thought wrongly that it had lived in this canal backwater throughout its life, whereas in all probability it had hatched in the Sargasso Sea, a stretch of the western Atlantic, and as an elver at three years swam instinctively to the mouth of a river.

The nearest seaward meandering river, that was still unbeknown to me, was the Trent, the second longest in England. Here, if nature had ran true to course, the eel survived while journeying for four or five years and presumably by travelling overland around the staircase of lock gates, as eels do, it had entered the Wollaton section of the Nottingham Canal and languished in its last place of sanctuary, the backwater.

On Wednesday mornings, the ironing done, shirts and dresses placed on hangers and returned to the wardrobes, blankets and sheets folded and stowed into the broad oak chest on the upstairs landing and the bread made, Mum and I ventured beyond Hoggs the grocer's and carrying a few items from there, crossed the factory darkened Radford Boulevard to continue shopping along Hartley Road.

Before entering the cobbler's, where at least one month Mum took several pairs of shoes to be repaired, we usually studied the stills for the films currently showing at *The Windsor* cinema and mentally noted those that we wanted to see. We would then enter the cobbler's, the sounds and smells of which I found intriguing but in a different way to those which I had by then familiarised myself at the grocer's.

The smells of leather, rubber and gas jets blended with the whirr of the belt connected machinery which was hidden from view by a screen of glazed windows, framed shuttered for when it was necessary and beautifully varnished.

The narrow section of the cobbler's counter faced the opened door of the shop. Sometimes Mum rapped lightly on the mullioned glass partition to let the cobbler know that he had a customer.

'Okay! Hello there! I'll be right with you,' the cobbler used to call out cheerily.

Seconds later he was facing us in greeting and talking briskly and fluently. A smart, hazel-eyed, bustling but efficient type of man, with a pink complexion and a mass of thick, curly chestnut or auburn hair. He smiled with every word he spoke, this man, as breezily he exchanged pleasantries and studied the shoes with Mum. His nose was narrow, well-formed, and his cheekbones so pronounced they became silver sheened by the light each time that he turned or lifted his head from the shadow.

He was a craftsman, having inherited the business from his father who used to cycle around Wollaton and Radford collecting shoes from his customers or delivering them after they had been repaired, the shoes being stowed in the carrier at the front of his bicycle.

But now the cobbler's son, the man with whom Mum was dealing, had moved into a modernised shop with the sophisticated machinery that his father had watched come to the fore but which he could never have afforded.

Unlike Dad, whose shirts were always starched white, the cobbler wore a checked shirt like my silver screen heroes, Gene Autrey and Roy Rogers. The shirt sleeves were also rolled to his elbows and his waistcoat was protected by a long leather, belted apron.

After several visits to the shop, I realised that this cheery man worked with a variety of hammers and various sized tacks, shoe soles and leather trimmers. He had, Mum explained, a trade and those were the tools of that trade.

When he was well ahead with what he called his "orders", the cobbler placed the repaired shoes in brown, screw-topped bags on his counter. Each bag was tied with string and decorated with a coloured ticket, usually dark red or blue, and on which was written the customer's name and address.

Many of his customers worked in the factory and offices of the nearby Players Imperial Tobacco Company and took their shoes in to be soled and heeled first thing in the morning.

On leaving the cobbler's, Mum and I then crossed to the butcher's while I secretly attempted to overlook such signs as someone having spat onto the pavement or thrown down a colourful but empty and unwanted cigarette packet earlier that morning.

Before going into the butcher's shop, I would look at the artist's impressions of cattle and sheep - always in blue - emblazoned on the white tiles below the spacious product packed shop window, while at the same time wondering how the artist had gained such an exact likeness of the animals.

Sometimes the butcher, Mr. Burroughs, would be wiping down the window with a chamois leather or the frames and woodwork with a piece of cloth.

As I came to accept, the butcher's shop door was complemented by a bell and the smells as one entered were those of bleached white overalls, dried blood and sawdust, a little of which was always scattered onto the floor. Sides of meat, usually a half cow about three times my height and breadth, hung leg joint suspended by hooks from silver rails. The dressed carcasses were deep yellow and dark red in colour but Mum explained that the deep yellow was fat and that it was the dark red, the meat, that most of the customers sought.

Mr. Burroughs, the butcher, was a stockily built man with a shock of iron-grey hair. He had seldom much to say to children, although once, and smiling while addressing me, he said, 'Aye if we win this damned war, you youngsters are going to have easy lives compared to what the rest of us have had to go through.'

Mum smiled but quickly silenced him by making a "shush" sound between her lips before steering him onto another subject.

Later Mum told me the Butcher had experienced hard times throughout the First World War, so she had heard. But, I thought to myself, why pick me out? Is it my fault that I was born between two horrific wars?

From then on I was always a little wary of Mr. Burroughs, although never nervous in his presence. After all, I thought in a retaliatory way, he's only here to cut up and sell meat.

However, he was in his way a craftsman and as I watched the butcher cutting up his joints, expertly dividing his pork and lamb chops or trimming streamers of yellow fat from the sides of hook suspended beef, I realised that there were skills attached to butchering just as there were to cobbling shoes. And unlike my visit to the cobbler's, I could watch Mr. Burroughs working while at the same time pick up such mouth-watering terms as brisket, neck or leg of lamb, shoulder of mutton, steak, tripe and those ever delicious kidneys that Mum bought and served up at least once a week.

Other names were straightforward; self-explanatory. Oxtail, pig's head, sheep's head, pig's trotters. And Mum again had to produce the ration books for certain items and I watched and heard the sharp "twirk, twirk" sounds as the scissors cut through stiff paper.

What I found secretly fascinating about Mr. Burroughs was the way that he always worked with a cigarette dangling out of the side of his mouth. Moreover, he conversed with his customers *without once removing* the cigarette from between his lips.

Usually he removed the cigarette only when his wife or a member of his family brought him a mug of steaming hot tea from the living quarters, curtain screened and situated at the back of the shop. When such instances arose, Mr. Burroughs paused in his chopping or knife and skewer sharpening, then removed the cigarette and placed it lit end upwards between his fingers and bridged by the palm of his hand alongside his hip. His other hand he used to firmly clasp the mug from which he seemed so gratefully to drink.

Not infrequently, Mr. Burroughs divided pork and lamb chops or placed customer-selected slices of liver on a wrapping paper and scale pan with a long taper of cigarette ash lengthening the cigarette clasped between his lips. Yet never once can I recall seeing the ash plummet down onto the counter or a joint of meat.

The carcasses, Mum explained, were prepared and divided in an abattoir where the cattle, sheep and pigs were killed. She also recalled running the gauntlet of central Nottingham streets, on what were then called "errands" for her mother, and seeing carcasses of prepared meat hanging *outside* the butcher's shops, flies, dust and contamination regardless, although at intervals throughout each working day the butcher or one of his staff swilled each carcass down with a bucket of water.

After leaving the butcher's, we continued up Hartley Road and by a large, red-bricked house surrounded by gardens of yellow privet and high walls with railed tops. It had once been a gentleman's residence, Mum explained, but since she and Dad had moved into our home on Chalfont drive the building had been assigned to the Social Services Department and used as an orphanage.

When Mum then explained the reasons for maintaining an orphanage, I was so stunned that further words refused at first to form within my mind.

'*A home for children who have no mothers and fathers!*'

It took me seconds to recover from the shock.

'No, but they have friends there in the orphanage. Friends of their own age who they may know all their lives, as well as the people who look after them.'

Yet still my mind was reeling.

'But......but.......'

'And sadly, there will be a lot more children without mothers and fathers by the time this war is over. Not just in Britain, but in France and Germany as well,' she continued.

I thought then of the anguish collectively imprinted on the faces of those many children being evacuated, particularly from London. I had seen them on the cinema newsreels. On the page of the *Daily Sketch*. Children already dazed by the horrors of the blitz and uncertain whether they, their parents, *or anyone* could be credited with a future. Yet daily they continued. Thinking. Hoping.

And sometimes, although I was personally unaware of it, praying.

At the "top of Hartley Road", as it was known locally, three other roads split off into different directions. Opposite another grey stoned church on the Hartley Road corner loomed another high building that looked like the type of prison I had by that time seen in films, except that there were no towers and no bars at the windows, which were tall and could be opened inwards and outwards.

With trolley buses purring and rushing by, swirls of brown dust and sheets of discarded newspaper caught up in the maelstrom of bus and lorry wheels, I learned that this brooding place was a school. But to me, no ordinary school because, Mum told me, Dad used to go there as a boy.

'Why though, Mum? Why did Dad want to go *there*?'

'He didn't *want* to go. He *had* to go.'

'*Had* to go! Why did he *have* to go?'

'Because everybody - every young boy and girl - had to go to school.'

'*What? Even me?*'

'Yes, everybody. I went to school. Your Dad went to school. Aunty went to school. Your sister Betty goes to school.'

'Yes, but *I'm* not going.'

'You are, mu lad,' murmured Mum reproachfully.

'When?'

'Oh, you've got a couple of years yet. I'll tell you when it's time to go to school.'

My stomach locked. I went hot. And then cold. Seconds later I calmed because I had an answer. *I simply wasn't going to school and that was it*! Thus the matter was dropped from my mind.

Turning right, we progressed for a few yards in the direction of Nottingham along Alfreton Road, which I rightly assumed eventually took one, if one travelled it, to Alfreton, Derbyshire.

I was not aware, of course, that Alfreton was in Derbyshire, although I occasionally glimpsed the place name in the destination panel of a blue and cream Midland General bus. To me, Alfreton represented "a somewhere", just like Nottingham was "a somewhere", and school "a somewhere" to which I had no intention of going.

I might became a grocer, a cobbler or a butcher, but I wasn't going to school!

Our first call on Alfreton Road was to Mrs. Harrison, the baker's. Here, in a shop that always seemed empty and over-decorated with immaculate display cases, Mum purchased what she called "a home-made brown loaf". Sometimes a Hovis loaf was also added to the shopping list. Mum or Aunty could, I suppose have baked their brown loaves in our home installed ovens if they had wanted. Yet Mum called at this shop at least twice a week but usually purchased the brown loaf on a Wednesday, while on Friday calling in to briefly talk and discuss in whispers with the proprietor, Mrs. Harrison, the latest bombings and national or local war associated tragedies.

Mrs. Harrison had attended the same school as Mum, the Bluecoat School in Nottingham. How this lady acquired the shop on Alfreton Road, I had little if any idea.

She was by the time war broke out, however, widowed and from then on nursed her ailing mother whom I never saw but presumed lived in the rooms behind and above the shop. A quietly spoken ladylike woman, Mrs. Harrison's oval and slightly freckled face projected a calming affect. Like Mum and Aunty when they were working in the kitchen, she wore a flowered smock and long skirt.

Sometimes she smiled at me but seldom addressed me in any form, even less used my Christian name. She and Mum conversed quickly, in low voices and in all seriousness. It became clear that despite her becalming expression, Mrs. Harrison was worried and in all probability about how to get her sick mother down to a street corner air raid shelter when the sirens wailed out their dreaded message.

On one occasion, with tears in her eyes and hands widespread, she referred to every person grounded and victimised by war as "sitting ducks". That was the first time I had heard such a term. And always the pale blue eyes of this once so obviously serene lady were veiled with tears.

After leaving Mrs. Harrison's, we continued again in the direction of Nottingham. The road widened. The shoppers were more noticeable. The traffic heavier.

At a war illuminated Belisha beacon we crossed, always at the same place as do territorial animals, and called at the last two shops.

The first was a greengrocer's aptly called Onions. Usually there were two people serving: the son, Stanley, and daughter, whose name I think was Barbara. I liked to watch one or other of them take the large scale pan, wedge it sideways into the pile of carrots, potatoes or brussel sprouts as they were required and then lift the pan clearly from the pile with pretty close to the amount that was needed riding intact, unbroken and moving swiftly to the scale's pointer so that a price could be agreed upon.

Here the atmosphere was relaxed. Mum was called by her Christian name. The hushed, secretive telling of stories that Stanley one day told me were not for the ears of little boys took place as I stood placidly in a corner.

It was here at Onions that I saw, quite regularly, a side of Mum's personality that was for instance unlike the one that Mrs. Harrison knew. Thus it seemed as if Mum, perhaps like most people lapsed into a personality change according to whichever establishment she was calling at.

When one morning I asked her why she was different with Stanley and Barbara Onions, Mum looked surprised and told me that in the years she and Dad lived at Roderick Street she used to work at Onions to help pay the bills. She also worked at Hallam and Wilson's, the confectionery next door. Here she bought chocolate eclairs and my all-time favourite, a cream bun. And here, as in Onions, she was called by her Christian name and there was always low voiced banter taking place between Mum and one of the three women assistants.

One bespectacled woman with a florid complexion and dark blonde hair seemed always to make a point of seeing Mum and having a word whether she was serving her or not. The woman's cheeks were healthy, glowing and seemed to swell whenever she laughed, which was often.

The war? It might well have been fought on a different planet for all these friends of Mum's seemed to care. But I make these observations in a kindly way. Like Mum and countless other working-class British people, they did not for one minute think the Germans toting the banner of war would ever set foot in this country. Being bombed out of their homes might have been another story. Yet on the surface there was not a hint, *not a shred* of worry outwardly displayed.

When loaded with bags Mum and I left the confectioners, we had then to cross Alfreton Road and catch a 16 or 13 bus at the corner of Bowden Street, which if Mum had not been with me I would have found due to the corner foundry chimney, the likes of which I had never before seen, striking up to the sky.

When the bus arrived, we went downstairs with someone usually offering a cheery word. Or, alternatively, saying nothing.

After a five minute semi-circular ride through Radford and Bobbersmill, we arrived at Aspley Lane island then walked the quarter or so mile along Western Boulevard with the lime trees and allotment gardens either side to the first road on our right, and home having completed a full circle.

Thursday was storytelling day. Aunty played her Nelson Eddy and Jeanette McDonald records. Mum busied herself around the house.

Friday morning was the last in the week for walking again over the New Bridge beside the derelict and long forgotten pleasure grounds of Radford Folly, before shopping along Hartley Road and Alfreton Road.

At a corner newsagent's Mum bought me a comic or two, *Mickey Mouse* or *Film Fun* usually and sometimes smelling strongly of print. Having five minutes earlier browsed the stills outside *The Windsor* cinema, my head was swimming with images by the time Mum and I arrived home and I was given my cream bun.

Snow White, who like Bambi had long black eyelashes. Goofy, the hound "dawg", with his long snout, flappy black ears and prominent black nose. George Raft, James Cagney, Humphrey Bogart and Alan Ladd. Tough guys each with a revolver hidden in his overcoat pocket, cigarette dangling from the side of his mouth, ready to kill or be killed while in the meantime catching the eye of Rita Hayworth, Jean Peters or Veronica Lake.

Film Fun furnished me with pictures of Abbot and Costello, Laurel and Hardy or Flanagan and Allen. There was also a feature page allocated to the "The Adventures of the Lone Ranger and Tonto."

The Lone Ranger was a black masked and gloved American Frontier version of Superman, except that he didn't or *couldn't* fly. His horse Silver was deep chested, magnificent and pure white. His native American sidekick Tonto timed to appear at exactly the right moment.

In the few Lone Ranger films I had seen, the masked hero had seldom if ever called Tonto by that name, but used the deeply drawled and often impersonated, "Thanks, Tonno".

Between reading stories and nursery rhymes with Aunty, I rode a white horse. Fired a silver revolver. Told Veronica Lake that she was safe so long as she stayed with me. But to my weekly dismay, Friday night was also bath and toenail cutting night. The hot soapy bath soon after Uncle Mac's *Children's Hour* I thoroughly enjoyed. The warm towels, smell of freshly ironed pyjamas, comforts of my pink or blue dressing gown and matching slippers also.

Having to sit on the settee, lean back and put my feet onto Mum's lap as she sat beside me, however, was another matter. And the scissors snipping coupons out of the ration books? Surely they were smaller and daintier scissors than those Mum used for trimming my toenails? Sitting perfectly still as I was told, I squirmed inwardly and winced noticeably but silently.

Then horror upon horrors! If Betty realised I was having my toenails trimmed, she would sneak accidently-on-purpose around the settee, pounce onto the cushion next to mine and when Mum had finished, and despite my laughing protests, take each toe of one foot in turn while chanting,

'This little piggy went to market,
This little piggy stayed at home.
This little piggy had roast beef,
This little piggy had none.
And *this* little piggy went wee...eee....eeee all the way home!'

The last line, of course, ended in a toe-tickling session which seemed to last an eternity and throughout which I didn't know whether to laugh or cry.

On more than one occasion our smiling neighbour Mrs. Teather was around for my toenail trimming session but, much to my silent chagrin, Betty pounced on me just the same.

CHAPTER 17

Emerging briefly into the haze between sleep and early morning darkness, I was suddenly probed into full wakefulness by the sound of something approaching. Something passing over the house. Something that in its passing, or on its journey, produced a rhythmic, almost haunting song. For the second time in those formative years I experienced the hair suddenly stiffening and chilled on my nape as the sound tapered into the unseen, *unknown,* distance.

That something was travelling. Unfettered by war and instinctively exploring a flight path merging between the land below and the starlit threat zone established by the Luftwaffe. But what was it? And how was the *sound* made.

As anchored between the blankets I conceived these questions, I heard the familiar and welcoming sounds of Mum coming up the stairs. When she opened the bedroom door, as always round faced and beaming, she asked, 'Did you hear the swans going over?'

'Swans? What are swans? And it's still dark out there, so how do you know they were swans?' I piped.

As she accompanied me down the stairs with Scamp waiting, his tail wagging, by the bottom stair alongside which my pig drawing still decorated the wallpaper, Mum explained that she used to see and hear swans flying when she lived in the house at Claude Street, Lenton, because the backyard was situated near the canal.

'We used to see pairs flying at this time of the year, just as it was getting light,' said Mum.

'Are they big birds then, Mum?'

'Yes, big and white with long necks and broad wings. That was what made the sound you could hear; their wings or rather the air passing through them as they flew.'

After I had knelt beside the hearth and tickled Scamp's tummy as he lay on his back, tail thumping against the fender, Mum reminisced about her days living beside the canal and how in the midwinter when she was a young girl she, her sisters and their friends used to walk with arms linked along the canal's hard frozen surface to the munitions factory where they worked.

Aunty during the day told me that before the flood banks for the River Leen were established around Whitemoor and Bobbersmill, swan pairs used to nest in the reed and willow breaks and hold individual territories there.

In the evening Dad similarly reminisced about the Daybrook which brought surface water from the areas of Mapperley and Arnold down to the millponds that, in his boyhood, were actively used until the housing estates were built and the Nottingham ring road system, known as The Boulevards, was laid with future and disturbing volumes of traffic in mind.

He told me that the railed pond in Vernon Park where Joey Duck was buried had originally been a millpond but with an island built in the middle to attract wildfowl, particularly a swan pair, and additionally that alongside Roderick Street where I was due to be born there were two tracts of reeded floodwater either side the railway with a swan pair tenanting each.

He then said that it may have been a pair from there that I heard flying over the house, perhaps moving to the canal or the River Trent passing through the low-lying fields beyond.

Putting his newspaper aside for a moment, Dad in his armchair reminisced about a tract of water which as a boy he had been particularly fond. It was again a millpond situated about a mile and a half from his boyhood home, bordered on one side by a mill and carpeted in the summer months with white and yellow water lilies. A swan pair nested in the reeds there. The millpond was called Farrands Dam.

'It's all been built on now, though,' Dad sadly added.

Nevertheless, I asked him to draw me the map that to this day I carry within my mind. I also persuaded him to take me to the site the following Sunday morning. Farrands Dam had been situated just off the Boulevards and a good two mile or so direct walk from our home.

At the corner of the Boulevard and Ventnor Rise we paused while Dad pointed to a sturdy oak tree towering from the corner of someone's garden. 'It was in the fields just behind this oak. A track led off from beside this tree and took you straight across to Farrands Dam.'

For the life of me, I could not understand why a housing estate had been built on so lovely a place as Dad had described. And at so early an age I realised that the conservation of land and places, at least until after the war, meant nothing. Was almost non-existent. People came first. People and houses.

'Well people have got to have somewhere to live,' said Dad quietly as we retraced our route home.

'Yes, but why there?' I queried, and am still querying.

When earlier that week I asked if I could be taken to see swans, Aunty and Dad assured me this would be possible. However, as the lighter evenings were nudging in and perhaps by way of an appetizer, Aunty said that there was a swan pair she and Dad had in mind but first why didn't I look at a book. She then produced a coloured cover edition of Hans Christian Anderson's *Ugly Duckling.*

On the front cover picture, across a lake paddled by ducks, sailed a bird with wings arched like the sails of a ship. The bird's neck was long. Its bill was orange. At the base of its bill was positioned the distinctive black knob or "berry", just before the black beady eye highlighted the downy whiteness of the swan's head.

On the back cover sailed a swan with flatter wings and Aunty explained that during the summer months swans, ducks and geese preened out their old feathers and grew new ones in time for the beginning of the autumn. During this time these birds are flightless and the wildfowler's term for the moult is "eclipse".

Both Dad and Aunty agreed that the book's artist knew what he or she was about and it was then I realised that while one person wrote books and told stories, another usually illustrated them. The book was illustrated with drawings in black and white. One in particular related to the sounds I heard that morning. The artist had depicted a swan - "the ugly duckling", but by then transformed into a swan - lifting its head from between its wings as from the reeds it watched three swans flying over.

Their necks were held tautly; their wings appeared longer than their submarine shaped bodies. I imagined them flying against a starlit, pre-daybreak sky. When could I see swans?

Aunty lifted a forefinger indicating patience, while Dad again told me that they might both have a surprise for me in the days and weeks to come.

Early one Saturday morning, Dad and I set off for the Huntingdon Street covered market in the centre of Nottingham. We were, Dad told me, going to buy a dozen chickens and keep poultry in a long corner of the back garden. At least until the war was over.

The bus from Middleton Boulevard after many twists and turns lasting for half an hour, stopped directly outside the market. The poultry stall was situated facing the outer pavement and within sight of the bus stop.

Across the road a bulky building of cream brickwork blocked the light from the market's east side. The building was, Dad explained, the Palais-de-Dance where Betty had started going with her friends on Saturday night. A dance hall. Lights. Music. Couples by the hundred perhaps dancing to the rhythms of a guest dance band such as we sometimes heard on the wireless.

As we then made our way through screens of people to the poultry stall, I wondered why on earth Betty and her friends, or anyone, would want to go dancing on Saturday night when they could go to the cinema and watch cowboy films.

The poultry stall sold coops, pot eggs for inducing hens to lay, all manner of grain, spices and poultry and pigeon meal as well as day old chicks, the focus of Dad's attention that day.

The stallholders, whose names were boldly emblazoned on the sides and front of every stall, wore khaki front coats or smocks over their everyday attire.

The stall fronts were painted cream, the lettering green and the awnings and canopies designed in plain green and white stripes.

The yellow bundles of fluff, that incredibly to me and only a day or so before had each pecked and thrust forcefully from within the shell of a hen's egg, were packed tightly into cardboard boxes. Each box, with the inquisitive turnings one way and the other of the many newly hatched chicks, nurtured within its four walled space a collective movement; a gentle swaying and bustling movement as the chicks looked at one another, jostled and rubbed against each other but knew of or could see nothing more.

Without handling them, Dad selected twelve chicks and the stallholder placed six in one cardboard box and six in another, put a lid on each box and looped both effectively with twine. The boxes had air holes in the top and sides which the yellow fluff of the nearest chicks blocked.

Tentatively I carried the box I was given across the busy road with Dad and we caught the homeward bus, a number 45. We sat the boxes firmly on our laps. The bus conductor smiled. The chicks would be heard cheeping inside.

Dad and Mum had already decided that the chicks could spend a week or so in a corner of the dining room, in "Jerry's Corner" which backed onto the kitchen ovens and was also situated near the kitchen end of the french windows. That way the chicks would gain the warmth from both the sun and the ovens. Dad blocked one end of the corner off with the settee but placed rugs underneath it so that the more inquisitive of the yellow, disorientated throng were prevented from going under. He then put a wooden board across another section and the chicks makeshift quarters were intact.

After gently releasing the chicks, Betty put down a saucer of chicken feed and another of water while Dad and I set off on our second walk of the day over the New Bridge to Worthington's old farmyard where Dad purchased a sack filled with straw and chaff.

In Worthington's yard I stood looking at the derelict and long forgotten milking sheds, the stables with half open doors, the shuttered house with its cobwebby windows, while a middle-aged man provided Dad with the sack of straw and chaff for which a price was soon agreed.

Ivy adorned sections of the farmyard walls and other plants flowered from occasional cracks in the brickwork.

Leaving the man and his derelict yard we turned eventually for home, Dad as always in his suit and trilby but on this occasion carrying the sack of straw on his shoulder. Nevertheless, when he saw my interest in the waterfall as we neared the colliery lane entrance, he murmured, 'Do you want to go and have a look, Little Man?' and I lost no time in running to the rails from where I could see the Leen's surging water crashing white edged over the sills of the weir.

Trails of green weed, sometimes known as "Mermaids Hair", adorned the willow shaded flow over which swallows and house martins flickered. Mum and Aunty called them "blue birds" and at the age I was then I too used to that term as I watched the birds spiralling, dipping and rising - 'catching flies' as Dad put it - between the bowered willows and the water.

When we arrived home, Dad dumped the sack in the yard near to the back door and Scamp immediately investigated. The instant the scents of the sack's contents flowed into his nostrils his tail began to wag.

'These are the smells he knew as a puppy. The smells of the stable yard where I brought him from,' smiled Mum, fondly watching Scamp while standing with one hand placed to her hip.

While I was telling Aunty about the blue birds, Scamp entered the dining room and with head uplifted in the manner of a dog proclaiming territory, he went to the boarded sections of the french window corner containing the chickens and put his head over.

Here, I should add, a corner of the carpet had been lifted and rolled back and sheets of newspaper put down for the chicks to walk and defecate on.

I watched Scamp's moist muzzle pulsing as he inhaled the varied scents of house furniture and poultry. But as I stood, so his muzzle suddenly nudged me beneath the elbow. As I turned to stroke him the expression in Scamp's eyes read. '*Come on!* Don't be giving *them* too much attention. What about me?'

After dinner, eaten as always in the English working-class tradition around midday, Dad and I set off again. On this occasion we walked the more favoured route, so far as I was concerned, over Colliers Pad and through Radford Woodhouse to Wollaton Road. We were not, unfortunately, going to the deer park but to an ironmonger's and hardware shop to buy rolls of wire netting and fence supports, and the following Saturday planks of wood and rolls of weather-insulating tarpaulin which would form the basics of Dad's quite sizeable fowl pen.

The hardware store, standing to this day but beneath a different banner, was a long fronted shop with a brick and cement frontage. It was, I should imagine, privately built with living quarters at the back. The relative dark interior carried the aromas of rubber mats, metal chippings and tarpaulin, several rolls of which Dad ordered for collection the following Saturday.

The proprietor was a small, thick-set man, who wore a grey overall with low wide pockets into which he habitually plunged each unusually wide hand. Like all shopkeepers of that time, he kept a pencil stowed behind his ear and had a rule and tape measure protruding from the top pocket of his overall.

In the shop were dustbins, hand and soft bristled brushes, dustpans and seemingly every make of cleaning utensil. Drills, planes, saws, hammers and chisels were displayed on racks arranged along each of the long, low walls.

Dad bought a variety of nails, staples and tacks and stowed the bulky boxes, some into his jacket pocket and others into mine. Between us we lifted and carried six or eight lightweight fence supports strung together and two or three rolls of wire netting, which the proprietor inter-looped and Dad again slung over his shoulder. And in this manner, awkwardly yet progressively, we walked the mile or so home ignoring the canal backwater and the prospect of glimpsing geese in Jackie Matthew's farmyard. Just walking, walking, until thankfully we arrived at the front garden gate.

All the newly bought materials we piled into the shed Dad had erected at the kitchen end of the open yard and alongside Teather's high privet hedge.

Our day, however, did not end there. After tea, and surprisingly whilst it was still light, we went to the *Forum* cinema. To my delight we walked Cherry Orchard Lane from the thicket sides of which blackbirds fluted while song thrushes whistled repetitively yet pleasantly from the allotment trees and hedgerows facing the fields. The Aspley Hall dairy herd, comprising some thirty red and white liveried Shorthorn cattle, grazed the extensive parkland fields.

When about two hours later we left the cinema, an usherette handed me a long stick on the ground end of which was welded a walking Donald Duck. The strange rattling sound made by the cartoon character's webbed feet was, I think, supposed to be an imitation of a duck quacking.

The Aspley Hall Shorthorns were grazing heavily and close to the railed fence as we walked the narrowest stretch of Cherry Orchard Lane. I was still walking Donald Duck and the sound clattered unceremoniously beside the allotment hedgerows. Yet, surprisingly, not one heavy bodied cow lifted her head from the feast of grass and clover stretching below her rubbery muzzle.

The next morning when with Scamp I inspected the chickens, Scamp again nudged my elbow. Dad joined us and pointed out a single chick standing alone, shivering and alternately opening and closing its eyes.

'Dying on its feet,' Dad murmured.

'Aren't we all?' quipped Mum, as she laid the cutlery at our place settings in readiness for breakfast.

It took Dad two Saturdays to complete the fowl pen, the last acquisition being the main house equipped with perches on which the hens roosted at night and the side boxes where, given time, they laid their eggs. A sloping plank connected the door of the hen house to the pen. The tarpaulin Dad used to insulate the roof. This end of the pen levelled with the entrance to the air raid shelter and screened the gap in the privet through which Mum periodically conversed with Mr. and Mrs. Fisher who lived on Westholme Gardens, the cul-de-sac running parallel to the road on which we lived.

In a matter of days the eight or nine surviving chicks that were still kept in the dining room corner developed minute wattles and combs and by the time Dad transferred them to the hay and straw-lined hen house, their coverings of fluff had taken on the smoother appearance of embryo feathers.

While Dad's attention at the weekends had diverted to getting a War Effort poultry-keeping routine underway, his vigilance had not strayed throughout the weekdays and although he mentioned each evening having seen "coveys" of partridge out on the fields of the Nottinghamshire-Leicestershire border and pheasants, hares and rabbits, the connection to Hans Anderson's story of *The Ugly Duckling* he kept to himself.

On his early morning walks to the bus terminus he probably saw the swan pair in flight that earlier in the season I had heard, for unbeknown to us both at the time, I suspect, breeding swan pairs when they have selected a territory fly often at first light or by starlight or moonlight and circle the boundaries of their bond selected territories in a bid to keep them free from interloping swans and rival breeding pairs.

What Dad obviously saw as the lighter mornings made his Boulevard walk more comfortable was a swan pair flying or sailing arch winged on the canal pound by the boat builder's derelict yard on Radford Bridge Road. It was in the boat builder's yard beside a brick storage barn that the male swan or cob eventually built the nest of dried grass and reeds, and where every other day the pen laid an egg until the clutch was complete. Then she began her thirty-five day period of incubation.

The hatching of the cygnets coincided with the longer warmer days and when Dad saw the family out for the first time on the canal, he gently alerted every member of the family except me and we all tramped down to the backwater arm on a sunlit Saturday evening.

Our destination was again Wollaton where Dad intended to call over his beloved horses, but the swan family were scheduled as my surprise, which indeed they proved to be. The excitement that precedes exploration surged through me when we reached the backwater arm for gentle hands, perhaps Betty's, Aunty's or Mum's, guided me onto the narrow path that climbed a steep man-made embankment grassed over and levelling with the lock gate ahead.

Dad picked me up and by inching gingerly one behind the other, the family crossed the lock gate holding onto its single railing, as Mum had done so often when she was a girl.

When we were on the towpath, Betty and Aunty walked down the slope and I walked, as usual, between Dad and Mum. We were walking towards the bridge which Aunty and I frequently crossed when we went to Cunnah's.

The boat builder's yard on the opposite bank carried the same sense of dereliction as Worthington's farmyard.

Betty and Aunty still walking together looked back smiling. And again. It was then I saw the water rippling as Aunty stepping aside said, 'Right, Keith. You wanted to see swans. Well, here they are.'

Dad's face was also alight.

The swan pair were just as those depicted on the cover of *The Ugly Duckling.* Hissing, the pen arched her wings and with neck swelling turned her head from side to side indicating that we should not step closer. Fascinated, I noticed how the black knob or "berry" surmounted on the cob's bill shone in the sunlight, due to him submerging his head and pulling up weed for the seven cygnets bustling between them to feed on. Water also dripped from the end of the cob's hooked bill.

The cygnets were greyish-buff in colour. They had black bills and black paddles with which each created its own wake. But collectively they pecked at every floating object, some of which shone like water beetles, and as the cygnets sorted through the weed, the cob and pen alternately pulled more from the canal bed and rested it on the water surface before them.

Much of the entire canal pound was at this time of the year carpeted by the green floating weed that some people called "slime" but which is, in fact, duckweed and contains a sugary substance beneficial to the diet of ducklings, cygnets and moorhen chicks. Consequently, there was no shortage of natural food for our local swan pair and their cygnets that summer.

CHAPTER 18

In April 1942 the Mediterranean island of Malta was targeted by the Italian and German air forces. The British base was particularly sought for it was from there that the convoy routes between Egypt and Libya were planned and maintained. The British Navy also installed a submarine base there and "harassed" the enemy ships.

On April 15th King George VI awarded the George Cross to the entire Maltese population for their fortitude throughout the bombardment.

From the middle until the end of April the Luftwaffe bombed the British cities of Bath and Exeter in the reprisal Baedekar raids following the Royal Air Force attacks on Lubeck and Cologne.

In May the Japanese using a combined force of native labourers and Allied prisoners-of-war began building the Kwai Railroad which when completed linked Burma to Bangkok. During the railroad's eighteen month period of construction, over 90,000 native labourers died alongside an estimated 15,000 Allied prisoners.

The United States Navy then overturned a Japanese plot to take and commandeer an Allied base at Port Moresby situated in the Papuan territory. The naval battle that ensued was historically listed as The Battle of the Coral Sea.

Meanwhile in Libya the British 8th Army led by General Sir Neil Ritchie fought the German and Italian forces, both of which were under the combined leadership of General Erwin Rommel.

By June the United States' President Franklin D. Roosevelt had set up an Office of War Information and with Winston Churchill discussed further military strategies and war materials production at the Washington Conference.

In Czechoslovakia the German Gestapo eliminated the village of Lidice because the famed Czech resistance fighters killed Nazi "protector", Reinhard Heydrich. From this village ninety-eight children were deported, 184 women transported to Ravensbruk concentration camp and 198 men shot.

By mid-June Rommel's forces had regained control of Tobruk, the all important Libyan port, and the British retreated east with the intention of staging a defensive at Mersa Matruh. The Commander, Sir Neil Ritchie, was recalled and his position succeeded by Sir Claude Auchinleck.

Early in June the British 8th Army under his command blocked the advance of Rommel's German troops whose mission was to secure the tracts of Egypt under British control. This much needed victory was listed as the First Battle of El Alamein.

By the 26th of that month Britain made ready for reprisal raids following the Royal Air Force bombing raids on Hamburg.

Ship building in Britain was really underway with body parts construction taking place in inland factories then being transported to the shipyards and the final slipway once they were assembled. Incredibly, a 10,000 ton merchant ship was launched in Great Britain every three weeks. Some shipyards strove to achieve building targets of twelve to sixteen ships a year. Newspaper photographs and Pathe News cinema reels featured newly assembled warships being pulled into a basin or dock for fitting out by a fleet of tugs.

The Ministry of Aircraft Production were equally busy, turning out fleets of magnificent Spitfire aircraft.

***

When I wasn't reading *The Ugly Duckling* from cover to cover or sitting in Aunty's lap watching fascinated as she showed me Uncle Charlie's beautifully varnished home-made cigarette box, I was kneeling on a chair at the table and reading more names from *The Daily Sketch*: Bath, Exeter and Rommel, who the War Department and media nicknamed "The Desert Fox".

Both the newspaper photographs and cinema newsreels continually illuminated a monochrome world but one in which every adult and a great many children, some around my own age, were in some way affected by or involved in the war.

Occasionally, we were startled by an explosion that shook the glass panes in the french windows, yet we had not heard the air raid siren. Wide-eyed, I met Mum's equally startled gaze.

'Quarrying. It's men blasting a quarry with dynamite,' she several times assured Aunty and me.

In retrospect, I think it was the Ak-Ak guns going off from the partially concealed ARP base situated on the far side of Shepherd's Wood just beyond Aspley Hall. Mum probably surmised this too, and Aunty. But they weren't letting on.

When with Mum and Aunty I went one afternoon to the Food Office to sort out some query relating to the ration books, my attention focused upon the wall posters and the pictures arranged along the wall - the paintings and artists' impressions of the Land Army girls.

The one to which my attention kept returning was headed *TO BE A FARMER'S GIRL*. Below these words a smiling, ample haired young woman wearing a wide brimmed hat tilted to the back of her head, stood with her right shoulder free and her left bowed by a sheaf of oats or barley. The girl wore a sweater with sleeves rolled up to the elbow, a shirt open at the neck and collar flipped over her shoulder. Her face was strong but delightfully feminine. Her eyed filled with good humour. But then, as Mum may have pointed out, she *was* posing for a photograph.

While Mum dealt with the family ration books, Aunty returned to my side and told me that I was looking at a recruitment poster which as I studied it filled me with a sense of inadequacy, especially when I realised that people I attempted to draw in my jotter had round faces and single lined bodies, arms and legs.

Betty drew people that way too. By the time I moved on to gaze at another poster, I had made my mind up to draw real looking people. After all, my pig adorning the wallpaper at the foot of the stairs seemed proportionate. So why, I asked myself, shouldn't my people be too? I noticed, for instance, that the Land Girl's arm was a drawing within itself. Something I had heard the grown-ups call a work of art.

A second poster depicted Land Army girls working together with hay forks, stacking the stooks and sheaves higher onto the hay cart.

Each member of the Women's Land Army or WLA had left home, travelled, filled in wads of forms, sat tests and attended a training centre before being assigned to a farm perhaps several hundred miles away. Usually they were welcomed as a family member but lived in a stockman's cottage adjacent to the main buildings. Some were poorly rationed but afraid to report the matter to the relevant authorities. Several were assigned the regular task of mucking out the stall or stable of an untrustworthy bull or stallion and they could hardly refuse.

Although I understood that most of the nation's healthy young men had been conscripted or "called up", I was under the impression that girls and young women could volunteer or stay at home and continue with their jobs and evenings spent at a local dance hall. I was unaware that the conscription, concerning an average seven or eight out of every ten young women, commenced a few weeks prior to the Christmas of 1941, although not every young woman chose to become a land girl.

Women air raid wardens were not unknown. Others worked, as Mum and her sisters had once worked, in munitions factories while both industrial and war historians have in recent years highlighted the prowess of those many women employed as welders throughout the shipyard network of Great Britain. And yet, *and unfairly*, they were still paid less than the men doing the same job.

Of the eighty thousand or so trainee Land Girls, not all chose to work on farms or holdings. Some were employed as pest controllers and others as sawmill workers, producing among much else, pit props and railway sleepers. Those in the Timber Corps doctored, selected and felled trees.Because we youngsters saw posters of young women working on the land, that is what we assumed them to be doing.

Those closest to my home worked on crop planting and harvesting the land acquired by the War Commission on Wollaton Park. My late friend Wilf Widdowson recalled there being one 'big bosomed lass in a green jersey and fawn knee breeches who spread manure across the paddocks with a bucket and rake and excelled at other jobs the War Office officials considered well beyond the physical capabilities of the average land working woman'.

I sometimes wondered why my sister Betty showed little or no enthusiasm for working on the land. She was, however, being trained as a Pitman shorthand typist at business college level while still attending school.

Refugees I had seen photographs of. Children of my age and older gathered at specified centres or on railway stations in queues or groups and sometimes waving goodbye to a parent or guardian.

They carried baggage and were to some extent name badged and labelled. They also carried boxed gas masks looped over their shoulders and almost banging their knees as they walked or were quietly, yet firmly, urged to a destination of considered safety. They were just one part of the war that I would look out on, I decided.

One morning, with Scamp barking in the yard and growling as he thrust his muzzle beneath the lattice gates, Mum answered the knock on the front letterbox then called me into the hall. In the porch smiling were two girls - sisters, who Mum knew as Jill and Shirley Pearce. Freckled and blonde with thick curly hair, Jill was the oldest. Shirley had brown hair, thick and straight, and her eyes I realised were green.

With them was a boy. The first I had ever spoken with. He was about the same height as myself and wore a black jacket and short grey trousers. His thick brown hair was brushed forward. His name was Ronald. He was a refugee.

'From London!' I echoed, as minutes later he sat with me on the settee and I showed him my books.

The Pearce sisters had brought Ronald over because they thought matters would be good for Ronald if he had a boy of his own age to occasionally play and converse with.

Yet as Ronald confirmed that he was a London refugee, the capital city that I saw in my mind was that which, again, I had seen only in newspaper photographs and on cinema newsreels. A blitzed and shattered capital.

For some weeks, Ronald and I met and looked at books or roamed around the garden in the company of Scamp. I did not see Ronald every day because I was, as usual, taken over Radford Folly to the shops, particularly on Mondays. And on Sundays he attended church with the Pearce family, from what I could gather, yet I never knew or was told for what reason.

Some hot afternoons I crossed the road to the Pearce's house but was never asked inside. Instead, Ronald and I read books on the rear lawn.

I liked very much the houses on the opposite side of the road to our own because not only did they face south and the eventual full meridian light, but they also backed onto the New Aspley Gardens which were, in fact, allotments.

With Ronald then I was aware of rambling hedgerows of hawthorn at the end of the garden rather than the regimental privet hedges with which I was by then accustomed. There were butterflies, varied and colourful but which were nameless to me at the time. There were also blackbirds and song thrushes, some of which obviously flew between the houses and across the road to our own garden. The blue tits and great tits which explored the hawthorn thickets for insects with which to feed their broods I could name, because quite frequently one or other of these titmice species fed while clinging to the ball of suet which Mum or Aunty suspended from the branches of a rear garden apple tree. So to be in someone else's garden, and with a boy of around my age, I regarded as something of an adventure. Yet still I coaxed stories from Ronald, as I did habitually from Aunty, but these developed into a series of question stories prompted by each of us asking in turn, 'Have you been here?' or 'Have you been to there?'

One place to which Ronald had been taken before becoming an enlisted evacuee was London Zoo. When he uttered those two words I became riveted to the spot.

'A zoo?'

'Yes, there are wild animals in there like lions and tigers. They're in cages and enclosures but you can get quite close to them.'

Moreover, Ronald had among his belongings a map of London Zoo. *In colour!* That fact alone placed a higher value on the map so far as I was concerned. Briefly he went into the house, brought us both back a glass of lemonade but with the map tucked under his arm.

I was elated, never having seen a map before, although the two-page spread was actually a ground plan. With it we could trace the places, *the cages and enclosures* where the animals were kept. So my further questions began.

'Did you see one of these? Did you see one of those? Did you see one of......?'

The polar bears were kept on a rocky escarpment called Mappin Terrace. I surprised myself by reading out the name aloud and Jill, who came to join us and was four or five years older, told me that I was right. It was then we saw, on a path, the diagram of a man with woman's hair and wearing a frock coat. He was laying on his back, bearded chin tilted to the sky. At his side was something that resembled a long slender knife.

'It's a sword,' Jill confirmed. And the man was a cavalier.

I had no idea where such a person fitted in the jigsaw of world history. Or how far back from the then current war and Ronald and myself his era spanned.

Then I remembered Captain Marryat's novel, *The Children of the New Forest.* Surely Prince Rupert had been a cavalier!

A caption beside the artist's impression of the dead Cavalier informed us that when the flagstones of the original path were removed in readiness for building the zoo, or zoological gardens as they were officially known, the skeleton of the cavalier "in full regalia" was found beneath.

'He was probably killed in a duel. In a sword fight,' Jill told us.

I couldn't wait to tell Mum and Aunty!

Early one warm evening when Ronald and Jill were for some forgotten reason still in the house, I found myself sitting at the top of Mr. and Mrs. Pearce's garden facing Shirley. She was dressed in a green pleated skirt, pink blouse and grey cardigan. She was also entwining lengths of pink wool around her hands and fingers.

'What are you doing that for?' I asked, while thinking that it would be much better if we were looking at an interesting map.

'It's called a cat's cradle,' said Shirley.

As she spoke so I looked into her wide green eyes and found myself trapped, unable to avert my gaze. Shirley was staring at me in the same way. Suddenly unaccustomed bands of warmth filtered pleasantly through my tummy. Bands of warmth that I somehow knew had to do with Shirley's eyes, her face, *her presence.* Momentarily we were held by this then unexplainable force and there was no one in the green leafy world around us but she and I, who knew this.

When Ronald came down the lawn carrying books and our much treasured plan of London Zoo, his first spoken word broke the spell. Mrs. Pearce I seem to remember remained a background figure, white haired I think, and lingering. Sending Jill or Shirley to communicate with Ronald and me, informing us that Ronald had a meal waiting or it was the time Mum had asked that I be sent home.

Mr. Pearce appeared, briskly striding and immaculately dressed, about six-thirty in the evening. A man wearing a three-piece business suit, a bowler hat and carrying a briefcase in one hand and black umbrella in the other. Like Dad he walked in a straight backed manner. Or rather marched.

'Here's my Dad,' Shirley once or twice whispered as if in awe and from whatever was occupying us on the lawn we turned as Mr. Pearce greeted his family.

'Good evening Jill. Good evening Shirley. Good evening Ronald.'

Not to be left out, I ventured, 'Hello Mr. Pearce,' at which he barely returned his gaze in our direction but acknowledged me with a clipped 'Hullo', which indicated surely that I was a stranger in the camp.

Shortly after Mr. Pearce returned home, my three friends were called into the house thus indicating it was time for me, *the stranger*, to go home. As I crossed the drive to our front gate, I looked often towards Three Nail Tree silhouetted against the sun gilded westering light and paused to hear rival cock blackbirds fluting from the stand of rowan trees opposite our house. Later, with perhaps the supper time drink before me, I would secretly mull over the power that momentarily flared and lingered within a young girl's eyes and caused welcoming pains to sear through the tummy of a young boy, yet about which I would tell no one.

To some degree, I began associating the different directions leading to and from the house with certain members of the family. Mum with shops on the Hartley and Alfreton Road; Dad with the Vale of Belvoir, which I had not by then explored, and the ridgetop village of Strelley where his Home Guard Unit was based. Aunty I connected to Bobbersmill and Hyson Green because when she was walking with me in this direction she was at her most exuberant, perhaps because she had spent her childhood there and was, as we walked, reviving old memories of her family, schooldays and beloved Charlie.

But Dad's presence I felt to some extent whenever we reached the point where Aspley Lane met Nuthall Road because *The Nag's Head* where at weekends he played the piano, although screened by the roadside frontage of *The Wheatsheaf*, was unmistakably there. Piles of colliery dumped shale - 'slag tips' Aunty called them - bordered the railway from which we looked down onto weather rusted lines.

A private lane with a house alongside segregated the Bobbersmill colliery dumping ground from the tightly fenced field that was also segregated by the River Leen with its deep flood banks, which were relatively new to the people of Dad and Aunty's generation. If the road had not been private, we could have followed it and the river's course to Radford Folly and the waterfall by St. Peter's Street.

The river segregated field was always high with docks, thistles and nettles. But someone, perhaps from the row of houses extending from the field to *The Capital* cinema grazed a couple of tethered War Effort goats there.

The nanny goat who, Aunty explained, provided the milk, was never within range when we walked by. But because the Billy bore horns, I considered him the more interesting of the two.

If the Billy goat happened to be tethered close to the railings Aunty stopped and called him over, as she had with each of the dogs on Chalfont Drive. 'Right, Billy. Come here. Let's have a look at you then.'

Straining forward, the goat thrust his muzzle between the fence uprights and I felt his lips and tongue brushing over extended fingers as at the same time he explored our knuckles and finger nails. Aunty each time attempted to slide her slender hand between the rails and pat the goat's forelock and I did the same.

The goat, Aunty told me, was an English Billy. His fur cascaded long and brown in the winter and he had a woolly undercoat. Intrigued by his horns, I too touched them. Pulled them a little. The horns branched outwards and backwards and were set widely apart. They felt solid and serrated around the outer casing.

Aunty gently tugged the Billy goat's chin beard as he attempted to nuzzle my fingers, expecting food no doubt. He smelt sweet yet sickly, if the two can be combined. After rain I surmised that his coat would smell beyond all reasoning.

Leaving the goat's field, we would sometimes cross the busy road and divert around the back of a timber yard then continue by a series of bleacher and dyer works to a lane which connected Bobbersmill with Aunty's girlhood home on Berridge Road.

She, Dad, their brother Albert and Mum used to walk that way to picnic in the fields close to where we now lived. The lane Aunty called a 'snicket' or 'jitty'.

Where the wall terminated on the left, the meanders of the fast flowing River Leen wound between stands of reed, osier and willow thickets. Aunty told me that when she was a girl and the river flowed unchecked before the flood prevention scheme was put into operation, a swan pair used to nest there each year and rear their cygnets. There were still a few pairs of mallard and moorhens. And rats. There had *always* been rats!

I wanted to know why the terrible smell was in the air. The aromatic tangs that smelt stronger than cubes of Dolly Blue and Monday morning's washing.

'It's the bleacher and dyer's you can smell. They need fast running water like this to drive their machinery. That's why they're here,' Aunty explained.

She also told me that from here and for about five or six miles north to the Leen's source in the grounds of Bryon's famed Newstead Abbey there were about ten Victorian bleachers and dyers firms in operation. The offices and yards of the firm of Lindley and Lindley faced the river to our right and although I was never to see them, I despised the people who had allowed such places to be built.

Returning to the main road, and bypassing the goat's field, our usual road took us across the front of Betty's favourite local cinema *The Capital.* The cinema's draped stage curtains always fascinated me. The smells of plush red carpeting and upholstered seats were to me, and perhaps Betty, locally unique. On intermittent Monday evenings I went with Mum and Aunty to see George Formby films here, a prominent toothed comedian whom I tolerated rather than liked but who played the ukulele, sang and smiled while looking directly into the camera. The films of Old Mother Riley were also shown at around this time. The action, if such it could be called, bored me. The humour was clean-cut, simplified, but for adults. It was also domestic, literally orientated around the kitchen sink.

Old Mother Riley was, I decided, someone whom I wouldn't want to meet in the dark. Riley's lovely stooge, dark haired Kitty McShane, by contrast held me spellbound. Always carrying a handbag and dressed smartly in what was then known as a "two-piece suit", Kitty induced me to study her every move, every facial expression.

Beyond the cinema a wide pavement, bordered on the right by a block of shops, took us to the traffic island and the division of three major roads. Here we crossed, still with our backs to home, and walked a good way along Gregory Boulevard. Aunty always looked at the houses - the windows, the curtain arrangements of the three-storey properties, while I studied the differing patterns on the trunks of the pavement edged London plane trees.

At the crossroads of Hyson Green and Radford Boulevard, I knew that if we went to the left we would bypass *The Lenos* cinema, the locally named "flea-pit", where we had seen *Bambi.* I also realised that small boy though I was described as being, I could walk this far from home and return there unaccompanied if ever the circumstances arose.

When we crossed at the traffic lights, Aunty always angled over to a shop called Beecrofts which, I think, sold kitchenware and hardware items and from where, she told me, she intended one day to buy several rolls of lino.

Disappointed, I then walked with Aunty across a flat, sandy tract of land towards a long tree-lined hill. We were, she told me, crossing Nottingham Forest. But where were all the trees? Was that the best my natal city could do? Off to the left stretched acres of mown and treated grass bordered by a Tudoresque sports pavilion 'That's where your Dad spent all the summer evenings and weekends of his boyhood playing cricket and football,' Aunty pointed out.

'Oh I didn't know ......'

'Oh yes. He was captain of the local football team and a left-handed spin bowler and batsman with the cricket team.'

'But I thought he wanted to be a jockey?'

'He did, more than anything. He spent other days at the Nottingham Racecourse, Colwick Park. He *worked* as a stable lad and groom for a time. Next to your Mum, horses were his first love. But it was cricket and football he excelled at.'

And so another place that connected to a member of my family occurred.

Out of sight, hidden by the green ridged avenues and the bordering lime trees, was the Mansfield Road cemetery and a maze of sandpits from which the strange sounding name of Hyson Green derived. A hundred years or so before when the sportsfield was a recreation field and a picnicking ground, children played in the sandstone hollows and this green area was then called High Sands Green.

With the sportsfields to our left, we climbed a steep, broad cobblestone path which I considered steeper than the eastern path I sometimes climbed with Betty and our girl cousins when we visited Wollaton Hall. At the top of the hill stood what I first decided was a statue but which Aunty explained was a memorial to the soldiers who had fallen in the Boer War.

Fallen? Didn't she mean killed?

Wearing a saddened expression, Aunty nodded. 'It's an expression people use; fallen. But yes, it means the same thing.'

'Will there be memorials for people when this war is over Aunty?'

'Yes, I expect so.'

'When *will* it be over, Aunty?'

Aunty shrugged then said, 'Not yet a while, I shouldn't think.'

After crossing a ridgetop main road, we walked downhill by houses surrounded by high walls to the gates of the Nottingham Arboretum.

Here Aunty and Dad's generation had gathered in their dozens during the weekend afternoons of their childhood and youth.

Old postcards today on display in newsagents and stationery shops confirm this and while some of the boys may be slouching and standing with their hands in their pockets, the majority appear to be smartly dressed. In retrospect I wonder quite often if, as youngsters, Mum and Dad met here.

Aunty pointed out the bandstand surrounded by lawns where she and Uncle Charlie listened to brass band concerts on summer warmed Sunday afternoons.

Why wasn't a concert being held there on the day of our visit?

'Because all the men are away in the war or resting from a six day week job that is in some way affected by the war,' Aunty explained.

'Perhaps some of the men have been killed?' I suggested.

'Yes, who knows? They might have been.'

To my delight The Arboretum, between its shrubbery walks, harboured a pond. Railed like the one to which I had been taken in Vernon Park. There was a centralised fountain and two islands connected by a wooden bridge. And, of course, there were ducks.

Fascinated, I watched the rings ducks made in the water as they paddled and, at the same time, constantly interrupted Aunty's thoughts with such questions as, 'Why is there a fountain? Why are there two islands? Does the duck keeper walk over the bridge? Are the islands where the ducks sleep at night, Aunty?'

Turning from the pond, Aunty then pointed out the aviaries. They looked dilapidated, needing a clean out and a coat or two of paint as Aunty explained. But there were no men or women available now to look after them on a regular basis. And again these circumstances had arisen due to the war.

Here I was shown my first colourful fleets of canaries and budgerigars. There were also several sulphur crested cockatoos. It was these aviaries and the birds within that had conceived Aunty's fetish to one day own several parrots and cockatoos, which as a young woman she had.

'Before the war there were monkeys in one aviary. Red squirrels another. There were cranes and spoonbills and herons, as well as all the parrots and macaws,' Aunty reminisced.

Years later Dad reminisced by the pondside in the same gentle, dreamlike manner. Consequently, from that day I associated both Aunty and Dad with the small but always interesting pleasure grounds of The Nottingham Arboretum.

CHAPTER 19

One hot, sunlit afternoon I was gently ushered into the shade of the rear garden plum tree with Scamp and a galvanised bowl of water alongside in which to splash and cool my feet. Aunty and Mum arranged folding chairs and deckchairs in a semi-circle on the lawn. They conversed excitedly and both wore new flowered smocks.

All the bedroom windows of the house were open and the sparrows were perching on window ledges or flying to and from their nest, which again had been built in the crock of the drainpipe. Trails of straw and grass being woven haphazardly in the threads of a breeze. The sky was blue. The tree foliage green. Our elongated shadows were black. And a sailor called Bernard was coming.

'Betty is bringing him,' smiled Mum. 'At first she started bringing other people's dogs home. Then it was baby sparrows. And today it's a sailor.'

'Why is she bringing a sailor,' I piped.

'Because she's met him at the Palais de Dance and wants to bring him home for tea.'

Suddenly I experienced a wave of fear; shyness.

'Will I see him?'

'Yes I should think so. He'll be sitting with us here, I hope.'

'Will I have to speak to him?'

'Well all you need say is "Hello Bernard" and that's all.'

'But what's Betty bringing him here for?'

'I've told you. To have some tea with us. She feeds everything and everybody, does Betty. Then after tea they're going to the Palais.'

Nudging my elbow, Scamp sank onto his belly beside me, pink tongue lolling sideways over his jaw-line. Fur almost hot to the touch. While the adults seemed ravenous for the sun and heat, he and I sought the shade.

Eventually Betty came from the house. Dressed in a pink sleeveless blouse and grey and black pleated skirt, she walked smiling ahead of the young, dark haired sailor, whose height startled me.

Betty introduced Bernard to everyone including me, who mustered a hesitant 'hello' while grasping Scamp's studded collar for my dog was growling low and bristling.

'It's all right, Scamp. It's Bernard,' Betty explained to Scamp as if she was addressing a human being. But Bernard didn't approach Scamp. Nor did Scamp immediately welcome Bernard.

I was much taken by the sailor's uniform, particularly the flapping bottoms of the bell bottom trousers which also seemed to fascinate Scamp, who viewed them with his folded down ears slightly raised and eyes querying every movement almost as if he expected a mouse to dart suddenly from both the trousers and Bernard's long shadow.

When the family were settled with Betty and Bernard in the semi-circle, I pulled up tufts of grass, floated them in my bowl of water and thought of the canal, the reeds, the backwater arm, the swans and cygnets. And so began the ache that I was to know so many times in the years to come. The being in one place but wanting to be in another. The sufferance, as I silently and secretly looked upon it.

Aunty went into the house and returned holding the Brownie box camera which I disliked because it was black. She photographed Betty and Bernard and Betty kneeling beside Scamp, one arm over his back, and offering him a digestive biscuit.

When Aunty turned the camera in my direction, I protested. Didn't want it! Couldn't do with it! And no, I *wasn't* going to smile.

Strolling over to me, Bernard gave me a postcard of the aircraft carrier *Ark Royal* and I pointed out to him the house sparrows' nest which I considered fair exchange.

Then Dad arrived. He and Bernard shook hands, while Betty and Aunty returned to the house to select glasses and pour cold drinks. Scamp was given a shallow bowl of water.

When on one occasion I glanced up from stirring the grasses in my water bowl, I became instantly piqued on seeing that Bernard was considerably taller than Dad who matched in height our neighbours Mr. Ellis, Mr. Smith and Mr. Bennett when they were infrequently together walking and talking.

Sipping my orange juice, I heard Dad telling Bernard that he had been a soldier in the First World War. He worked first as an ambulance aide but transferred to a cavalry unit which, along with other soldiers, needed the many horses and ponies from Exmoor, Dartmoor and the New Forest broken in after they had been transported to Aldershot which, Dad explained, was on Salisbury Plain.

Such place names were music to my ears. I listened fascinated, Scamp still panting beside me yet cooled to some extent by the plum tree's shade. Dad then reminisced about his months spent in Egypt and when he mentioned the Sudan, a place name that I had not by then heard, the hairs shifted on my nape as they had when I read the words *'in the dead of night'* and heard the swans flying over.

Saturday tea, eaten at around five, usually comprised of seafoods like, prawns, lobster and crab meat with fresh green salad. Due to the summer heat, variations sometimes occurred by way of a home-made cream cheese or two which I saw first as a parcel of souring milk fastened to the water taps of the kitchen sink. And there were always rounds of bread and butter. The white bread, home-made and tasting delicious. The brown bought at Mrs. Harrison's the previous day.

I liked spring onions but tolerated radishes. Could see no point in spending time over them. Nevertheless, I ate pretty much of what was put before me.

At the tea table with Bernard, the talk had more to do with his home life than the war. Yet I was aware, as probably Bernard was himself, that like him thousands of young men and not a few children, including my new friend Ronald, were disorientated by the many unforeseen and tragic events which were taking place around them.

Walking one Tuesday evening to Cunnah's with Aunty, I saw sitting on the grass bank of the backwater arm a solitary cygnet. It sat facing the water but with head turned to one side as it nervously logged our movements. One black paddle rested over its back. The cygnet was long necked and the stubby brown appendages of its embryo wings gave its dark brown body an uneven appearance.

'As the cygnet is now, about three or four months old, is how one must have looked in Denmark and inspired Hans Christian Anderson to write *The Ugly*

Duckling,' said Aunty.

'But I don't think cygnets are ugly, Aunty. Not the ones I've seen anyway,' I replied.

I then asked Aunty why the cygnet was alone and she surmised that the adult swan pair had led the brood away from the backwater and up the steep grassy hillock which levelled with the lock gates, then resettled on the canal stretch fronted by houses and Jackie Matthews' farm. But perhaps because this particular cygnet was not aware that stretches of water were to be found elsewhere, it had turned back to the canal, the reeds and the carpets of edible waterweed which it had known within days of having struggled from the confines of the egg from which it had evolved.

'So it's surviving on its own. A lone cygnet,' said Aunty.

'A lone cygnet?'

'Yes, a cygnet on its own. Or solo, if you like. And that's what we'll call it if we see it on its own again, shall we? Solo.'

'Yes, I like that Aunty. Solo the cygnet,' I confirmed.

On another hot Saturday afternoon, Dad took Ronald and me on a coach trip - my first - to the riverside village of Gunthorpe, situated south-east of the city and some six or eight miles from its people thronged centre.

Whether Dad had known Guthorpe in the past, or whether one of his work colleagues had told him about the village, I have no way of knowing. Coach trips, so far as I was concerned, could go on forever such was my interest in the surrounding countryside. But when eventually the three of us alighted at Gunthorpe, I was much taken by the span of the bridge taking The Fosse over the River Trent. I had not seen a bridge of such stature before nor a river so wide and shimmering as the Trent.

We strolled The Green which extended alongside the river to the lock gates, lock house and weir, with the wooded ramparts of East Bridgford and Kneeton blazing green beneath the blue sky.

Glancing across at the detached houses facing the river, I momentarily wished that I lived in one and was of course not to know that thirty years hence I would befriend someone there, who at the time of my first visit was teaching at the nearby village school.

We glimpsed swallows and house martins hawking for insects over the river then when we strolled back to Gunthorpe Bridge, Dad gave me some money and pointing to the white kiosk van told me to buy three ice-creams, which importantly I lost no time in doing.

While we licked our ice-cream cornets, the three of us sat. Dad in his quiet way then pointed out the channels that years of flooding and floodwater had gauged out of the opposite bank. It was cattle pasture. He told me to look longer. Eventually, a white object appeared above the bank and then disappeared. Seconds later another white object appeared. The raised and lowered heads of swans?

'There's a pair of swans feeding along those channels, probably with cygnets following them,' said Dad.

Tucking into his ice-cream, Ronald seemed less interested. And so we sat for long after we had finished our ice-creams. Dad was probably tired after a full week's working and evening Home Guard meetings, because that afternoon and until the next bus to Nottingham arrived he just wanted to sit. Whether he was thinking something out, a problem at work, a strained relationship - perhaps with my mother, Betty's then considered underage relationship with Bernard, I have no idea. Contentedly he gazed across the river and into the green hazed distance.

In retrospect, he could have lapsed into a meditative state much as I have done when sitting in the glade of an English covert or beside certain sequestered lochs in south-west Scotland. And most certainly after I had chewed on flapjack while wedging myself into a fissure within yards of the Cairngorms summit. Here in this often considered "stoniest place in Europe", I sat in meditation as I have never done before. Therefore it would not be unreasonable to suggest that Dad was similarly meditating by the Gunthorpe riverside.

When an hour or so later we stepped off the bus at Middleton Boulevard, Dad looked over the canal bridge and saw four or five cygnets, by then long necked and brown feathered, feeding on the duckweed.

'Let's go and have a look,' he said and swung open the grey gate that took one down the ramp and onto the towpath.

Solo the cygnet was obviously reunited with his or her family. The cygnets fed on the duckweed with black bills lowered to the water surface and making a slapping sound. At intervals, one or two would lift their heads and raise their chins.

'They look as if they're talking, Dad,' I ventured.

'Well yes Little Man, I suppose swans must have a language of their own much like most other birds and animals.'

When we arrived home Ronald thanked Dad for taking him to Gunthorpe then crossed the road to the Pearce family's front gate, while I made ready to tell Aunty about the cygnets having returned to the canal pound on which we first saw them.

Each morning after breakfast, I went with Scamp down to the fowl pen to collect the three or four eggs, warm, nestling in hay and often brown shelled.

When our eight or nine chicks had reached the pullet stage of their lives their feathers turned white, except for the tail which was black. They had also black flecks and dashes on the upper neck. Dad then told me that the hens were of a strain known as Light Sussex.

An addition to our Friday morning shopping list, which usually included visits to the cobbler on Hartley Road after which Mum bought my comics, was two tightly packed cartons of Karswood Poultry Spice. It was apparently a specialised diet which needed mixing with the existing food. The bags were stiff papered, the seal always flattened tight, the words clearly printed along with the instructions in dark red.

All this in order to get a regular intake of fresh eggs, I quietly mused.

Some evenings, often overcast and with the dusk filtering in at the onset of autumn, I would stand beside Dad's vice in the garden shed and watch him crunching up dried bread crusts and egg shells, which the following day one of us fed to the hens.

When I asked Dad if he knew why white hens laid brown eggs and brown hens frequently laid pale shelled eggs, Dad told me that he didn't know but emphasised that it was a fair question anyway.

The shed sometimes smelt fusty - high, and Dad said that he thought it may have been due to mice. He showed me two traps baited with cheese but, so far as I'm aware, the baits were never taken.

Then along with the weekly packages of Karswood Poultry Spice, Mum collected a weekly magazine called *Poultry World.* After reading my comics, I would flip through the pages and study photographs of the different varieties of hens and ducks while attempting to read and pronounce their names. On at least two Saturday mornings, Dad took me on a single-decker Barton bus out to such South Nottinghamshire villages as Cotgrave, Colston Bassett or Car Colston.

Here on farms or in village cottages lived one or two of his work colleagues. These knowledgeable countrymen then took us through their stockyards or gardens to the fowl pen and shed where Dad, on each occasion, was given or purchased a hen.

The ones that had been recommended to him were called Buff Orpingtons which were known to mix well with Light Sussex.

Dad carried one hen packaged with its wings held fast by sacking and twine, close to the body and the legs put through holes in the sacking, and I carried the other.

We timed it so that we would be at the bus stop in good time for the return journey and travelled sitting side by side, each with a hen on our knee.

Some passengers smiled. The majority spoke or acknowledged. The hens sat immobile, their red combs back-lit by the sun and only the occasional blink of a hazel eye betrayed the fact that they were alive.

When we arrived at the market where Dad had purchased the chicks, we had then to catch a second bus. A jerking, purring tram-type trolley bus which was usually packed, although we managed to get a seat and alighted at the terminus. But we were still not home, for we had then to walk through Radford Woodhouse and when I stopped to adjust my feathered load Dad merely smiled and said he could carry one hen under each arm for the rest of the way, a suggestion to which I offered no protest.

According to Dad, when we stood again crunching and mincing toast crusts and eggshells in the garden shed, the Buff Orpingtons had settled in well and it was from him, his colleagues and the *Poultry World* magazine that I picked up the term "point of lay," although I had never the occasion to use it.

Our next door but one neighbours, Mr. and Mrs. Bishop, adopted a pair of ducks. A duck and drake. Brown feathered and known as Khaki Campbells. From Mum's bedroom window I watched one afternoon the drake following the duck round and round a galvanised bath filled with water. Fascinated, because the drake literally dogged the duck's steps, I wondered why.

'Why doesn't he just go off and do something on his own?' I asked Mum who, smiling widely, admitted that she didn't know.

Then one afternoon Mum gestured towards the dining table on which a pale green egg rested on a blue napkin. 'Mr. and Mrs. Bishop have sent you a duck egg for your tea,' she announced.

I had the egg boiled and supported in a blue egg cup. The yolk was a deeper, richer yellow than that expected of the average hen's egg. I ate the duck egg with two rounds of bread and butter. It was as it appeared at first glance; delicious.

On 13th August 1942, General Bernard Montgomery took command of the

British 8ᵗʰ Army in North Africa.

Six days later, British troops and Canadians journeyed into north-east France and laid siege to the important port of Dieppe. The siege, however, was thwarted and by the following day considered "an operational blunder". Many troops were taken prisoner, wounded or killed. The Canadian casualties numbered some 3,370 men.

August 30ᵗʰ saw Field Marshall Erwin Rommel striving to break the British 8ᵗʰ Army's position at El Alamein. Egypt was again the prime target and in the ensuing Battle of Alam Halfa the 8ᵗʰ Army proved themselves superior. By September 2ⁿᵈ Rommel's troops were no longer advancing. The British and American tanks were considered superior to those used by the Germans, even though anti-aircraft guns and anti-tank guns were used by the Germans in the historical bid to halt Montgomery's advance.

Erwin Rommel was still mentioned by everyone involved in the North African offensives. He was considered an expert in tank and armour warfare. The 88 mm anti-tank guns he used against his British and American adversaries were cursed and feared. And Rommel's legendary title of 'Desert Fox' still held fast.

***

In the early mornings as I became used to seeing groups of people, women mostly, walking the pavements of Chalfont Drive, Mum told me that they were clerks and administrative staff employed at the Ministry Buildings, newly opened but with gated entrances, at the top of the drive where my cousin Peggy and I had seen the trees being felled the previous summer.

They arrived by a double-decker bus, a number 53, which ran the length of the Clifton, Middleton and Western Boulevard circuits.

Just after five the groups retraced their steps to the 53 bus stops, one of which had been installed at the bottom of Chalfont Drive close to where the New Aspley Gardens began.

'We are getting quite modern, aren't we? *Two* buses running along the Boulevard now,' Aunty observed.

In the early afternoons if we weren't going out I became aware of the weekly post bags, the intake of brown envelopes that were stacked on the darkly varnished hall stand which was two-tiered and easy to manoeuvre because it was fitted with castors. Inside most of the envelopes were folded instructions relating to the different situations a family might find themselves facing according to the national and localised conditions of war.

Some of the words and sentences I attempted to break down as I read them - *No-ti-fi-cation of In-juries*, or '*De-pen-dants of Men In the Services*, neither of which meant anything to me even though I mastered the sentences.

There was also a drawing depicting stirrup pumps and hoses, sandbags and buckets stacked on a shelf. It was worded THE GOOD CITIZEN.

Aunty then explained that it had to do with everyone knowing what to do if their house or neighbour's home was set on fire or bombed.

Early one afternoon when Aunty and Mum were as usual in the kitchen washing the pots together, a sudden clattering of the letterbox enticed me into the hall. On the lino, to my delight, was a book, poorly printed perhaps and disappointingly with no pictures, although there were signs and figures which I didn't understand.

Dutifully I took the book into the kitchen, while asking, 'What is it, Mum? What is it, Aunty?'

'Oh, it's only Old Moore's Almanac,' Aunty replied.

'Was that Old Moore who's just posted it through the letterbox? I asked.

'No it's just some delivery person going from door-to-door.'

'But what are all the strange figures and signs in the book for?'

'Oh, they're the signs of the zodiac.'

'What's a zodiac?'

'Oh, you'll learn when you get older,' said Mum, turning from the sink dishes and tea towel in hand, using a gentle yet affirming tone that indicated the end of yet another one of my questions and answer sessions.

I loved the gamey smell of rabbit even when one such animal was dead, destined for a pie and being handed to Mum or Aunty by the rabbit-catcher.

On one occasion the rabbit-catcher held me spellbound when he asked Mum if she had heard or read in the newspaper about the London family who lost everything in the Blitz and over a period of weeks walked from and through London, Hertfordshire, Bedfordshire and Northamptonshire to their relatives in Leicester. So far as I could ascertain the family comprised of the married couple, three children normally attending school, and a baby in a pram.

They left their home when the air raid sirens sounded and went to the communal air raid shelter. They knew the bombs had struck close because the ground trembled as if in the throes of an earthquake. When they emerged at the "all-clear", they saw through the smoke-screened rubble a gap where their house had stood.

All their possession were burnt or entombed due to the explosion. They had no money, only the clothes they stood up in and the pram which they had taken and left outside the air raid shelter. Relying then upon the kindness of strangers, they began their walk to Leicester where they were at least assured of a welcome because their relatives had already offered to take them in if they were bombed out of their home.

In retrospect, I would think that these determined folk were not the only family on the roads. There were probably others journeying to outlying areas from Coventry, Norwich, Birmingham and possibly every city that had been blitzed in both Great Britain and Germany.

On a breezy autumn Sunday morning in late September, Dad and I walked Woodyard Lane along which I stopped now and again to pick up the acorns that had been felled by the night wind.

In the ditch, against the stands of hawthorn and banks of ground ivy to our right, stood a gaggle of geese. They were alert. Ready to waddle back to the field in front of Heap's canalside farm. But I moved in close enough to see that the solid chested gander had blue eyes.

As I pointed out the gander's eyes to Dad, I realised the canal bridge was up ahead, ran to it and hauled myself, legs swinging and resting on my elbows up the bricked parapet.

On the round pound below the bridge sailed a lone cygnet. Solo? I urged Dad forward.

The cygnet drifted in arch winged display towards the bridge, its furled neck shaped like a letter S, its black bill and eye gleaming in the sunlight, black paddles almost caressing the harvest of aquatic weed over which it sailed.

The cygnet's plumage was the same fawnish brown as that of a Khaki Campbell duck. The front of its neck was pale grey and layers of white feathers were lifted by the continuing breeze.

It was then that I saw the connection between a cygnet, or swan, and a boat or ship.

'But where are the *others*, Dad?' I queried.

Dad told me that some swan pairs keep their cygnets with them right through the winter, whilst others fly to other stretches of water with their broods at the onset of the autumn. That way they can disperse their offspring and keep them free of the swan's breeding territory.

Solo's parents had flown, probably with all seven cygnets originally, but the homing instinct was strong within Solo and she (for Aunty had decided that the lone cygnet was a female) had returned but settled on a higher stretch of the breeding territory to that in which she had spent the summer.

Our intention that Sunday morning was to look over the Wollaton Park wall at the newly established prisoner-of-war camp which was taking in and rehabilitating a large number of Italian and German prisoners.

Not surprisingly perhaps, I told Aunty about Solo's arch winged splendour as soon as Dad and I arrived home to a Gracie Fields radio show background and Mum preparing dinner.

Then about an hour before tea one dusky midweek afternoon, Aunty took me in hand as usual while explaining that she had gathered together some bread crusts which she was going to feed to Solo. Between that and my last visit Solo had again flown. We came upon her on the penultimate canal pound to the Woodyard Lane bridge. Arch winged and hissing with bill agape, the cygnet surged towards us then snatched from the water surface the bread crusts thrown by Aunty. Suddenly, and for me alarmingly, Solo then stood in the shallows and took the bread from between Aunty's fingers. Solo was, I discovered, a little taller than me. We were almost beak to face. Pointing to Solo's neck, Aunty showed me the nodules of bread which were outlined and travelling slowly down Solo's gullet. I stood fascinated before noticing that Solo had a slight cut on the left-hand paddle, as if while sailing with the cygnet brood she had snagged the paddle on a coil of submerged barbed wire. Aunty said we would use that as a recognition factor for when hopefully in the future we would see Solo amongst other swans.

At intervals Solo gave out a sound that would best be described as between a rasping whistle and a grunt. She also lifted her chin repeatedly, as I had seen the cygnet group doing six or seven weeks earlier.

'She's talking, Aunty.'

'Yes, like Oliver Twist she is asking for more.'

Later on another afternoon I went with Aunty across the Boulevard to a newly opened grocers and off-licence, called Burleys. Aunty and I had again been reading *The Ugly Duckling*. Consequently, swans, reed beds and wild tracts of water were on my mind as Aunty purchased a tin of pilchards.

As we walked home beneath a metallic grey sky, I imagined the houses were mountains of red rock and that the Boulevard, although tree-lined, was a natural waterway which no man or woman had explored. It was a wilderness place, about which I would tell no one. And no one could penetrate it because it existed only in my mind.

Then I suddenly wanted to know how one opened a tin of pilchards.

'With this,' said Aunty, pointing to the key fastened to the side.

Satisfied I then asked her where we were going the following day.

'I don't know yet. It depends on the weather. See - it's going to rain. But we'll just get home in time,' Aunty smiled reassuringly.

Because the autumn was in Dad wanted to dig over the garden plots on Saturday and Sunday mornings. Betty therefore offered to take me to Wollaton Park. On that particularly bright and frosty morning, she suggested that we walked a good length of Middleton Boulevard and entered the park by the formal Lime Avenue entrance.

We saw no one. There existed a great sense of peace, yet the leaves were drifting - drifting without really making a sound.

Eventually over to our left against the distant background of Arbour Wood, red deer came into view. Hinds in silhouette. And then a stag with wide spreading antlers, pronounced shoulders and tucked in rear quarters appeared. Using the horizon, he trotted one way and another, pausing at intervals to roar, head lifted and antlers aligned with his back. Time and time again the stag roared, but that morning there were no challengers

I asked Betty then if the four rows of lime trees that towered above and extended the length of the avenue had been planted by people, although when I said people I had men in mind.

'Yes, I expect so,' answered Betty, but she could tell me nothing more.

Despite our girl cousins spending the afternoon with us, the freshness of the morning, the splendour of the roaring stag and the monumental atmosphere created by the limes remained with me.

When after tea the time came for the usual goodbyes, Rene, Alice and, *I think,* Peggy instead of saying as usual, 'We'll see you next weekend or the one after,' to my surprise said, 'We'll see you when we see you then, good people.'

Then Dad and Aunty joined Mum, Betty and me in the hall and although we were not a hugging and kissing family, I sensed a sadness and saw tears in the eyes of one or two of our cousins.

They waved. We waved. I glanced up at Mum and saw that her eyes were brimming.

When they had left the family went their separate ways, Aunty to put on her Nelson Eddy and Jeanette McDonald records, Mum to finish off a few pots in the kitchen.

I followed her in.

'Mum, aren't Sylvia, Rene, Alice and Peggy coming again?' I piped.

Without looking at me, Mum answered, 'Oh, they'll be coming again. But.

'

'Yes, Mum?'

'Separately perhaps. Or with Sylvia. Sylvia will be coming as usual because she's the youngest. She's not much older than Betty.'

'But ... ?'

'Well, Rene, Alice and Peggy are older than Sylvia and — '

'Yes?'

'They're going into the war. Into the forces.'

'When?' I asked, startled as a portrait of Adolph Hitler flooded into my mind.

'Next week,' Mum answered with her usual clipped tone indicating finality.

CHAPTER 20

Since March 1941, weapons and sophisticated equipment had been transported from America to Great Britain in accordance with the Lend-Lease Act. The Soviet Union was included into this Act when America decided to fight alongside the British. For the next two or three years military equipment and civil aids were transported continually, until eventually 2,000 divisions of infantrymen were equipped. Victory in Europe then seemed to be based on the size and continuing wealth of the American economy.

In 1942, the first four engine bomber aircraft were rolled onto the British airfield runways. These were fitted with radio and navigation equipment, the like of which had not been used before.

Under Bomber Command's Air Chief Marshall, Sir Arthur Harris, these Avro Lancaster, Halifax and Short Stirling aircraft were selected to bomb the German cities in which war equipment and munitions were being manufactured.

Besides equipment, America again came to the fore when over a three-year period one million or so American troops were assigned to Britain either to serve on the Bomber Command bases or be stationed at the British controlled bases in Europe. Thus some stayed, others were transported and if fortunate brought back. Because their equipment was stamped G.I. indicating General issue, that is the name they soon came to be known by.

They were much better paid thaN the average British soldier or "Tommy", were exuberant, nurtured attractive accents and gained access to the PX store nylon stocking market. They were also generous with their cigarettes, and could afford to be. Consequently, they were popular with the women of Great Britain but only tolerated by the men.

The Luftwaffe bombing raids continued across Britain and on the 3rd October in Sussex twenty-six schoolchildren were buried in a communal grave after German pilots allegedly targeted not only a village but its school. In Libya and Egypt in the same month, many German and Italian infantrymen were captured by the British.

On November 4th, the British succeeded in forcing Erwin Rommel's troops and tanks west across the desert.

A week later the Germans had occupied Vichy in France. On the 13th, with Rommel's army still in retreat, the British 8th Army re-entered the port of Tobruk.

***

The threat of an air raid or not, I still loved wearing a warm overcoat and being taken by Mum and Aunty in the early evening darkness to the cinema. Retracing our steps through the city connecting streets of Hyson Green, we followed the cinema usherette's torch down the aisle to three appropriate seats positioned like varnished surface islands within an ocean of black outlined living bodies. The cinema was packed. The film was *The Adventures of Robin Hood* starring Errol Flynn, Olivia De Havilland and Basil Rathbone, whose name, once I had heard mention of it, I could not free from my mind. The film was made the year I was born, Mum had explained earlier, and again I experienced a slight shock at the thought of the world having started without me.

Apart from *Bambi* and the usual newsreel accompanying cartoons like Mickey Mouse and Donald Duck, I had not seen a Technicolor film, even less a dashing, swashbuckling adventure film like *The Adventures of Robin Hood.* I relived every second, every scene, from the fight with pikestaffs on the plank bridge between Robin and the Sheriff of Nottingham, or Errol Flynn and Basil Rathbone. If I hadn't been separated from him by a screen, he was a man I could have rightly been afraid of and I was thankful that he was an actor and not a Nazi officer descending upon the district around which we lived.

In retrospect, the role of the Sheriff of Nottingham was surely the one which proved to have been the pinnacle of Rathbone's long career.

The villains, King John and the Sheriff of Nottingham, I truly disliked as I was meant to. But fearless, almost taunting Robin Hood I, like every boy, saw myself as being if I had lived in those times.

I noticed that both the villains ate their meals, and in particular the mouth-watering venison sausages, without using a knife and fork. I noticed too how they used their voices to portray power, which included ordering the men at arms to escort Maid Marian to the dungeon.

But until that time I had never been captivated by a scene so vivid, so magnificently staged and directed, as the staircase sword fight between "bold Robin" and his arch enemy.

The scene repeated itself within my mind on the trance-like walk home, not that Aunty and Mum escaped my customary questions and answer session. Where *was* Sherwood Forest? How far away? Could we go there tomorrow? And where was Nottingham Castle?

Mum explained that, yes, there was a castle in Nottingham but it was nothing like the one in which the Errol Flynn epic had been filmed. (The staircase and many other scenes were, I believe, filmed at the still splendid Warwick Castle). The present Nottingham castle was *and is* disappointing, to say the least. But the rock on which the castle had been built, that was something quite different and, yes, they would take me one day.

The following day when Mum's shopping expedition permitted, I knocked on the Pearce's front door and presenting two bamboo canes asked if Ronald could come out to play.

The bamboo canes, borrowed from Dad's woodshed, were of course our swords and in the ensuing fight from the Pearce's front gate, across Chalfont Drive and to our lattice gates from beneath which Scamp growled and barked excitedly, I portrayed Robin Hood. Fence with those bamboo canes though we did, I was disappointed because our "battle" was staged on flat ground. There was no magnificent staircase. the only staircase that I knew was out of bounds and within the fifteenth century confines of Wollaton Hall.

The following Saturday at breakfast, Betty came downstairs in her blue dressing gown. Beneath her arm she carried the film book version of *The Adventures of Robin Hood.* No it was *not* for me! It was *hers*! Yes, I could look at it but after my bacon, egg and fried bread breakfast when I had washed my hands.

The book was illustrated with stills from the film, one half or full plate still to each page. I studied them, as I did many times after, and the different expressions used by Errol Flynn. At all times such expressions interpreted optimism, bravery, perhaps here and there even a touch of foolhardiness. And certainly mischief.

The illustrations again afforded me the opportunity to study the interior of a motte and bailey castle. The costumes were worn by kings, outlaws and serfs. The sturdiness of "the green wood" oaks.

One picture depicted a grinning Robin Hood standing before the dining table of King John and the Sheriff of Nottingham with a deer strung across his shoulders.

Rightly or wrongly, I gleaned from both the film and book an overall mind picture of leaf canopies, sturdy oaks, endless sunlit glades and herds of red deer such as roamed at will in nearby Wollaton Park. The stag on Robin Hood or Errol Flynn's shoulder, however, was of a different species. It carried antlers but its muzzle was snub and its forelegs and belly were off-white. Dad explained that this was probably a fallow buck, the other type of deer that roamed at will in Wollaton Park, and indeed many an English tract of forest, but which always trotted away when they realised humans were approaching.

'But it's clever of you to have noticed, Little Man,' Dad murmured while smiling directly into my eyes.

As Christmas approached, Ronald and I, well out of guardian and parental earshot, discussed the possibility or not of there being a Santa Clause. We decided there was not. *Couldn't be.* He'd be covered in soot if he came down our chimney and a great many others. So who fills our stockings and pillow cases with presents then? One's Mum and Dad. It just has to be. But why at this time of the year? Because it's Christmas we concluded.

To break the monotony of books as presents, but for which I was always grateful, someone stowed packets of sweets into my pillowcase and a small hound dog with body segments connected to hidden strings. It was called Wackeroo and I was shown how to press the underside of the toy which resulted in the hound moving its head, bending its legs and supposedly wagging its tail - all at the same time. Dad I noticed, to my secret amusement, was quite taken with it.

Mrs. Teather came as usual on Christmas Eve bringing two books for me and our girl cousins came on Christmas day having, I think, completed their training sessions at various camps.

In the evening around the front room fireside, cracking nuts, eating figs and dates, the girls compared the necklaces and wristwatches they had been bought.

'You youngsters today don't know you are born! All I used to get in my stocking was a threepenny piece, an orange and a pink sugar pig. And that was it!' smiled Mum.

I was too full of the extra large Christmas meals to want nuts and figs. Consequently, my hands were clean and Betty again allowed me to look at her *Filmgoer* and *Silver Screen* annuals. From these I learned that new cowboys were emerging from the Hollywood scene; Tim Holt was one, Charles Starrett another, and William Boyd, who played Hopalong Cassidy, another.

He had white hair, William Boyd. He was also photographed with his pure white horse Silver rearing into the air and pawing space. Yet William Boyd smiled for the camera and held his hat in one hand, and so I decided that riding a horse would be easy. If Gene Autrey and William Boyd could do it, then so could I! And look at Dad! He had broken in horses and ponies from somewhere that grown-ups called "the wild". Unlike Dad, however, I would wear a Stetson, cowboy outfit and six guns. Moreover, like Gene Autrey I would sing.

Pouring over Betty's film annuals, which smelt deliciously of new print, I decided there and then that I would become a Hollywood cowboy. But I would tell no one as yet. Not even my evacuee friend, Ronald.

The Hollywood West aside, those film annuals again fascinated me because they not only named the films of that year but also the actors and actresses. There was a full portrait study of one of Mum's favourite male actors called Frederic March. Another of a beautiful but seriously expressioned actress called Patricia Roc.

Film titles like *How Green was my Valley?* continued to interest me, as did *The Glass Key* and *This Gun for Hire* which starred Alan Ladd and Veronica Lake.

I couldn't for the life of me see why actors like Alan Ladd, Humphrey Bogart and James Cagney preferred roles in which they walked the streets and hotel rooms wearing suits, raincoats and trilbies pulled almost over one eye, when they could be riding horses, *galloping* and shooting. Perhaps there was some attraction about holding a long cigarette between the lips that I wasn't by then aware. Having your cigarette dangle sideways almost out of your jaws. And the raincoat pockets! Deep enough to hide a revolver, which they almost *always* did!

There were films that became cinema-going classics released around this time, not the least of which was Michael Curtiz's *Casablanca.* The male cast of Peter Lorre, Sidney Greenstreet and, of course, Humphrey Bogart, a boy named Brian and I did our utmost to impersonate months later whenever we met in the school playground.

Bogart's co-star, Ingrid Bergman, had to my mind the face of all faces. The face, I decided, of a goddess.

Dad also had his favourite films and filmstars, the latter being just one that I can recall - Gary Cooper, and if he discovered that a Jack London novel or Alexander Korda script was being filmed, then Dad lost no time in going to see it. Ernest Hemingway he occasionally mentioned with the exuberance one would use if attempting to describe a literary god, which is why Dad, Mum and I hurried to an early evening showing of *For Whom the Bell Tolls* at the Forum one starlit Saturday. Not surprisingly for one so young, I could not understand the story and had never heard of the Spanish Civil War. There was, however, much horse-riding, shooting and outdoor scenery to keep me occupied. It was, Betty assured me over breakfast the next morning, 'a very serious film'.

Another film that to my eyes appeared "very serious" was *Lassie Come Home*, which one overcast afternoon Aunty took me to see. This was, of course, filmed in Scotland which I had only a notion of by studying the landscaped sketches backing the stag portrait on the blue exercise book back home.

I had not seen mountains or heather, water cascading unevenly over naturally evolved rocks. The grey stoned villages. Lonely roads. Wide lochs. So immersed in this film did I become that I almost cried when the road mender picked up his dead terrier from the laneside and felt warm tears brimming when Lassie the collie (which was actually Pal, a male dog) was seen to be walking with paws bloodying the ground and rocks on "her" long homeward trek.

Facing the glare of headlights and the rush and breaking of traffic on the late afternoon walk home, I was almost overcome with anxiety when I realised that Scamp could also become separated from us in that way. But what chance would

he have with traffic increasing at a rate that Mum and Aunty's generation had never before experienced?

Scamp still waited at the bottom of the stairs for me every morning and his tail wagging continued to thump the bottom of the stair panelling or brush my artistic attempt at a pig, which was still boldly displayed on the wallpaper. When Mum was putting my breakfast onto the table, I lowered onto all fours, Scamp rolled over onto his back and I tickled his tummy while he moved one leg in a circular motion, which to me suggested that he was thoroughly enjoying the sensation. Frequently I sniffed his tawny forepaws and inhaled through my nostrils their warm, almost sweet smell. I then felt the undersides of his paws; the hardening pads.

Perhaps because he was "teething" as Mum put it, Scamp occasionally chewed on a nodule of coal or coke and according to Mum this sometimes lodged in the back of

his throat. I had then to put one hand into Scamp's warm, watery mouth and feel with my knuckles his serrated gums or jaw-line. I then located the nodule, withdrew and threw it onto the fire.

As the moistened nodule hissed, Scamp rolled onto his tummy and looking at me wagged his tail he then nudged my arm and I would fondle his hound-like head until Mum told me to go upstairs and wash my hands before starting breakfast.

CHAPTER 21

1943. From January 14 -24, Prime-Minister Winston Churchill and U.S. President Franklin Roosevelt staged a conference in Casablanca, almost as a way of celebrating the German withdrawal from Morocco and the North African battlegrounds. At this conference they decided to invade Sicily in an attempt to emphasise the success of the Allies, again in North Africa. They also agreed to step up their combined bombings of Germany.

On January 18th the Luftwaffe returned and bombed London.

By the month end, at Stalingrad in the USSR, the Germany 6th Army, led by Friedrich von Paulus, surrendered to the Soviet armies which in a long affray captured or killed 200,000 German troops. With the Soviet armies experiencing several more outstanding victories, the Royal Air Force joined with the United States and the leading German cities were bombed, as agreed at Casablanca, on a daily and continual rate.

On March 28th the British 8th Army in North Africa successfully attacked the Italian and German operated Mareth Line.

April 4th was the all important day in which the combined air forces of Britain and the United States continually bombed and disrupted operations in the industrial districts of Ruhr, Germany.

***

Early one Monday afternoon when Mum and Aunty had done the washing then shopped at Hogg's the grocers, Mum announced that she was taking me to the pantomime. Staged at the Theatre Royal in the city centre, the performance of *Alice in Wonderland* was intended to be specifically for children. A matinée performance Mum emphasised, as we walked towards the traffic island and canal where we were to catch the bus. Suddenly two swans came flying from right to left and following the waterway towards the Trent flood-plain. They flew, one slightly ahead of the other. Necks outstretched; taut. Wings cleaving the air.

'Mum, look! Swans!' I yelled.

Against a build-up of cloud they appeared white which reverted to golden grey as they crossed a tapering path of watery sunlight.

'Yes, they're following the canal. When we lived near the boat builders we used to see them flying like those or hear their wings as they came over the house.'

'Was it the same canal, Mum?'

'Yes. We lived in a house on Claude Street when I was a girl, in the same direction the swan pair are flying.'

On the bus to the city I was still looking at the swans as they travelled the flight paths of my vivid imagination. I felt trapped, grounded. Having to comply with a timetable, whereas they were in every way free *and wild* so far as I was concerned.

I had not read Lewis Carroll's *Alice in Wonderland* and when as we walked between the ornate pillars of the Theatre Royal Mum told me there was "a sleepy dormouse" featured in the story, I replied, 'Oh good! I've never seen a dormouse.'

Suppressing a smile, Mum then explained, 'Well you won't today. It's not a real dormouse. It's somebody dressed up to *look* like a dormouse. There's a white rabbit too. But again, it's someone dressed up.'

'Why do people want to dress up to look like animals?'

'Because they're actors and actresses like you see in the films, except that those in our pantomime work from the stage.'

'Well, why do they want to do that then?'

'Oh sometimes they *have* to do it, because they want the money.'

'Do they get paid then, like Dad?'

'Oh yes. Nobody works for nothing,' Mum assured me.

The theatre was half full and lighter than the cinema.

Chewing the nougat toffees Mum bought at the foyer kiosk, I enjoyed the pantomime, particularly the ravings of the White Rabbit. Yet occasionally, the stage, the set, the entire pantomime, became overshadowed by my earlier vision of the swan pair in flight.

When we returned home, Aunty and Betty crowded around. Did I enjoy it? Were there many people in the audience? Did I want an *Alice in Wonderland* book?

I answered each question while Mum carried away our coats then barely able to contain myself, I blurted, 'And we saw two swans flying along the canal!'

'*You did?*' shrilled Betty.

'Yes. We were walking on the pavement and they were flying - flying.'

'Well there would be something wrong with you and your mother if you two suddenly started flying,' quipped Aunty, at which Betty giggled.

'I know but they don't have to go to the shops or do what they don't want to do,' I answered.

'I know, but they haven't got a house to live in, or books. And *they* never went to the pantomime, did they? Now let's see what we're having for tea,' Aunty answered whilst ruffling my hair.

For some unexplained reason, Mum decided that we should alight from the bus at Grassington Road, the stop before our normal stop, one morning when we were returning from our usual circular to Alfreton Road.

Perhaps she had heard that "The Man" was prowling the lonely tract of Western Boulevard between the usual bus stop and our home.

Alighting at this stop meant we had to walk by the extensive sports field of the Imperial Tobacco Company, or Player's Recreation Ground as it was locally known.

I liked to look across at the Tudoresque sports pavilion with its half timbered front, tennis courts and bowling greens. The cricket and football pitches were at the far end, or near end if one took into account our destination.

On these pitches a flock of gulls were foraging and among them stood a cygnet. Was it Solo flown over from the canal? And on seeing the white gulls, had she become visually disorientated and taken them for swans?

Mum, of course, couldn't tell me, although she assured me that a groundsman would probably come along, entice the cygnet over with bread, grab it, place it into a van and take it to the canal or river.

Even today, according to most bird recognition books, it is believed that a swan cannot take off unless it is on water. However, providing the wind is in a favourable direction and there is a long clear viewing field ahead, a swan can take off on land, and I am a first-hand witness to such events. It happens infrequently, but it can *and does* happen.

This cygnet then may eventually have left on its own accord but we did not see Solo on the canal again, at least not while she was a young bird.

As we accepted Gracie Fields' singing on the Sunday lunchtime wireless programme and Bing Crosby's show on later winter Saturday afternoons, so Mum and Aunty, the family's wireless enthusiasts, tuned in to Tommy Handley's ITMA or *It's That Man Again* each Saturday lunchtime.

Tommy Handley's was not a voice that I particularly liked. The radio script portrayed him as a non-stop talker and non-stop talkers I didn't like because they failed in giving one time to think.

The family laughed loudly at Handley's jokes but I didn't understand them and could not therefore join in. Another voice merged into the family scene around noon on Monday. It was the voice of Mr. Stevenson, the insurance man.

He arrived on a sit-up-and-beg bicycle, his insurance books stowed into the waterproof saddlebag. He wore a trilby, glasses and a long raincoat over his three-piece suit.

Being used to dogs he came to the lattice gates which Mum unbolted. He knew Scamp's name and called out to him the instant Scamp began uproariously barking, 'It's all right Scamp. It's only me lad. It's only me.'

On opening the gate and stepping into the yard then closing the gate behind him, Mr. Stevenson would find Scamp standing directly before him, grumbling by then and wagging his tail.

Once Mum had answered Mr. Stevenson's knock, our insurance books in hand, Scamp calmed and trotted to his favourite spot beneath the widespreading plum tree.

Mr. Stevenson had no script. His voice, like his manner, was slow, easy; enquiring. He and Mum commented on the war - the bombings mostly, both in this country and Germany.

Mum seemed to prefer visitors or callers on Mondays, including her friend Mrs. Doughty, and as the evenings drew out another Monday voice merged into the house-calling scene.

The voice was that of Mrs. Lowe who went from door to door selling National Savings stamps. As she did with the insurance man, Mum unbolted the lattice gates before Mrs. Lowe arrived and on the first visit told her what to say to Scamp and, more importantly, to continue talking to him as she inched tentatively through the lattice gate while looking into the bewhiskered and bark contorted face of the family's self-elected guardian.

Mrs. Lowe was always asked into the kitchen where Mum or Aunty were usually arranging the washing they had earlier taken from the garden strung line. She spoke clearly and cheerfully, seldom if ever mentioning the war - at least not in my presence.

Her hair was black and curly, her features small, her face pretty. She wore black rimmed glasses and a smart bluish-grey business suit. She also mentioned her daughter Barbara and one sunlit evening invited me to the house so that we could meet and talk.

The Lowes lived on the opposite side of Chalfont Drive to ourselves and closer to Cherry Orchard Lane, about which Barbara knew nothing and had never walked with a parent or relative.

In the Lowe's sunlit garden, backing onto the allotments, Barbara and I sat on the rockery and talked about nothing, yet about everything. Barbara's pale blonde hair, held to one side with white ribbon, was smooth and sheened with condition, her yellow dress the same colour as the light. She was a steady speaker who measured her words. Thought about what I had said before answering. Her eyes were narrowed by that same light, therefore I failed to become enmeshed as I had with Shirley. Yet I felt strangely and pleasurably empowered by her presence.

The routine walks to the shops with Mum, and on Monday both she and Aunty, were on two occasions dramatised by incidents concerning a carter's horse and a white paper bag.

On the first occasion, Mum and I were nearing the corner of the street on which Hoggs the grocer's was situated, our heads lowered due to the fierce gale that was seething through the streets, when a white paper bag drifted phantom-like against a stationary cart in the shafts of which stood a black cart horse. The carter wasundoubtedly in the opposite street corner café. Fortunately, we were walking uphill and the horse and cart were on the opposite side of the road and similarly facing uphill.

Although the horse was fitted with blinkers, it saw the white paper bag hovering into a portion of its vision, took fright and with the bag wind-lifted and hovering alongside, sprang forward dragging the empty cart behind it.

Startled Mum grabbed me by the collar and hurried to the grocer's door, while yelling, 'Come on, Keith!' as the horse lunged onto the pavement relatively close to us. A corner of the cart struck the red stone wall at which bricks, mortar and dust exploded in all directions.

Neighing in fright, the horse alerted the carters all of whom ran from the relative comforts of the café yelling, 'Runaway! Runaway!'

The horse and cart were heading straight for the busy crossroads of Radford Boulevard and Hartley Road, along which buses rattled and lorries were driven. Through Hoggs the grocer's glass door and in the sanctuary of the shop we watched as a man walking downhill sprang across Hartley Road and all but hurled himself at the head and muzzle of the horse, while no doubt speaking in soothing tones. By this time the cart was surrounded by excited carters, the stranger having averted a potential disaster in seemingly a matter of seconds.

With Mr. and Mrs. Hogg looking on, Mum pointed across at the wall — 'If someone had been walking or standing there, they'd have had their ribs crushed,' she emphasised.

The second incident occurred on a Monday afternoon when, for some forgotten reason, Aunty wasn't with us. With Mum carrying a basket, its handle tucked over her arm, we left Hoggs and turned downhill towards home. Several horses and carts were parked in line along the kerb to our right. Suddenly a bay horse, again fitted with blinkers and sporting a long white blaze, swung its head sideways and lifted the white bag filled with teacakes Mum had bought, clear of the basket and proceeded to eat them, paperbag, teacakes - the lot.

Mum swerved in a startled action while angrily resorting, 'Hey! *I'm* not buying teacakes to feed somebody's damned horse!'

Nevertheless, we did not return to Hoggs to buy more teacakes, our weekly ration or financial outlay probably having been used. But on future visits, Mum was careful how she packed the bags and baskets and in a gently authoritative way checked that Aunty arranged them likewise.

With so much happening on a Monday, one would think there was little time for adventure and exploration. Yet as the evenings grew noticeably longer, more people came into our lives; the Kittoe sisters and the Pearce sisters to be exact. They were joined by Ronald and came to call for me when they had a local walk or journey in mind. And these, it seems, were always planned for a Monday evening because on other evenings they had homework to do and attended Girl Guide meetings and events staged in the church hall.

The Kittoe sisters and Jill Pearce were, I think, junior schoolgirls, while Ronald, Shirley and I had yet to step inside a classroom. Nevertheless, mixed assembly though we were, we all shared the urge to discover something. See and find something different.

Our first Monday evening walk was a circular. We needed to know where the path from New Bridge led and discovered that as we walked with our backs to Radford Folly, Hoggs the grocer's and Hartley Road, that it was an allotment holder's path with periphery hedgerows fringed by a clear water stream. The path led us onto Ascot Road where we turned left onto Aspley Lane, then left again to walk the then familiar Grassington Road fringed by Lombardy poplars and the Imperial Tobacco Company Recreation ground, as I had done already several times.

On the walk the senior girls paused as we climbed the steps of New Bridge and turned in the direction of the city and the high rise blocked horizon where stood the Imperial Tobacco Company factories and offices.

'Goodness me! Can't you smell the tobacco from here? I bet all the houses smell of it around Churchfield Lane,' said Barbara, and her sister Vivienne agreed.

'*I'm* not going to smoke when I grow older. It smells horrible, tobacco,' Barbara continued.

I studied them. Vivienne always laughing, excitable, pale skinned, hair thick, auburn in the late autumn sunset and curling boyishly at her blouse collar. Usually wearing a navy raincoat, white ankle socks and black laced shoes, Vivienne was alert like her sister Barbara, but perhaps the quieter, slightly more studious of the two.

Barbara's hair was long, raven black and often tied or clasped at the nape. Her complexion was dark, compared to Vivienne's. Her eyebrows were black and doll-like, her nose straight, eyes blue and mouth generous. On our sometimes chilly Monday evening explorations, Barbara wore a blue overcoat.

By the allotment holder's path that first Monday, one or other of the sisters found a cluster of yellow petalled flowers.

'Coltsfoot!' she exclaimed.

They knelt to examine the minute yet vivid petals. Stroked them with their fingertips. Spoke in hushed tones as if they were discussing priceless gems.

On another Monday evening, at my suggestion perhaps, we walked the Boulevard to the canal bridge. But our senior leaders chose not to cut through Radford Woodhouse. The evening was overcast, which brought in the dusk. However, on the canal pound behind Jackie Matthews' farm we saw a swan pair sitting the darkened water surface.

On the next pound, perhaps two hundred yards long and straight, sailed a single swan.

'I've heard that one swan of a pair has been shot along here,' Vivienne told us.

Alarmed, I wondered if we would be seeing a cygnet brood later in the season.

Sometimes if we arrived back at Chalfront Drive and the light was still lingering, we played games suggested and supervised by the Kittoe sisters, like Dobbie or What time is it Mr. Wolf?

If the rain came before the darkness, such games were abandoned and quickly as we all hurried to our respective houses. I loved to think that I could reach the front porch before the rain came down heavily.

On the half field where each evening Dad took Scamp, who still continually sniffed out the hare trails. Vivienne found one Monday evening several small purple petalled flowers which she immediately recognised as violets.

They were clustered in the hedge bottom close to the single hedge gap oak. Delighted with Vivienne's find, I went up with Dad and Scamp the next evening to show him the violets and the following Sunday took Betty and Sylvia.

Then followed a lighter sunlit Monday evening when upon the utterance of a single word, Mum and our neighbours, the Bennetts and the Bishops, hurried down their garden paths, clothes baskets tucked into their hips, and began unpegging the washing.

That word, that name, was 'gypsies' who, Mum said, sometimes entered people's gardens and yards and stole the washing that had been left out overnight. Mrs. Lowe coming around with the National Savings stamps? Yes, she too had been told about the gypsies and has taken in her washing accordingly.

'They might come knocking on the doors tomorrow or the next day wanting you to buy clothes pegs. I shall set Scamp onto them if they do,' threatened Mum.

I remained calm, unperturbed, and although I had never seen a gypsy, I did not believe that they would steal washing off people's clothes lines one day and go to those same houses selling pegs with which to hang washing out on the line the next.

'Yes, let's go and look at the gypsies,' the Kittoe and Pearce sisters enthused, as with Ronald and me they turned from our front porch.

'Careful they don't kidnap these little lads,' Mum called out, at which all four girls assured her that neither Ronald nor I would be allowed out of their sight.

The black figurine dog did not sit outside his owner's gate in the evenings I observed, as chattering we made our way across the Boulevard and down to New Bridge.

The gypsies were camped to the right of the path that led directly to the embankment steps. We hurried by seeing several brightly coloured living wagons or "vardos", children swarthy but brightly clad carrying buckets from the clear water stream, piebald and skewbald horses, and a grey haired woman who stood smoking a pipe.

As we walked, rudely pointed and squealed with delight, several dogs appeared - "long dogs" and lurchers which were not known to any of us then. The dogs began barking. The children put down their buckets and stared at us until the pipe smoking woman called them into the encampment circle.

Were they *real* gypsy children or kidnapped children, we discussed excitedly amongst ourselves.

Despite the wind drifting tangs of tobacco, the Kittoe sisters led us up the steps which I was by then climbing three mornings a week. But on that single occasion, I decided that we were being led to safety.

From halfway up the steps, where the corner turned, we saw a centralised fire being lit by tweed-coated men who look weathered and had dark hair. Women came from the vans carrying cooking pots.

'They're going to make supper,' one or other of the senior girls announced.

I was much taken by the red and yellow scalloped artwork adorning the sides of the "vardos" and carts. One or two of the vardo windows blazed yellow, suggesting therefore that the vardos were lit at that time of the evening by oil lamps.

On the thickets by the stream and all along the post and rail fence bordering the busy railway line, rugs and much washing - brightly coloured sheets and blankets mainly, were spread out to dry.

So, I asked myself, why if the gypsies liked colours in the way they so obviously did, would they want to relieve all the local washing lines of starched white sheets and cream coloured blankets?

One gypsy boy, older and taller than Ronald and I, came running between the nettle beds and stems of burdock to look at us. His face was tanned, his hair thick, black and unruly. His eyes dark and enquiring.

The horses and ponies were each tethered to a long chain, fastened to a stake which had been hammered below ground level. They had thick manes and long yellow edged tails, suggesting that they inadvertently sprayed themselves with urine.

They were all brown skinned, these gypsies! All brown skinned and black haired. The women in particular wore colourful clothes and golden tinted flashing earrings.

The boy ran back. Or perhaps he was called back to collect his dish or plate in readiness for the communal meal.

Camping in the suburbs and on the edges of towns and cities as they did, bands of true Romany, such as we considered ourselves to be spying on that evening, must have seen the bombings, the Luftwaffe and subsequent desecration night after night after night. And, in retrospect, by camping near railway lines they were risking being bombed by a poorly aimed missile themselves.

When in the deepening dusk I arrived home, I told Mum that the gypsies wouldn't be wanting our sheets and blankets because they had plenty of their own. I also wondered what it would be like travelling in a coloured house on wheels.

The next morning Mum and I walked across the field to the shops. Women wearing shawls carried babies from one vardo to another. Men checked the ponies and horses, called the dogs to heel. In the centre of the encampment stood a canvas tent, the likes of which I had not seen. I looked for the woman who smoked a pipe, wanting to point her out to Mum who walked with her head lowered, thus giving me the impression that she wouldn't have looked anyway.

The dogs barked, wagged their tails. Several men wearing grey trousers, tweed jackets and cloth caps stepped from the edge of the stream.'They've been collecting watercress,' Mum told me.

The gypsies left just after daybreak on the Friday morning of that week.

With the usual shopping, my comics and two or three cartons of Karswood

Poultry Spice in mind, Mum and I crossed the field at our usual time.

Elderly men from the nearby houses strolled to the widespread piles of horse dung and shovelled it into sacks to use as fertilising manure on their garden plots and borders.

A few charred circles in the field grass were all that remained of the gypsy encampment. There was not a shred, not a glimmer, of domestic litter. A sense of routine disorientation accompanied me on my next exploration with the Kittoe and Pearce sisters because we went on a Sunday morning to find, and look across at, Bobbersmill.

To do this we had to climb the steps of a wooden railway bridge from where we looked down onto the swirling flow of the River Leen and the derelict mill, which we presumed had belonged to the Bobbers family and in my parents' time been used as a corn mill.

The mill was built as late as 1907 when the employees' cottages were registered locally as a "hamlet community". There was originally work there for 250 people. The corn threshing industry, however, was short-lived locally and the mill existed for little less than thirty years.

Dad and his twin brother, Albert, had explored it as boys when, like the derelict Radford Folly, the millpool was regarded as a local attraction. Mum had often told me that such places were overrun with rats and, as if to endorse her word, one such mammal worked its way through the reeds heedless of our yells and exclamations re-echoing from the bridge that morning. There was no doubt about the animal being a rat. It had a long hairless tail but never before or since have I seen a brown rat that was gingerish fawn in colour.

Seeing the rat was the pinnacle of that particular foray and when I entered the house after leaving the Kittoe and Pearce sisters, those were the first words I used with which to greet the family —

'We've seen a *rat!*'

I was with the Kittoes on another overcast evening when in the hedgerow on the far side of the Half Field and where the single oak presided in late foliaged splendour, Vivienne fell to her knees as she exclaimed, '*Oh look!* Violets!'

Encircling the minute purple petals with her long white fingers, Vivienne spoke again as if they were priceless gems. Fascinated, I stood watching the violet clusters and long grasses swaying in the wind.

We left the violets and both Vivienne and Barbara said they would check on their progress every few days.

The following Monday, Ronald and I went with the four girls to see them and again the wind swayed the grasses and branches of the by now familiar hedgerow that struck inwards from the ditch side of Cherry Orchard Lane.

Stepping around the violet clusters, Vivienne surveyed the long arable field, then yelled, 'Quick! Run! It's The Man'

Always able to resist the temptation to look back, I did exactly as I was told. *I ran.* Vivienne, Barbara and Jill raced beside Shirley, Ronald and me then ahead of us, while yelling our names and urging, 'Run! Run!'

We followed the hare paths threading through the dense tussocks towards the four detached houses positioned offside to Colliers Pad and Three Nail Tree.

I brushed by clumps of nettle, stands of thistle and dock. One of the girls half turned, squealed, 'Come *on* boys! *Run!'*

153

It seemed incredible that the legendary Man, about whom I had heard mentioned since I was lowered from the pram, was now actually behind us. Running. *Chasing us!* I heard the crash of vegetation. His heavy booted rhythm closing in. *Closing in!* Then his strangely guttural voice half said and half gasped, 'Come here little blond 'n. *I* want you.'

Ronald was the darker blond of we two small racing boys. The Man was focused upon *me!*

His voice spurred me on. I hadn't known that I could run before that evening. Hadn't *needed* to run before that evening.

I could hear The Man's uneven breathing. Then he was gasping, 'Sod it! Sod it! Bastard! Bastard!'

And still without turning I knew instinctively that I was free. Still I ran.

The girls, who *were* looking back, spilled across the road to the gate of the first house situated within twelve strides of Three Nail Tree. We could seek shelter there if need be.

There was no question, however, of anyone telephoning the police, simply because the house that had a telephone connected was throughout working-class Great Britain the exception rather than the rule. But we could at least knock on the house-holder's door. Or alternatively, if we chose not to swing left down to my parents' home situated about one hundred yards away and risk being cut off by our gasping assailant, we could have crossed the Humps and Hollows Field then connected with Beechdale Road and described a complete circle.

At the low wall in front of the house the girls turned, Ronald and I with them.

The Man, tall, square shouldered, wearing a cloth cap and long black overcoat, stood shaking his fist.

'Go away and leave people alone!' yelled Jill or Vivienne.

Pointing to Vivienne and her sister Barbara, The Man bellowed, 'YOU TWO! I'M AFTER YOU TWO NOW! AND I'LL SHOW YOU GOOD AND PROPER WHEN I CATCH YOU!'

Panting, I turned to Ronald, 'What do you think he'd do if he caught us, Ronald?' I asked.

'I dunno. Thump us, I expect,' shrugged Ronald.

Led again by the girls but at the same time watching The Man retrace his steps towards the oak, we made our way to my parents' house.

'We've all been chased by The Man,' one of the senior girls told Mum.

'What?! Where is he? Where is he!' blazed Mum.

'Oh, he's gone now,' we told her.

'I'll put Scamp onto him if I see him,' Mum continued, then overcoming her surprise advised, 'You'll have to be careful where you go in the future. Stay away from Cherry Orchard Lane and the fields for a bit.'

Within a matter of days the threat of The Man was lessened considerably and the following Monday the two sets of sisters and Ronald called for me as usual.

The Man, however, was still on the prowl. Over the next fifteen years I came across him face-to-face three times. He continued to terrorise the occasional woman foolhardy enough to cycle along Cherry Orchard Lane and was thought responsible for the bizarre death of a teenager.

Wearing always the same clothes and striking from ambush, The Man cunningly allowed time to pass between his assaults and incidents.

Descriptions were issued to the police, but The Man was never caught.

CHAPTER 22

May 16th 1943. A squadron of British bombers carrying bouncing bombs designed by Barnes Wallis, a British aeronautical engineer, breached two of the three Ruhr dams targeted in the Operation Chastise exercise.

By July most of the German troops were engaged in warfare around Kursk in the USSR. Here the deadliest tank battle scored a high placing in the annals of world war history, thus severely weakening German defensives along the Eastern Front.

On 10th July combined units of the British and United States Forces landed on Sicily which was occupied by the Germans.

By 3rd September the Allied Forces (British and United States) arrived unchallenged in Italy. The leader of the "new" Italian government, Marshal Pietro Badoglio, who had succeeded the deposed Benito Mussolini, signed an armistice with the Allies.

***

Dad assured me as we walked behind the unsightly gasometer on Triumph Road one warm Saturday evening that he would take Mum and I home along the canal towpath. My parents were out for a walk and an early evening drink. Children were not allowed in pubs, which meant that when Dad came out of The Rose and Crown carrying a tray of drinks the three of us had no choice but to sit at a forecourt table. Not that I minded, because as we crossed the bridge over the lower district meanders of the River Leen, house martins and swallows hawked colourfully for insects between the willow bowered banks. Blackbirds fluted. Here and there between the houses and yards I glimpsed white and creamish swathes of apple and pear blossom.

The lemonade sparkling in the glass Dad handed to me pleasantly made my nostrils tingle. Just one glass, Mum had told me, or I would be going to and fro all night.

When we left the pub and walked towards what previously had been the formal entrance to Wollaton Park, I was suddenly and pleasantly aware of a lock gate beyond which stretched a long tract of reed fringed canal.

'Here we are then. Along here, Little Man,' Dad softly indicated.

I followed him through a set of ornate gates that led on to the canal towpath. On our left was the high wall of red brick that had once served as the south-eastern boundary of Wollaton Park. The height of the wall became extended by the lime and Lombardy poplar trees that had been planted along the length. On the other side of the wall was now a recreation ground and an estate of bungalows.

The reeds either side of the canal were so high, thick and extensive that I could not see over them, only peep occasionally at the water between.

The waterway was secretive. The reeds intriguing. And that stretch of towpath remote and seemingly cut off from the present to the extent that when walking it regularly in future years I never seeing anyone along it. The diaries that I maintained throughout my youth also confirm this.

At intervals we heard the "crook" or "carr-uck" calls of a moorhen. Then when we ascended a steep section of the path that accompanied the next set of lock gates onto a higher stretch of what was once known as The Wollaton Flight, the reed jungles deepened, the tree foliage darkened into a dusk haze of green and the stillness made me feel like an impostor.

Ahead of us, Dad put up a finger, turned and pointed to the reeds. It was then I heard it; something nibbling.

'Water vole!' Dad exclaimed by shaping his mouth.

Moorhens continued to call. We heard the "ee-sp" of newly hatched moorhen chicks. The strange and nasal croaking of frogs. Occasionally, a moorhen startled me as it crashed through the reed stems.

Presently we came to a place where barges had once been loaded and unloaded. A wharf, its twelve or fifteen feet high wall built from local stone. The wharf had been designed in the manner of a recess and there were steel rings fitted into the wall to which the narrowboats and barges had been moored so that the cargoes of coal or night soil could be loaded and unloaded by a crane and jib.

But neither the wharf or recess had been used for many years. Both were unreachable unless, as in the past, one was travelling by boat. Consequently, a great mass of green reeds had sprung up in the recess and it was in that direction that Dad again pointed.

The swan pair had built a nest, a large and high island of reed stems and aquatic weed against the wall. One swan incubated an egg clutch. Facing us she hissed with orange bill agape, her head turning from side to side. Before her in a reedy channel leading directly to the nest her mate was anchored and dozed with head slightly lowered.

Dad's smile widened, probably like my own, and in retrospect he was probably back at Farrands Dam in the days of his boyhood and looking at the swan pair nesting by the mill wall there.

I then followed his gaze to the top of the wall on which a young man sat in silhouette.

'How long will they be sitting?' Dad shouted across to him.

'Six weeks,' the young man answered.

'We'll come and see the cygnets then,' Dad called back.

'Yes they make a nice sight, a family of swans,' the man confirmed.

And so we walked on, blackbirds and thrushes fluting in the deepening dusk. Grass and reed stems reaching almost to my waist, the canal bending widely in accordance with the wall to our left.

Then the many storied warehouse of the Imperial Tobacco Company blocked out the watery sunset and although green lawns sloped down to the canal's reeded banks, I wondered why people had been allowed to erect a building alongside so quiet and lovely a place.

Where the canal levelled out, I recognised the rooftops of the Middleton Boulevard shops and wondered which was Cunnahs. The thought occurred to me then that the swan pair I had seen flying when Mum took me to the pantomime had been following the canal down to the stretch on which the swans were now nesting. But was it the same swan pair, I wondered?

After Mum, Aunty and I had journeyed to the shops the following morning, Mr. Stevenson the insurance man called around lunchtime.

He asked Mum if we'd been anywhere interesting throughout the weekend and she relayed the visit to The Rose and Crown and seeing the swan pair.

'Ah, a pair of swans nesting at the back of Triumph Road, eh? Good place for them there, the old wharf. It's a fire station now, you know. By the way, the male swan is called a cob and the female a pen,' Mr. Stevenson enthused.

Mum thought I hadn't heard because I was at the dinner table, but I'd heard all right.

When she came into the room, insurance books in hand, she asked, 'Did you hear that, Keith?' Then with Aunty listening, she continued thoughtfully, 'So that young man sitting on the wall high above the swans' nest, he was obviously a fireman.'

'And perhaps a plane watcher too, on the look-out for enemy aircraft, because according to the wireless bulletin just now the Germans haven't finished blitzing us yet. They're coming back,' Aunty told her.

Along with this news several changes occurred within the family. Betty, who periodically brandished a notepad before my eyes filled with dots and lines whilst telling me that it was Pitman shorthand, was about to leave school. Moreover, there was a job waiting at the Barlock Typewriter Company Ltd. which was situated north along the Boulevards and near Dad's oak. His singular reminder indicating the bygone whereabouts of Farrands Dam.

One exceptionally overcast evening, Mum reminded Betty that she had to visit Betty's school sometime in the coming week to attend Betty's medical.

'What's a medical?' I piped.

'Oh, it's when somebody has to see the doctor to make sure they're in good health,' Mum explained.

'Can I come with you, Mum?'

'No, you will have to stay here with Dad and Aunty. It's at Betty's school and after all you don't want to sit looking at a bunch of young girls running about with no clothes on.'

Excitement seethed like fork lightening through my head and stomach upon hearing those words.

I stood disappointed because Mum was not taking me with her and stunned by the biological reaction to her words. It was almost as if a much older person living secretly within me was reacting to them because I had never thought of any girl or woman as someone 'running about with no clothes on'. The thought of how anyone looked nude or naked had never once entered my head.

So I inwardly queried as I returned to my books and toys, had I been here before? Had I once been a man, like Dad?

Soon after Betty's medical, Dad bought her a bicycle with semi-dropped handlebars. With it was a yellow waterproof cape, hood and saddlebag. That is the way in which she would be travelling to work and coming home for dinner, then travelling back in the afternoon. In all she would be cycling, Dad reckoned, about eight miles each day.

With the sudden surge of warm weather came another change. Early one weekday afternoon I travelled with Mum and Aunty across the crowded traffic-filing city to Trent Bridge.

Having at intervals throughout my life wandered the towpaths of the Derwent, Wye, Soar, Thames and Severn, I have concluded that the river promenade or esplanade of the Trent just upstream from Nottingham is about the finest in this country.

The shaded walk, or Victoria Embankment, is lawned, sylvan and follows the Trent's breeze swept meanders for about a mile, bypassing the Suspension Bridge and the locally famed Toll Bridge at Wilford. The walk, or embankment, is wide with the Trent to the left and the tree-lined road to the right. There are ornamental gardens, playing fields and in April daffodil displays equal to those of any English city. But since television sets were installed en-masse throughout the city, the summer strolling crowds have ceased, whereas in wartime and before the Victoria Embankment was crowded with strollers, people sitting the length of concrete steps as they watched the boaters or feeding bread to the large non-breeding flock of swans.

As Aunty and Mum led me towards the river and I was taking in my surroundings, one or the other of them explained that Aunty would be staying, whereas Mum and I were returning home as we came - on two buses.

Mutely negotiating a space between the many groups and families sitting on the steps, Mum and Aunty said we would sit there awhile and watch the forty or fifty swans until it was time for the kiosk to open.

'The kiosk?' I queried.

Just across from the bus terminus and within sight of the wide arches of Trent Bridge, a brick and glass confectionery and ice-cream kiosk stands to this day.

The kiosk was, on my first visit to Trent Bridge, due to open at one-thirty and Aunty, dressed in a lovely blue flowered working smock that I hadn't seen before, had the key. She was going to work there four or five afternoons a week. Selling ice-creams, cakes and sweets. At least throughout the summer months.

I was stunned and uneasy. Dad at work and now Betty and Aunty at work. That would only leave me, Mum and Scamp at home throughout the daylight hours!

Aunty interrupted my thoughts by gesturing towards the swans preening, wading and sailing alongside the steps below and suggesting that "our" cygnet Solo, of the previous summer, may well be among them.

Suddenly swans swirled aside as a pair sailed together with their small buff-grey cygnets clustered tightly into a flock and bobbing between them.

'This breeding pair are exercising dominance because they have cygnets. Normally such pairs don't join a breeding flock when they have cygnets with them, so they *could* be a young, inexperienced pair.'

Standing, I turned to face the swarthy young man on the steps. His shirt sleeves were rolled to the elbows and I was surprised to see that he wore neither tie nor waistcoat. Nor were his trousers pressed in the way that Dad's normally were. But he spoke unfalteringly and with authority —

'If another dominant pair are in the flock, they will try to kill these cygnets.'

'Kill them? But how?' someone asked.

'They'll try to drown them. It's to do with the pecking order and authority,' the young man continued.

I was impressed. Who was he? And how did he know all this about swans when he was a man? It was there and then that this other person within me arose again and vowed that I, or he, would be similarly equipped with evolutionary knowledge and concern by the time that I, or he, was the young man's age.

Aunty glanced at her watch. It was time to go. Time to open the kiosk. Time for her to smile at children other than me.

As we stood, and until we were on the second homeward bus, I experienced for one of the exceptionally few times in my entire life, jealousy surging through my mind.

Aunty talking to other boys and girls! Smiling at them! Selling them ice-creams! But not telling or reading them stories, I hoped.

When we arrived home a sense of loss prevailed. At least until Betty, Dad and Aunty returned separately in the evening. Yet the sense of loss seemed equalled by my having recognised someone upon whom I could model myself. Someone who knew exactly what birds, animals and possibly people were doing.

In my narrow viewpoint of the world, the young man's presence that day had eclipsed that of the singing Hollywood cowboy, Gene Autrey. Dad! Betty! Aunty! I couldn't *wait* to tell them that I had seen the man I hoped one day to become.

Betty cheered considerably once she had left school. Saturday mornings at the breakfast table were less argumentative. Usually I was able to feed Scamp under the table on bacon scraps before Betty joined me and I was careful to sneak him the lean pieces, keeping the lightly grilled, thinly cut and deliciously trimmed edges of fat to myself.

I never fed him the slightest portion of fried egg but the crusty corners of fried bread were a different matter. Scamp fared well, especially if Dad fed him likewise before he went to work.

Betty's mood was light and smiling. When after washing my hands I asked if I could look again at *The Adventures of Robin Hood*, it was handed to me willingly, almost eagerly.

One Saturday morning, Betty, seated across from me, tossing her head and smoothing back her hair, told me that the previous evening she had been down a coal mine.

Riveted suddenly to the chair, I awaited her next quiet but enthusiastic outburst. Sharing the office and typists' pool with Betty at the Barlock Typewriter Company was a girl called Iris who lived at the Bestwood Colliery village. She and Betty had become good friends.

Iris's father was obviously either a collier or a "top man", or office administrator employed at the colliery, and it was he who had arranged for Betty, Iris and her younger sister, Dilys, to go down.

Betty described how before they were taken down in the cage, colliers coming off shift and going to the pit baths wolf-whistled at the three girls as they were being handed and told to wear a safety helmet.

The ride in the cage was uncanny for it seemed as if they were going down into the bowels of the earth. Standing caged and embarking upon an endless descent surrounded only by the smell of coal and the colour of midnight. Their guide handed them each a torch on this memorial descent. And when they left the cage they travelled along what Betty described as 'black streets beneath the ground.'

There were miles and miles of these streets and dozens of colliers hacking at the coal face. Crawling on their hands and knees; attempting to squeeze fissures; spading coal onto trucks drawn by ponies.

'Ponies! Under the ground!' I exclaimed.

Betty assured me that there were and as Mum put the breakfast cups of tea besides our plates, she chimed, 'Pit ponies; yes. And before they used ponies, they had women and children hauling and pulling the carts to wherever they needed to go.'

Having explained this, Mum returned to the kitchen while Betty and I sat staring at one another for I think we were both stunned, yet believing.

Iris and Dilys, or their father, kept hutched rabbits in the garden of their house in Bestwood Village. I had not seen rabbits kept in hutches, not even while visiting the poultry stall in the market as I periodically did with Dad. I had, however, seen a wild rabbit such as the rabbit men brought round to the house, except that this had been very much alive.

Dad and I were on Woodyard Lane one Sunday morning looking at the brightly painted but redundant farm carts parked beneath an open-sided barn when Dad suddenly whispered, 'Rabbit,' swung me onto his shoulders and told me to look across the field to the tightly fenced Harrison's Plantation. I saw the white scut of the rabbit as it ran towards the overgrown banks beyond the barbed wire.

However, I had not seen what Betty called tamed or hutched rabbits but my sister and her new friends rectified this situation one exceptionally hot Saturday evening. I had spent the afternoon wearing only shorts and sandals in the shade of the rear garden plum tree with Scamp. He had chewed relentlessly on a broad leg bone that we had brought from the butchers for him, while I sailed a model boat in a bowl of water, imagining myself to be a frog, moorhen or swan thriving in such reed beds as we had seen bordering the canal towpath.

After tea Betty announced that she wasn't going dancing on this particularly hot night. Instead, Iris and Dilys were coming in their car, or the family car, and taking Betty and me back to Bestwood village to see the rabbits.

That was my first car journey. And perhaps Betty's. After Mum had stood talking and joking companionably with Iris and Dilys, Betty and I were gently directed into the back of the four-seat saloon and with Dilys at the wheel we drove north along the Boulevards to Bestwood.

With Betty's arm around my shoulders, I sat directly behind pretty and small featured Dilys, who in looks reminded me of Alice Faye, a filmstar whose portrait graced a page of one of Betty's growing pile of film annuals.

When the car was turned off the Boulevards and we journeyed along sunlit Vernon Road, I sensed home as being over my left shoulder. When we turned north again in the sandstone town of Bulwell, my homing instinct told me that home was at my back. When we climbed a steep bridge that Betty told me was Moor Bridge I sensed that home was still at my back, then as we turned into Moor Road it was again on my left, but some distance away. The colliery houses were mostly built from red brick. They were built in couples or blocks of four and some had the date the colliery opened or the insignia of the land-owning family to whom the pit once belonged deeply inscribed above the front door.

Betty pointed out the pit entrance, the baths, the headstocks, winding house and the cage down which she had travelled to the underground city of black streets and yellow colliers' lamps bobbing in the darkness.

We did not go into the house owned or rented by Iris and Dilys's parents, but followed a narrowly paved path to the small rear garden. Here were stacked about six hutches, wire fronted, creosoted, tarpaulined and with a rabbit in each. I was allowed to open the door of each hutch and stroke the occupant. The warm, glossy fur was different to that of a dog I discovered, while bringing Scamp to mind. And the scents of straw, hay and chaff reminded me of the sacks Dad periodically carried over his shoulder from Worthington's for our chickens, on the Saturday morning he was allowed off from work. A few weeks before our visit a stoat, a small reddish-brown member of the weasel family with a black tipped tail, had worked its way under and into the wire netting front of one of the rabbit hutches, Iris told us.

Normally hutched rabbits scream and stamp their hind feet if they are threatened, but the family in the house had not been aware of any such warnings. Nor were they certain that the stoat had appeared at night. If it came by day then there was seldom anyone at home, because every member of the family was by then working. Consequently, the stoat had gained access to the hutch and killed an obviously terrified and squealing rabbit. Moreover, the stoat had fed on the flesh exposed by its bite and also the belly. It had also drank some of the rabbit's blood then curled up and slept on the still warm body. When one of the family went down the garden to the hutches, however, the stoat awoke, wriggled back through the wire and made its escape.

'But a rabbit is usually safer in a hutch than in the wild if there's a stoat about,' Dilys assured us.

Had we but known it, many of the sheds and lean-tos in the rear gardens of those colliery houses contained ferrets and here and there a flock of homing pigeons. And it was the same for every colliery community, including our close-to-home Radford Woodhouse. But besides ferreting, most colliers took an interest in football, gambling, pitching the horseshoe, fishing and flying racing pigeons.

Most racing pigeon enthusiasts built a loft in the yard or rear garden of the back-to-back house in which they lived. Therefore, it was commonplace on a Sunday morning to strap a wicker basket filled with pigeons on the pannier of one's bicycle and cycle out to some high point then release the pigeons, for racing pigeons were an emblem of freedom to a collier. While taking in great lungfuls of air, he watched the birds flying free. And yet when the weekend was out he always returned dutifully to his self-elected prison.

Watching the sunset as Dad had told me always to do, I sat quietly in the rear seat of the saloon as Dilys and Iris drove Betty and me home.

'One day I will drive a car like Dilys and Iris,' Betty quietly assured me when we were home with Mum and Dad.

Our parents looked at her fondly, but as if in disbelief. But within the next few years Betty was sitting in the passenger seat of a green and black Morgan sports car owned then by Peter, her fiancé. Not many years were to pass before she was driving the car that belonged both to her and Peter as together they worked and with a young family in tow built up their own reputable business, Betty being the receptionist, negotiator and secretary.

CHAPTER 23

Due to Allied technology, the menace of U boat invasions decreased considerably and sea transported cargoes were aided by escort carriers equipped with High Frequency Direction Finding modes designed specifically for U boat detection. At last British American vessels were no longer seen as floating targets. The Germans eventually discovered this to their cost.

In Britain the film industry experienced a much needed revival, due to films being made as documentaries about the war or dramatisations highlighting the lives of a single soldier and his girl or the strains experienced by a working-class family.

One hugely successful film, described as "realist drama", was *Millions Like Us* starring Patricia Roc and Gordon Jackson. The setting was an aircraft factory. Humphrey Jennings then directed *Fires were Started* which was regarded as a fitting tribute to the Auxiliary Fire Service and the sterling work of its members throughout the London blitz.

The 'DIG FOR VICTORY' campaign encouraged people, and families in particular, to grow their own produce. Some schools turned their lawn areas and grass verges into vegetable plots. Acres of derelict land and plots once designated as public spaces were transformed into allotment gardens which reached an astounding '1,4000,000 allotments *in use*', according to a survey in the summer of 1943.

In August a ten-day conference of Allied leaders was held in Quebec. Here the British Prime-Minister Winston Churchill planned with Franklin Roosevelt to concentrate on defeating Germany and invading France in May 1944. Once these operations were completed, then defeating the Japanese would see an end to this 'War to End All Wars'.

***

One morning after playing with Scamp and finishing breakfast, I asked Mum if we were going as usual over New Bridge to Hoggs the grocer's.

'*I'm* going over New Bridge to Hoggs the grocer's, but you m'lad, you're going to school. That's where you're going.'

Astounded, I turned to face her. *School! Today!* Surely that hadn't been Mum speaking. Using the term m'lad? True she had never called me love or darling, thank goodness, but neither had she referred to me as 'm'lad'.

'But I don't want to go to school!'

'You're *going. Today.*'

'But what happens if I don't go?'

'Then me and your Dad will go to prison.'

I saw them both, plunged into the dungeon depths of the type of castle fortress I had read about in my story books. Behind bars. Squatting on flagstones. Food bowls beside them. Rats closing in. Dad's white hair gleaming like a beacon in the darkness.

'Now go upstairs. Wash your hands and face, then clean your teeth and put your coat on, because that's what you'll be doing on every school day morning from now on.'

'But what about Scamp?'

'Never mind about Scamp. I can look after him. And never mind about your story books, you can look at those when you come home tonight. Go on upstairs, or you'll be late!'

Late! I *was expected* to be attending school then? But, I inwardly queried as I washed, how did people know about me? Who had told them? And how did they know about anyone? The soldiers in the trenches. The sailors out at sea. And what did they *look* like, these people whom I was hating?

My stomach was churning as with Scamp alone and locked inside the house, Mum and I walked north along Western Boulevard. We were heading in the direction of the built-up area of Basford. It was not the direction of my choosing but *someone else's* choosing. And I was having to walk it that morning. The morning that some faceless person with a set of documents and a typewriter had decided, or worked out, that I *should* be attending school.

My chosen direction was south towards the canal, the deer park and the sun. But that morning, because of the faceless person, I was walking with my back to the sun and having to walk with my back to it because I didn't want Mum and Dad to go to prison.

There were two busy main roads to cross, the first being Aspley Lane along which double-decker buses rumbled by the allotment hedgerows to the council estates of Bilborough and Strelley. The second was a busier road connecting Nottingham to the villages of north Derbyshire, the City of Derby, the Pennines and Manchester. Blue and cream liveried Midland General buses travelled this route and lorries, the size and like of which I hadn't before seen. Today extra traffic lanes and traffic lights have been added but accidents are still so frequent that it has been locally nicknamed "Kamikaze Island".

The lime tree bordered roadside and grass verges, along with the shaded central reservation, continued in wartime all along the Boulevards and this at least made my enforced journey bearable.

School? Mum pointed sternly up the hill. This was the district of Whitemoor. There were council houses on both sides of the Boulevard. Council houses and traffic.

It was halfway up the Boulevard hill that I suddenly decided that I wasn't going to school. *I wasn't going to be told what to do by faceless people* who sat at desks with typewriters in front of them.

I turned for home. A hand settled onto my shoulder like a vice. 'Come on,' Mum ordered.

'No! I'm not going!'

'Oh yes you *are*!'

The hand singularly spun me round to continue up the hill. Suddenly I was in tears and enraged. The tears hot; rage simmering.

I turned again, 'I'm *not* going, Mum!'

'Oh yes you are, m'lad.'

Again I was spun around, while at the same time empowered by both the determination in Mum's tone and the sheer power of her grip. There was only one way to fight determination and that was with determination, I decided. Ducking aside I turned and again the hand descended like a vice but this time on my collar.

'Look, you will be coming home at dinnertime and I'll have your favourite meal waiting for you. White cod, potatoes and parsley sauce.'

'B-but have I got to go back this afternoon?'

'Oh yes and you can walk back on your own this afternoon. But this afternoon you leave again at half past four.'

It looked like it was going to be a long day! I *wasn't* going.

Thus the altercations, the turnings, grippings and crying continued until we reached the top of the hill. 'Bracknell Crescent. Here it is! And there's your school,' said Mum, pointing to a building with a formal entrance and short gravel drive situated on

a plateau at the top of the hill leading off from the Boulevard.

There was a crowd of children outside the school. They stood with their backs to Mum and me, but facing two or three women. I was aware of boys wearing laced boots. Girls wearing cardigans. Some girls with bows in their hair.

We drew closer.

'There. You go and stand with those children, listen for your name being called and do as the lady tells you,' Mum advised.

Lady! I was already confused because I didn't know to whom of the three women I should be giving my attention. Far easier for me to go home. Yet none of the other children were turning for home and less than a handful were accompanied by their mothers.

Suddenly I realised that I was standing alone. Alone for the first time since I walked to Mr. Kirk's off-licence at Radford Woodhouse!

I spun round. Mum was hurrying away. She turned, pointed to the right and down the hill. 'At dinnertime you walk this way and just keep walking. You'll come to Chalfont Drive eventually and I'll have your dinner on the table.'

She was glowering. Wearing a severe expression.

For the first time in my life I was not with or destined to be meeting a member of my family. I was outside of school; among strangers!

A woman stepped forward. Bespectacled, round faced, grey hair back-swept and held in a bun. She wore a grey cardigan and a long pleated skirt. In her hand she held a wad of papers.

'Right children. I'm Miss Jones. Listen for your name being called and then stand in the line I put you in.'

Surely my name wasn't among the many she intended to call out! And if it wasn't, then I was definitely going home. There was no question of that! In her slightly rasping voice, Miss Jones began calling out the names — 'Barrett.......Bradley......Ewin'

Children put up their hands calling out, 'Yes Miss,' and went and stood in the line Miss Jones indicated.

Presently there were only a few of us who were not in formation. The names continued — 'Selby......Settle......Smedley......Strutt.'

I was almost ready to turn, heart beating, a feeling of freedom and well-being prevailing, when my name cut through the air.

Miss Jones pointed to the end of the line, as still hating the faceless people who had put my name on the list I joined those children standing with their backs to me and realised that Miss Jones had not only replaced Mum but also Aunty. On future schooldays she was to be the guardian-woman in my life.

About half of the other children lived close to the school along its periphery road Bracknell Crescent, or nearby Raymede Drive and Wilkinson Street, and at least two of them in houses fronting the Boulevard. Others had been brought by a special bus from the colliery village of Bestwood, which I had recently visited, and also the surrounding Bestwood housing estates.

'Right, let's go into school. This line first and then the others following just a little behind,' rasped Miss Jones, pointing to the line that I was in.

'Forward, march!' Miss Jones barked lightly.

March! I thought that only soldiers, sailors and airmen marched! But, of course, we didn't mrch. We walked, in single file between the imposing gates and towards the darkly shadowed corridors of the unknown.

Opened on 26th September 1935, the school was designed like several in the district on the scale of a Roman villa. There was a lawned area and quadrangle fashioned corridors. Classrooms led off from three of these and a fourth housed the storerooms, staff room and cloakrooms. This fourth corridor never saw the sun. It was shaded or shuttered according to the season and cool or cold accordingly. It was also a slightly foreshortened corridor, which ended abruptly at the cloakroom corner and the double-door entrance to the assembly hall with its well raised and impressive stage.

Miss Jones showed us first to the cloakrooms, which were painted pale green. She advised us to always use the same peg and added that sometimes we might have to share the pegs because the school, I later learned, was intended to accommodate 460 pupils.

The classroom smelt of sugar paper, ink, polish and glue. We sat in couplets, each with a desk before us. Some desks carried discreet initials or ink blots and smudges that could not be erased. The inkwells, I noticed, were manufactured in Hemel Hempstead which set me wondering how far away that was and if it had survived the bombings.

Addressing a mixed class of some forty to forty-five pupils, Miss Jones told us to try always to sit at the same desk then she could gradually learn our names. Squirming inwardly, I told myself that I didn't want her to know *my* name.

We were told to lift the lids of our desks.

'Have you all got a gas mask inside?' asked Miss Jones.

Collectively and in a three syllable rhythm, we chorused, 'Yes, Miss Jones.'

'Put up your hand if there *isn't* a gas mask inside your desk.'

No one moved. All was well.

Pointing out of the french windows to the playground, Miss Jones explained that the brick buildings, one each side of the playground, were air raid shelters. But we were only to rush into them if the siren sounded when we were in the playground. At other times, we would assemble in turns and walk calmly *behind* Miss Jones to the shelter allocated to our particular class.

She then gave us all a blue exercise book, pen and ruler. The first thing to do was draw up a timetable of the lessons we would be attending. Some I didn't like the sound of: sums, handicrafts (one which I disliked because I didn't know the meaning of the word, let alone the subject). Reading, writing and singing, they were different: I considered them important.

Halfway through this classroom period, Miss Jones glanced twice at her watch, then murmured, 'Good heavens!'. Clapping her hands together twice, she made yet another announcement, 'Right boys and girls, it's milk time. Right, I'll have two boys go out into the corridor and bring in two crates of milk.'

I was just about to shrink behind the boy in front when she pointed to me and the grinning boy next to whom I was sitting. 'Right. You two. You'll do. Off you go. And after the timetable, we'll fill in a milk monitors' roster. Two different boys each day. Right?'

The boy sitting next to me was broader shouldered and had thicker wrists than I. His name was Billy I discovered, as holding a milk crate each with both hands we struggled in first with one and then another. While Billy and I were busy at our task and surprising ourselves because, under duress, we could between us carry a milk crate, one of the girls went round to all desks and handed everyone a straw.

'When you drink the milk, drink it quietly. I don't want to hear those horrible glugging and sucking noises when you're near the end,' Miss Jones told us.

Each day I wanted the milk to last because then the lesson, *the period* as the teaching session time was called, wouldn't seem so long. I thought of how one could keep Miss Jones preoccupied so that we would collectively work to that sort of schedule. But Miss Jones would have none of it.

Billy had an expressive face and an irrepressible sense of humour. He was, I think, the son of a collier. His deep auburn hair rose to a carefully combed quiff at the front. And with Sam, his street-wise companion who sat in front of us, he indulged when lessons allowed in a non-stop repartee.

Sam was red complexioned and wiry, sporting a semi-crew cut hairstyle. Like Billy, he wore long sleeved sweaters and like us all short, grey flannel trousers, usually with grey socks to match. But unlike me, most of the Bestwood boys wore black lace-up boots which were studded and afforded their wearers the opportunity to slide across areas of the school playground when chance permitted. By contrast, I wore black shoes.

At playtime I was traumatised. Never had I seen boys and girls racing one way and then the other, playing "dobby" or " cops and robbers". Never had I seen *two or three hundred* boys and girls playing in this manner. It wasn't just the mêlée of twisting, bending, twirling and running children that surprised me. It was the noise. They yelled, shouted and screamed for no reason that I could see. Consequently, I shunned the groups and wandered in a daze.

Eventually I was befriended by a tall, broad boy, black haired and suntanned, and considerably older than me. His name was Barry and although he wore lace-up boots, he lived across the boulevard from me in a house looking out onto the unsightly New Bridge and the field where, with the Kittoe and Pearce sisters, I had gone to see the gypsies.

Barry explained in his kindly manner that the playground was always noisy like this. Furthermore, he advised me to find some of my classmates, like Billy and Sam, and join in with whatever game they were playing.

I thought him a kindly person and thirty years later after a footpath exploration of the Byron and D.H. Lawrence country I stood waiting for the hourly bus when a van pulled into the lay-by and the driver offered me a lift. It was none other than Barry. He was by then in the building trade and we conversed without either of us mentioning school. Whether he recognised me as that traumatised little five-year old whom I advised in the school playground, I shall never know.

167

But he gave me a lift almost to my front door.

When at twelve fifteen the bell sounded, Miss Jones told us to finish what we were doing. It was dinner-time and we were not due back until a quarter to two.

I walked home alone, practising my road drill at both the busy main roads I had to cross, and Mum, looking a little more relaxed, gestured to my promised dinner which was waiting on the table.

With a furiously wagging tail, Scamp sniffed my knees, socks and shoes as I sat on the chair, his eyes and nose seeking my past whereabouts.

By a quarter past one I was walking back to school, watching the starlings hop running along the grass verges, studying the cloud formations, the differing texture of the tree trunks and wondering where all the cars and lorries were coming and going.

I was desperate to get back to school, wanting the company of Billy, Sam, Fraser and Harry, all of whom I believe stayed school dinners. I didn't want to miss out on *anything*. By playtime that same afternoon, I was one of the shouters and whoopers, imagining myself a pilot on a bombing raid or Gene Autrey pursuing a gang of black hatted baddies.

About half an hour before we were due to leave, Miss Jones left the classroom and was replaced by a younger teacher. Her mass of black curly hair framed her round, fresh complexioned face. Her name, she told us, was Miss Gibson. I recognised her as the lady who had cycled past Mum when I was remonstrating about attending school that morning.

Miss Gibson pulled up a chair, took a book from the teacher's desk and told us she was going to read us a story. All we children had to do was sit quietly with our arms folded in front of our chests and listen. The story was about a rabbit called Peter who lived in a briar patch and a gardener called Mr. McGregor.

Warmth surged through my stomach as I imbibed every word of Beatrix Potter's classic tale. If every school day ended like this then yes, I decided, school *was* acceptable. I would go just to have a story read to me. Further stories, however, were few and far between but at half past four I left school beaming inwardly with pleasure.

Wait until I told the Kittoe and Pearce sisters, Betty, Dad and Aunty. But, I also wondered, would Mum or Dad one day buy me a pair of studded lace-up boots like Sam and Billy's?

CHAPTER 24

Because of school the weekends were now precious and after each Saturday breakfast I went down to the fowl pen with Scamp and gently removed the three or four new-laid eggs from the laying boxes while holding my breath because I disliked the acrid smells of poultry faeces. If Dad was not working we went over to Worthington's and brought back a sack of hay and chaff for relining the laying boxes and Dad, having by then changed into his old clothes, entered the fowl pen, scraper and bucket in hand, and cleaned the perches and floor to the best of his ability.

One Saturday we journeyed by bus to a village near Langar and came home with a magnificent Rhode Island Red cockerel. With its wings held down by sacking and tied with string, the cockerel sat on Dad's knee, its red comb and long wattle conspicuous along with its magnificent rufous and russet plumage against the dull interior of the bus seat and Dad's gabardine raincoat. Fascinated, I studied the cockerel's malignant expression, the threat of war in its unblinking eyes.

Passengers smiled on alighting and boarding the bus and in the city Dad and the cockerel won further speculation. When Dad opened the fowl pen door and removed the string and sacking, the cockerel swiftly backed up and attacked him with its elongated spurs. 'Dash you,' muttered Dad as he slammed shut the fowl pen door. He then examined his hand. The cockerel had drawn blood. We were back to the Polly and Aunty situation for within minutes Dad was bathing the wound in the bathroom and preparing to dress it with iodine and plaster.

Mum also experienced repercussions due to keeping poultry but in a different way, for quite often I would see her, fork in hand, mixing a bowl of Karswood Poultry Spice with used egg shells, toast crumbs and brussel sprout leaves which had been through the mincing machine.

She would stand rubbing her nose but with her eyes watering as if she was peeling onions. 'Spicy! Oh, it's spicy all right!' she frequently exclaimed between the tears. Yet she and I both loved the smell and I jokingly once suggested that she made us all a Karswood Poultry Spice cake.

Within two days of starting school I had picked up, but never repeated, more expletives than were good for any five year old.

I had not heard the words before but knew by the way in which one or other of the boys at playtime delivered them that they were not words used in the everyday language and certainly not by the adults I knew. The words were delivered either cynically, jokingly or with venom, and I knew instinctively that if I repeated them at home I would get a clout, probably from Mum, although all the rebukes I had received in the past had been verbal. I was never slapped, hit or 'thumped' as it seemed had the boys who came from the colliery communities.

From one of these communities came a girl we will call Anne. In sunshine, freezing fog or teeming rain she came to school without a coat, her hair cut to shoulder length and wearing a grey, sleeveless summer dress, white ankle socks and black plimsolls.

By the other girls she was shunned, the more so perhaps after one of the boys announced that Anne's father was a collier - yes - but also a drunkard.

One girl in the class, as best she could, befriended Anne. Her name was Pat. She was quiet and pretty. Dark skinned with eyebrows and hair black as a raven's wing.

Two or three days a week Pat came to school in a different dress and lovely machine knitted cardigans. And like all girls, except Anne, she wore a different coloured bow in her hair. Poor Anne wasn't allowed a bow.

One morning Pat appeared in the classroom with two or three machine knitted cardigans under her arm. Miss Jones, who was about to call the register, hesitated then smiled because Pat went over to Anne, said something to her and gave her the cardigans. Tears flashed through Anne's eyes as she emphatically thanked Pat. The class, including myself, were momentarily stunned into silence.

The next day Anne arrived wearing one of the cardigans. Pat then gave her a parcel. It contained socks and underwear. Perhaps even a pair of weatherproof shoes.

Warmth stirred through my stomach. I thought that a lovely gesture, as I suppose did we all, as Pat explained that her parents were both employed as machinists in the hosiery trade.

The following Monday morning Anne came into the classroom, shivering and again wearing the grey sleeveless dress, the white ankle socks and black plimsolls. Pat looked shocked dismayed, and with good reason, because Anne never came to school in the clothes Pat had brought for her again. It was *always* the grey sleeveless dress, white ankle socks and black plimsolls for Anne, and there was precious little anyone could do about the situation.

There dawned an autumn day of icy drumming rain in which I donned my galoshes before leaving for school at the usual time of eight fifteen. But even wearing galoshes, a navy raincoat that covered my jacket and short trousers, and a cap, I arrived soaked and until the bell sounded admitting us into the classrooms I stayed beside the cloakroom radiators.

It rained heavily all morning. There was no let up. I envisaged Mum walking over New Bridge to the shops with Aunty, who by the summer's end had been made redundant until the following summer.

When at twelve fifteen I came out of school, prepared for the usual long walk and another soaking, a voice stopped me in my tracks — "Keith."

Turning I saw our neighbour, Mr. Nahori, a man perhaps in his late thirties with Byronic looks, shepherding his daughter, Suzanne, and her brother into a maroon Ford type saloon car. I hadn't realised that Suzanne, to whom I'd never really spoken, was attending the same school as I.

"Jump in! We're going home in style on a day like this," urged Mr. Nahori.

That was my second experience of a car journey. With rain drumming on the car roof, we drove along the Boulevards awash with surface water. I was fascinated by the rhythm of the windscreen wipers. The blurred images of lime trees discarding their leaves in the rising wind. The surging splashes as the car tyres broke across the small pools and ponds, the likes of which we youngsters had never seen.

On pulling up outside the Nahori family's gate , which was three below our own, Mr. Nahori told me to call back when I had eaten and he would drive us back again.

"They're lovely people, the Nahoris. They're Jewish," Mum hailed as she eased hers and Aunty's umbrellas aside in the front porch so that I could get by.

Mum imparted this information as she did similar pieces of information. She told me in a way that suggested I knew exactly which culture or about whom she was speaking. The fact that the Nahoris were Jewish meant nothing to me. But Mum knew them better than I and at least once a week took new-laid eggs from our poultry around to the house and exchanged them for bags of rice, which explains why I was given rice pudding as seconds at least twice a week. But how I enjoyed them! Especially if there was a pale brown skin on the top.

Much though I hated Thursday afternoon and its handicraft lessons spent cutting shapes out of folded coloured paper, Friday afternoon was very much my friend for in the latter half after playtime we were allowed to look at books. Our own books. Those we had brought from home.

Both Terence and Peter, who were unrelated but looked alike being dark haired and well-made, brought thick books that were illustrated. As we could swap books amongst ourselves, I discovered that at least two of the volumes were about the London Zoo.

The photographs were printed in black and white, sepia and, alarmingly to me, green and white. There were photographs of animals and birds I had never seen in books or on film. Marmosets, warthogs, armadillos. All the many and varied antelopes. Giraffes and okapis.

I was particularly interested in the photographs featuring people involvement. There was staged at London Zoo daily at four p.m., weather permitting, a chimpanzees' tea party. Children queued to have a ride on an elephant. Or rode in a gig at the helm of which stood a peak capped zoo keeper guiding the llama that was pulling the gig.

Where did my friends get such books? They were given them as Christmas presents I was told. There was, I should add, no mention of Santa Claus.

***

The Allied Conference of Foreign Ministers held in Moscow agreed to form the European Advisory Committee, its purpose being to negotiate with and advise the Soviet, American and British Ministers involved in the war. This was held in the last two weeks of October 1943.

In November, the British Royal Air Force began a five month night blitz of Berlin. The damage caused was insurmountable but throughout those five months close on six hundred bombers and their crews were lost; presumed shot down.

A further offensive lasting four and a half months was staged in the Ukraine by the Soviet army who on having regained a large proportion of the Soviet territory there, decided to claim the rest from the Germans. Throughout the autumn wounded Italian soldiers arrived in England and 230 of them were sent to Nottingham. They were described as being 'surprisingly cheerful', even those who were severely wounded.

Telegraph boys, on red motorcycles, were busy delivering official envelopes to families, girlfriends and fiancées informing them that their son, brother or boyfriend had arrived in Britain after being released from German prison camps. Not infrequently the news was bad, informing a family of the death of a loved one.

Films continued to be made about the war. Starring Greer Garson and Walter

Pidgeon, *Mrs. Miniver*, released in 1942 and directed by William Wyler, won the Best Picture award. Wyler won the Best Director award, Greer Garson was voted the Best Actress and the film won six Oscars.

Winston Churchill publicly described this film as being 'more valuable than the combined effects of six army divisions'.

While the bereaved wept in privacy and some in public places, the singing continued. Songs such as *It's A Long Way To Tipperary, Roll Out The Barrel, Pack Up Your Troubles* and *Daisy, Daisy* were heard on the wireless everyday with audiences, *people* singing en masse.

Still the radio comedians Vic Oliver, Charlie Chester and Flanagan and Allen entertained those audiences. Jokes were exchanged in the trenches, tanks, lorries, aircraft, aboard ships and in Forces' canteens.

***

With the chill, mist and rains came the autumn and the fresh, clear, sunlit days that I loved.

Needing like me to be amongst trees at this time of the year, Dad suggested, as I had hoped, Wollaton Park for a Sunday morning walk. As was usual so early in the morning, the oak ride known as Digby Avenue and along which we walked was deserted.

Leaves drifted ceaselessly from the trees. Yellow, buff, red ochre, and the scents of tree musk, leaf decay and woodiness again infiltrated my nostrils. Far better than the smells emanating from a school classroom those!

Dad pointed across to the wood known as the Family Plantation. It had been planted, like all the woods, as game covert and was thick with rhododendrons. Bracken surrounded the wood and on a series of hillocks stood a group of red deer hinds and calves. To their right, backed by the rhododendrons and facing the avenue, stood a stag, dunnish-grey in colour, long backed, full maned. His head was high and his antlers, carrying twelve to fourteen tines, appeared pale, almost silvery, against the background of dark vegetation.

So far as Dad and I were concerned, the stag was standing sideways on but as the eyes of most animals are positioned at the side of the head, the stag may well have been watching our approach, for deer are known to be extremely long-sighted.

Suddenly the hinds and calves were standing, wheeling and racing through the bracken, blocked from our view by the trees of Lime Avenue.

The stag wheeled and as always took up a rear position, his antlers travelling like elongated antennae against the background trees.

Simultaneously, Dad and I swung round as two mongrel dogs romped side by side in the direction of the swiftly departed deer. I was still memorising their buff rears bobbing above the bracken fronds when Dad exclaimed, "How did these two get in?! There'll be some trouble if a keeper sees them."

There was no question of Dad and I having left open the single park gate because that was affixed to a spring which slammed the gate shut behind one then as it does today. The dogs we then decided had entered the park by way of one of the house rear gardens backing onto the park. Dad explored the possibility of them being regular deer chasers and if they were they would one day undoubtedly be shot.

Scamp still stalked and tracked hares which fed in the fields, ditchside and disused allotments situated within a hundred yards of our home. He had become an habitual hare stalker. And although there were hares in the deer park, those two dogs had instinctively taken to chasing deer. At least that was how the situation appeared to Dad and I.

On our future visits to the park we would bring Scamp, we decided, but he would always be on the lead. We were both aware of his capabilities and his instinctive capacity for hunting.

As for the owner, or owners, of the two dogs we had just seen, they were obviously unaware of their dogs' capabilities. Or perhaps like many of the irresponsible people I was to meet in the future, they just didn't want to know.

Such situations were, Dad reflected philosophically, a sad reflection on society.

CHAPTER 25

Usually I kept my books under the settee cushions because, as I mentioned earlier, there was no room for a book case in the house filled though it was with other types of furniture.

When sometimes exasperated because I couldn't find a book, Aunty would say, "You'll find it when you're not looking for it." And quite often her experience proved its point.

In the evenings and at the weekends I still spent time on the settee reading and browsing books. But Aunty, now that I was reading alone, worked steadily on her sewing machine, sometimes with Betty looking on, while I glanced occasionally at the bright blue, green and orange lengths of cotton wound tightly around the bobbins. One overcast Saturday, the darkest that I remember, Aunty did not join us for dinner or the midday meal, which was eaten in relative silence.

Soon after the meal was over, Dad, who appeared to be in an uncharacteristically agitated and nervous state, told me to put on my hat and coat because he was taking me to the Aspley Lane shops to buy me some toy farm animals. To my delight, and despite the sky with black clouds gathering en masse, we went along Cherry Orchard Lane where the grasses and ditchside thickets shuddered due to the force of the wind.

Dad, again uncharacteristically, was in no particular hurry. Consequently, we strolled rather than walked and several times I wondered if 'The Man' was watching us, although I was not afraid because I was with Dad. We stopped to watch the Aspley Hall dairy herd grazing the parkland meadows and Dad told me that most of the herd consisted of the red and white liveried Dairy Shorthorn cattle.

Closer to the Forum cinema than to home, Dad went into the newsagent's and sweet shop and came out smiling and carrying a perspex wrapped card on which were slotted several minute lengths of fencing, some pigs, sheep and cattle. "There you are, Little Man, you can have a farm of your own now," said Dad.

He then told me that we were going to call on his twin brother Albert and his wife Alice. They lived with their two sons, much older than I, in a cul-de-sac on the nearby council estate. When Dad and his brother greeted one another I was pleasantly shocked because they were almost like identical twins. Dad took off his trilby and my aunty, whom I hadn't met before, sat me at the kitchen table and put before me a plate of sugared biscuits.

This lady, this *new* Aunty as I thought of her, just couldn't stop smiling. She wore glasses, had a fresh complexion, thick brown shoulder length hair and wore a blue sleeveless dress fronted by a starched white apron. Dad, I noticed, wasn't with us. He had gone into the dining room to talk with his brother and they had quietly closed the door.

The house interior was immaculate and smelt of polish. My new Aunty asked me about school. What lessons did I like? What lessons *didn't* I like?

Then Dad and his brother came into the kitchen and Dad said, "Right, Little Man, we'll be going."

My Uncle Albert fondled my hair. He looked down at me, his blue eyes twinkling. He and my new Aunty seemed a compatible and therefore contented couple and that contentment permeated throughout the neat and orderly rooms of their house.

When we returned home I played at the table with the newly bought farm toys which was not unusual, except that Betty or Aunty were not in the room.

Betty came home in time for tea but there was still no Aunty. Was she working at the sweet kiosk on a dark wintry day like this?

Sunday continued as normal with Dad and I walking up to and exploring more of Strelley Village, but by early evening the question as to Aunty's whereabouts was burning on my lips.

Betty had, I think, gone dancing with Sylvia, who was obviously missing her sisters. I was acutely aware as I played with my farm set at the table of there being three people in the house instead of four.

I was not sitting in my usual place but across from it and facing the glowing fire. Dad in his favourite armchair to the left read from the pages of *The News of the World.* Mum sat on the other side of the hearth facing him. She darned socks. Neither spoke.

Unable to contain myself I asked, "Where's aunty?"

"She's dead," answered Dad slowly and without lifting his eyes from the newspaper.

Shock enlarged my eyes. Forced open my mouth. I nearly fell from the chair, which I was habitually tilting back from the table.

Dead!

The word screamed through my ears; my mind. Burning tears pricked my eyes. Dad and Mum remained composed. Not once turning a head in my direction. The ensuing silence was uncanny. Lips trembling, I didn't know what to say. What to do. Where to go.

Eventually, Mum put down her darning mushroom and said without looking at me, "Right, mi lad. I'll get your drink ready then it's up to bed."

And still Dad continued looking at the newspaper, whereas I felt around me a great space. Moreover, I felt *utterly alone.* The space was cold, vast and silent. I knew instinctively that from then on the books and stories of the future would have to be of my own choosing. That or my sister Betty would attempt to fulfil Aunty's role as my consistent friend and guardian.

Nor did I cry in front of Mum and Dad because I knew instinctively it was not expected. But I cried later between the blankets and silently within my mind for seemingly hours afterwards.

Early the next morning Mum woke me. There was no school for a week. It was half-term. I would therefore have to go with her to Hoggs the grocer's and the other shops. But early that afternoon she was taking me to see another Aunty. Her sister, my Aunt Alice, who had three sons of around Betty's age and lived in a bungalow near Wollaton Park with her husband, Tom Brown. Thus I discovered I had an Aunt Alice and Uncle Tom. When I had been to Aunt Alice's with Mum, she wanted me to go again on the Wednesday. And go alone. In retrospect, this was probably the day of Aunty's funeral but of which again I was told nothing. Monday morning was still wash day and there was just as much washing for Mum to do and so we were later going to Hoggs.

That said there was no such time or term in Mum's life as 'elevenses'. When one job was finished there was another waiting. And always would be while she had a husband and family.

Elevenses! Mum and other women of her generation would have scoffed at the idea! When after our midday dinner Mum walked with me to Aunt Alice's, she pointed out the route that I needed to take when on Wednesday I retraced my steps.

I was afraid of meeting Aunt Alice, yet wanted to be walking in the direction of the canal and deer park.

Mum made me promise that I would not linger by the canal lock gates, my beloved backwater arm or the towpath. Nor must I on any of my future walks speak to any men. Beyond Cunnah's and the Middleton Boulevard shops, which I by then associated with Aunty, we carefully crossed the tree-lined Boulevard and walked by rows of bungalows, one around which I experienced particular delight because it was surrounded by a spinney of mature Scots pine trees.

"That was once a spinney in Wollaton Park," Mum explained. "Scalford Drive. You turn here by the privet hedge and then.....walk up to......Farndon Green."

This was a railed green set within a circular road with several roads leading off abacus fashion. On the corner of one road stood a white stuccoed post office "Toston Drive. This is where we want, look. You need to have the post office on the corner to your right," Mum continued.

Aunt Alice's bungalow was situated in the far corner of a spacious, well-tended garden.

Mum knocked at the solid back door which faced vegetable plots, privet hedges and the main road. When the door was opened, I heard someone saying to Mum, "Don't knock. You're family. Just open the door, call out and come in."

Aunt Alice stood taller than Mum. She was quietly spoken, straight backed and had her ample black hair pinned high upon her head. Her feminine features were distinguished. Her eyes pale blue; kindly, laughing. Like Mum, she wore a flowered smock for working around the house.

When following Mum I walked into the dining room, I met with the unfamiliarity of a piano, windows edged with vines and creepers, a caged canary and a black enamelled cooking range and fireplace. Besides an oven complemented by its stew pot and stock pot, buckets filled with coke or coal were placed in the hearth where kindling from the park and boulevard limes could be dried.

Pairs of boots and shoes were positioned in front of the fender above which was placed a rack for drying socks, scarves, gloves and hats.

Aunt Alice made us coffee, gave me biscuits and conversed with Mum as she went from this main dining room to the kitchen and although Mum occasionally joined her in the kitchen and the two women conversed in low voices, the dividing door remained open. I was part of the small gathering: the family.

On the piano stood several framed photographs, each depicting a good looking but serious expressioned young man. These were, Aunt Alice explained, my cousins.

Alan, who was a frogman diver on active war service out at sea, and Geoffrey and Derek, who were soldiers.

On seeing rays of sunlight tapering across the table, Aunt Alice took the birdcage down from its hook by the window, placed it in front of me and into the paths of light and told me that the canary would soon be singing. Canaries loved sunlight and that is what induced them into song, she further explained.

I sat alongside the cage and studied the yellow bird; noticed how its toes locked effectively onto its perch and how one deft movement changed its pose entirely.

The canary sprang from one perch to another with surprising agility. Its yellow plumage, I decided, was the colour of the sun. Its eye kindly in expression. Its beak designed for picking up seeds and husks of small fruit.

Suddenly the canary perched facing the light, opened its gape and issued from its pulsing throat a series of liquid notes that drew me like a magnet closer to its cage.

I wanted to call out to Mum and Aunt Alice, who was preparing something in the kitchen, but the words would not, *could not* form. I was literally speechless, kneeling on a chair beside the canary's cage, arms folded on the table edge before me while the little bird produced sounds from some tiny vestibule at the back of its throat that were nothing short of pleasurable to the human ear.

I had not by then heard of a larynx. Nor was I aware that at daybreak from April until the middle of June countless male songbirds fluted from perches to attract mates and then define their territorial boundaries.

Dad, and others on their early shifts, was obviously aware of 'the dawn chorus' as it was known but I was unaware of its existence, due probably to Mum not waking me each morning much before seven. Those minutes with Aunt Alice's canary then filled me with yet another startling but pleasurable aspect of the natural world. Had me wondering *why* small birds sang so beautifully, then further wondering if people stopped to listen.

Eagerly I returned to Aunt Alice's on the appointed Wednesday morning but I did not walk there alone, memorise the route though I had, for Aunt Alice was walking down the Boulevard's long bridge within minutes of me having patted Scamp goodbye and latched the front garden gate.

It was on this second visit I noticed the mature lime trees rising above the bungalow rooftops, perhaps two hundred yards from Aunt Alice's garden.

"Aunty, is that Lime Avenue on Wollaton Park?" I piped.

"Yes, and we'll be going there soon."

Later that morning, Aunty Alice took me by the hand and walking slowly and straight backed led me to the top of the road where we turned right onto Sutton Passeys Crescent. This crescent was named to commemorate the whereabouts of a village that like many in England appeared to be flourishing in medieval times but which appears to have become 'lost'. There is no trace of it today nor of its exact whereabouts. But at least bygone local historians conferred with councillors and planners around 1929 when the bungalow estate was nearing completion and the name Sutton Passeys was used accordingly.

To my delight, a high railed fence bordering the periphery grasslands of Wollaton Park had set within it a hand gate through which Aunt Alice guided me. We walked then across the grass and beneath the winter silhouetted lime trees towards the hilltop Hall. Of the red deer we saw nothing that day, except sets of hoof prints or 'slots' engraved in the sandy earth of their chosen crossing places. However, as we walked I learned something about Aunt Alice.

She was taller than Mum by perhaps three or four inches. And whereas Mum

177

worked to a daily and weekly timetable or routine, Aunt Alice gave one the attitude that she spread out over two weeks the chores that Mum crammed into one. What didn't get done today would get done tomorrow. Aunt Alice was confident and serene, whereas Mum, the second eldest of the two, was the hustler and bustler. When I was out shopping with Mum I was expected to walk at her pace, whereas Dad, Betty and now my new friend and guardian, Aunt Alice, walked at *my* pace.

Dad perhaps only hurried when on alighting from the Middleton Boulevard bus he had a live hen or cockerel tucked beneath his arm. And that was understandable!

I had the midday meal at Aunt Alice's and in the early afternoon she carried, in two journeys from a bedroom, a set of blue encyclopaedias and put them on the settee beside me.

"There. Have a look through these, Keith. There should be a lot to interest you there," she smiled.

Each page of these encyclopaedias was illustrated with a monochrome or sepia photograph. Enthralled, I read about Napoleon and the Duke of Wellington. General Gordon of Khartoum. Captain Scott of the Antarctic. 'Buffalo' Bill Cody. Historical events and people of whom I had never heard. There was an occasional feature that I liked called *Tales the Woodsman Told* and from it I learned about the animals of North America such as porcupine, racoon, bear and white tailed deer.

As I browsed the pictures and pages featuring the Boer War and the First World War, Aunt Alice putting another plate of sugared biscuits beside me, said, "Your Dad and your Uncle Tom were in the First World War." Uncle Tom, whom I had not by then met, was Aunt Alice's husband. But when she mentioned both men, I saw Dad's smile and twinkling blue eyes and was quietly grateful that he had come through it unscathed.

The encyclopaedias also contained maps of continents and of the world. Fascinated, I studied photographs of the Canadian Rockies, the Dolomites and Yellowstone National Park.

The great painters such as Cezanne, Picasso and Matisse meant nothing to me, but when I saw a print of Edwin Landseer's famed *Monarch of the Glen* the volume stayed open at the page as I read of Landseer's prowess as a sculptor, engraver and painter. Knighted in 1850 and said to have been the favourite artist of Queen Victoria, Edwin Landseer was best known for his sporting paintings and fewer sentimental Victorian studies of dogs and dog groups.

He sculpted the lions at the foot of Nelson's Column in London's Trafalgar Square and his best known work, *The Monarch of the Glen*, was displayed in the House of Lords.

Landseer was the first artist I was really aware of. I marvelled at his animal form correctness. His every detail of fur, tail position and eye expression. The dog-like muzzles, eye, shape, secretion glands and antler proportions of his stags.

At teatime when Mum came to fetch me, I thanked Aunt Alice for having me as I had been told. Aunt Alice, however, waved my thanks aside —

"You can come any time you like, Keith. Any day, any time. You're family. And so is your Mum."

And as with Mum I left the small bungalow estate, I realised gratefully that I had discovered my second home and had learnt more in one day than I had in those weeks spent at school.

The next day Mum was excited. Her niece and my cousin Rene had written saying she was home on leave and coming to see us that afternoon.

By the time Rene arrived, the dining room smelt of polish and the slim books I was not currently browsing were placed discreetly beneath the settee cushions.

Scamp was as excited as Mum and I when wearing a new flowered dress Rene arrived. With me she enthused about the country estate where she was billeted in Arundel, Sussex, and the relative tameness of the red squirrels there. With Mum, in the kitchen, I would think she learnt of Aunty's death, the funeral for which had taken place the day before when I was with Aunt Alice.

When she returned to Scamp and I in the dining room Rene took from her leather bag a brown covered book which she handed to me — "Present for you, Keith."

Thanking her, I resettled onto the settee to study the embossed title of *The Children of Other Lands* but only for seconds because I was soon turning the book's pages.

Each chapter was written in the first person and as if from a boy or girl who lived in Brazil, China, India or a village in the heart of the Belgian Congo. Each page was illustrated with a monochrome photograph depicting some form of activity taking place within that village or encampment.

I particularly liked two chapters, perhaps because the narrators were literally Poles apart and their lives so extreme and comparable. The first described the life of Tuk-Too, an Eskimo boy who lived in an igloo. Furs and seal oil were, I learned, the foremost commodities relating to an Eskimo's survival. And the equivalent of going shopping, as I still sometimes did with Mum, was for Tuk-Too to take up a harpoon and kayak and go searching for a seal.

Like most young readers, I could barely imagine the experience.

The other extreme was described by a Bedouin girl called Herfa. She was particularly responsible for the sheep and goats, the providers of wool and milk, kept by the elders of the tribe.

The survival of Herfa's people again revolved around animal substances, particularly hide, cheese and milk. Herfa milked goats, made cheese and occasionally herded the tribe's camels and dromedaries.

Having already familiarised myself with the existence of the local gypsies, I was much taken by the idea of wandering from place to place and for many weeks after Rene had given me the book, both Tuk-Too and Herfa hovered within the unexplainable realms of my imagination.

In that one mid-term week I learned so much from a set of encyclopaedias and one book. Matters, *learning matters*, however seemed to slow when in the dark days of winter I returned to school and with the prospect of Christmas dominating our thoughts. The Christmas with Santa Clause, I discovered, belonged to home. Imagery relating to the house. Here at school a new person was introduced into our lives, or at least into *my* life. Someone called Jesus of Nazareth.

Enthralled, like every child in the classroom, I listened to the bible stories relating to his birth and memorised the carols Miss Jones chalked line by line up on the blackboard.

On the classroom's back wall we between us drew and painted our versions of the nativity scene, then on another section of wall put up pictures relating to a

Christmas window and stuck daubs of cotton wool dipped with glue across it in an effort to depict snowflakes.

Leaving school at half past four, I walked the Boulevards alone in lamp-lit darkness but drew comfort from the headlights of passing traffic. Had there been an early air raid, I would have ran all the way because I knew of no air raid shelter along the route.

The song that we children all loved that Christmas was *Away in a Manger* followed by *The Holly and the Ivy*. In the carol *We Three Kings of Orient Are*, I never asked but each time we sang I wondered why three kings ruled over two cities, one city being Orri and the other Tarr.

Mum was one of the mothers who attended our carol service on the afternoon the school broke up for the Christmas holiday. She walked to the school with a lady called Mrs. Coombes whose son Terry attended but unlike me was allowed to stay school dinners. Throughout the carol service Mrs. Coombes sat smiling as we sang but Mum, probably ten or fifteen years her senior, sat with tears brimming in her eyes. Yet I never asked why.

After the service the four of us walked home together, the war forgotten and Christmas looming colourfully and excitedly on the horizon.

On the night before Christmas Mum and Dad called me into the kitchen. They were about to wring the necks of the three oldest hens. Scamp was to stay in the dining room beside the fire.

Sitting side by side on chairs taken from the dining room Mum and Dad had a hen placed between them and one on each knee. Facing outwards the hens sat perfectly still, combs and wattles gleaming, eyes unblinking but not blazing with fury like those of the cockerel reigning dominant in the pen alongside the remaining hens.

"This is what you have to do to kill a hen, Little Man," Dad explained. Gently he fingered the feathered neck of a still, unprotesting hen, felt for the space between the vertebrae then guided my fingers along the same route. When he found the appropriate space, Dad, while concentrating, asked, "Are you looking?" He then positioned a finger and thumb in the space and gave a sharp tug. The hen's head lolled slightly forward. She had known nothing.

Mum repeated the process with the second and Dad the third. There were no squawks, no fluttering, no blood. At Mum's bidding, I then returned to the dining room, Scamp and my books.

Some time later they called me again into the kitchen. Mum was laughing because feathers and minute particles of down tickled her nose. Around their ankles on sheets of newspaper dozens of beautiful russet feathers were spread as Mum and Dad each plucked the crops and bellies of the freshly killed hens.

Following this they carried the plucked hens to the draining board and deftly decapitated them. Mum gave me a head to study. The eye was as bright as if the hen was alive. She then gave me the severed legs and feet, yellow scaled and with singular spurs evolved at the back for scratching through soil, pebbles and chaff in an effort to find food. Mum singed the wing quills with tapers of paper lit from the gas cooker. The smell was acrid. She then showed me the family famed parson's nose.

Replacing the three plucked hens on the draining board, Mum and Dad each standing aside so that I could see put one hand into a chicken and withdrew the innards.

"That's what you do, see. I'll let you have a go next Christmas," said Mum, then nodding sideways at the innards, she said "Our insides must look something like that."

I looked at the conglomeration of pipes and organs and Mum found the dark red atom that was the hen's heart.

"Incredible when you think that the lifeline and *lifetime* of almost every living thing depends on this," Mum murmured while again rubbing her thumb sideways across the end of her nose.

When the hens were cleaned and dressed they were placed onto the kitchen cold slab for the night, each on a plate. I helped Mum and Dad sweep all the feathers into the sheets of newspaper and Mum made a parcel of the innards, heads and feet. We then dumped the lot into the grey waste bin placed in the backyard recess.

The next day Dad and I walked to Mrs. Doughty's with one oven-ready hen. My cousin Sylvia came for the other.

"Is Mrs. Doughty *buying* the hen off us, Dad?" I ventured.

"No. She might offer us money but we won't take it. You must never take money from people worse off than yourself. Besides which, it's always a pleasure to give and often a bigger pleasure than to receive," Dad confirmed.

Mum told me that feathers were used to stuff pillows and eiderdowns and that night I found a curled white, black and russet feather poking from a corner of the pillow which I carefully examined.

"That will be the feather of an eider duck. No, they don't live around here. They congregate along the coastlines and out at sea," explained Mum while anticipating my further question.

On Christmas Eve feathers were far from my mind. Pillows by contrast were *very much* on my mind because two pillowcases had been placed side by side on the landing in readiness for Santa to stuff with presents. One pillowcase for me and one for Betty.

Mrs. Teather had called earlier, 'ahead of Santa' as she put it, and presented me with a book called *The Tailor And The Mouse*. And that, I decided, was the night in which I would discover if there really was such a person as Santa Claus.

I planned to stay awake between the blankets. Listen for every footfall. Every creak of the stairs. Every muffled sigh, indicating that Santa was successfully completing his task.

And surely Scamp would bark. Surely.........!

Suddenly my eyes opened. *I had fallen asleep.* I was surrounded by darkness, silence, the solstice chill. Had I missed him? Had Santa been?

I was by this time sleeping alone in Aunty's bedroom above the front door. I could hear my heartbeat yet knew that I could do *without* sleep. Leaving the bed, I switched on the bedroom light and padded onto the carpeted landing. The two pillowcases bulged with parcels. *Presents!*

I went to mine and began hauling it into the bedroom while addressing Betty's closed bedroom door with the words, "Come on Betty, he's been!"

Chuckling to herself while recalling that incident years later, Mum told me I had called out to Betty at two in the morning!

The pillow slip contained packets of sweets, a toy car or two and, as expected, books. Not surprisingly, I unwrapped and opened the bulkiest - 'A present from Mum and Dad'. So how had it fallen into Santa's hands? Moreover, *why* had he allegedly delivered it? And by coming down the chimney? The book was called *The Daily Mail Annual.* It was an encyclopaedic volume of stories and informative articles and, to my delight, like Betty's film annuals one could smell, *could almost savour* the print, especially attached to the full page monochrome photographs of birds.

There was a pair of long eared owls, featured with the female incubating eggs in an old crow's-nest. There were also two studies of a barn owl, one capturing the pale winged bird in flight, the second a full sized portrait depicting the owl perched, facing the camera and with a dead mouse or vole clutched in its talons.

In later years these and other such photographs became classics and by reading the captions that Christmas morning I learned that the photographer's name was Eric Hosking, who had been photographing birds for twenty years. Twenty years! That seemed an incredibly long time.

I imagined Eric Hosking to be a tall, lean man who wore glasses and sported a head of black curly hair.

The captions explained that he carried most of his sophisticated photographic equipment in a shoulder bag and pannier attached to the back of his bicycle.

Looking at the owl photographs I was again aware of the surrounding silence within the house. The darkness beyond the curtained windows. Birds such as the barn owl, and at around a quarter past two on that Christmas morning, I associated with Dad's daily bus rides out to the villages of south Nottinghamshire and the Vale of Belvoir. Little did I realise that a pair of tawny owls hunted the hedgerows and ditchsides of Cherry Orchard Lane less than three hundred yards from the house. Or that a pair of barn owls, which reared an annual brood at Aspley Hall Farm, skimmed over the night blackened fields and spinneys close to Shepherds Wood. Another pair of barn owls left, each dusk, the deserted stables of Woodyard Lane and quartered the canalside fields. Only in later years did I learn there were owls much closer to home than I had realised.

Eric Hosking had also photographed oyster catchers and a pair of stone curlew and as I turned the pages of the book I wondered if, when I was a man, I would become a singing cowboy like Gene Autrey or a bird photographer like Eric Hosking. Which would I, *should I*, choose?

The second bird panel in *The Daily Mail Annual* featured the superlative work of an artist whose name I have forgotten, if indeed I learned it in the first place. These were the birds of the garden and woodland. Some birds, like the chaffinch, bullfinch, great and blue tit, that I had seen on my walks to and from school, I had become used to seeing. The song thrush, with its mud-lined nest in which four bluish green eggs with black spots were visible, was beautifully portrayed with the warm honey yellow of its crop holding those black blotches that rendered the bird so conspicuous and recognisable.

The artist's song thrush was singing. I imagined its tongue flickering and throat pulsating, but unlike Aunt Alice's canary this bird was portrayed totally wild.

The painting of the blackbirds nesting in honeysuckle I quietly revelled in, for the artist had included every detail including the yellow orbital ring of the cock bird as well as its tail and wing flickering stance.

Disappointment then clouded my vision when I noticed that the plumage of the hen bird incubating the eggs was black, whereas in truth the plumage of the hen blackbird is dark brown. Hadn't the artist noticed that?

Ignoring the continuing chill, I turned more pages of the book but stopped again when I saw the monochrome photographs of *The Cutty Sark*. Launched in 1869, this clipper ship was photographed in dry dock at Greenwich Pier. I compared the height of the masts to the length of the ship. Wondered who its captains and crews had been. Admired its figure heads. Its sheer height and size. At Greenwich, the book continued, the naval history of Britain could be traced back to Tudor times.

Eventually, I realised that not only my hands but my nose were cold. But at least I knew Santa had been! Closing the book, I returned all my presents to the pillowcase, put out the light and snuggled beneath the blankets and eiderdown.

When Mum came to tell me breakfast was almost ready, I was again studying the photographs of *The Cutty Sark*. "I see that Santa's been then," she smiled.

"Yes! *Look at this!*" I enthused, while brandishing with two hands *The Daily Mail Annual* before her eyes.

"Yes, I'll look at it later. After breakfast," laughed Mum, and it was then I detected a look of mischief in her eyes that told me she had looked at it before fitting it into my urgently waiting pillowcase.

That evening, in the front room with Betty and our cousins Rene and Sylvia, I learned more from the *Silver Screen* and *Film Review* annuals.

The actress Greer Garson had won an award for her part in *Mrs. Miniver* and a film, *The Song of Bernadette,* starring a pretty dark haired girl called Jennifer Jones had been released in the USA.

I was, however, still baffled by such film titles as *The Life And Death of Colonel Blimp* or *The Gentle Sex* and *Stage Door Canteen.*

After a while I thought, 'Why bother?' They weren't cowboy films anyway!

CHAPTER 26

January 1944. Amphibious tanks rolled off British production lines. Tanks designed to act in shoreline defensives against the enemy.

On the 22nd British and American troops beached at Anzio in Italy. The plan was to break the German Gustav Line, but the Germans remained fighting and steadfast. Joined by the French Corps, the British and American troops made a second attempt on January 24th. The battle, by then being fought at Monte Cassino, ended on February 12th. Three days later the British and Americans destroyed the monastery by bombings.

On the 19th February, and for the first time since 1941, the Luftwaffe returned to bomb London. The bombings lasted until the 26th and although known as 'the little blitz', there were many casualties. At Lake Tinnsjo, Norway, the Germans' water supply used in atomic research was blown up along with a ferry. No force or battalion claimed responsibility, therefore the 'culprits' were labelled saboteurs.

'Big Week' followed this raid. The combined American and British air forces flew intent on bombing selected targets aligned to the German aircraft industry. Around 21,000 tons of bombs were released in this 'surprise' and well thought out campaign.

In March, the United States Air Force released their P-51 Mustang fighters, equipped for long range combat, out with the squadrons of bombers which bombed Berlin, the German capital, by daylight.

On the 24th, seventy-six Royal Air Force officers escaped from a Polish prisoner-of-war camp. Three made it to England. The remaining seventy-three were recaptured. Showing no mercy Adolph Hitler, the German Chancellor, ordered that fifty of those officers be shot.

***

Sunday evening. The threat of snow beyond the curtained french windows. Snow according to the wireless forecast. Not at all portraying an aura of romance as the Bing Crosby recording of *White Christmas* suggested.

Dad sat in his fireside chair reading the newspaper. Mum again sat opposite darning socks. With books beside me and an increasing stock of metal farm animals in front, I sat to the table. Little or nothing was said.

So used had I become to the background wireless that I had acquired the knack of tuning in when my brain and ear demanded, which was infrequently. That evening proved an exception.

As I placed my metal animals in paddocks and corrals then changed them about, my brain and ears became attuned to a steady, 'harum, thrum, thrum' rhythm being transmitted through the wireless grille.

It was a marching rhythm. A column of solders marching through a misted and uncertain horizon were coming into view. There was snow underfoot and the deep mystique of a forest either side the track along which they marched. Yet they were singing, *singing.* And singing in harmony, in tune.

Suddenly the room, table and metal farm animals before me meant nothing, for I was out there singing with the soldiers. Marching to war. *To my death perhaps.*

Years later our neighbour Mr. Teather, who became my choral master at the secondary school I attended, once explained to the school assembly the surveyed and eventual world-wide agreement that while an audience can listen intently to a woman speaking for longer than they can a man, the reverse occurs when they are listening to a singer.

A man speaks, converses, usually in monotone, whereas a woman's voice varies according to the points she is making or instructions she is giving. By contrast, in singing the average woman's scale range is to some extent limited and the high notes are not always easy on the ear even though the woman singer appears to have reached the notes effortlessly. Men singers, on the other hand, are able to demand more from the attention span of the average audience and the renderings of a male voice choir, were, and still usually are, considered preferable from a listener's viewpoint.

When that evening the soldiers with whom I imagined myself marching began collectively singing, the haunting words and rhythm of the song forced me to sit, metal farm animals in hand, and listen.

Mum, Dad and I were the audience. The room's audience. The *silent* audience. And the men? They were singing words describing *a somewhere* out there in the snow.

There was a lamplight. A barricade. And a girl who waited for them there. A girl whom they needed. The only girl or woman remaining in the life of each one of them. A girl called 'Lily Marlene'.

"Are they real soldiers singing, Mum?' I asked.

'No, it's a male voice choir. They are singing from a recording studio. But there are soldiers out there in the snow tonight and cold," Mum answered. Then suddenly she was crying. "Poor lads! They don't *want* to be out there but they *have* to be. Hundreds of miles away from home most of them, and not knowing if they'll ever see home again."

Dad continued reading the newspaper but I suspected he was as much startled by Mum's outburst as I was myself.

"Is it an English soldier's song?" I continued, while thinking that when she gave me the answer Mum would stop crying.

"Well, that's an English male voice choir singing it, but it's a German song really."

Baffled, I wondered how and why an English male voice choir had learnt and chosen to record a German song.

"It's a Marlene Dietrich song. But I should think there are hundreds of poor young soldiers singing it."

"What, *our* soldiers, the British?"

"Yes, but it doesn't matter whether they're British, Italian, Yanks, Russians or Germans. All those poor lads, they don't want to be fighting in the war. They want to he home like we are tonight. Home with their Mums and Dads and brothers and sisters. It's a terribly cruel war." Removing her glasses, Mum then began dabbing her eyes.

Shifting uneasily in his armchair while turning the newspaper pages, Dad added,

"That's true. It's nothing short of cruel is war. And the trouble is, Little Man, and always has been, it's the politicians and dictators of this world who start the wars but the hundreds and thousands of working-class people like ourselves who have to fight in and finish them."

By this time the male voice choir, the soldiers, had marched by and were fading into the distance. Marching to so-called glory....to war......or......

In the school playground with Terry, Brian and Fraser, I played shooting and dodging games inspired by the latest films we had each been taken to see. The games were originally called cowboys and Indians or cops and robbers but then a new phase, including again the shooting and dodging theme, merged in and was called spies and secret police.

More demonstrative lads spread out their arms and made machine gunning noises while yelling, "Look out! I'm a Spitfire!" whereas occasionally another attempted to circle and shoot him down, while loudly informing 'the enemy' that he was a Luftwaffe day bomber.

If Dad had to work on a Saturday morning, Mum was left with no choice but to take me shopping with her to the city. Betty, who could have stayed home and looked after me, often met her friends and like Mum and I went to the city but to go around the departmental stores looking at clothes, buying sweets and a weekly or monthly film magazine.

The first section of the city centre with which I became acquainted was Beastmarket Hill, for here beneath a row of ornate balustrades Mum queued to reach the glass display counters of Elizabeth King, who advertised 'high-class pork pies and delicatessen commodities'.

After leaving the bus one morning and walking by the Odeon Cinema to Elizabeth King's, I studied a railed statue situated in the centre of the road. It was the statue of a woman, heavily robed and bearing a dour faced expression.

"It's Queen Victoria," said Mum in answer to my question.

"But I thought the King lived at Buckingham Palace."

"He does but with the new Queen and two Princesses. Queen Victoria, she's dead now. But she was on the throne when I was a little girl."

This answer furnished me with an awareness of continuity and family lineage, although the present King and Queen *did* smile I was about to say but thought the better of it. However, I secretly decided that Queen Victoria had been portrayed looking purposely stern and displeased. But then, as I told Betty, so would I be if I had to sit on a throne all day wearing long robes and a crown.

Suddenly, I was hit in the face by the corner of a leather carrier bag swinging from a woman's uplifted arm. Smarting with indignation, I yelled out and looked back but so far as the woman was concerned there was no one walking the streets of the city but she.

Mum resorted to the bantering tones to which I was gradually become accustomed as she guided me to the long queue outside Elizabeth King's.

"Look, you mustn't expect too much from the people of *this* city. They walk, as I suppose they have always walked, as if everybody else is invisible. I know because I was born and bred here and as a little girl I had to run errands for my parents. I was hit in the face with a bag more than once. They're just plain ignorant most of 'em, mi lad, so you might as well face up to it now and get used to the idea."

Mum and Dad had taught Betty and I that if as a family we walked four abreast and someone came from the opposite direction, two of us would drop back to allow them to pass. Because the pavement was there to be shared; it belonged to everyone.

In the city centre, however, no such pavement etiquette existed. "All talk, sweaty under the armpits and fat as bacon pigs, m'lad," was how Mum described some of the people she envisaged me meeting in the city of the future.

Once we were in Elizabeth King's queue and later the shop, however, the people Mum had just described passed by and beyond the counter display cases where various sized pork pies, trays of sausage rolls, ham and veal or steak and kidney pies enlivened the appetite, the girls and women serving were slim, polite and smiling.

In retrospect, I believe that these shop assistants were on the books of or had been recommended to the firm by domestic agencies. They were young ladies in every sense of the word. Moreover, they seemed to glide across the floor and were incredibly straight backed.

"They've had lessons in deportment or how to walk properly," Mum explained.

One girl shop assistant, tall, slim and probably not by then in her early twenties, unwittingly earned my constant attention. Her hair was black, sleek and clasped at the nape. Her face was pear shaped. Eyes blue, twinkling. Teeth even and white. Mouth and lips small and beautifully formed. Complexion fresh, sheened. Wide eyed, I expect, I studied her every move. Her every twist, turn and uttered word.

"I like *that* lady, Mum," I ventured.

"Yes, she *is* nice. I expect she's of Irish descent."

I was then reminded of Bing Crosby and the Irish ballads that spasmodically enhanced the Saturday afternoon wireless programme centred around him. Surely the girl would rather be in Ireland, which according to Bing was always green and to which every dreamer wanted to return.

"Then why isn't she in Ireland, Mum?" I whispered.

"Oh, I expect she's come over looking for work. A lot of them do. There's not a lot of work in Ireland from what I can gather. And people have to work to live," Mum explained.

In the weeks and months of the future the name Elizabeth King was, to me, synonymous with the image of the girl. Not surprisingly then, I looked forward to going there with Mum.

On leaving Elizabeth King's, we crossed between the buses and delivery lorries to Slab Square which was overlooked by the prestigious and domed building known as the Council House. As we walked, or as I dodged waddling people and food bulked leather carrier bags or wicker baskets, I glimpsed between moving bodies the pigeons pecking at the cracks in the flagstones.

"They taste very nice do well browned young pigeons, son," grinned an old man sitting on a seat watching the pigeons, people and buses go by.

Mum looked at the man and smiled. She stopped because she sensed that I wanted to stay a short while. She also explained that even in a war such as we were experiencing, pigeons had their uses because messages were sometimes fastened to their red stubby legs and a pigeon carried these probably hundreds of miles to the place from which it had been taken.

"They're called homing pigeons," Mum assured me.

In the school playground I had learned about spies. "Do spies use pigeons too, Mum?"

Mum looked surprised. "Well yes, I expect they could if they wanted," she confirmed.

Built from stone hewn from the quarries of Portland in Dorset, the Council House in Nottingham's city centre resembles at first glance St. Paul's Cathedral which was also built from Portland stone. Mum and Dad knew the previous building which was called the Old Exchange. In fact, every Nottinghamian knew it for within the offices all the general rates, various taxes, rents and market stall fees were administrated.

Close by stood another building known as The Shambles. The annual Goose Fair had been held on the area in front of these buildings and extended along Long Row, South Parade and on to Chapel Bar.

Designed by architect Cecil Howitt, the Council House dominated the site of the Old Exchange and the foundation stone was laid in 1927. In May 1929 the prestigious building was officially opened by the Prince of Wales. A golden key was used to open the doors. The building has several memorable features, not the least of which is the dome. But as she stood with me in the Old Market Square (known to many as Slab Square) that Saturday morning, Mum pointed out the clock positioned beneath the dome. The clock was called Little John.

The hour bell, weighing around ten and a half tons, carries the reputation for being the deepest toned bell in the country.

When the wind was in the right direction, Mum said she heard it chiming from hers and Dad's bedroom but the bell clock with which I was most familiar chimed high from the church tower on Churchfield Lane and had a mellower, singular clanging tone.

Some Saturday mornings we walked the Boulevard to the bus terminus at the Middleton Boulevard shops, Mum's explanation being that she needed to go straight to the Central Market. Having gone there with Dad to buy the day old chicks, I thought it an intriguing place and loved the striped awnings over and around the stalls, the banter of the salesmen and saleswomen dressed in khaki smocks and the displays of green vegetables, lettuces, cauliflower and watercress.

If for some reason I failed to become a singing cowboy like Gene Autrey, I might work in a market I decided. Have a stall of my own. My name displayed and painted above it.

The fish market, with its saline odours, I could have explored for hours. Mum often bought several pounds of black, dripping shelled mussels here which together with me she split open at the kitchen sink to accompany the green salad which, with sliced boiled egg, the four of us enjoyed each Saturday teatime.

When purchased in the market the mussels had to be wrapped in several sheets of newspaper, then put inside a paper carrier bag. Then the smells of the sea blended with those of soaked newspaper print which I considered less attractive.

As Mum led me between the fish market stalls, she noted my interest in the size and shapes of the fish displayed there and pointed out to me the silver grey cod, the rotund halibut - the white fish she prepared for me with mashed potatoes and parsley sauce on Wednesday, and the flatter plaice with its red spots which Mum shallow fried on Fridays.

Just as stallholders swept cabbage, lettuce leaves and paper wrappings from the front of their stalls in the main market, so the fish market stallholders between serving and straightening the fish displayed on their slabs periodically moistened their wares by each using a small watering can or small bore hosepipe.

When we left the market by the doors on Huntingdon Street, I was reminded of Dad, if ever he was far from my mind, when I saw the red and cream liveried Barton and Trent buses leaving or pulling into the bus station.

About every third or fourth visit to the market entailed Mum guiding me for about five hundred yards along Huntingdon Street or nearby Glasshouse Street without really explaining where we were going. However, when we came to a shortened cul-de-sac, cobble-stoned and darkened by a low wide bridge which connected one to the railway, I was in no doubt as to where we were going and who we would be seeing. And in what state we would be leaving. On my first visit I was surprised and apprehensive. Where were we? What were we doing there?

To the right on a street corner was a door with a clean brass knob. A door which, to my surprise on that first visit, Mum opened by turning the knob then directed me to the left and into a dark room with one window looking out into the bridged and cobbled street and the other facing east but overlooked by a stable yard. The house smelt of dust, damp and wood rot, especially the eerie staircase at our backs. Then we were in the room; potted plants, palms and dog statuettes on shelves and window sills. To our right stood a broad table beyond which was a fireplace. And in the corner, seated in a high back chair, draped from head to toe in black and facially resembling my mother, Elizabeth Alice Bonser, my maternal grandmother, prepared for greeting. Bonser was my grandmother's maiden name, for she had married Sam Wheat, my grandfather, whom I saw only twice on those visits and who, like most men, worked Saturday mornings.

I soon learned to refer to both grandparents as Grandma and Grandad Wheat.

The instant she saw my head bobbing above the table, Grandma Wheat's round face lit up but her greeting psychologically cut me off at the knees. "And what yo come for?" she would hail.

So weren't we welcome, Mum and I? And if we weren't, then *what* were we doing there?

When Mum and Grandma Wheat looked at each other their faces darkened. They scowled and inwardly both women prepared for war.

Clutching the zipped leather shopping bag, Mum sat opposite her mother and the interrogating and raging began. Why hadn't Mum called before this? Why, her mother and father might have died. Just because Mum was living in a big posh house now, did she think herself too far up the social ladder to be calling on her mother? Mum, quietly snarling in the same way as Grandma Wheat gave her answers. She came when she could, which was usually when she was visiting the market. After all, what time had she for heaven's sake? She had a husband and daughter to pack for work. A son to get to school. Shopping to do! The weekly washing and ironing to do! Breakfasts, dinners, teas and suppers to daily prepare. So what time had she for visiting, eh? Besides which, she lived on the other side of the city now.

In her scowling and gesticulating defensives, Grandma Wheat mentioned my Aunt Alice and her other daughters who were, of course, also my aunts but each of whom I had never met. Amy, Nellie, Harriet. There were uncles, John, Les and Fred, too. They came to see Grandma Wheat. Came *especially* to see Grandma Wheat. *They* didn't call in on the way to or from the fish market. *And* they took all their children with them. The grandchildren who Grandma and

Grandad Wheat were entitled to see.

Perplexed, I examined the table legs, the chair to which I was steered. I disliked the palms and pot dogs as much as I disliked the ongoing argument that each time Mum took me there, both women seemed to thoroughly enjoy.

It was remark for remark. There was no hesitation and no expletives uttered. Had they been given boxing gloves I think, even today, both women would have gladly set about each other.

On one occasion Grandma Wheat broke off and gesturing towards me said to Mum, "And see to your lad. He's looking upset."

The truth was I didn't know how I was *supposed* to look and *where* to look. Grandma Wheat then stood, went to the window and unhooked a birdcage from a pedestal. She brought the cage across and put it on the table in front of me. "Say 'sweet' to my canary," she coaxed.

Not knowing what else to do, I did as I was told and while I studied the canary the women continued their argument. Word matching word. Outburst matching outburst. No pause for breath. No loss of words. Neither would give way.

On one occasion, Grandma Wheat retorted, "I don't know where you get this snapping and snarling attitude from," to which Mum answered —

"Why from you, of course. Didn't that ever occur to you? Your days of bullying me are over. I'm a match for you *any* day and I'm not going to be treated like this."

I never expected tea and biscuits to be placed before us, nor were they.

Eventually, and much to my relief, Mum stood and said, "Right, come on, Keith. We're getting out of here."

Gently but purposely Mum guided me in front of her while Grandma Wheat sang out her farewell, but to me.

Still seething, Mum usually slammed the door. But never once did she use her aggression on me. Instead she guided me left, across Glasshouse Street and along Cairn Street to the wooden footbridge with its steep steps and bustling people, which took those many pedestrians over the noisy, intriguing and soot scented platforms of the Victoria Station.

Sometimes I looked through the steel sections and saw on the platforms, or boarding steam hazed trains below, groups of soldiers or airmen lifting kitbags, smoking and talking.

It was then I felt the jab, the start of reality, because previously I had viewed such scenes in grey, black and white on the cinema's twice weekly *Pathe News*. But below us on those Saturday mornings lingered the truth. The reminder *that the war existed*, was being fought, while on the descending stairs Lord Kitchener stared balefully from a poster, his finger pointing, filling one with trepidation as his eyes spoke the words emblazoned below his portrait, 'YOUR COUNTRY NEEDS YOU'.

Grandma Wheat? Lord Kitchener? Or Mum on the defensive? Who was the strongest? The most determined?

Leaving the Victoria Station, Mum shepherded me across to a grey church and told me we were in Trinity Square. As we crossed to a row of shops, Mum then pointed to Forman Street. "When I was a little girl about the size you are now, I had to dodge in and out of the traffic and take pudding basins into a pub along there to have the landlord fill them with pork dripping which we spread on slices of bread at teatime. It was either that or jam . And late Friday and Saturday evenings, I had to get to the shops just before they closed and buy the leftovers; the loaves of bread, cakes and slices of bacon or corned beef that would otherwise be thrown away. They were sold to me cheaply because the shopkeepers were glad to get rid of them. There's Reville's Yard. I had a friend lived there in a tiny, poky house situated *right in the middle* of the city. Her family were badly off, too, and sometimes she and I would run the gauntlet of the streets together, pudding bowls in our hands, almost begging. Even at that young age I felt *so* ashamed."

Mum then directed me to a short paved street that sloped down to meet traffic-thronged Parliament Street. This short street was called Trinity Walk. Off to the right, about halfway down where the street curved slightly, we joined people queuing outside another shop. Here fresh fish, some game, poultry and seafoods were sold. The shop was owned by Maud Anderson and was, of course, referred to by that name. The queue could never be compared to that which assembled daily outside Elizabeth King's but a queue was always there nevertheless.

In Maud Anderson's shop window crabs, pink, cream with black foreclaws and looking like waxen toys, crawled on damp white tiles. Fascinated as always I checked that each had eight legs. Attempted to locate the eyes and wondered why and how such strange looking creatures had evolved. What were they doing on this earth? Where did they come from? Mum explained that these were edible crabs. They lived on the edge of the sea and sought the pools of rocky coastlines. Their meat was clean and good. Which was why we were having crab meat for tea.

The women serving behind the shop counter lacked the grace of those I secretly admired serving in Elizabeth King's. They were, by comparison, older women. Around Mum's age perhaps.

It was not, however, the women behind the counter who controlled my interest once Mum and I were inside the door of Maud Anderson's but a sightless object positioned high on the wall. The skull and antlers of a red deer stag, or 'the head' in hunting and taxidermy parlance.

The antlers were black with ivory white tips. Each antler carried seven or eight perfectly formed tines. In retrospect, I would estimate the stag to have been shot in its sixth or seventh year.

A neat rounded bullet hole defined the centre of the stag's forelock. When seen in a certain light the antlers created a wall shadow.

I stared at the black eye sockets wondering if the stag had once roamed the walled parklands of Wollaton within walking distance of my home. Or had it graced the glades and plucked overhanging foliage from the oaks in Sherwood Forest?

Mum couldn't say. Nor did she ask the women serving behind the counter. "Because it will only hold the people up who are queuing behind us and Maud Anderson's assistants might not know anyway," she explained.

I have heard it said that when a live crab is selected for the table then plunged into the pan of scalding hot water, which kills it, the crab in its death throes screams. If this is so, I heard no such screaming after Mum had picked out our particular crab and when it was handed to Mum, the crab was inert and wrapped tightly in newspaper.

On arriving home with our saline scented bundles, Scamp stood wagging his tail while probing the leather bag with his broad muzzle.

"No, Scamp. None of this is for you," Mum told him, then stepping into the pantry and extracting from the cool slab a singular meaty bone brought the previous day from Burroughs the butchers, Mum added, "But this *is*."

Without hesitation, Scamp took the bone between his jaws while I opened the back door and let him out into the garden.

Scamp always chewed on and broke up a bone in one specific place when he was in the garden, and that was under the plum tree. Tummy to the grass, he positioned the bone upright between his forepaws and began chewing, grinding, turning his head sideways his eyes half closed, but whether due to effort or gastronomic ecstasy I could never ascertain.

When every sliver of meat had been swallowed, Scamp licked the bone then broke into it. I can hear the feverish crunching of bone against teeth as I write and see his tawny whiskered muzzle rising and lowering according to the play of his jaws.

As for the altercation that had taken place between Mum and Grandma Wheat, I gained the impression that Mum had forgotten by the time we left Maud Anderson's.

When later after each visit I told Dad about the stag head positioned on Maud Anderson's wall, he always smiled and said, "That was on Trinity Row, wasn't it, Little Man? Well, a place called New Yard used to stand there and that is where a famous boxer was born."

"A boxer!"

"Yes, Bendigo. Have you heard about him at school?"

I admitted that I hadn't.

"Well, I'll tell you about him when I'm not gardening as I am today. And I'll take you to his grave. It's not far from Trinity Walk."

"When are we going then, Dad?"

"We'll go one Sunday morning. There's a lovely statue of a white lion on Bendigo's grave. We can catch a bus to Trent Bridge from there," Dad told me, as smiling he returned to his spade work.

CHAPTER 27

Each Saturday afternoon varied but often Betty and cousin Sylvia would take me back to the city on a number 13 bus and we visited one of two cinemas situated less than fifty yards apart.

Both the Odeon and the Ritz were carpeted, beautifully upholstered and plush in every sense of the word. Each dressed in their best two-piece, Betty and Sylvia walked with me between them holding one hand. Consequently, I felt safe. Had few, if any, leather carrier bags to dodge or be assaulted by. And the bus stopped in front of both cinemas.

Usually we went to see the films of Bing Crosby, Bob Hope and Dorothy Lamour, the films known as 'The Road Series'.

There is little that I recall of *The Road to Utopia* but *The Road to Morocco* carried a distinctive sing-along type title tune and the talking camels had been allocated lines that had almost the entire audience laughing including myself, although I failed to understand the jokes. Between the years 1937-1947, although they were probably not aware of it, British cinema going audiences were seeing, *were experiencing*, the best films that cinema historians claim to have been made and the audience ratings obviously confirmed this. The Saturday afternoon cinemas were packed to the hilt and quite often the torch-bearing usherette had difficulty in finding three seats together. However, in respect of this we were always fortunate.

No matter how early in the afternoon we arrived at the cinema there were only a scant few seats left and if the film was that of a serious nature, a drama perhaps, the audience participation was intense.

Not infrequently the preceding *Pathé News* depicted battalions of young soldiers, airmen or sailors going about their training. *Being trained for warfare.*

One sequence that had me worried, and which throughout the war was screened several times, involved a training exercise in which soldiers in single file, helmeted and carrying full packs had to negotiate a rope bridge strung across a gorge.

The camera work was, for the time, sublime. The plunging distance. The awesome landscape of skull breaking rocks. The awareness that rope could break, *does break* or snap if badly worn. The prospect of German aircraft appearing as the soldiers filed tentatively over this swaying, uncertain, *frightening* bridge never failed to hold the attention of the audience. Would I one day be expected to do that?

After the *Pathé News* on Saturday afternoon, the 'B' film, as it was known, was a documentary about Whipsnade Zoo. I had never heard of such a place.

At Whipsnade, we learned, few if any of the zoo's inmates were caged. Instead they were kept in spacious paddocks or enclosures. It was due to this film that I saw my first lion. A magnificent male; scenting the air. Full maned, high shouldered, long backed and in grey, black and white. A thread of excitement shot through me. As if sensing this, Sylvia, sitting on my right, whispered, "Keith, we've got a zoo book at home that you can have. I'll bring it the next time I come."

"Oh thank you! Are there any lions in it?"

"Yes, lions, tigers - everything." Then Sylvia's gaze returned to the screen.

Following the Whipsnade documentary, the film was shown that everyone there had gone to see. The multi-award winning *Mrs. Miniver* starring Greer Garson and Walter Pidgeon. Not a word of dialogue did I understand. Yet I remained quiet in my seat for that unaccustomed, yet lovely warmth spread through my tummy as I studied Greer Garson. The thickness of her hair, shape of her small featured face. And those curling eyelashes. The way she tilted her head, lifted her chin. Much prettier than Bette Davis, the actress whose films I had also sat through without understanding a word, and again with my sister Betty in a seat on one side and Sylvia the other.

Greer Garson. I was still turning her name over in my mind when in the late afternoon we left the cinema. The prospect of owning a zoo book was also on my mind as we joined the crowds walking beneath the prestigious balustrades of Long Row in the centre of Nottingham.

There were still women, middle-aged and sombrely dressed, visiting the food shops. Those who were window shopping meeting at cafés or visiting and leaving the cinemas were well-dressed. At my height I was aware of well-pressed trousers and thick overcoats worn by the men, the majority of whom when seen twenty or forty feet away also sported trilbies, scarves or cravats. Some middle-aged men I thought looked like the film stars Clark Gable or Don Ameche, the more so because they sported short, dark moustaches.

Girls and women in two-piece suits and wearing court shoes linked arms as they looked first in one shop window and then another. Beneath the balustrades of Beastmarket Hill people still queued outside Elizabeth King's.

Reverting back to the films, I wondered firstly why grown-ups found so much to discuss and, secondly, why these discussions appeared so serious in films. I wondered then how the actors and actresses knew what to say and when to say it. It seemed a very sophisticated business.

As we crossed the end of the Market Square, I suddenly realised that we were partially surrounded by young men. Talking in groups. Smoking. Sitting on the low, periphery walls. And wearing uniforms. Some looked at us and grinned, or winked. I couldn't for the life of me think why.

A two-syllable whistle induced me to turn. And another. Betty and Sylvia also turned and smiled; *laughed.* Some of the uniformed young men winked and beckoned, but to Betty and Sylvia. I then remembered Betty bringing home her sailor boyfriend, Bernard, of whom we heard nothing more.

"What's that whistle for?" I asked, while wondering if I could do the same.

"It's a wolf whistle," answered one of the girls.

"What's it for, though?"

"It means that they like us."

Panic swept through me then. Surely my sister and cousin were not going to abandon me! Leave me standing while they went to the young men!

"Who are they anyway? Soldiers?"

"They're Americans; Yanks. G..I's. From the camp at Wollaton Park, I should think," Betty explained softly.

One stepped towards us and to Betty and Sylvia's delight gestured towards their handbags. "Got any gum, chum?" he asked which, as Sylvia repeated later, sounded to us like, 'Godd'ne gurm churm?'

Giggling, the girls opened their handbags while each giving a negative answer. The G.I's next question was, "Whaddya doing tonight then, ladies?"

"Going dancing; to the Palais," Betty told him.

"The Palais. See yer there about eight," he said.

I resented his intrusion. His forthright manner of speaking, *of asking.* The two girls, however, guided me by the groups of G.I.s to the 13 bus. Here I experienced a degree of relief because I knew that home waited a hundred yards or less from the bus stop. All we had to do was board the bus and sit down.

Inwardly comforted, I was grateful to Betty and Sylvia because they hadn't abandoned me after all. And if they *did* later meet the G.I.s? It didn't matter because I would be safe and at home with Mum and Dad. But next time she came, would Sylvia remember to bring the zoo book?

On March 10th, 1944 paratroopers of the 508th Regiment of the 82nd Airborne Division arrived in Nottingham. The two thousand or so young men were billeted in Wollaton Park and delighted with their surroundings.

On their first visit to the city, most found the time to be photographed around or on the back of one of the two ornate white lion statues positioned either side of the Council House steps. From then on they made friends in the Nottingham pubs, *The Jolly Higglers* on Ilkeston Road and *The Cocked Hat*, Broxtowe, in particular.

They were welcomed into the community and invited to eat with families, despite the food rationing enforcement. In family homes the G.I.s singly, or in pairs, listened to the wireless, especially the news bulletins, then went with the husband and wife, or often just the husband, to the pub of their choice. Beer, both mild and bitter, was rationed as the pub landlords were all too aware. Yet the evening party atmosphere was retained.

Towards midnight and perhaps throughout the small hours, the once quiet, almost forgotten lanes connecting Aspley and Beechdale to Wollaton resounded with the footfalls of parachutists heading from the pubs to their new home in Wollaton Park. Many no doubt sang and were drunk. But all were accounted for and appeared fresh and well-groomed at roll-call each morning.

CHAPTER 28

Mum announced one Monday tea-time that as the evenings were lengthening it would be a good idea if she and I walked the canal towpath to the wharf behind the fire station yard. The swan pair, she explained, might be nesting there again.

Dad's dinner? She would arrange things so that he could help himself.

As we walked the length of the Boulevard, cloud gradually obscured the sun. The gate opening onto the ramp which led one down onto the canal towpath with the bridge at our backs was painted grey, I noticed. The same colour as the clouds. The gate squeaked when between us Mum and I forced it open, probably because there was not a member of the British Waterways staff around to oil it for they had heeded Lord Kitchener's advertised warning and joined a section of the Armed Forces.

Blackbirds fluted from the lime and poplar trees rising above the wall to our right. Between the bridge and a little school that backed onto the canal a few rusted machines languished like russet cattle in a railway sleeper enclosure. Here, on the opposite side of the canal, once stood a row of dilapidated cottages, Mum explained. She remembered a blacksmith and farrier's workshop and a cottage resident, Mrs. Voce, who kept a bedraggled donkey in a relatively small shed.

The school backing onto the canal fascinated me because it housed a clock tower. If my memory serves me correctly, there was a clock on all four sides.

"Why can't I go to that school, one that backs onto the canal?" I demanded.

"That's it You'd be sitting gazing out of the window all day," Mum confirmed. I felt piqued until I saw a white ball easing round the tight canal bend that wound behind the lawn edged gasometer. The ball shape was achieved by a cob swan arching its wings high and wide over its back in a display of territorial aggression.

The swan's boat shaped body was propelled due to the forceful thrusts of its black paddles which co-ordinated with its rounded crop cutting forcefully through the cloud reflected mirror of water before it.

"Here's a swan," murmured Mum as the cob lurched forward, its neck taut and outstretched and seven feet wingspan finally breaking the water mirror.

We heard and saw its wings flogging the water, the cob lifting, coming closer, *closer*, with spray cascading in all directions, black paddles describing a running motion and a lane of suddenly disturbed water evolving in its wake.

Mum hesitated. The cob was flying *at us!* She and I were the reason for this sudden eruptive outburst.

"We don't want it to come on the towpath. They come padding down after you when they're protecting a nest like this," Mum said. Mum thought it better that we turn and walk back towards the bridge because with a wall on one side, now to our left, she felt vulnerable.

Here was Britain's largest and heaviest flying bird uncomfortably closing the gap between itself and us. The wall held the rhythmic echo of wings hitting the water, as amazed I watched the cob rise above the canal surface then again begin skimming it with its black paddles staccato fashion.

Once it was alongside, the cob braked like a *Pathé News* seaplane then momentarily mantled the water surface with its outstretched wings before resetting them over its back and sailing unhindered towards us, Mum and I still walking the towpath.

"We'll keep walking, Keith. It's not going to let us get as far along the towpath as its nest."

"What will it do to us, Mum?" I was alarmed, walking quickly with Mum, the cob patrolling fiercely alongside us.

Mum explained that a swan can flog a human with its wings. Moreover, she had seen it happen years before in a Sheffield park. Her sister, Amy, had strayed close to a swan pair preening on the grass with newly hatched cygnets and the cob or pen had struck out with its wings and caught Amy a blow on the leg. This caused a bruise that, according to Mum, never went away.

"Male geese, or ganders and turkeys, sometimes attack in the same way."

Arch winged and exercising the display known to the Victorians as 'busking', the cob swan sailed beside us. As we neared the bridge, Mum grew bolder and stepped closer to the cob which hissed with half-opened bill.

"Well I never!" Mum exclaimed.

"What, Mum?"

"I *know* this swan. He was lower down the canal on the Nottingham-Beeston stretch when I was a girl. Our family and everybody else called him Jack."

"How do you know it's the same swan, though?"

"Come here and I'll show you."

Turning I faced the cob who sat the water surface in front of us. His orange bill carried a black tip and was slightly hooked to enable him to pluck aquatic weed from the river or canal bed. The black knob or 'berry' surmounted at the base of the bill gleamed with moisture. His comparatively small, black and rounded eye was expressionless. Smears of ginger or orange swathed the top of the cob's head. His neck was yellow plush, shaped like an S. His full crop smeared with mud and weed. His wings raised cradle fashion with all the different shaped feather layering emphasised by the evening light.

But Mum was pointing to the black paddles of the cob, resting below the water surface like oars positioned in the row locks.

"See that paddle, the one on the right? That's how we children learned to tell Jack apart from the other swans."

The paddle was badly scarred; surely, I decided, with teeth marks.

"What's done that?" I queried.

"Well something has had a hold of him when he was a cygnet. It might have been a pike. Or it could have been an otter. But something grabbed Jack and tried to pull him under; eat him."

"He's much older than me then?"

"Oh *much* older. I can remember him when I was a girl, and I'm forty-five now."

Mum then told me how some of the narrow boat people claimed to have known Jack and his mate when as a young swan pair they annually reared a cygnet brood on a reedy lake in the grounds of what is now the Nottingham University campus.

Each autumn and winter Jack and the pen flew the short distance to Lenton Marshes, fields bordered by hedgerows but underwater in a particularly low section of the Trent flood plain and close to Mum's home. Besides aquatic weed, the swans fed on submerged field grass there. When in 1929 the lake was elongated, transformed into an ornamental boating lake and many swans flew in, Jack and his pen began nesting in a willow break at Harrimans Lane on the Nottingham-

Beeston canal.

"We used to see them sailing between Abbey Bridge and Treverthick's boatyard," Mum told me.

A decade or so after Jack had successfully turned Mum and I towards home, I learned from Ted Eales, a Wollaton water bailiff, that Jack used sometimes to nest in the reed beds of Martin's Pond situated about a mile from our house and similarly fly directly from the reeds and across the expanse of water the instant he saw someone walking along the bank.

As we turned again towards home, Mum said, "Yes, he's known and been fed by the narrow boat people has this old cob swan. He's known some hard winters, too. Snow and ice, just like I have. *And* he's lived through two world wars. We *both* have. Or *are* doing."

The greenish-grey dusk was coming in. Blackbirds and song thrushes continued to flute. Several feet to our right on the canal we heard the quiet 'lap, lap' of water as Jack sailed arched winged across our reflections.

In a change of mood, Mum began to recite. Not nursery rhymes, as years before I had learned to accept, but a poem. The first lines of poetry I had heard.

"There saw the swan, his neck of arched snow,
And oar'd himself along with majesty;
Sparkled his jetty eyes; his feet did show
Beneath the waves like Afric's ebony....."

Again the hair stiffened on my nape as it had when I read the sentence 'in the dead of night' and heard the swans, which I hadn't by then seen, flying over the house in the winter darkness.

"What's that called?" I shrilled.

"It's the poem *Imitation* by a poet called Keats. We used to have to recite it at school and then I recited it alone, on the stage, at a Thanksgiving Day. And I won a prize. A little bible that I still have. I had to go on the stage again to receive it from the school's headmaster."

The thought of going alone onto a stage to collect a prize with the entire school looking on intimidated me more than had the threat of Jack taking off at full flight down the canal. But the poem..... And the way Mum had recited it.

"Do you know any more poems, Mum?"

"Oh lots," she answered, smiling and with her eyes glistening.

By this time we had reached the awesome cave of the canal bridge and the ramp leading up to the squeaking gate.

"Bye, Jack," I called as the cob swan turned in the direction of the little school and his mate incubating on the high nest of reed stems that I saw only in my imagination.

"We'll have to come back at the weekend when your Dad's with us. We'll feel safer then," said Mum.

Dad, I by then knew well enough, would have continued walking had Jack flown towards him. He would smile and put a screen of reeds between the cob swan and the family so that we could stand and watch Jack and his mate in relative safety.

Suddenly I wanted another poem.

"The poems that I know aren't all about swans," smiled Mum.

"Well it doesn't matter. Just.....anything. Say another poem Mum, please."

"You mean *recite* another poem," Mum corrected then added, "I have to think of one first. Let's see. Oh I know......"

And together we walked, Mum thinking rhythm, thinking cadence, into the gathering dusk.

We returned to the towpath on a warm Saturday evening, Mum, Dad and I. As we walked, listening to the alarm calls of moorhens in the reed stems, I watched the bend ahead. Prepared myself for Jack's visual assault. Jack, however, failed to appear.

The wharf by the fire station wall was thick with reeds. Undisturbed save perhaps for the peregrinations of moorhens and water voles. The swan pair were not nesting there that year. But in the thicker reed jungles ahead, and still on the opposite side, blazed two islands of white.

"There they are!" Dad enthused.

Jack, possibly the largest and heaviest cob swan I have yet encountered, stood one side of the nest and his mate the other. Both were engaged in rearranging dried stems around the nesting hollow. The huge nest, an island of reed stems and fewer twigs, was raised well above the water level. Yet reeds were so prolific and high elsewhere, both the adult swans and the nest would have appeared obscured when seen from the far bank. At that time such a venture was, in any case, impossible because the bank was screened by a fence of barbed wire. Consequently, Jack and his mate had remained undisturbed.

Between these two heavy swans preened three buffish-grey cygnets. Balls of fluff with black paddles and black beaks. Dad thought they had hatched in the heat of that summer's day. And it was beside the cygnets and his mate Jack chose to remain. Occasionally, like his mate, he stretched his neck upright and pole-like as he surveyed us with head turned to one side. But he did not take to the water.

There dawned an overcast Monday evening when, to my delight, I realised on awakening that I didn't have to attend school. It was again half-term. And instead of doing the washing and going to the shops on Hartley Road, Mum had made an appointment to visit a solicitor's office in the centre of Nottingham. She carried with her a black, box type attaché case, slender and expensive looking and with the words 'EXHORTS OF MRS. AMY SHAW' printed on the spine.

The attaché case, Mum explained, contained important papers to do with Aunty's Will. Aunty had left the house in which we lived to Mum and Dad and also two shops and five terraced houses situated at Heanor in Derbyshire. Over the weekend, both my parents had signed all the appropriate forms and Mum was due to return them to the solicitor in Weekday Cross that morning.

Usually Mum walked whenever she could, as did Dad, but on that particular morning she took me for my first and last ride on a particular Nottingham bus route. We were only going a matter of stops, she told me. When we alighted, the bus pulled away and we stepped around the roadworks. Mum said, "Right, that was your first and last ride on a bus down here because it's all going to be pedestrianised."

In retrospect, I think Mum had taken me on the bus for the experience while so far as she was concerned it was the end of yet another era, another stage in her life. But she took that Monday morning opportunity to have one last bus ride, which is understandable.

We had only to hand all the encased and official documents to a secretary and after receiving a receipt Mum took me a tour of parts of Nottingham I had not visited while pointing out such places as The Fountain and an intriguing, narrow street comprising of walkways and steps that she told me was called Narrow Marsh.

She realised that we had enough time to shop at Hoggs the grocer's, especially if we caught a bus on Castle Boulevard.

I was amazed that Mum knew her natal city so well. That *anyone* knew it well.

Sitting downstairs on a double-decker bus, myself nearest the window, I looked at the houses, street corners and people until a stretch of railings came into view. Beyond the railings loomed the sullen waters of another canal stretch. I then saw on the other side of the towpath a reeded backwater and as the canal dipped away from the road, a swan pair escorting an exceptionally large brood of twelve or fourteen cygnets slid onto the water.

When the canal was hidden behind the houses, Mum explained that had we walked a mile or so along that towpath we would have arrived at the communal yards, streets and the house that she had known as a girl. It was there she became aware of the cob swan Jack and attended school with members of the Treverthick and Clayton families who owned the boat repairs and builders' yard.

As a family, the Wheat brothers and sisters had a pet pig called Ginny, who lived in the house and slept beside the hearth like a dog. When Ginny became large and cumbersome their father, Sam, transferred her to a sty on his Harrimans Lane allotment. About a year or so later the Wheat family ate pork with vegetables for their Sunday dinner.

"Did you enjoy your pork, boys and girls?" asked Sam Wheat.

"Ye-es," chorused Mum, her brothers and sisters.

"Good, 'cos that was Ginny," Sam Wheat announced.

Mum then told me that she was so upset that when household chores permitted, she went up to the bedroom she shared with her sisters and wept.

Clinging as always to stories like this, I attempted to imagine the scenes as Mum and I alighted from the bus and walked towards Hoggs the grocer's, the factories and warehouses blocking out the light and the reek of tobacco lingering unpleasantly on the tendrils of a breeze.

CHAPTER 29

Although she complained that it was too hot and sunny to be visiting the cinema, Betty took me with her one Friday evening to *The Capital*. The film showing was *Cover Girl* starring Rita Hayworth.

I had already decided not to enthuse in the school playground about the film on Monday morning because my friends Joey, Billy, Fraser and Brian might think me a sissy. Being familiar with the magazines *Silver Screen* and *Filmgoer*, I knew a little about cover girls and understood this film more than I had those starring Greer Garson and Bette Davis.

On the way home Betty walked slowly along Grassington Road, making use of the shade created by the unbroken line of Lombardy poplars bordering John Player's recreation ground. She wore the pink blouse she had worn the previous summer when Bernard, the sailor, came. Her skirt was pleated with a dog's tooth check design.

We talked about film stars like Rita Hayworth who often starred in 'swimming pool' films, as we called them. Betty told me that Esther Williams *always* starred in swimming pool films but Rita Hayworth only sometimes.

So who was the best and most famous girl film star at the moment, I wanted to know.

"Betty Grable," answered Betty.

"But why Betty Grable," who, I had heard on the wireless, was entertaining the American troops serving abroad.

"Because of her legs. All the men love her because of her legs," Betty answered as the pleasant and secretive warmth spread through my tummy when I remembered the cover photograph of Betty Grable in a swimsuit and wearing high heels.

Yet when it came to faces I would still have chosen Greer Garson, but failed to admit this to Betty.

Early one Sunday afternoon, I left Dad sleeping in his fireside chair and joined Sylvia, Mum and Scamp in the kitchen. In the background the wireless show was centred around Ann Shelton, who like Betty Grable, Bob Hope and Gracie Fields was touring abroad and singing for the troops.

The mouth-watering aromas of freshly baked apple pie persuaded me to think of teatime even though we had just eaten dinner and standing between Mum and Sylvia's hips I stared at the warm brown pastry and the pale green traces of stewed or cooked apple oozing invitingly between the cracks.

Taking a knife, Mum scraped these gently aside then wiped her eyes with a white handkerchief. She and Sylvia had shared a joke; Sylvia was still chuckling and grinning. But neither of the women would tell me what it was about.

As I urged, "Tell me then. Can't you tell *me*?" I noticed the way in which the warm sunlight highlighted the red and black mottled tiles and the black enamel surrounds of the ovens built above the small kitchen fire. Mum told me she was leaving the oven doors open to let the warm air out. She told me that but not a shred of the joke she and Sylvia had shared in those seconds before I entered the kitchen. Yet I derived a degree of inner pleasure because the two women were laughing. I liked to see it. When Betty came down from her bedroom she sensed the mood immediately and began smiling, looking from Sylvia to my mother, while asking, "What is it? What are you laughing at?" But I knew that she wouldn't be told while I was standing in the kitchen. Nor was I *ever* going to be told.

Mum then asked if I wanted to sit with them in one of the deck-chairs on the lawn.

Like Scamp, I preferred the shade of the wide spreading plum tree. Sylvia used our Brownie box camera to photograph Betty, kneeling with one arm around Scamp's neck as she fed him a digestive biscuit. Immediately Sylvia stood after taking the photograph, Scamp retreated from the glare of the sun and joined me beneath the plum tree's shade.

I was lying on my back listening to the house sparrows talking from their nest wedged behind the drainpipe alongside Mum and Dad's bedroom window. After a while, I decided the best place to be was beside water and imagined myself a moorhen or water vole exploring the sanctuary of the reed beds close to where Jack the cob swan and his mate had nested.

There was no breeze. After a while, the sun seemed somehow to have infiltrated the shade. I stood while complaining that it was too hot and entered the house by way of the window step and the open french window which Mum or Dad had pulled the curtain across in an attempt to keep the room cool.

The dining room was surprisingly shaded. Dad slept on in his armchair. Quietly I positioned myself on the settee and found there the zoo book Sylvia had promised me.

I heard then a scrabble of paws as, panting, Scamp followed me up the window step and into the room. On seeing Dad and I, the dog wagged his tail before sliding quietly into the shadows beneath the table. My attention, although on the zoo book, was also on Dad because I estimated that within a few minutes he would awaken then smile, while greeting me softly with the words, "Hello, Little Man," seconds before Scamp crossed to nudge his knee and lick his hand.

CHAPTER 30

April 1944. The Allies repeatedly bombed occupied Europe alongside Germany. On 1st May, Spain signed an agreement with the British Government. The agreement ensured that, while Spain continued exporting tungsten to Germany, the consignments were considerably reduced, a move which slowed down the production of Germany's armaments.

On the 9th, the Germans evacuated Sevastopol, a port in the Crimea. Two days later and throughout the following week, Allied troops at Monte Cassino, Italy, broke gradually through the Gustav Line and pushed the Germans clear of Rome and the Anzio beachhead. On May 18th, Polish infantrymen forced the remaining Germans to evacuate the Monte Cassino monastery. All such strategic moves throughout the month were considered successful.

By the 4th June, General Mark Clark of the United States 5th Army had entered Rome.

On the 6th, the Allied Forces comprising of the United States, British and Canadian Army divisions began the campaign called Operation Overlord.

At Normandy in north-west France, and faced continually with German opposition, the Allied Forces mounted the first amphibious attack and landing having gained a foothold ashore at 6.30 p.m.

A tally which closed at midnight revealed that 75,000 British and Canadian troops had landed. They were backed by 57,500 troops of the United States divisions. The Germans were dug well in at the Omaha Beach, which was soon nicknamed 'Bloody Omaha' by the United States V Corps who, while making a breakthrough, left an estimated 2,400 dead in their wake.

Six weeks of hard warfare followed before the Germans began to retreat.

Also involved in the Normandy landings were 2,056 parachutists of the 508th Regiment of the 82nd Airborne Division, the parachutists who had been billeted in Wollaton Park, Nottingham. 995 of these men returned to Nottingham on 13th July. They left behind in hospitals 1,754 men who were wounded and 307 who were killed or mortally wounded.

**

Despite having to attend school five days a week, the fields at the top of Chalfont Drive were seldom from my mind. Nor far from the minds of senior girls like the Kittoe sisters, apparently.

One golden lit Monday evening after Mrs. Lowe had called with the National Savings stamps, the Kittoes came. They had a bird's nest to show me. *A blackbird's nest!* They had seen the parent birds flying to and from the thicket, then explored accordingly.

The thicket was high, green foliaged and bordering Cherry Orchard Lane. Vivienne and Barbara guided Ronald and I along paths weaving through the masses of dead nettle and wild bramble. Then one or other of the sisters lifted me clear of the ground and as high as her strong young arms allowed. She instructed me to peer beyond the first screen of hawthorn foliage and suddenly, surprised, I found myself looking into a darkly shaded nest where four young blackbirds cowered within. One of the sisters told me to put my hand gently over the top of the nest and to my amazement all four young blackbirds opened their gapes.

"Because you're creating a shadow they think it's the mother or father bird coming in with food," I was told.

Doubtless there were many other nests about, especially in the allotment hedgerows backing onto the Kittoes' house. But it was the comings and goings of the blackbird pair on the field corner of Cherry Orchard Lane the sisters had noticed, then called for Ronald and I because they thought it important that we saw it. And despite Dad leaving the house at first light every morning and returning home between seven and half past in the evening, he was sometimes keen to go for a walk with Scamp and I alongside. It was usually along to Shepherd's Wood that we walked; that familiar route between the hedgerows of Cherry Orchard Lane, the disused allotments to the right, long tract of arable field with the Government buildings or 'Ministries' beyond on our left. Where the arable field ended and the parkland grazings of Aspley Hall began, a stile invited us over and a slender path ran alongside by the arable field boundary and the mysterious 'Ministry buildings'.

Scamp trotted carefully beneath the rungs of barbed wire, cutting across a corner of the arable field rather than squeeze between the rungs of the stile. I loved the distant spinneys - of pine mostly. The thick grasses carpeted with buttercups. The sturdy, red and cream liveried Dairy Shorthorn cattle with their bulky heads and pink, rounded udders. The chewed grass, warm cream and dried dung smell of these same cattle, which Scamp totally ignored.

Through a post and rail gate, which was always left open, beckoned an elm spinney rising on a grassy hillock. The splendid white farmhouse and outbuildings of Aspley Hall blocked the horizon about two hundred yards to our right.

Ahead, a matter of strides beyond the spinney, rose the green barrier of Shepherd's Wood.

If we arrived before sunset, Dad and I slipped between the strands of barbed wire then picked up a slender path between the rhododendron thickets and bracken fronds. We then leapt a clearwater stream, from which Scamp drank noisily, before easing out into the light. Ahead were sandpits and dug out trenches. A local branch of Home Guard were based here, or some similar defence unit. Two or three 'ack-ack' guns stood beyond a cluster of sheds and tents, the gun barrels pointing skyward.

It was from there we retraced our steps, always with the meadow grasses cushioning our feet, the cattle grazing without once lifting their heads, and Dad and I arriving home ten or fifteen minutes ahead of the sunset.

Such evenings I never wanted to end. It seemed incredible that I should have to face the contrasting boredom of a school classroom the following morning. And boredom nurtured by a school situated just a mile away.

One Sunday morning I first saw Dad standing grinning, hands in his pockets beside the dining room fireplace, then the brassy glint of several objects tied with strips of red, white and blue string to the ornate candlesticks positioned on the mantelpiece.

"It's shrapnel," Dad informed me before swinging me onto his shoulder to examine the destructive artefacts of war.

After breakfast we walked to Woodyard Lane where from the railway bridge Dad pointed out a nearby bomb crater, burned black and wide into the earth. "It was a near thing for the people in those houses," he explained.

An explosion twenty miles from London occurred a few hours before dawn on 13th June, 1944. On investigation, the Civil Defence and Army bomb squads discovered a scaled down missile aircraft with shortened wings and a gyroscopic automatic pilot. Experts identified it as a flying bomb or V1, a Revenge Weapon or Vergeltungswaffen produced by the Luftwaffe. In a planned bombardment of London, the Luftwaffe intended to send 500 over throughout each twenty-four hour period. In Britain the V1 was known as a 'doodle-bug'. At night Londoners vacated their houses and sought shelter in the tube stations, for this period was regarded as a third Blitz.

By the beginning of September some 21,000 Londoners were listed as killed or maimed by the V1 bombardments. These bombardments were eventually halted by the British anti-aircraft battery assault fighter aircraft and the Allies discovered and captured the France-based launching pads. But in the autumn a new menace descended after making a seventy mile ascent before plunging at an estimated four times the speed of sound. This was the V2 rocket, designed by the German Army, the first of which literally hit London on the 8th September.

In all some 9,000 people throughout England were killed by the V1 and V2s which continued through into 1945 and ceased on March 27th of that year.

In the school playground boys making whistling or whining noises spun around on their heels then crashed into their peers while hurriedly explaining, "Sorry, I'm a doodle-bug," or "*Watch out!* I'm a V2 rocket!" the seriousness of the V weapons never having been explained to us, except by the unseen narrator on the Pathé News. And even then, we who lived outside of London found it difficult to take in all that we saw on the cinema screen, often relating the incidents to a somewhere beyond our combined imaginations.

One story that we *did* take the time to mull over concerned a man who stood looking out of a window at his garden vegetable plot the morning after a bombing raid. Seeing a rounded pink object nestling within a row of cabbages, he went out to investigate while glancing at the roofless remains of several nearby houses. The pink object was a man's head. When finally the householder recovered from the shock, he went to his shed, made a small coffin which he lined with curtain velvet, placed the man's head into it, nailed up the lid and took the coffin to the local vicar.

In the classroom I sank low in my seat, but not due to the threat of a V2 rocket. Sitting with arms folded across my chest as we were told always to do, I stubbornly refused to accept mental arithmetic. In retrospect, I believe this stubbornness to have manifested in a psychological bid to avoid ridicule. I was afraid to put up my hand and answer Miss Jones' continual mental arithmetic questions because I feared that if I gave the wrong answer I would be laughed at. Consequently, I never volunteered an answer. Miss Jones, I decided, would hardly know of my existence if I failed to put up my hand. Little did I realise that not putting up my hand and attempting an answer was enough for Miss Jones to single me out, along with one or two others, and give me a poor assessment when that time of the educational year came around.

Mental arithmetic? I *hated* it! Saw no reason why the subject should be thrust at us three mornings each week, especially if we were one day expected to take a rifle and pack and hold a position in a trench until a bullet put an end to it all.

CHAPTER 31

On the first Friday afternoon in October we went, Betty and I, to the Goose Fair which was held then, as it is today, on the tract of low fenced parkland known as the Forest. Betty had been given a half day holiday and much to my delight our school had similarly closed at midday.

The day was dry and mild. At Betty's suggestion, we stopped at Towlson's sweet shop situated just across from the Capital cinema. She bought a bag of Dolly Mixtures for me and a second bag of Liquorice Allsorts that we shared. From my Dolly Mixture bag Betty selected as we walked the sweets in the collection which she called 'duck and green peas'. The Kittoe sisters had on occasions, I remembered, also selected these. To me, however, a sweet was a sweet. I liked them all. Goose Fair, Betty explained as we kicked through the leaves of the London plane trees hiding the pavements of Gregory Boulevard, was one of the biggest fairs staged in the British Isles, if not *the* biggest.

I didn't know what to expect. Had been told nothing but for this. Minutes later we were in the fairground dawdling by stalls and side shows with striped awnings. I loved the powerful throb created by the great Vulcan engine that drove such rides as the Waltzer, the Dodgems and the Galloping Horses. And it was on the Galloping Horses that we first rode. Betty had to lift me into the saddle of our chosen mount, then calling out 'Just a minute, please!' to the ride's operator and clutching her skirt, she swung somehow up behind me.

And so around we went, me clutching the solidified mane and neck of a golden painted horse and Betty holding onto a supporting pole with one hand and me the other. She would not, I knew, release her hold on me while ever we were seated there.

The Dodgems I enjoyed because we sat together, Betty and I. I smelt grease, fumes and talked for the sake of it as she steered the car expertly between the others while telling me to keep my hands inside the car in case another collided with us and my fingers got crushed.

On the walk home, Betty surprised me by announcing that she was returning to the fairground with cousin Sylvia that evening. There was no question of me going. The fairground at night was beautifully lit but *very* crowded. I wouldn't like it because, Betty surmised, I didn't like crowds. Mum had told her that.

Sunday morning. A brisk northerly wind. Blue frosted sky. Dark green, yellow and golden foliaged trees.

We were again into the autumn and because I so loved that season, I nurtured no thoughts of home, the past or the future. Living for the present I walked alongside Dad on the moat side path which divides the ornamental gardens of Wollaton Hall from the south slopes of the deer park and golf course. Away to our left in a tussocky valley, that in later years I learned was called Deerbarns Hollow, a darkly wallowed stag roared as he attempted to herd several family groups of hinds and calves. Between the path and the stag stretched the fold of land over which several autumns earlier I had watched with Betty and our cousins the two stags interlocked in battle.

The stag roared; resonant; travelling on the wind.

I wanted to know why the stag was black. Why had it wallowed, as Dad thought, in the moat fringing the east bank of the lake or the lake shallows?

Then across our path from left to right bounded the doe of a deer species that carried a fawn coat, dappled Bambi-like with white spots. But the boy naturalist that I had become saw the doe in a clear-cut sense; marvelled at its turn of speed as unhindered it continued down the green parkland slopes to the paddocks and fields extending beyond the seventeenth century courtyard block. Dad told me that the doe was a female of the fallow deer species, whereas the stag roaring from the tussocks of Deerbarns Hollow was a male red deer.

About red deer I already knew, due to my previous deer park visits. Fallow deer were a different proposition for neither a male or buck or female, known as a doe, were displayed in the Natural History museum. This was probably because the red deer superseded the fallow in size, natural stature and ornamental value as the shield mounted heads and antlers in the Cockburn Mammal Room so obviously interpreted.

Dad asked if I'd noticed the longish tail of the fallow deer; black and white. Its rump was also white. He then explained that most hoofed animals like deer and antelopes displayed pale rear quarters so that the members of the herd and the young could follow the route taken by a leader or parent when they were pursued by a predator.

The twenty-five acre lake, bordered on three sides by thick belts of woodland, nestled in a hollow north-west of the Hall and ornamental gardens. Because of its proximity to woodland, it had always appeared a formidable place when viewed from the garden footbridge. That morning due to the freshness and blue sky, however, the lake and woods beckoned and to my delight Dad and I turned our backs on the Hall and gardens and walked downhill, between two widely spaced lines of orange foliaged lime trees, to the lake.

There was a path extending the length of the woods. A path divided from the water by screens of rhododendrons. Here, where leaves drifted like golden flakes of snow and hid the path surface over which we walked, I quietly revelled as before in the scents of humous, dampness and natural decay.

Where a stand of magnificent beech trees overlooked a wide tract of sandy based shallows, eight swans drifted with the lake's flow. Dad pointed to their greyish black or dull pink bills and identified them as young swans. Two to three years old. I then thought of Solo, the cygnet. Perhaps she was among them? They had probably flown in from the River Trent, Dad told me.

But for the hunger that would be gnawing at my stomach, as always by midday, I could have stayed in the deer park with Dad. Spent the entire day there. Going home only when it was getting dark. There was something to see with every turn of the head. Something to *marvel* at. And subsequently to ask questions about.

Every walk I decided surpassed those dreary hours spent in a school classroom. Why, the outdoor world within itself *was* a 'classroom'!

***

In mid-August 1944, the town of Falaise in north-west France was regained by Canadian troops who, along with the United States Forces, broke through German defensives. The United States troops crossed the River Seine at Nantes, whereas the Allied troops circled a sizeable unit of armoured Germans south of Falaise in a strategic move linking the British, United States and Canadian forces. Around fifty thousand Germans were taken prisoner.

The Dumbarton Oaks Conference was held in Washington D.C. Britain and the United States were successful in persuading the USSR and China to negotiate a proposal for a New World United Nations assembly.

On August 24th, the United States Army entered Paris which was then freed from German occupation. The Parisians were jubilant and a unit of the French army led the official celebratory procession the following day.

September 3rd saw British troops entering the Belgian capital of Brussels. The following day further British Army units captured the important port of Antwerp. Between the 11th and 16th Winston Churchill and Franklin D. Roosevelt attended the Octagon Conference in Quebec, Canada. There they planned an advance by the Allies into Germany.

The 17th - 28th September were earmarked for the Operation Market Garden based in the Netherlands. As part of this operation, British troops landed unsuccessfully at Arnhem. Meanwhile, airborne United States troops landed at Nijmegen and Eindhoven, their instructions being to control the river bridge over the Rhine, Maas and Waal.

In France, Resistance forces and workers amalgamated to swell the ranks of the French army and became part of that army accordingly.

On the 25th, Adolph Hitler announced that all males between 16 or 60 who were not involved in the fighting would be required to serve as members of the Volkssturm, a force designated to defend Germany against the by then feared Allies.

Three days later troops of the Canadian army liberated Calais.

In Poland the bloody and destructive Warsaw Uprising ended on 2nd October with surrender to the Germans, the city almost razed to the ground and an estimated 250,000 Polish residents believed killed.

British troops landed in Greece on 4th October, despite the German occupation. Ten days later they had liberated Athens, the capital. On 14th October, German Field Marshal Erwin Rommel made world headlines for the final time by committing suicide rather than face the court martial served upon him for taking part in the plot to kill Adolf Hitler.

United States General Douglas MacArthur returned with his units to the Philippines which he had been forced to abandon in March 1942.

British and Greek forces declared on November 11th the full liberation of Greece. The following day the German battleship *Tirpitz* was sunk by British bombers in the Norwegian fjord of Tromso. This all important bombing ensured that Britain's large warships could enter the Pacific.

Strasbourg, a city in eastern France, was stormed by the Allied forces and freed of German occupation on November 24th.

***

When I was in my fifties and Betty her sixties, we discussed one evening at her home our upbringing and subsequent roles in the small family unit. We also agreed that both Mum and Dad were gently instructive and keen for us to learn something out of school every day.

Then arose the question of whether we were hit or slapped by our parents and I had to admit, gratefully, that although Mum on that first morning half dragged me off to school, neither she or Dad used their hands as a form of punishment.

Betty then confessed that Dad *had* slapped her on one occasion only. "Oh he was lovely, Dad, he really was. And it was my own fault," she explained.

She recalled how one Friday or Saturday night she had gone to the Palais-de-Danse and missed the last bus home.

Our home was situated about two and a half miles north-west of the city and the Palais-de-Danse about one and a half miles to the south-east of it. The homeward trek, if like Betty one missed the last bus, entailed a walk of four and a half to five miles. Betty decided to follow the bus route. In those times theatres and cinemas closed around ten or half past and dance halls a little later, although Betty couldn't remember them open after eleven. Quite a lot of girls were expected to be home by ten but Betty, who loved dancing and socialising, usually persuaded Mum and Dad to expect her by half past.

I was, of course, upstairs in bed but as Betty described this particular evening to me, I saw in my mind's eye Mum and Dad sitting in their armchairs, one each side the blazing fire, Dad reading the newspaper and Mum darning socks. Scamp was probably curled on the red hearth rug between them.

Although the bombings had ceased, almost every adult thought and talked about the dreaded 'doodle-bugs', Mum and Dad included.

By half past ten Betty had not returned. By a quarter to eleven I don't doubt that Mum or Dad, or both, became gradually aware of the gentle ticking of the mantelpiece clock. At ten past eleven the silence became sinister. Both began to worry. Yet typical of them both, neither would admit this to the other.

Beyond the house was the threat. The darkness. The slight possibility of a doodle-bug assault. The stronger possibility of the prowler. The Man, by whom I had already been accosted.

At twenty past eleven anxiety forced Dad to his feet. He was going out to find Betty, he announced. And even if he had to walk all the way to the Palais and back then walk a section of that route to catch the works bus the following morning, he was going. Moreover, he assured Mum, hiding her fears behind her darning glasses no doubt, that he would be returning *with* Betty.

He set off for the bus terminus at Middleton Boulevard, a lone man striding the pavement, walking the route he would need to walk again in six hours' time. He was anxious. Pent up. *Frightened.*

Then from the down slope, with the railway bridge at his back, Dad saw a solitary figure rounding the bend by the council houses.

A girl! Surely it was a girl!

He felt like running to her but thought the better of it. Then as with beating heart Dad began to assure himself, the anger set in replacing anxiety. And yes! It *was* Betty. She had walked those four and a half to five miles. Had seen no one after leaving the Palais. Betty expected Dad to be smiling but instead he looked angry, an experience which was new to her and a side to him that I never throughout his lifetime knew existed.

Dad walked straight up to Betty, slapped her across the face and said, "You know what that's for."

As Betty reeled with pain and surprise, Dad looked shocked as if he had never believed it of himself. Lowering his head and not uttering another word, he turned and walked alongside Betty. Neither spoke.

"Bless him, I think the slap on my face hurt Dad more than it hurt me," Betty recalled those forty or so years later.

When they arrived at the house I imagined Mum addressing Betty, as in my teenage year she often addressed me, with the softly queried, "And what have you been doing until now?"

Dad did not take off his trilby and overcoat but went to the kitchen gas meter cupboard and took Scamp's lead from the hook. "Come on, Scamp. One more little walk before bedtime." Scamp as usual stood wagging his tail as Betty stroked him and Mum asked if she wanted supper.

"Dad? Well he left the house with Scamp but his head was lowered which wasn't, as you know, characteristic of him. I thought perhaps he was crying," Betty gently explained. "Nor was the matter raised again. I don't suppose I was the first and last teenage girl to worry her parents beyond reason in wartime. But Dad and me, we were friends again the next day," my sister said reassuringly.

As Christmas approached, I wanted every day to be standing in the school assembly hall singing the carol *Away in a Manger.* I loved every word; every line. The hymn portrayed colour, love and warmth. Especially warmth.

Then hardly had we seemed to have broken up from school than I was standing again in the kitchen watching Mum and Dad plucking, singeing and dressing four freshly killed hens from our garden pen.

On Christmas morning I awoke about 2 a.m. and in a freezing bedroom, but propped up by two pillows, poured through the pages of the new and print scented *Daily Mail Annual.* I also had a film annual of my own, with the actual stories of the films printed therein and photographs of singing cowboys like Gene Autrey and the newcomer Roy Rogers, who rode a palomino horse called Trigger. The film stories of *Gunga Din* and *Tarzan of the Apes* were also featured. There were few, if any, glamour girls.

A third book contained stories and drawings instead of photographs. One illustrated account was about a swan and two cygnets. The drawings I thought superb. However, instead of children looking at the swan family, the artist had chosen, in keeping with the story, to portray two chimpanzees dressed as children. And to these I couldn't relate, although I told no one. Swans and chimpanzees just didn't meet each other, I decided.

After breakfast in the dining room trimmed with streamers and tinsel, Dad wandered over to the french windows. Mum and Betty carried the breakfast pots into the kitchen and began washing them while quietly conversing.

Dad stood, hands sunk into his trouser pockets and legs braced. His immaculate waistcoat took on a grey sheen.

Suddenly I surprised myself by asking, "Dad, what year is it?"

"Nineteen forty four, Little Man," Dad replied without turning.

It was then that twenty or so gulls hovered and bickered above the garden rockery where Mum or Betty had thrown out bread scraps for the sparrows. With raucous cries and on scimitar wings, the gulls dived and swooped to within feet of the french windows beyond which Dad stood statuesque.

His stance, his silence, worried me. I had gained the feeling that he was looking *beyond* the gulls. That he was thinking. But about whom or what? Was he missing Aunty? Thinking back to his own boyhood Christmases? Was he thinking of the gaps left in countless homes where young soldiers, sailors or airmen had waved goodbye, never to return? Or was the relationship between himself and Mum on a less secure footing than first met the eye?

After what seemed a considerable time, Dad turned, smiled and told me that the following day - Boxing Day - he was taking me to a village called Bingham, where the hounds and huntsmen of the South Notts Hunt were meeting before moving out to hunt the fox at eleven a.m. precisely.

"And we'll be there, Little Man. We'll be there to see them," smiled Dad before announcing that he was going to the bathroom for his morning shave.

Sylvia and Rene, our girl cousins, arrived after lunch. The sunlight was noticeably warm as it penetrated the panes in the french windows and, according to the weather forecast on the wireless the following day, promised to be just as sunlit but cooler. There was going to be a frost.

Dad made up and lit the fire in the lounge then after tea, as usual, we all settled in there, the bay room chillier of the three main downstairs rooms. And not just Betty, but I, had a film annual to pass around on that occasion.

Again I was intrigued by some film titles: *This Happy Breed*, a film adapted by David Lean from a Noel Coward play; *To Have and Have Not*, based on a novel by Ernest Hemingway; *The Song of Bernadette*, starring Jennifer Jones. How did the screenplays comply with the titles?

The names of film stars stuck in my mind. Dana Andrews. Orson Wells. Cary Grant. Why couldn't I have a name like those?

Boxing Day morning was, as forecast, frosty and sunlit. I quietly revelled in the light as the four of us breakfasted together.

The bus leaving Huntingdon Street for the South Nottinghamshire village of Bingham was to my delight a double-decker. Dad and I were its only passengers and chose the front seat on the upper deck.

At Lady Bay, West Bridgford, the road ran parallel with the canal where a swan pair 'up ended' with tails and rear quarters only showing above the water surface and supported either side by their black feet or paddles. With them three or four piebald cygnets similarly fed. A work mate of Dad's had told him that the swan pair hatched off an exceptionally large brood of thirteen cygnets in the May or June months of that year.

As we travelled, so I reacquainted myself with the intriguing place names of the villages, a few of which I had already visited when with Dad we had journeyed out to collect a hen apiece for the poultry pen. Gamston... Cotgrave...... Cropwell Bishop....Car Colston.... Cropwell Butler. Like the titles of the films I browsed the previous evening, I wondered how such names had come about.

From the bus windows I studied the differing shapes of fields, positions of cottages and farmsteads. One farm that I always looked forward to seeing is set back off the road in a fold of land near the Fosse Way and Saxondale Island. A path leaves the road and curves gently along to the walled farmhouse and outbuildings, partially surrounded by trees and with a pond cradled in the hollow field below the wall.

The traceries of trees outlined against the frosted blue sky I also found fascinating, particularly when I saw what appeared to be a lone skyline tree that, as the road turned with and through the contours of land, I discovered was outlier of a spinney in which seven or eight such trees had been planted.

When we alighted from the bus in Bingham Market Place I was surprised to see many people assembled around the hunting folk, each mounted on a well-groomed horse.

Dad was in his element, especially when he learned that the hounds were on the way.

"On the way from where, Dad?" I piped.

"The kennels," he replied and I imagined then a red roofed place, a group of buildings where the hounds were kept specifically. In the side roads horse boxes were parked. Some members of the hunt were saddling up. Dad pointed out the roan, chestnut and bay horses. Sleek, arch necked. One or two champing at the bit, or impatiently scraping a fore-hoof over the worn tarmacadam. Again Dad estimated the height of each horse in terms of hands but I was studying the pink or red jacket and cream breeches attire of the huntsmen.

Presently a cry went up, "Here they come!"

Longer legged than I expected, tri-coloured and with sterns feathering the hound pack, watched over by the whipper-in, surged into the market place. Suddenly a hound was sniffing and licking my fingers and I lost no time in caressing its chin, muzzle and those two hollows behind the ears that I sought our each morning when at the foot of the stairs I was met by Scamp. Hound after hound came along the edge of the crowd to be fussed. Someone gave one a bone. The hound sank promptly onto its belly and, like Scamp, held the bone upright between its forepaws seconds before it began to chew. Other hounds closed in. The hound possessing the bone clamped it to the road surface but continued peeling slivers of flesh from it. Then an interloping hound sniffed at the bone and narrowly missed being scarred on the muzzle.

This was my first experience of seeing hounds *or animals* thriving within a pack.

I had watched swans as a family and in a flock. The Wollaton Park red deer as a herd. Our penned hens and strutting cockerel as a group. I had become aware of the pecking order. And now the foxhounds before me were also working within an order - of superiority.

Presently a pub landlord appeared with drinks on a tray. "The stirrup cup," Dad explained. There was some talk between the landlord and the hunts folk, particularly the Master who raised his glass in a toast.

The hounds were still around us. Sterns stiff, feathering. Muzzles pushing out and into the hands and fingers of anyone's they could reach. At least until the whipper-in, realising one or other of them was astray, located and called it in.

When the landlord returned with drinking glasses and tray in hand to the pub, the low surge of background voices changed pitch. The crowd quietened. Some people looked at a clock that I couldn't see. Dad took from his pocket his gold watch and showed me the numerals while saying, "This will be yours one day, Little Man." But I didn't want a gold watch! I wanted Dad! I didn't want that 'one day' to come! He then said, "Only seconds to go....."

"And then what, Dad?"

"They're about to move off. At eleven. All hunt meets throughout Britain now move off at eleven," he explained.

Then the clock began to chime. The whipper-in firmly brought the hound pack to heel. The low collective murmur of the crowd subsided. Everyone seemed tense and inwardly excited, including Dad.

"Right, that's it! The eleventh chime! They're off," said Dad.

The huntsmen and whipper-in guided their mounts steadily down the street, the hounds around them. As the rest of the hunt members took up their positions, the people in the crowd turned and followed or walked alongside.

"Is everybody going but us?" I queried.

"No. Most people will just follow the hunt out of the village, but a few - the stalwarts among them - *will* follow, on foot. "

"How far do they go, Dad?"

"They'll go on and on until they put up a fox."

I saw then the dog fox the taxidermist had set up for display at the Wollaton Hall Natural History museum within walking distance of our home. I saw also, in my mind's eye, the hens and the Rhode Island Red cockerel in the garden fowl pen.

Foxes killed poultry so the huntsmen took out hound packs to kill the foxes. Lions and leopards killed zebra, wildebeest and antelope out on the African veldt. Killing something, strange though it seemed, was part of the ritual of living.

On the bus journey home I revelled again in the surrounding landscape while talking to Dad about foxhounds and other hounds. Dad asked me then if I had heard of a greyhound and I gave him a negative answer.

As a boy and young man, Dad had not only captained his local football team and been batsman and left-handed spin bowler with the cricket team but had also gone to both greyhound and horse race meetings and, when they were both young, sometimes with Mum.

He told me further that there were packs of cigarette cards featuring both outstanding race horses and greyhounds and that at school I should look out for and collect these cards.

If ever I was given a cigarette card featuring a greyhound called Mick the Miller, he would love to see it.

"Why?"

"Well because Mick the Miller made a nice lot of money for me when I was a young man. I used to gamble you see, Little Man. Put money, *bets*, on greyhounds and racehorses. *Well, I still do,*" Dad grinned mischievously.

He had worked as an Army enlisted horse breaker during the First World War and seen action in the Sudan. He had raced both horses and camels or dromedaries. And although after the war he was just a little too tall and heavy to become a jockey, he merged with horses, and later greyhounds, whenever he could.

He loved the excitement created by a race. *Any race.* Greyhounds, like Mick the Miller, had created that excitement for Dad and many other gambling or betting men.

Mick the Miller had won races which, of course, I had never heard. The Cesarewitch, Derby and St. Leger. Moreover, he chalked up a total of *nineteen* consecutive wins! Dad's eyes twinkled and his face was aglow when he told me that. Almost as if he had trained or owned the much celebrated greyhound himself.

So interested was I in learning of the achievements created by animals that were probably unaware they were actually racing or competing, I forgot to look over the hedge of the Grantham Canal for the family of swans.

Then as continuing our bus ride we crossed Trent Bridge and re-entered the city, Dad told me of another animal which had been given the name Miller. This was a racehorse called Golden Miller. He was based in Ireland and considered a slow starter on the track, but was bought by Miss Dorothy Paget, whose name,

Dad told me, I should see on the backs of many cigarette cards relating to horse racing. Golden Miller won five consecutive Cheltenham Gold Cups and weighing 12 stone 1 lb. in 1934 won the Grand National. It was the second Grand National this horse had been entered for.

And so Golden Miller conceived a new course record which remained unchallenged until the magnificent Red Rum pounded by the winning post in 1973, although to Dad and his generation Golden Miller was unsurpassed, the racehorse of all racehorses.

Moreover Dad, I understand, won a considerable amount of money when Golden Miller romped home in that Grand National of 1934 and knowing him portions of his winnings would have gone to Mum, his brother Albert and perhaps some friends who gathered to sing around his Saturday and Sunday evening piano playing sessions at *The Nag's Head*, Bobbersmill.

"But how do you know what horse to back," I asked.

"You read form. Read the fixtures in a racing paper. Work out how many races a horse has won, then look at the achievements, if any, of those who are running with him. Then you go to the bookies and begin hoping," grinned Dad.

"Do you always win money then, Dad?"

"Not *always*, Little Man. But I seem to win more than the people I know and work with."

"Because you read form?"

"Well, partly. Anyway, I'll teach you how to read form when you're older. Show you how to make some money," Dad assured me as the bus pulled in at the terminus.

On the next bus, the one that took us to within half a mile or so of home, I was riding in my imagination. Sitting in the saddle of a fine horse, following the hounds as they pursued a fox through the frost smarting chill of the winter countryside.

The next day we regarded as a Sunday, except that we were not expecting our girl cousins and Mum's nieces. I spent the day with my books and in the evening went with Dad to the Elite cinema in Nottingham to see Judy Garland in *Meet Me in St. Louis.*

Situated on the busy central thoroughfare of Parliament Street, the Elite buildings were prestigious, the cinema by far the most spacious I had visited.

Surprisingly, the cinema was about three quarters full but whenever I went with Dad to see a film we always sat from the beginning, whereas with Betty and Sylvia or Mum and Aunty if what was called 'the big film' was on when we arrived we saw it through to the end then sat through the part at which we came in. Dad, however, didn't work that way. He was extremely time-conscious, just as I am today and have always been. He studied the film starting times in the evening newspaper and arranged our meal with Mum and travelling times accordingly. There was no such term as 'arriving late' in Dad's daily schedule, nor has there been in mine.

CHAPTER 32

In December 1944, the U.S. Congress awarded the distinction of five star general to General Dwight Eisenhower, George C. Marsh and Douglas MacArthur.

In Italy on the 5th, Allied Forces liberated the city of Ravena which had previously, but briefly, been held by the Germans. On the 16th, the German forces launched their last offensive stand in the Ardennes, Belgium. This became known as The Battle of the Bulge. Battalions of United States troops were trapped in the offensive which lasted ten days.

On the 26th, however, more battalions were sent in and successfully routed the Germans, thereby freeing the town of Bastogne and the troops who were trapped there.

***

One Saturday morning on a thoroughfare that I now know to be Bridlesmith Gate, Nottingham, Mum recognised a young soldier and grabbing my hand cut through the crowd to have a word with him.

She introduced him as my cousin Geoffrey, the middle one of Aunt Alice's three sons. He was suntanned, smiling and in full uniform. As Mum and Geoffrey exchanged pleasantries, I studied his highly polished boots, immaculately creased khaki trousers and webbing belt, all the items of Geoffrey's attire that were below or on a level with my six and a half year old gaze.

Back thumbing over his shoulder, Geoffrey told Mum that he had just been to the NAAFI for a cup of coffee, quiet smoke and a haircut. This last available service surprised Mum, who was further surprised when Geoffrey told her that this particular NAAFI branch was the largest in the country and was opened by the Sheriff, Lord Mayor and Lady Mayoress of Nottingham who were also joined by Lord Belper.

Reminiscing, Mum asked Geoffrey if he remembered going on the boating lake at Titchfield Park with his mother, herself and his brothers. She then asked him if he knew that under John Player's old cigarette factory, close to where she shopped, was a communal air raid shelter that could take in an estimated five thousand people. That was Geoffrey's turn to look surprised.

He told Mum that he was drinking at the American Red Cross Club in Nottingham one night when he recognised Clark Gable, who had played the romantic lead Rhett Butler in the film epic *Gone With The Wind*. Gable was serving as a Captain in the 8th Army Air Force and reportedly devastated by the untimely death of his wife, the actress Carol Lombard. He was drinking with some fellow officers but, according to Geoffrey, when the group left 'so did everyone else'.

Off-duty soldiers, sailors and airmen followed Gable and his party to *The Flying Horse* hotel in the Nottingham city centre where the revellers reassembled. Gable, however, was taciturn; abrupt. Suddenly he was recognised by a woman similarly enjoying a night out. "That's *him*, look! Clark! It's Clark Gable! Rhett Butler!"

Gable's party were then assailed by a group of excited women and girls. There was nothing to do, they decided, but leave. But as they made for the doors so too did the women and girls. They were screaming. Wanting to touch Gable. Wanting to be in his company.

Peck Lane cuts alongside *The Flying Horse* hotel and it was down this that Gable and his friends ran, then crossed St. Peter's Street to seek shelter in the nearby church. The women and girls remained outside, still excitable, until the police dispersed them and escorted Clark Gable and his group to their next secret destination.

Mum, laughing, admitted that she too would have pursued Gable had she seen him out in the street, while I stood alongside puzzled and slightly shocked by this admission.

Eventually she and Geoffrey drew apart, Mum asking him to remember her to her sister, while adding that she would be going round to see Aunt Alice within a matter of weeks. It was then that we turned our separate ways and again faced the crowds.

My second meeting with a soldier occurred a few weeks later and at the house in which we lived.

After descending the stairs to meet Scamp and begin our ritual of Monday morning greetings, I turned when Mum said, "We've got a young man stretched out on the settee; a soldier."

The unfamiliarity, *the very admittance* that my usual routine was about to be interrupted conceived waves of uncertainty within my stomach. *I didn't want to meet him!* Didn't know what to say to him! What was he doing *here,* anyway?

"What am I going to say to him, Mum?"

"Just say, 'Hello Harry'. He's a lovely young man. His name's Harry Philips. He's a Welshman."

"But what's he doing here?"

"Oh, he's cousin Alice's young man. And he's stayed over. Just for one night. He's on his way to the station then rejoining his unit."

Cousin Alice. She of the raven hair, porcelain cheek bones, blue eyes and husky laugh. Suddenly I wasn't shy about meeting Harry. Scamp ahead of me, his curled banner of a black and tan tail wagging, made straight for the dining room door, nudged it aside with his muzzle then went for a further fuss from Harry with whom he had probably been acquainted for several hours.

Dressed in khaki uniform, Harry was stretched out on the settee, head propped by pillows, his body covered by thick blankets and an eiderdown. The usual welcoming fire was blazing in the hearth.

"Hello-o, Keith," hailed Harry as I gulped out my reply before easing into my chair in readiness for breakfast.

Harry's darkly handsome face was alight with laughter. His mahogany tan emphasised the whiteness of his smile. His hair was black; cut short, Army style. His dark twinkling eyes were slitted, so pronounced was his smile. Scamp nudged Harry's equally suntanned hands. Harry stroked and patted him as Scamp had indicated he should.

As I turned to face my breakfast surprise arrested me for the second time. Pinned
to the wall opposite my place at the table were about a dozen coloured spreadsheets, each illustrating animals against a white background.

"Wow! What are these?"

"Pictures for you from cousin Sylvia," laughed Harry as I climbed from the chair and went around to them.

Sylvia worked at Thomas Forman's, a Nottingham printers, and on seeing these spreadsheets that were eventually to become the pages of a book had begged a set from her boss, specifically with me in mind.

Every wild and domesticated European animal was featured on those spreadsheets. Horses, cattle, sheep, goats, pigs, deer. Beneath each animal its breed was clearly printed. There were dolphins, whales, seals porpoise, snakes, bats. Animals that, although I had familiarised myself with *The Zoo* book that was also a gift from Sylvia, I never knew existed.

The Dairy Shorthorn, Ayrshire, Lincolnshire, Redpolled and Blue Albion cattle I recognised immediately because it was from individuals of each of those breeds that the dairy herd at Aspley Hall farm was formed. But there were also Highland Cattle, Friesian and Jerseys of which I was also unaware.

Sheep I had only seen when Dad and I watched the sheep dog trials in a show staged at Wollaton Park one summer weekend. Until that morning when I studied the spreadsheets, I thought that sheep were sheep and pigs were pigs. There were thirty or so breeds of sheep featured and an estimated thirty million grazing the hills and fields of Britain during wartime, although I was not then aware it.

The pigs varied in shape, size and colour enormously. The Berkshire, Wessex Saddlebacks and Tamworth strains. I had only to see a picture of one and I memorised the name and didn't forget it.

When Mum came into the room and saw me studying the spreadsheets, she told me to eat my porridge whilst it was warm and that the pictures would still be pinned up on the wall when I came home at half past twelve.

As I ate, Scamp sitting beneath the table at my knees, I realised there were also many horse breeds featured on the spreadsheets and envisaged Dad looking at them before he left for work.

When it was time to leave for school Mum suggested I shook hands with Harry, something I had never done. Grinning, Harry clasped my one extended hand between both his palms and looking into my eyes said that we would be meeting again soon and at this assurance, a lovely deep warmth passed through my tummy.

In the classroom I sat, as usual, with my arms folded throughout the mental arithmetic session with Miss Jones, while thinking smugly that I was the only boy in the class - *in the school* - that morning with spreadsheets featuring every mammal, reptile and amphibian in Great Britain pinned to the wall so that I could study them while I ate my meals. And how many boys and girls knew what a Derby Gritstone represented or a Landrace? Mental arithmetic or any arithmetic I had little or no interest in. So long as I could count money, what did it matter? Yet knowing the breeds of cattle and sheep one was passing in a field I secretly regarded as being of extreme important. This, however, I admitted to no one.

CHAPTER 33

January 1945. A soldier of the United States Army, Private Eddie Slovick, was executed for desertion. The Western world was shocked for no such execution had been carried out since the 1861-65 American Civil War.

On January 3rd, the British 14th Army waged war on the Japanese Forces in Burma.

From the 17th to 19th, Soviet forces liberated the Polish capital of Warsaw and then Krakow.

The Allied Army on the 22nd reopend the Burma Road along which munitions consignments were then transported to China.

After liberating the Polish town of Tilsit from German occupation, on the 23rd the Soviet Forces reached the famed and dreaded Auschwitz concentration camp.

By February the United States forces were concentrating, as previously planned, on the Japanese defensives in the Philippines.

On the 8th, Operation Veritable began; the combination of British and Canadian Forces driving in to secure defensive positions and clear the German troops from the regions of the Upper Rhine.

From the 13th to 15th the Royal Air Force and United States Air Force began a bombing siege on the historic city of Dresden, a mission intended to disperse the German troops which were being transferred into Soviet territory. Over 60,000 people were killed in these three day assaults.

On the 7th March, United States troops took possession of the Ludendorff railway bridge at Remagen in Germany. By the evening one hundred or so troops had crossed the Rhine.

On the 23rd Veritable was considered a success when the British and German troops also crossed the Rhine. By the end of the month the Soviet forces were still liberating towns and the port of Danzia.

Field Marshal Harold Alexander on 9th April led an Allied assault across northern Italy, their purpose being, as elsewhere, to rid the land of German troops. On that same day the German born anti-Nazi Pastor Dietrich Bonhoeffer was taken from the prison cell he had occupied since April 1943 and hanged by the Nazis.

The following day United States troops were in control of Hanover, but the Germans held fast to Bremen despite fierce fighting.

**

As the warmer days came in I looked forward to visiting Aunt Alice's bungalow close to Wollaton Park, but by contrast became afraid to enter my grandparents' house attached to Boultby's Yard on the corner of Great Freeman Street near the city centre. Not that I was by then visiting alone, for Mum was always with me. Yet each time, Mum ushered me through the dark doorways ahead of herself almost as if she was using me as a shield.

One bright morning in the early week we found Grandma Wheat sitting, black clad as usual, in her fireside chair but at the same time that we entered directly from the cobblestone street my Grandfather Sam came in from the stable

yard of which until that day I was totally unaware.

I warmed to Grandad Sam Wheat the instant I saw him. A stockily built man with a shock of iron grey hair, wide blue eyes, silver moustache and side whiskers. To a tie-less striped shirt he wore a waistcoat with watch and chain like Dad. His trousers were charcoal grey.

Smiling, he took my hand and softly suggested that he and I had a look around the stables, "After all, we don't want to be around when two women are facing each other daggers drawn. Let 'em fight, little fella. Let 'em get on with it. And me and you? We'll keep out of the way," he gently persuaded as he led me through the dark and sparsely furnished kitchen, or scullery, then opened the solid back door.

Grandad Sam Wheat was employed as a horsekeeper for the Coal Delivery department of the Nottingham Co-operative Society who had leased Boultby's Yard and the adjacent stables as a tied property. Following in the occupational line Sam succeeded George Barlow but whether aware of it or not, he was the last horsekeeper to be employed by the Society because flat backed delivery lorries were on the increase and considered more economical. The Nottingham Co-operative Society therefore were by this time no longer looking for stable yards but garage premises.

I acquired in later years the picture of a man who loved pubs, socialising and had a number of like-minded friends.

How my grandfather acquired the position of horsekeeper at Boultby's Yard was explained to me by my mother a year or so before she died at the age of ninety-two. The family were at the time living at Claude Street, Lenton, close to the canal, boat builder's yard and munitions factory.

The Nottingham Co-operative Society's No. 1 branch shops, a grocer's, butcher's and greengrocer's were situated on the main Nottingham-Beeston road near Abbey Bridge. Here the canal's locally famed staircase of lock gates began. The towpath was open to all pedestrians.

One afternoon, Sam Wheat was on the towpath, probably walking to or from the *Rose and Crown* pub situated close to the next bridge along on Derby Road, when as he approached Abbey Bridge he smelt the smoke and then saw a great plume arising from the rear of the Co-operative shops.

Like Boultby's Yard, a section of the Coal Department's stables was situated at the rear of these premises and on the afternoon that Sam and other local folk realised the stables were on fire, they also realised that the dray or delivery horses were stabled inside. Because of this, one gains the impression that the afternoon was a Saturday or Sunday.

People were looking on from nearby Cloisters Yard. Others were grouped, perhaps with a few narrowboat people amongst them, around the canal lock gates. Men, women and children.

The fire was well underway. Horses kicked at the stable doors and neighed incessantly. The smoke cloud created excitement and fear.

When he reached the crowd, Sam Wheat asked if anyone had gone to rescue the horses. The answer was collective and negative. Someone had sent for the

Fire Brigade. Surely *they* would rescue the horses?

Eyeing the roof structure of the old buildings, Sam Wheat said that he didn't think the Fire Brigade would make it in time, so it was up to himself and the crowd - the onlookers - to release the terrified horses. There were, however, no volunteers. Disgusted, Sam Wheat went in alone and as he ran through the smoke he thought for seconds that the ground was moving before he realised that the movement he was looking at was created by hundreds of rats vacating the blazing premises.

"Rats by the hundred ran out and your Grandad ran in," was how Mum explained the situation to me. Whether the buildings were in a state of near collapse or Sam was drunk (a condition of mind that wasn't entirely unknown), Mum never learned.

But what everyone watching from the safety of the canal towpath learned was that Sam Wheat single-handedly released and thereby rescued all the horses that would otherwise have been trapped within the stables.

Once the horses were out and standing nervously in nearby Cloisters Yard or on the towpath, Sam, jacket over his shoulder, continued on his way.

When the Fire Brigade and a Co-operative Manager and Director arrived, someone asked the onlookers who it was had released the horses. And Sam had apparently not been amongst total strangers. His name and addressed was given to the Co-operative Director and days later Sam received a letter thanking and informing him that the horsekeeper at Boultby's Yard was about to retire and asking Sam further if he would be interested in the job.

On the day that Grandad Sam Wheat showed me around the stables I knew nothing of this. I just experienced a tremendous warmth. A feeling of safety - *confidence,* just so long as he and I were together.

Besides feeding and mucking out the horses, Sam Wheat had also to ensure that each set of harness or tack was in working order and that every horse had been backed and harnessed between the shafts of a cart when the coal delivery deliverymen arrived on the five weekday mornings.

When Sam, holding my hand, took me into the stables I was aware of the hay, bales of straw, scents of oatmeal, chaff and horse urine that the stiff bristled sweeping brush had failed to dispel. Every stable was lined with fresh hay. Moreover, each nurtured several strokeable occupants that were much smaller than horses. These were, to my delight, domestic rabbits which would normally have been kept in hutches.

Kneeling, Sam and I coaxed the rabbits over and it was then I amazed both Sam and myself by memorising the rabbit page of the wall chart cousin Sylvia had pinned up for me on the night Harry Philips stayed over.

"That's a Dutch rabbit!" I exclaimed when I saw the splendid black and white.   "And that's an Old English."

"Ah, but what's this one then?" chuckled Grandad Sam Wheat as he pulled in and stroked a rabbit with drooping ears.

"That's a Lop Eared," I told him.

"Well, I never," he chuckled while ruffling my hair.

"And that...... isn't that a Belgian Hare, Grandad?"

"*It is* an' all," Sam Wheat triumphed.

Slowly we went from stable to stable. Quietly opening the top section of each door and sliding in. Kneeling in the hay to fondle the rabbits, some of which nibbled lettuce and cabbage leaves. Sam Wheat was, to my mind, a man fond of horses and rabbits. *Especially rabbits.* Never once did it occur to me that he was also fond of rabbit pie, served with home-grown vegetables and rich gravy two or three times a week!

Mum, Dad, Betty and I still enjoyed rabbit pie. But, in all honesty, I thought that Grandad Sam Wheat kept rabbits as pets.

When we had completed our tour of the stables, Sam Wheat again took my hand. "We'll go and see if those two have calmed down now that they've said what they have been wanting to say," he explained while winking at the same time.

On re-entering the house Sam asked, "Is it all right now? Have you got it off your chests? Has the thunderstorm passed over?"

Grim faced, Mum and Grandma Wheat indicated that they had said all there was to say. We left minutes later.

Grandad Sam Wheat? I didn't want to leave him. Within his stocky frame, he nurtured love, warmth and a gentle yet unflinching strength.

In later years I heard Mum quietly chuckling, as she told Aunt Alice that when their parents married, "Elizabeth Alice Bonser found she had met *her* match and Samuel Wheat found he had met *his*."

Grandad Sam Wheat, I later learned, had his faults just like everyone. But in writing thirty six years later, and thinking of him after our first and sadly penultimate meeting, I conclude by admitting that he has remained the most charismatic person I have met throughout my entire lifetime.

***

On April 11th, troops of the United States Army arrived in the Elbe Valley situated north-west of Berlin. The following day the American President Franklin D. Roosevelt died. Vice-President Harry S. Truman succeeded his position.

Vienna, the Austrian capital, was abandoned by the Germans on the 13th when Soviet forces marched in. With Karl Renner as Prime Minister a provisional government comprising communists, Christians and Social Democrats was established.

The Soviet forces further scuppered the Germans along the River Oder as they continued moving towards Berlin. By April 25th, the Soviet forces had joined with troops of the United States Army at Torgav in the Elbe Valley. Ministerial headlines were made again on 28th April when Prime Minister Benito Mussolini was assassinated with his mistress Clara Petacci in Italy. The Italian Resistance claimed responsibility. the following day the German forces in Italy had no choice but surrender to the Allies.

On the 29th the German dictator Adolf Hitler and his mistress Eva Braun descended into their Berlin based bunker where they were married. The next day the couple committed suicide in the same bunker by taking poison.

***

Mum persuaded me to stay around home while she went to the city shopping on

Saturdays. However by law, so I believe, she could not leave me alone in the house. There was a kindly lady called Mrs. Robinson, she told me, who had a daughter Dorothy of around my age and a younger son Geoffrey.

Dorothy and I were kindred spirits. We both loved books and were interested in animals. Wouldn't I prefer to stay with Dorothy and her mother while Mum did her shopping? Particularly since I'd admitted I disliked crowds and being slammed in the face by carrier bags.

"What kind of animals does Dorothy have?" I asked.

"Well, just a rabbit in a hutch at the moment. But there's a round pond in the front garden. It's the house on the boulevard corner. You've passed it many a time," persuaded Mum.

To satisfy her, I knocked on the front door of the large house with a garage, side yard and double bays the following Saturday and was admitted by Mrs. Robinson. She wore glasses, often had her fair hair pinned up and, like Mum, spent considerable time working in the kitchen.

Dorothy, who like myself sought whichever part of the settee the sunlight was emblazoned upon, smiled and said, "Hello," when tentatively I entered the sitting room which looked out onto the Boulevard.

Dorothy had fair hair which she wore in plaits and marble white skin. Her eyes were blue. Her voice soft but expressive. She liked to wear sleeveless dresses, often of a small check design.

The Robinsons, I discovered, came from Stourbridge near Birmingham.

"Why? Why did you come from Stourbridge? Isn't it nice there?" I queried.

"Yes, but Dorothy's father has a job here in Nottingham. Well that's his main office. He's a traveller. Comes home around Saturday lunch time and leaves Monday," Mrs. Robinson explained.

Dorothy and I exchanged books. Talked about, *discussed* stories. Wondered why the authors had chosen to write them. And asked were they true or not.

I told Dorothy about the films I'd seen. Particularly the animal films, the most recent then being *My Friend Flicka* starring Roddy McDowall and Preston Foster. I went with, I think, cousin Alice and the soldier sweetheart Harry Phillips, whom she married; her sisters, Rene and Sylvia; and Betty.

The film was, like Anna Sewell's *Black Beauty*, the story of a horse. But an American horse, just one individual among the large herds that roamed wild across the prairies of Montana. However Dorothy's mother, understandably, would not allow her daughter down to the canal, nor to go with me or any other child to watch the deer on Wollaton Park. Dorothy's contact with her Dutch rabbit left me with little doubt that she loved it, as she had loved her dolls. Together we stroked and fondled the rabbit while I told her of those many in the spacious stables managed by my Grandad Sam Wheat at Boultby's Yard.

From the rabbit hutch we next went to the pond side, knelt side by side and saw our reflections distorted by several stick-like insects that appeared to row across the water surface.

"Water boatmen," Dorothy told me.

"But from where?"

She couldn't say. They had just appeared.

As a pair of house sparrows continued to nest in the crook of our drainpipe, a pair nested likewise in the drainpipe crook of Dorothy's home. Trails of straw blew in the breeze from that high nest facing east, the Boulevard side of the house, and as I explored a corner of the lawn Dorothy's older sister came out of the house wheeling her younger brother in a pushchair.

Dorothy's brother, reined into his four wheeled carriage, reared upwards pointing to the nest and exclaiming, "Dicky birds! Look, dicky birds!" as undoubtedly I had done myself when I was his age, but with Betty at the helm of my pushchair.

Whether Mum called in to see my grandparents on those Saturday morning visits was never made known to me.

On the Saturday afternoons, despite the splendid early summer weather, Betty still took me to one of the two city cinemas: *The Ritz* or *Odeon*. Sometimes Sylvia joined us. Sometimes not.

Twice we saw the same film: Dorothy Lamour starring in *Madonna of the Seven Moons*. It was the story of an island jungle girl who faced sacrifice to appease the gods controlling a volcano. The scenes, in colour, of the volcano erupting I found particularly exciting. These eclipsed the factual newsreel accounts depicting the Soviet and American troops breaking through the German lines or, in this instance, of the Soviet forces on 2nd May storming Berlin.

One overcast evening, with the threat of school the following day lingering in the background, Jill and Shirley Pearce brought my friend Ronald the evacuee over to say goodbye. He was leaving for home, for *London*, early the next morning.

"Shake hands then like two little gentleman should," urged Mum.

I clasped Ronald's outstretched hand and looked directly into his eyes. They were clear eyes. Smiling eyes. The worry, threat or terror that may once have lingered within them was removed. And in London, at the railway station or evacuee centre, his mother and father would be waiting.

When with the girls Ronald turned, he looked back. And again. Then waved for the last time from Jill and Shirley's front gate.

CHAPTER 34

On May 3rd 1945, Japanese forces occupying Rangoon in Burma gave in to troops of the British and Indian Armies. On the equally historic 4th, Field Marshall Sir Bernard Montgomery accepted the collective surrender of German forces under arms. The Germans surrendered to the Allied forces of whom Montgomery was the prime commander. The Official World War II Surrender of Germany took place in Reims, France, at 1.41 a.m. on May 8th. The United Stages General Dwight Eisenhower was present with allied officers when General Alfred Jodl signed the surrender. May 8th was then celebrated as V.E. or Victory in Europe Day by both the United States of America and the relieved and grateful people of western Europe.

***

Because there was no school I spent some of the hot May day at Dorothy's and returned soon after tea.

At Harrison's the Bakers with Mum the previous day, I heard such terms as, "Oh I knew owd Monty would get us through. I think we all did," being bandied around but had become used to hearing Field Marshall Montgomery and Winston Churchill mentioned in the affectionate context of 'owd', or old, and had ceased asking questions. After all, I decided, *The Daily Sketch* and the *Pathé News* would tell me all that I wanted to know. Not to mention the latest tale of terror, blood and spilled guts that frequently came my way in the school playground.

On leaving Dorothy's at sunset, I turned the walled corner onto Chalfont Drive and became immediately blinded by the intensity of the light. The sky was red as far as the eye could see. Then as I struggled with the light, I realised that people were standing at their front garden gates. People I had never seen before. They were talking excitedly, yet in hushed tones, with their neighbours. Some, mostly wives and mothers, crossed the road and greeted each other. Then, to my amazement, two women embraced.

On my side of the pavement, children of around my own age, whom I knew only as Michael and Cynthia Cox, Sheila Roscoe and Angela Johnson, stood at or climbed upon their gates to reach the same height as their smiling mothers.

Mrs. Johnson, black hair to her shoulders, classical cheekbones and darkly lashed eyes, stood with her family around her. She wore a smart white sleeveless blouse and long black skirt. Out of the front gate, which was ajar and on which Mrs. Johnson leaned with folded arms, trundled Whiskey the family's old Scottish terrier.

Stooping to pat and talk with Whisky, I asked, "Mrs. Johnson, why are all those people at their front garden gates? Why are they all talking? What's happened?"

Suddenly Mrs. Johnson stepped around the gate and swept me up into her strong, suntanned arms. Stunned, I found myself pressed tightly to her body and almost nuzzling her neck and cheek as she retorted, "What's happened, Keith? *What's happened?!* The war is over and *the men are coming home!*" And then Mrs. Johnson was crying openly as she hugged me to her and I tasted for the first time the salty warm tears of a woman.

I felt trapped, embarrassed and glad all at the same time.

"Mrs. Johnson, I'd better go and tell my Mum," I ventured and slowly and carefully she lowered me to the ground.

I said goodbye to them all, Mrs. Johnson, Angela, Whiskey, the Cox and Roscoe families, then ran towards the sunset. But if the war was over and if she was glad the men were coming home, why had Mrs. Johnson been crying I wondered?

Our front garden gate was, as usual, latched. When the latch clicked as I opened the gate I regarded the sound as the forerunner to the startling item of news I was about to relay to Mum. Opening the front door, I stumbled breathlessly into the hall as Scamp came from the kitchen to greet me.

Mum was, as usual, standing with her back to me at the kitchen sink.

"Mum, *guess what?!*"

"What?" said Mum half turning.

"*The war's over,*" I hailed.

"Oh, I know," Mum answered dismissively.

Disappointment travelled swiftly from my head to my toes. That was the second time in my life she had answered me that way. I felt unwanted. Useless. All that excitement - anticipation - wasted.

Taking off my jacket I went into the dining room to seek the refuge of the settee and my beloved books.

"The war's over. Did *you* know, Scamp?" I asked my black and tan friend. Wagging his tail Scamp accompanied me to the settee.

Hiding behind a book I attempted to stem the anger arising within.

Mum! Why hadn't *she told me* the war was over if she knew? Why hadn't *she* swept me into *her* arms and hugged me in the same way that Mrs. Johnson had? Why hadn't *she* smiled? Why didn't *she* look pleased like everyone I'd seen on that fifty yard walk from Dorothy's house to my home? Was I *so* unimportant!

When eventually Mum came into the room, I told her that Mrs. Johnson was crying and that I thought people cried only when they were unhappy or hurt.

"No, people cry often when the are happy, especially if they've been through a hard time. They cry with relief. And it's no shame to be seen crying even when you're a grown-up," Mum told me.

It was then I realised she was agitated. Mum and I were the only people in the house. Betty had probably gone dancing. But Dad? Where was Dad? Surely he ought to be home by now?

In retrospect, I believe Dad had either joined his Langar based workmates and colleagues and gone for a celebratory drink in a village pub, or stopped off for what was meant to have been 'a quick one' - but lasted longer - in one of the crowded pubs of the city.

Few, if any, of we children were aware that throughout Britain, the United States of America and Europe the adult populations were celebrating. Pubs, cafés, restaurants, dance halls and the city streets, squares and pavements were packed to the hilt with excited, *delighted*, people.

Some people attended private or quickly arranged services at their local church. Our neighbours, Mr. and Mrs. Teather, would undoubtedly have been among those. Others, dressed in mourning black and wreaths in hand, knelt beside cemetery gravesides. Some stood, just for seconds perhaps, looking at the mass of rubble that had previously been their homes.

After my supper-time drink of warmed milk, I said goodnight to Mum and Scamp and went upstairs to bed. The fires of my first peacetime sunset were cooling, fading slowly from the doorway corner of my bedroom wall. Tomorrow the *Daily Sketch* and a day or so later the *Pathé News* would tell me *everything*, if Mum allowed me time to see them.

The next morning I awoke to the sound of Mum pushing open my bedroom window.

My first question of the day was, "Mum, what are you doing?"

"Putting the flag out," laughed Mum.

Attached to the window catch by a tightened rubber band was a blue stemmed flag; a Union Jack. The coronet was painted gold. When still wearing my pyjamas I looked out, I saw the road on both sides transformed and the house fronts half hidden by Union Jacks. The flags were out as far as the eye could see, and ours amongst them.

When I was dressed and still unbelieving I again looked out of the window, regiments of Union Jacks were still there. Still intact. A sense of pride swept through me then. An unaccustomed wave of patriotism. Almost as if single-handedly it was I who had fought and won the war.

Later that morning cloud obscured the sun as I studied my books on the settee. Did the Arabs and Eskimos featured in the book *The Children of other Lands* know that the war was over I wondered?

Then Scamp barked when someone knocked on the front letterbox. Mum answered, her manner light, welcoming, as she asked 'the someone' to come into the hall.

Minutes later when our visitor had left, Mum beaming peered around the dining room door. "That was our friend Jill Pierce. The Pearce and Kittoe sisters are organising a street party. We're going to have our tea outside in the drive with almost everybody else."

"When?"

"Today; this afternoon."

"Are Dorothy and Geoffrey and Mrs. Robinson coming?"

"Oh, I should think so. Everybody who can come. And then tonight...."

"Yes....?"

"We are going to be dancing around a bonfire."

"What for?"

"As part of the V.E. Day celebrations," Mum explained.

She then produced a cardboard Native American head-dress. A banded hat, painted, made from cardboard and carrying five cardboard feathers. I would rather they were real feathers. *Eagle feathers.* Tonto, the Lone Ranger's sidekick, sometimes wore a headband with a single eagle feather pinned stiffly to it and facing the prairie wind. It would be better, I decided, to wear one natural eagle feather than five cardboard cut-out feathers. But I chose not to quibble and decided instead to let matters take their course.

Mum, suspecting perhaps that someone would organise a street party, had bought the Union Jack and the Indian hat from the Hartley Road newsagent's when I was at Dorothy's the previous morning.

"People were queuing for them - *queuing for them!*" she enthused.

Around four that overcast afternoon, Mum, Jill Pearce and Vivienne Kittoe each carried a chair from the house to the line of tables positioned in the middle of the road. Union Jacks were everywhere. With Mum on one side and Jill Pierce on the other I was helped onto a chair, while noticing that all the neighbours and their children were there and how excited everyone seemed.

Our house was considered central amongst those lined along the drive and so three or four tables joined together spanned the width of our front garden. In all there must have been some fifteen or sixteen tables joined and out in the road. Tables spread over with tablecloths, serviettes, condiment sets, bowls, plates, cutlery, teapots, and glasses for those who wanted lemonade.

Mum was beside me. Neighbours smiled, said hello. The Kittoe sisters acted as usherettes while Jill and Shirley Peace ladled out portions of jelly, trifle and cake assisted by our mothers.

Apprehensive though I had been, I was soon enjoying communal eating and 'tucking in' as the grown-ups called it. That is until our next door neighbours, Mr. and Mrs. Teather, stepped from their gate accompanied by the vicar. All three in their hands cradled a bible.

Sidling up to me, Jill Pearce whispered that we were going to say a little prayer. By then I was used to prayers but always administered in the school hall.

With Jill alongside I closed my eyes, put my hands together and despite the Vicar's short and gentle sermon, dreamed only of finishing the red jelly on my plate. The single prayer amounted to two or three, during which time both Mr. Teather and the Vicar of St. Margaret's Church convinced me, red jelly still waiting, that the mysterious someone called Jesus who beamed down on us from the sky in the school hall was now hovering above the entire nation and watching them about to recommence their street parties.

We were asked to stand around and alongside the tables while the Vicar took a series of photographs. The 'little ones', said the vicar, could stand on their chairs.

The resulting photograph of our elongated and people surrounded table depicted Jill, hands around my waist and supporting me as I stood on my chair. Neither Jill nor I were looking at the camera but were engaged in whispered conversation, my eyes connecting directly with her warm and friendly face. I was still wearing the Native American hat and my 'special' green sweater with the two stags clearly emblazoned and showing clearly on the finished print.

The Teathers and the Vicar came around and spoke with everyone, Mrs. Teather, as always, quietly spoken, smiling and deeply sincere.

When eventually we disbanded and the tea things were taken back to the houses, Mrs. Robinson and Dorothy said they would call for Mum and I on the way to the bonfire that evening.

Holding onto one of our chairs that one of the Kittoe or Pearce sisters carried into our house, I realised that someone to do with my life at the beginning and middle of the war was missing. That someone, I realised when we reached the front porch, was Aunty.

The darkness, the hour to be seeing Dorothy, Geoffrey and Mrs. Robinson, seemed a long time in coming. When eventually they arrived, Mum left Scamp in the kitchen, placed a note on Betty and Dad's plates explaining our whereabouts, and locked the house.

Colliers Path, the fields - my derelict yet beloved wilderness - and Cherry Lane were unfamiliar territories to the Robinsons. And to them they remained unfamiliar. Yet familiar though they were to me, I experienced an inner release of excitement each time that I wandered there even if I had been earlier that same day.

Nowhere, I rightly decided, is ever the same. The mood of every field, wood, stable or house is changed and governed hourly, not due to its animal or human occupants, but the play of light.

When we walked the short distance up to the bonfire, however, there was no light, except from the street lamps. But I knew the trails used by the Kittoe and Pearce sisters that wound through the nettles, bramble stands, masses of elder and dog's mercury, and led the way. To our left the high rambling haw and blackthorn thickets, where Barbara and Vivienne had taken me to see the blackbird's nest, blocked off Cherry Orchard Lane, the Half Field, 'the Ministeries' - or Government buildings as they were known - and Shepherd's Wood beyond.

Ahead were minute beacons of light made by the torches, flash lamps and old

Kelly lamps of the people already assembled by the bonfire. Mr. and Mrs. Teather and the Vicar who, despite the darkness, I recognised immediately.

As the adults similarly recognised one another and conversed, I explained to Dorothy the whereabouts of the fields, farm, Vicarage and all important *Forum* Cinema, and she seemed to listen intently.

Then yellow torch lights bobbed along the paths. Came closer. We recognised and greeted the Pearce and Kittoe sisters, each with their mother and a lonely neighbour or two.

Probably some forty or fifty people were assembled there.

Then the fire was lit. Amazed, I stood looking at the pile of gale felled and autumn pruned tree branches, dry bramble stems, old boxes split to make firewood, and the base of dry rolled pages of newspaper. Someone, the Kittoe sisters perhaps who were in the Girl Guides, had lightly dug a circle of soil around the bonfire in an effort to ensure the flames didn't spread.

As the fire took hold and the tongues of flame hissed, crackled and were drawn vacuum-like skyward, I recognised neighbours standing or moving around the fire. I also secretly studied Dorothy standing beside me, a rapt expression soothing her Nordic face, her plaits, shoulders and bare arms outlined and paled by the red and yellow flames rising twice, then three times the height of us both.

Someone brought a bucket of coke. Someone else two cardboard boxes filled with straw and in what would eventually become jacket potatoes.

In time, besides the heat, we were aware of the smoke that made our eyes run, the warm aromatic tangs drifting beside and around us.

Mrs. Robinson stayed beside Geoffrey, her youngest son. Dorothy stood beside me and Mum I lost sight of several times as laughing and chuckling excitedly she moved into the darkness and from one group of people to another, for she loved company. She was naturally gregarious, sometimes a teller of jokes or an ad-libber. A singer throughout the house in which we lived.

Eventually Mr. Teather again introduced the Vicar. Just a prayer or two, not just for ourselves but the hundreds and thousands of people who weren't up to celebrating because they had lost their loved ones in the war. Standing alongside

Dorothy, my hands together, I thought of the entity I had come to know as Jesus now looking down on the hundreds of celebratory bonfires that were being lit throughout the land, and smiling because the war - *the terror* - was over.

After the Lord's Prayer, Mr. Teather, baton in hand, announced, "Right, come on! Let's sing it, ladies and gentleman. Let's have it. This is the time! This is the moment! Please join with us in singing *Land of Hope and Glory*."

For me, Dorothy and everyone around the bonfire this was a momentous occasion. We were unaccustomed to singing in the company of grown-ups and I for one hadn't realised that, church service and wireless staged concerts aside, they sang with such enthusiasm.

Everything was forgotten. All eyes were on Mr. Teather standing wielding his baton in the rising, expanding glow of our communal bonfire. He loved, *we loved*, our country, our island, and were proclaiming that love in song. Dorothy standing to one side of me and Mrs. Robinson the other felt for my fingers and each held my hand. It was then I realised that everyone was holding hands. Holding hands and swaying as they sang. We youngsters, who didn't know the words, followed as best we could.

When the song ended, people - Mum amongst them - shouted, "Again! Encore!" And so it was repeated. People were smiling, singing, swaying and a few cried as they sang and swayed. One group held up a Union Jack.

When the singing ended, people encircled the fire. More brushwood was heaped into the flames by someone using a garden fork and the songs differed, but without Mr. Teather and his baton. *Roll out the Barrel. It's a Long Way to Tipperary. Down at the Old Bull and Bush. Run Rabbit.* Songs that we heard on the wireless two or three days a week.

Mrs. Johnson then came round with cardboard plates and gave us all a jacket potato which we ate with our fingers; the cardboard plates we were to throw into the bonfire.

As we ate I laughed and talked. I looked beyond the bonfire and at the night blackened thickets screening Cherry Orchard Lane. Was 'The Man' out there, wearing his peaked cap and black overcoat? Was he peering at us through the few gaps in the foliage?

I wondered, too, if the families who lived in the four detached houses facing the Half Field had joined us, for there were certainly people there whom I didn't know. More singing followed, not the least of which was another song that had little trouble in persuading us to link arms and hands; mine and Dorothy's first experience of *Auld Lang Syne*, which with Mr. Teather conducting was repeated. And how we loved it!

More wood, more tree branches, nodules of coke, coal and rolled up newspaper pages were added to the blaze.

And again Dorothy, Geoffrey and I, like all the neighbours' children, could only follow the grown-ups when it was suggested we danced and, of course, sang the *Hokey- Cokey*.

We were in line around the bonfire, one behind the other. I had my hands on Mrs. Robinson's hips and Dorothy her hands on mine. This number was about swaying putting —

'Your left leg in, your right leg out ......'

The chorus during which we twirled and sang, resting our hands on the person in front's hips, was deafening. The Vicar and Mr. and Mrs. Teather joined the swaying, twirling caterpillar of people. All shapes, all sizes, all singing against the smoke and flames of our home-produced volcano.

Suddenly I saw someone on the slender path. A man wearing a grey suit and trilby. Dad? *Dad!*

He called out, "Hello, Little Man."

And then he was in the circle, in the caterpillar. Laughing and dancing. As he twirled so I stared as I sang and danced, for I had never seen anyone moving so gracefully. So lightly on their feet.

For all his small to medium height, Dad was built for speed, lightness of foot, and it was then I remembered that he had once been a locally famous cricketer. A batsman and left-hand spin bowler.

"Your Dad! He could turn on a threepenny piece," someone said of him in later years.

Every song and dance was repeated; every jacket potato and warm sausage bap eaten; every emptied box, plate or carton tossed to the flames. With Dad now among us we finished off the evening, Mr. Teather again conducting the singing of *Auld Lang Syne, Pack Up Your Troubles* and, of course, *Land of Hope and Glory.* Then as the bonfire decreased, became a sadly low and smouldering heap, the Vicar and Mrs. Teather joined her husband in the firelight's remaining glow as the evening was rounded off with the National Anthem during which rendering I thought of Buckingham Palace and the two princesses.

CHAPTER 35

The morning after the bonfire I couldn't wait to see the houses bathed in golden sunlight and the Union Jacks swaying gently in the breeze.

I was not alone. The children of our neighbours were gathered around their front garden gates, Sheila Roscoe's young brother pedalling a small tricycle. Cheerful, as always, Michael Cox, dressed in a brown corduroy suit, his shock of black curly hair gleaming with condition, exchanged pleasantries about the previous night's bonfire. His mother then recalled the morning when she and her husband having just moved in saw from the window a resplendent cock pheasant in the front garden. Mr. and Mrs. Nahori came to their front gate with their daughter Suzanne and her younger brother. As always, Mr. Nahori wore a suit but unlike Dad and most of the men thereabouts he preferred to be seen hatless.

Unbeknown to me, Mum and the Nahoris had remained good neighbours throughout the war.

Suzanne, on learning that I was addicted to animals, asked if I'd like to see the two stuffed stoats affixed to their fireguard. Minutes later I was in their sunlit dining room and studying them.

The stoats were positioned as if travelling to meet one another down the fireguard's outer frame. Both were identical; white pelted. I knew from the spread-sheets Sylvia had given me that with some stoats this was their winter coat, or pelt. They were said to be 'in ermine'.

The next surprise which Mrs. Nahori was so keen to show me was contained within a special type of box. When she opened it, I saw among the stems and green leaves several creamy-white worms. "Silk worms," Mrs. Nahori announced triumphantly.

Later that morning, the Pearce and the Kittoe sisters took a group of us up to the Humps and Hollows Field. Whether Suzanne was with us, I cannot be certain. But I doubt it because, understandably, few if any young girls were allowed out, including my new friend Dorothy.

For the next two or three years I lived under the impression that I was allowed out because I was a fast runner; I had outran 'The Man'. Neither he nor my sudden turn of speed, however, were on our minds that warm May morning. The girls wanted to collect wildflowers. Although I told no one, my reason for going was because I wanted to be near The Tallest Tree in the county and hear the skylarks singing over the fields, as I had those seemingly many years ago with Aunty.

The thickets were green with foliage, profuse with blossom. The Humps and Hollows Field a carpet of grass and yellow flowers. The girls were going to look for clusters of eggs and bacon or bird's foot trefoil.

When we reached The Tallest Tree I led the way down and up the ditch bank, the route I had been with Aunty. And yes, the larks were singing as they had every similar golden morning.

When we were out across the field it occurred to me that I had never seen the humps and hollows by which it was so named. Or rather I had never *explored* them. The humps were hillocks, short grassed, sheep cropped perhaps in bygone times. While the girls stepped carefully through the carpets of cowslips, celandines and buttercups, I made my way over to the humps and hollows.

On the lip of one sandy hollow a gorse bush struggled for survival and swayed gently in the wind. Then I sensed a presence, a girl older than I but delighted to see me. She was by the gorse bush. *By the gorse bush and yet I couldn't see her.* The hairs on my nape stiffened. A chill enveloped my spine. I wanted to speak to her. Yet how can one speak to an entity that cannot be seen? Leaving the edge of the hollow, the girl came towards me. I imagined her speaking with me. Was I there to pick wildflowers? She would pick some with me. Would I stay? Would I *please* stay with her?

The female presence was not that of Aunty. She was younger, my sister Betty's age perhaps. She had brown hair and an open country girl's face. That much about the girl *I sensed.*

Then one of the girl group called to me. Told me not to wander off. Asked me to join them so that together we could listen and perhaps catch a glimpse of the skylarks.

"Please don't go," the girl implored.

I turned, leaving her to the breeze and the solitary swaying gorse. Nor did she accompany me.

I wanted to tell someone - Vivienne, Barbara, Jill. Yet I could not. What had taken place back there had taken place between the girl and I.

But why wasn't she with me now? Why hadn't she followed me? Why hadn't she rushed over to meet the girls?

Why? Because, I told myself, she was somehow, in some way, rooted to the hillocks and sandy hollows. Yet she wanted to pick wildflowers and *intended* to pick wildflowers at that bygone picnicking spot.

Back at home I spread my books across my knees, as usual, and appeared to be reading. But I was thinking. Stunned into silence and thinking.

When dinner was over I asked Dad if we could take Scamp up to the Humps and Hollows Field. Cloud gradually obliterated the sun. A cool wind crept across the fields. Dad, dog lead in hand, wandered aimlessly out into the middle of the grasses. He appeared to be studying the square buildings of 'The Ministeries'. On the pretext that I was looking for bunches of eggs and bacon, I made my way over to the humps and hollows and the quivering, beckoning gorse bush.

As the wind whined uncannily and the grasses and countless flower heads swayed and trembled, I looked at the gorse bush and decided that had been the girl Something strange, that perhaps only grown-ups knew about, had taken place within my mind.

Then she was there! Rising from beside the bush. Coming towards me. She was smiling. "You're back! How nice to see you! We *could* pick wildflowers together. It was so lonely here. *So lonely!*" And she didn't know why, but she couldn't go anywhere else. Didn't I see?

The chill settling into my spine superseded that created by the wind. I felt sorry for the girl. But.......but........

Turning, I raced back to Dad and as I ran I wondered why the girl was bound to a certain place. Why, unlike me, she could not cross a specific yet unrecognised line. She was there and yet she could never be seen. At least not by me. Perhaps not by anyone.

Before Dad and I, with Scamp trotting ahead, arrived home, I decided to make the Humps and Hollows out of bounds. The girl was lovely and needed a friend. But I would not, *could not*, go near the hollows or the solitary gorse bush again because of the fear that I might learn more.

It was over. As a nation we were all due back to school and work on Monday. Standing at sunset beside the front garden gate, I realised that all the Union Jacks, including our own, had been withdrawn from the windows.

The gates and front doors of the houses were closed. But the remaining tree belt indicating the whereabouts of ever beckoning Shepherd's Wood remained etched against the orange red sky and unchanged.

Seven and a half years old and school on Monday. *Ugh!* And what was I going to do when I left school? Become a singing cowboy like Gene Autrey. I had always wanted to do that. But what about a cowboy actor who didn't sing, like John Wayne who played the Ringo Kid in John Ford's *Stagecoach?* True I couldn't ride a horse, But like Wayne I could drawl, "You're gonna be needin' me an' this 'ere Winchester, Curly," while indicating with my sun narrowed eyes that several bands of renegade Apaches were sending smoke signals from the uncomfortably close buttes. And by the time I was John Wayne's age, I would have been riding for years anyway.

Or, did I see myself as a market stallholder? Standing, one hand in my overall pocket, the other cradling the stem of my pipe, while silently staring into the distance until someone indicated that they wanted to buy a dozen day old chicks, a puppy or a packet of dog biscuits.

On the other hand, I might become a Field Marshall like Lord Bernard Montgomery. My eventual moustache might not be as dark as his but I would command the same respect when I inspected the ranks of infantrymen, or stood for the newspaper cameramen alongside a tank. Besides which, people would salute me if I became a Field Marshall and the thought of people saluting me furthered my premature decision considerably.

SUGGESTED FURTHER READING:

Britain at War. Maureen Hill. Pub. Parragon (Daily Mail unseen archives).
World War II in Photographs. Robin Cross. Pub. Parragon.
Children of the Blitz. Robert Westall. Pub. Macmillan.

BIBLIOGRAPHY

Accounts of World War II were gathered from various, mainly local, sources but checked alongside the concise mini-chronologies given in *The Modern World Volume IV (1901-1998)* of the *Hutchinson Chronology of World History* published by Helicon.